EDEN BURNING

OTHER NOVELS BY
BELVA PLAIN:

EVERGREEN
RANDOM WINDS

BELVA PLAIN

EDEN BURNING

DELACORTE PRESS/NEW YORK

Published by
DELACORTE PRESS
1 Dag Hammarskjold Plaza
New York, N.Y. 10017

Manufactured in the United States of America
Second Printing—1982

Designed by MaryJane DiMassi

LIBRARY OF CONGRESS CATALOGING IN PUBLICATION DATA

Plain, Belva.
Eden burning

I. Title.
PS3566.L254E3   813'.54   82-1452
ISBN 0-440-02412-9   AACR2

*To the garden, Earth, man's only home, and
to all those who would save it from the vicious
tyrannies of fascism and communism*

EDEN BURNING

AUTHOR'S NOTE

There is, of course, no island of St. Felice in the Caribbean area. Yet, as a composite of all the lands in and around that lovely troubled sea, one might say that St. Felice does indeed exist. So, then, and notwithstanding that its characters are entirely fictional, the tale told here is a refraction, a reflection, of the truth.

Prologue

On a winter afternoon in the year 1673, a fifteen-year-old indentured servant named Eleuthère François, of the family later to be known as Francis, saw the island of St. Felice rise up between clouds and sea. He was a waif from a peasant's cold home in Brittany, and despite all the sailors' yarns he had been hearing, had never imagined anything like this entrancing blue of water and sky, this warmth, this soft, unceasing wind. White sand lay spread like a silk robe, he thought, astonished at himself for having the thought; he was not in the habit of making comparisons, had indeed found little need in his life to do so. And stammered to himself as the island grew larger, It is a flower lying on a pond. Or the jewel in the bishop's ring that Sunday? The dark green shining, the deep, dark shining . . .

He knew nothing about the island where he was to remain and found a great family; knew nothing most certainly, of that primordial heaving of the earth's hot crust which had produced an arc of such islands between two continents. He had, very likely, no conception at all of a volcano, or of coral, or of the red-brown man who had preceded him there, the red-brown man with high cheekbones and black hair straight as a horse's mane who had come across the land

— 1 —

bridge from Asia some thousands of years before to wander eastward and southward, to scatter from what we now call Hudson Bay to what we now call Tierra del Fuego.

Eleuthère François thought of himself as a first-comer, although it had been a century since the first priests, armored soldiers, and buccaneers had arrived from Europe on their sailing ships. Under the tranquil leafage of these forests men had already been crucified and roasted alive for gold. In the ramshackle taverns of Covetown sailors and their whores drank out of emerald-studded stolen cups, gambled and stabbed each other for the possession of gold. He could not have known as he waited at the rail, while the ship moved in toward the wharf, that even now another kind of wealth was beginning to outmatch the metal: human wealth this time, black, out of Africa. He could certainly not have imagined how this wealth, so brutally seized, would in time produce such refinements as a stately portrait under the ceiling fan in a governor's mansion, or the tinkle of porcelain teacups on an English lawn, or a girl of his own blood dancing in white silk over a polished floor.

The anchor dropped. Men shouted. Gulls cried and swung about the rigging. Ignorant, hopeful, daring, and afraid, Eleuthère François stepped ashore.

Book One

BROTHERS

One

TERESA Francis, called Tee, was six years old when first she learned that St. Felice was not the world— and fifteen when she fled from it in fear and shame, for reasons that the most flamboyant imagination could not have foretold.

"The world is enormous, child," Père said. "It's a great ball spinning around the sun, and St. Felice is only a fleck of dust on the ball."

Père was her grandfather and her friend, more so than ever in that winter of 1928 when her father, he who was Père's son, had died. She understood Père's sadness, feeling it as a graver pain than Mama's was, in spite of the black dress and the tears.

"Look carefully, there—those two dark curves like clouds, you see? Those are St. Lucia's peaks. That way, there's St. Vincent. And Dominica, and Grenada—"

The child had a sudden image of these islands, drawn out of who knew what remembered words, an image of green turtles, mottled and domed, like turtles dozing by the little river where black women were even now beating clothes clean on the rocks.

"And down there's Covetown, follow my finger—you can see the careenage, and I think I can just make out a liner coming into the roadstead."

A liner. A great ship with smoke twirling from the funnels and a lovely name like *Marina* or *Southern Star*. When the ships came they brought good things: bisque dolls with real hair, Mama's beautiful hats and her kid gloves ("Unbearable in this climate," Mama said, "but a lady can't go very far without them, can she?"), and the glittery things in the Da Cunha shop on Wharf Street, and Père's books and Papa's suits from England—only there would be no more of those; his suits had been given to the servants.

She stood there thinking about all that, stood in a silence of wondering and trance, in a remote and midday silence, until a woman far below at the river broke it with a whooping laugh and Père spoke again.

" 'Full fathom five thy father lies, of his bones are coral made.' Our first ancestor here became a pirate. He came as an indentured servant and ran away from a cruel master to join the buccaneers. Have I ever told you that, Tee?"

"Yes, but Mama said it wasn't true."

"Your mama doesn't want to believe it. His name was Eleuthère François. When the English took the island the name was changed to Francis. . . . It was my great-grandfather who called this house Eleuthera, after a city in ancient Greece. He was an educated man, the first in our family to study at Cambridge. . . . I love this place. Your father loved it. It's in our blood. Two hundred years of it and more."

Père was tall. A child had to crane her head to see his prominent, thin nose. He carried a gold-knobbed cane, not to lean on, but to flourish. His name was Virgil Francis. He was master of the rising hills that mounted in tiers of jungle and cane toward the summit of Morne Bleue; master of all the looping fields that swept to the shore. Lands and houses miles away across the island were his also: Drummond Hall, Georgina's Fancy, Hope Great House, and Florissant.

For all this ownership, Tee knew, he was respected. In later life she was to wonder how she, a child kept in an unworldly ignorance so profound that it nearly destroyed her, could have known that ownership commands the most respect of all.

"But why ever he chooses to stay in this shabby, far-off hill place," Mama complained, "I will never understand." Her earrings sparked. Now that she was in mourning she wore jet instead of pearls or gold, but still they sparked. "Drummond Hall would be so much nicer, even though it's run-down, too. A pity, he's no manager."

Tee defended him. "He speaks Latin and Greek."

"Much good that does when it comes to running a sugar estate!"

But Mama would never have dared say that to Père. In all the pictures taken during those slow, long days it is he who sits in the fan chair on the veranda, Mama and the others who stand around him. Looking backward with these photographs (mounted in a black imitation-leather album with frayed corners), Tee, in another country where snow falls through gray afternoons, strains to recall the faces and the place which after so many years have grown unreal, yet which at moments can still be as painful and sensitive as fingertips.

Here she is herself in a dark skirt and a sailor blouse, the uniform of the convent school in Covetown.

"We are not Catholic, of course," Mama said. "But the nuns have the best school here, and as long as you go to the Anglican church on Sundays, it doesn't matter."

The twelve-year-old face is earnest, timid, and plain. She has inherited Père's proud peaked nose. Only her lavish hair is beautiful, lying dark on her shoulders. Later she will be told that this hair is aphrodisiac; certainly she would not have understood that then.

Here are the wedding pictures, the day Mama married again. Mama wore an enormous pink hat. There had been roast suckling pig and hearts of palm. A whole palm tree had been cut down to make the salads.

"A sin," said Père, who would lay his hand on a tree as though it could speak to him.

Mama's new husband was Mr. Tarbox—Uncle Herbert, Tee was to call him. He was a neat man who still spoke of England as home, although he had been living on St. Felice for twenty years. The servants said he was wealthy; he had been a commission merchant in Covetown, and now was to be a planter, which was a much more distinguished thing to be. He had money to invest in the Francis estates and perhaps he would make them pay more richly; he was known to be smart. They hoped he would get along with old Mr. Francis. Miss Julia was, after all, not a daughter, only a daughter-in-law. Still, there was the girl Tee to hold them all together. So they spoke.

Mr. and Mrs. Tarbox were to live at Drummond Hall. In loving memory of his son and to provide a home for Tee, Virgil had given a grand house to his daughter-in-law. But it was too echoing, too lofty for Tee.

"I don't want to leave Eleuthera," she said stubbornly. "I won't ever see you, Père."

"Of course you will! But you belong with your mother. And don't forget, Agnes will be going with you."

Agnes Courzon had come years before from Martinique, to work for the family. She had coffee-colored skin; her hair was fastened sleek-flat; she had gold hoops in her ears and on Sundays wore a flowered turban and a necklace of large gold beads. Tee supposed she was handsome.

She liked fine things. "When I worked in Martinique at the Mauriers'—oh, là! What a gorgeous house! Such damask and silver you never saw! But for the eruption I would never have gone away. Destroyed, that wicked Mount Pelée destroyed it all. It hurts my heart to think of it. But wait," she said, "wait and see what your mama and Mr. Tarbox will do with Drummond Hall. It won't be like this old place, tumbling down—"

Tee looked around the room. Really, she had never noticed that the plaster garlands were falling from the ceiling. Books were heaped on chairs. A small coiled snake lay preserved in a jar on the windowsill. Père studied snakes.

"I'll be glad to leave," Agnes said. "I should think you would be, too."

There are dozens of photographs of Drummond Hall. At the end of a lane it stands, between a row of royal palms. Twin staircases join at the top on a veranda, from which one enters into the gloss of parquet and dark mahogany.

The house was Mama's pride. But Uncle Herbert's thoughts moved out beyond the house.

"We shall need new rollers in the mill. And I'm thinking about turning the east hundred into bananas."

Mama said doubtfully, "I don't know why, I still think of bananas as a kind of Negro peasant crop."

"Where've you been these last twenty years? Have you any idea how many tons the Geest ships carry back to England from Jamaica alone?"

"But the old sugar families here—"

"Julia, I am not from an aristocratic sugar family, you forget. I'm a middle-class merchant." Uncle Herbert was not indignant, merely amused. "We're way behind the times on St. Felice and I mean to catch up. There's relatively no care with bananas. You plant the rootstock and in twelve months you're ready to harvest. There's no processing, nothing to do but pick, grade, and ship."

"It'll throw a lot of people out of work, cutting down on sugar," Père told Tee privately. "He doesn't care, though. A new man come to run things."

"Don't you like Uncle Herbert?"

"I like him well enough. He's a worker and he's honest. It's just that I'm too old to learn new ways. They don't agree with me."

But they agreed with Mama. Here in one deckle-edged snapshot after the other stands Julia Tarbox, gay and charming as Tee will never be: ruffled and flounced for a ball at Government House or smiling on the veranda with her two new babies, Lionel and little Julia, born only a year apart.

Tee knew, of course, that the babies had come from inside her mother, just as puppies and colts came out of their mothers. The question was, How did they get there? It was frustrating that there was absolutely no way to find out. Nothing was written anywhere and no one would talk about it.

"We don't discuss things like that." Mama's rebuke was gentle and firm. "You will find out when the right time comes."

No one at school knew, either. Vaguely it was understood that men had something to do with it. But what? Some of the girls used to gather around a daring, arrogant girl named Justine who could whisper odd things, but one morning the nuns caught her and after that she wouldn't tell anything. So Tee was troubled by unanswered questions. Of course, as Mama said, she would have the answers sometime, just as sometime she would wear high heels, or be invited to Government House. Until then she must simply try not to think about it too much. . . .

Meanwhile, here she stands with Mama and the two little ones. Père has taken the picture with his box camera; she is about to spend the summer of her fifteenth year at Eleuthera.

"The whole summer!" Mama objected. "Why on earth do you want to do that?"

Mama wanted her to go to the club, to be among girls from the right families, to be popular. Mama didn't understand, or didn't want to understand, that you couldn't make yourself be like that if you hadn't been born like that.

"But I love Eleuthera," Tee said. You could ride bareback into the hills; you could float on the river, just float and think; you could read all afternoon with no one to interrupt you.

"Well, you may go on one condition. Agnes will have to go along. You're too old to be without a chaperone."

"My books are getting mildewed," Père complained on the day he came for Tee. "I've got a cabinetmaker coming to build cases for them."

"Buckley doing it?" Uncle Herbert asked. "He repaired a settee for us. Did a splendid job."

"His apprentice is better than he is. A colored boy, no more than nineteen, I should think. Clyde Reed. He'll stay at Eleuthera. It'll take him most of the summer, I expect."

"All summer!"

"Yes, I shall want dentil moldings. And glass doors to keep the damp out."

"Still, the whole summer!" Julia repeated idly.

"Why not?" Père stirred his coffee. It was a way of ignoring Julia. "A most unusual boy, actually. I caught him reading my *Iliad*. I don't suppose he understood it. A pity, he wants to learn. Of course, there's a lot of white in him." He leaned toward Uncle Herbert. "Some of the best blood on the island, very likely."

Tee caught the whisper, caught Julia's frown. So there was something hidden here, something ugly?

"Reed," Uncle Herbert reflected. "Weren't there some Reeds who owned Estate Miranda for a short space? Gambled it away at cards in London. No scholars in that lot, I should think."

"Well, this Reed is, or could be, if the world were different. But it isn't. At least I can lend him some books, though."

Uncle Herbert said carefully, "If you'll allow me an opinion, with all respect, Père, I always feel that sort of thing's a kind of teasing. Offering an equality that you'll have to withdraw the moment it seems the offer might be taken up."

"Well," Virgil said vaguely, "we'll see." He stood up, ready to go. "Anyway, Tee and I will have a time for ourselves. It's a lot cooler in our hills than it is here, I can tell you."

"See that she invites some friends, do, please," Julia urged as they drove away. "I don't want her spending the whole time with horses and dogs. Or reading on the veranda. She is so like—"

Like my father, Tee thought defiantly. But I shall just read all day long if I want to. Or spend it with the dogs if I want to.

She knew nothing, nothing at all, that summer.

In the blue shade of late afternoon Père spread a large notebook on his lap.

"Quitting time, Clyde! You've been hammering and chiseling since breakfast. Would you like to listen to what I've got here?"

The boy Clyde came and sat down on the steps. It was odd that one called him "boy" in one's mind, for certainly he was a full-grown man. Tee thought, It is because he is colored, which seemed answer enough. Still, she mused, he is not very colored, is he? He was a shade or two lighter than Agnes, and like Agnes, quite clean. He wore a freshly washed shirt every morning and carried with him a pleasant scent of the wood on which he worked; sometimes a papery curl of wood shaving caught in his hair, which was thick and straight. White man's hair, it was. His narrow lips were the white man's. Only his eyes were Negro. White people's brown eyes were never that dark. It occurred to her that Clyde's had a wise look to them. Or perhaps a mocking look? As if even when he was being most respectful—and he was always respectful, Père would not have allowed him to stay if he had not been—as if his eyes were saying, *I know what you are thinking.* But then, she thought, that's probably silly; I am given to silly observations, Mama always says.

"This is a translation I made," Père explained. "From the French, naturally. The original is in my vault in town. It's crumbling, ought to be in a museum. Well, I'll get to that one of these days. Here it is: 'Diary of the First François.'

" 'We sailed from Havre de Grace on the English ship *Pennington* in the year of our Lord 1673, I being fifteen years of age and indentured for seven years to a Mr. Raoul D'Arcy on the island of St. Felice in the West Indies; he to pay my passage and clothe me, he to pay me three hundred pounds of tobacco at the end of my service.' "

Père turned some pages. "Fascinating. Here, listen to this. 'We labor from a quarter of an hour after sunrise to a quarter of an hour after sunset. I share a cabin with two black slaves. They are pleasant enough, poor creatures. They suffer, but I suffer worse than they do. My master admits to working the white man harder because after seven years he will part with him; but the Negro is his for life and must therefore be kept in health.' "

"I thought," Tee remarked, "our ancestor was a buccaneer."

"Oh, yes! He ran away to join the buccaneers. You can hardly blame him. And yet—what a devilish thing is human nature!—he became more savage than the master whom he had escaped. Listen to this. 'We came alongside the *Garza Blanca,* a merchantman sailing for Spain, sometime before moonrise. We boarded without a sound, surprising the watch, whom we threw overboard into a heavy sea. We bayonetted the captain, seized the guns, and put to shore, there to dispose of a goodly cargo: gold, tobacco, hides, and a great prize in pearls.' "

"I don't think," Tee shuddered, "I want to know any more about this François." She stretched out her arm, turning it over to regard the small cluster of blue veining at the elbow. "I can't believe his blood runs in my veins. . . . A savage like him!"

"Many generations removed, my dear," Père said complacently. "And anyway he became a gentleman before very long." He flipped through a few more pages. " 'I have resolved to become provident, having seen my lads squander a year's gains on brandy and' "—Père coughed—"other things. 'I mean to buy land and live on my property like a gentleman, to marry well—' " He closed the notebook. "And so he did. He married Virginia Durand, daughter of a well-established planter who had apparently no qualms about giving her to a reformed buccaneer. He lived, incidentally, to make a fortune in sugar before he was forty. Sugar's not a native plant; you did know that, didn't you?" Père frowned. "Tee, I'm feeling the signs of age. I was about to tell you about sugar and all of a sudden the facts have fled. Would you believe it possible that I can't name the place where it originated?"

"Excuse me, Mr. Francis, sir," Clyde said. "It was the Canary Islands. Columbus brought the first cuttings from there."

"Why, yes, you're right; of course you are."

"Yes, sir. I read it in the *National Geographic.* "

"You read the *Geographic?*"

"I've a friend. He was my teacher when I went to school. He keeps it for me."

"I see."

Clyde spoke eagerly. The words came out fast, as if he were afraid someone would stop him before he was finished. "I read a lot. I guess I've about read everything in the Covetown library. Well, not quite. I like history the best, how we all got to be what we are, you know—" He stopped, as if this time he feared having said too much.

He wants to show us how much he knows, Tee thought, sensing now not only the mocking pride which had been her first impression, but also something humble. It made her uncomfortable.

But Père appeared to be delighted. "Oh, I know you're a reader, Clyde! And that's wonderful! Reading is all there is to knowledge.

Reading, not classrooms. . . . Oh, I've been collecting books all my life. I've got books from as far back as when the English took this island from the French in—"

"In 1782, when Admiral Rodney beat the French at the Battle of the Saints."

"Listen to that, Tee! Listen to what the boy knows! Didn't I tell you Clyde was smart?"

He is treating him like a performing monkey, Tee thought.

Père stood up. "Well, Clyde, you may borrow all the books you want from me. Any time. As long as your hands are clean when you touch them. Come, Tee, it's time. We're having guests at dinner."

"Père," Tee said when they were inside, "that was insulting. Telling him about clean hands."

Père was astonished. She had never spoken to him that way. "You don't understand," he said. "They don't mind. They're not as sensitive as you are."

How could he know? How could he say such a thing? And yet he was so kind, Père was. Who else would invite a colored workman to sit down with them? Mama certainly would not, nor would Uncle Herbert.

"Bigotry, besides being stupid and cruel, stains the personality," Père liked to say. Yet there was this contradiction in him.

Another thing to puzzle over! The world, as you grew older, kept presenting things to puzzle over. There were many vague thoughts in her head, circling there like bees: thoughts about places beyond the island and times before the island and how people came to be what they are . . .

"You are much too serious," Mama complained, not unkindly. "I wish you could just learn to take pleasure out of life."

And Tee would think, Your pleasures are not mine. I'm not pretty enough for your pleasures anyway, even if I wanted them. And if I had your beauty, I wouldn't know what to do with it, how to laugh and touch Uncle Herbert on the cheek when he stands there adoring you in a room full of people. What I need is someone to talk to, really talk, without having to be afraid that I'm boring, or childish, or asking too many questions.

Père was growing too old for her. Suddenly that summer one saw that he was losing vigor and patience. Often he forgot what he was saying. He began to sleep away the afternoons. Eleuthera grew lonely.

So now, after the noon meal, Tee would wander into the coolness and sweet wood scent of the library to read or watch Clyde chisel a floral wreath on a cornice. There was something soothing in the tapping noises of the little hammer and in his soft whistle of concentration . . .

One day she read aloud from the ancient diary.

" 'July, seventeen hundred and three. Time of great woe. My wife's brother and four of his children dead of the fever. There is scarcely a family that has not suffered dreadful loss.' Whatever made people come to this wilderness in the first place, Clyde? I can't imagine myself doing it!"

"Poverty, Miss Tee. There was no work in Europe and what there was paid badly. These islands weren't populated by the rich."

He was reminding her that her ancestors hadn't been aristocrats. She saw the humor in that and didn't mind. Sometimes, lately, she surprised herself with her own insights.

"Also, a lot of convicts were sent here. It was called transport." He put the chisel down. "But you didn't have to be a criminal to be a convict. You could go to prison for stealing a few pennies, or for being in debt. You could be innocent, really. The innocent poor," he said queerly.

In the pause that followed, the words repeated themselves in Tee's head with a kind of grave dignity: the innocent poor.

"Well," she said, wanting to break this gravity that verged on sadness, "well, ancestors are fascinating, don't you think? You must wonder about yours"—and instantly flushed with the awareness of having said something awkward, something *out of place*. She apologized: "I'm sorry, I didn't mean—" making it worse.

"That's all right, Miss Tee." He picked up the chisel, setting to work again. "Yes, I wonder about mine. Not that it does any good."

"You could be a teacher," she said after a minute, wanting to make amends. "I think you know as much as my teachers know."

"I left school too early. My mother got sick and couldn't work, so

I took to this trade." He turned around, his shoulders gone proud. "There's no shame in working with your hands, as middle-class people, even among my people, seem to think."

"No, there certainly isn't. And has your mother got well?"

"She died."

"Oh. And your father?"

"I don't know whether he's alive or dead. I never saw him."

"Oh. My father died when I was six. Would you believe I still think about him? I feel as if— I miss him, even though I couldn't have known him well. I suppose it's because I'm not very close to my mother."

Clyde looked at her. His eyes were kind. "That's a great loss for you. And for her."

"She has two new babies and a new husband, so it probably doesn't matter." Her voice sounded bleak in her own ears.

"There have to be more reasons than that, Miss Tee."

"Oh, there are! We're very different, you see. My mother cares about clothes and entertaining and being invited places. She knows what families are important and who's going to marry whom and who's going abroad next month. But I don't care about that sort of thing at all!"

"What do you care about, then?"

"Oh, books and dogs—all kinds of animals, actually, and riding, and of course I'd like to go abroad, too, not to see the fashions but—"

"To see how other people live. To see Rome and London, the crowds and the great buildings— Yes, I'd like all that, too! And I mean to do it, someday."

"But then you'd want to come back here, wouldn't you? I know I'd always come back. This is home."

"It's different for you than for me," he said quietly.

Yes. Of course it was. His life and hers, both lived upon this little island, were different, indeed. And she had those queer feelings again: pity and a certain guilt—which was absurd; none of this was her fault!

Agnes remarked indignantly, "I never saw such an uppity boy, talking away with you by the hour—you'd think he was part of the family or something!"

"He isn't 'uppity,' Agnes. He's very polite. And he's one of the smartest people I've ever known!"

"Hmph," replied Agnes.

Agnes was jealous. Tee understood. Having no children of her own and having been scorned for it, Agnes had taken possession of Tee and couldn't share her. Yes, she was jealous of Clyde.

How strange it was that, outside of Père, a person like Clyde should be the easiest friend she had ever made! At school she had no deep friendships; there had once been a girl who read poetry with her, but she had gone to live in England and now there was no one.

Clyde appreciated poetry.

"Listen to this," she said. "It's by Elizabeth Barrett Browning and it's the loveliest of all, I think. Listen.

> *I thank all who have loved me in their hearts*
> *With thanks and love from mine. Deep thanks to all*
> *Who paused a little near the prison-wall*
> *To hear my music—"*

The room was very quiet. He had put down the tools. She was intensely aware of the quiet and the pure round tone of her own voice speaking.

"I wasn't quite sure at first what she meant by 'prison-wall,' and then I realized she meant her loneliness."

"She had a good deal of guilt, too. The family's fortune came from the West Indies, you know, from slave labor. That didn't disturb her father at all, but she was sensitive."

Clyde's face was soft. He's quite different when Père isn't here, Tee thought suddenly. Not stiff, nor humble either. Just probably himself.

"You read that very well," he said.

"Yes, Mama says I read with expression. I often think, if I were better-looking, I might be an actress."

"But there's nothing wrong with you, Miss Tee! You—"

"Look at me— No, no, you're not looking." For he had glanced quickly once and turned away. "Don't you see my nose? I've got my grandfather's nose. Can't you see?"

"I've never really looked at your grandfather's nose."

"Well, next time look at it carefully. Only I'd advise you not to let him know you're doing it."

The absurdity of this caution struck her then, and she began to laugh. Clyde standing there staring, measuring her grandfather's nose! And now Clyde, having, no doubt, the same picture in mind, began laughing, too.

"You know, Clyde, I'll really miss you when you've finished these cabinets."

"It's good of you to say so."

"Not 'good'! True! I never say things I don't mean. I wish we could stay friends. Maybe we will!"

He didn't answer. Intent again on his work, he bent to refine the spreading petals of a wooden flower. She thought perhaps he hadn't heard.

"I said I wish we might stay friends."

"That would be nice, Miss Tee."

"Clyde, you don't have to call me Miss. Don't you think that's silly? We're the same age, almost."

"It's the custom," he answered, blowing the sawdust away.

"But a custom can be silly, can't it?"

"You're not going to change it, Miss Tee, even if you want to. You'll only make trouble for yourself if you try."

Now it was her turn not to answer. Instead, she stood over him, watching the chisel flow along the soft wood, shaping a vine. He was right, of course. There was a rigid order in this world. A person knew where he stood in that order and how he must behave, how he must speak. In their different ways each fell into his place at birth, whether it was Mama's place or Père's or Agnes's. Money was part of it. Color was part of it. But—and this was very strange—mind, which should be most important of all, was not part of it.

A mind was a queer thing. Père had a book with a sketch of a brain, a gray lump, ridged and corrugated; you would have expected a brain to be more colorful, more like a mosaic, patterned with the pictures that your particular life had printed on it. And it seemed to her as if Clyde's mind and her own were of the same print, so that you could have set them beside each other in a continuous design, and there would be no jarring, no interruption.

Only their skins were different—and not all that different. Her sunburned hand, resting on the shelf a foot away from his working hand, was almost as dark as his.

He came to the end of the vine, curling it upward into a joyous flourish.

"There, how do you like that?"

"It's lovely. You're an artist, Clyde."

"Not really. I wish I were." But he was pleased. "There's a man in Spain, Antonio Gaudi, who does these flowers in stone. He's building a cathedral in Barcelona, all leaves and vines and even animal faces, a whole forest in stone. . . . The world's full of beautiful things."

How did he know of such things? He must have lived, must still live, in some village hut a world removed from Covetown, let alone Barcelona! And a soft compassion moved in Tee.

"That's all for today," he said, putting the tools away.

"See you tomorrow, then?"

"See you tomorrow."

So the weeks passed, and Tee was curiously happy, not lonely at all anymore. In the mornings at her bedroom window she watched the crows descending from the mountain to eat the *palmiche* of Père's royal palms along the driveway. The calm days stretched ahead. In the warm evenings after rain she stood at the window in her nightdress and heard the toads singing in the tree tops. She was so peacefully happy! She had no idea why. She did not even question why.

The hammock rocked gently between two acoma trees behind the house; so tall were they that their tremendous tops were shaken by a breeze, although at ground level the burning air was still. Yawning,

Tee laid the book facedown on her lap; in the house Père was taking his long Sunday nap; the whole world dozed.

She came awake. On the path beyond the rose beds Clyde was walking fast, swinging a bamboo birdcage.

"What have you got there?" she called.

"A parrot," he called back.

"Let me see!"

He set the cage down beside the hammock. In it stood an enormous parrot, two feet tall, a king of birds, marked splendidly in amethyst and emerald.

"Sisseron," he said proudly. "The imperial parrot."

"Where did you find him?"

"Caught him this morning. It was some job to catch him, I can tell you."

"What are you going to do with him?"

"I have a buyer. A sailor on an Italian ship, due back this month. I promised to get one for him, last time he was here."

The bird raised its wings and, there being no room in the cage to extend them, wearily dropped them again to stand in an attitude of patient waiting. Yet its round, alert, and curious eye seemed to respond to Tee's attention, and this aliveness was piteous, as though through the eye alone a plea were being communicated.

"He's so quiet," she said.

"He's not used to the cage yet. He's frightened."

"It's awfully sad, don't you think?"

"In a way, Miss Tee."

"When you think of how fast they can fly, how they love to fly! . . . They can live to be sixty years old, Père says."

"That's true. This is a young one. Two years, no more."

"So then . . . He has maybe fifty-eight years to spend in prison!"

Clyde looked down at the parrot, then looked away across the lawn.

"How much did the sailor promise to pay you?"

"I'm not sure. But a good price."

"Whatever he'll give, I'll give more."

"But—you want this parrot?"

"Yes. I want to buy him and let him go free."

Clyde was troubled. "If you feel that way about it, I'll let him go now, right here. I don't want any money."

"No, I'll pay. It wouldn't be fair otherwise. And we mustn't let him out here. We must take him home."

"He'll find his own way. It's just up the Morne."

"I want to see where they nest."

"They nest high up, in old palm trees. See his strong beak? He can bore a hole with that in a couple of minutes."

"I know. But I want to see where."

Clyde said reluctantly, "It's an awfully hard climb."

"You don't want to go? Then I'll go alone. Here, give me the cage."

"Miss Tee, you can't climb up there all by yourself. You'd get lost or fall or something."

"Come with me, then."

The way narrowed through ragged banana groves, then mounted steeply among palms and tree ferns which, fanning and crowning into the upper light, formed a crowd of green umbrellas under the sky. In somber shade, the path lay underfoot, dark as the bottom of the ocean. Tee climbed and stumbled. Ahead, Clyde strode easily, swinging the cage.

"I'll have to rest a minute!" she called.

He waited while she leaned against a tree.

"You know what kind of tree that is, Miss Tee? They call it candlewood because you can make a good torch with it for night fishing."

"Père says you're an expert fisherman."

"I like to fish, that's all. I like the sea."

"You like a lot of things. I wish I knew as much as you do, especially about this place where we live."

"Well, I do know this mountain like the back of my hand, anyway. I could show you things! I'll bet you've never seen the fresh water lake in the crater. Right inside the volcano. I've seen it."

"I haven't."

"And there's a pond not far from here, too hard a climb for you, though. A pond full of blind fish. It's in a cave. I went there with my teacher. There's a film on the water that looks like ice—my teacher's been in Canada so he knows—only it isn't ice, it's lime dissolving from the roof. You crack this film and you can see the fish beneath. Hundreds of them. They're blind because it's pitch dark in there and they've been there for generations. Come on, are you rested enough?"

Some minutes later there came a change, a feeling of great height. Coolness rippled through the air; the ground was wet and the rocks were covered with moss.

Clyde pointed. "Just about here is where the cane stopped. You can still see some of it, run wild."

"Cane, up here?"

"Oh, yes! In slavery days the cane covered the islands, halfway up the mountainsides. But now grass and jungle have grown back over whole plantations, whole islands even. Little out islands like Galatea and Pyramid, places like that, where they only pasture sheep today."

"What a wicked thing that was!" Tee cried.

"Wicked? What?"

"Why, slavery, of course! To own another human being! When I can't even bear to see this parrot locked up!"

"You're softhearted, Miss Tee. Don't you know there are people even today who wouldn't lift a finger to abolish slavery if it still existed?"

"I can't believe that! I can't think who would! Can you?"

"I can imagine, all right." Clyde laughed slightly. "But there's no sense talking about it."

She felt chastened, as if she had been scolded, the rebuke coming not so much from him as from herself. It had been really thoughtless of her to speak of slavery, to remind him of that terrible past! And she imagined that the knowledge of that past must be a secret, angry shame, attaching itself to a person like a painful burr. Yes, it would have to be like that.

Clyde whistled. Only a fragment of a tune, the few bars quivered into a plaint, thrusting a question into the neutral air. No, you will not get what you want, Tee thought with pity and foreknowledge, as if she were replying to his question. You're asking for music and color and brave things. I understand what you want. But you will probably die on this island with your tools in your hands. Père called you a scholar. Yet who will help you? If I could, I would. Yes, yes, I would.

The path dwindled and failed. Cracked limbs and trailing branches impeded their way. Great loops of lianas, thick as an arm, swooped overhead. Out of dark hollows, ferns cascaded like fountains. This was the world as God first made it, before man came. She felt their presence as intrusion here and was silent.

At last, abruptly, they broke into a clearing. It was a circular space about the size of a medium room, its floor a matting of low growth, its walls the embracing palms and acomas, tall as the cathedral in Covetown. From the topmost branches, a hundred feet above the ground, hung strong, green ropes.

"Kaklin roots," Clyde said, squinting upward. "Would you believe the roots are up there in the tree forks, while the plant grows down? The reason is, the parrots eat the kaklin fruit and drop the seeds in the trees."

"These look like roots in the ground, though," Tee said doubtfully.

"Yes, because they take root again. It's all planned out. You'd think the parrots knew what they were doing."

"Is this the place where you caught him?"

"Right here. Shall I let him go now?"

"Yes, do. Poor thing. Open the cage."

The door slid up. The bird, released, stood still a moment blinking into a shaft of light, as if not yet convinced of his freedom; stood flexing and stretching his brilliant wings; then, with a harsh and hideous cry, seemed to catapult himself into the air. Craning their necks, they watched his almost vertical flight: up he soared and disappeared into the crown of the highest palm.

An instant later the air was crisscrossed by a flight of parrots, a flapping and beating, a gorgeous flash and rush of wings. In seconds it was over and gone. And the stillness fell back.

Tee was awestruck. "This place is—is magic. I'll never forget it as long as I live, never. Or forget you for bringing me to see it." She took

Clyde's hand. "Aren't you glad you let the bird go?" she whispered.

"If you are."

"Oh, I am! Can't you see I am?"

He looked down at her, murmuring as if to himself, "You're like ivory. Like those little statues your grandfather keeps on the shelves."

"Oh, those! Those are white jade. They came from China, ages ago. We had a great-great-uncle in the China trade."

"White jade, then. Or milk," he said. "Yes, pale as milk." And taking her free arm, he turned it over, to stroke it gently from elbow to wrist.

She was surprised, so surprised as to know no affront, only confusion. No one had ever touched her like that, with such tenderness, for theirs was not an affectionate family; they did not demonstrate. This was almost hypnotic, this soft stroking. It made a warmth in her cheeks, it made a weakness in her. She wanted it to continue and at the same time wanted to pull away: there was a kind of embarrassment in being examined as closely as this, in not knowing how to respond. And as if casually, she tried to withdraw her arm, but could not: he had tightened his hold and taken the other arm, too.

"You're lovely," he said. "You're one of the loveliest things in all the world."

The warmth burned now in her cheeks, burned all through her veins.

"I don't know. I never thought I was—"

"You never thought you were beautiful because you're not like all the others."

How does he know that? she wondered.

"Because you don't chatter and preen and do your hair according to the fashion books—"

She looked down at the ground where dark stems and leafage frothed like ocean spray around their feet. From somewhere a fragrance blew, vanilla-sweet, clove-sweet, making her head swim.

"You have heart, you have spirit—"

He drew her to himself, holding her up; she had no strength; he had it all. Never, never had she felt like this, so helpless, so selfless, floating as in a dream. Her head fell back.

"I'm not going to hurt you," she heard him say. And she looked up into a face gone unfamiliar, gone stern and strange. She did not understand.

"I would never hurt you," he repeated softly. "I love you . . ."

Then suddenly alarm shot through her. Why, why? Something was wrong here, something— She came out of the dream.

"No, no!" she cried, but the cry was cut off by a hand on her mouth. She was picked up, laid down, stretched upon the ground among the froth and foam of green. Not roughly, but with gentle and determined strength, she was held fast.

"No, no," she cried again, struggling against the hand upon her mouth; the other hand had worked quickly, so quickly, on the thin fabric of her dress, beneath which, but for the thinner fabric and lace of her underclothes, she was naked. Her mind ran, clicking like a frantic, racing machine: Yes, yes, this is what it is. Of course it is. This is what Justine was punished for talking about in school. This is it, this was it all the time. And I not knowing. How could I not have known?

Pinned down, pinned, nailed, thrashing, with her yellow skirt over her head. Birds, now squawking in the trees. Awful pain, awful pain and shock. Her own voice muffled against the cotton skirt, against the weight that bore upon her. Terror. Outrage. Disbelief.

In a minute or two it was over. She felt release. She could look up to where he stood above her, where he stood horrified, looking down where she lay naked and weeping.

"Oh, my God," he said. "Oh, my God."

She heard him crashing down the mountain, heard the terror in his feet. A stone struck a rock; branches snapped. The heavy silence fell again. She stood up. I, I, she thought, and stopped crying. She pulled at the skirt, smoothing, smoothing, reached back then for the ribbon that had fastened her hair. In the morning Agnes ties the bow in my room where by eight o'clock the sun strikes between the jalousies and makes a dazzle in the upper right-hand corner of the mirror. Her hands trembled now but she managed a bow, not as neat as Agnes's. The bow and skirt are self-respect. It is all over and will never happen again, by God, now that I know what I know. But they will punish me for this.

And she began to run, run as though terror were still at her back, falling over a log where swarming ants stung before she could dash them away, speeding like mad down, down to where the trees ended and high razor grass whipped her legs. Ran and ran.

"Your dress is all grass stains! Where were you?" Agnes demanded. "Where were you?"

"I fell. There was a boulder on the path."

"Path? What path?"

"Up the Morne. I went for a walk."

"Up the Morne alone? Whatever for?"

"I wanted to. Isn't that reason enough?"

"Reason enough," she repeated arrogantly, and Agnes stared without answering, silenced by this voice of command which she had never heard from Tee before.

Of course, the arrogance was only terror and self-defense. For if I let go they will get the truth out of me. But why am I afraid if it was not my fault? But it was mine, partly, wasn't it? Oh, I could kill him, see him shot before my eyes, torn to pieces, and be glad of it. Still, it was partly my fault. Coaxing, inviting, stupid. Yes.

It crossed her mind that whenever there had been an accident, a near-drowning or a fall from a horse, they gave you brandy. Père kept it in a tantalus on the sideboard. It had a dreadful taste, bitter and burnt, but maybe it would stop the trembling. So she went to her room with the brandy glass, heard the evening-stir from the kitchen wing when dinner preparations began, heard wood pigeons coo on the lawn, and did not move. The brandy put her outside herself, so that she could see herself, withdrawn and secretive, curled like a cat, with a cat's wily, secretive face. . . .

Mustn't think of it. You can will a thing not to have happened. If you never think of it again, then it never was.

Père was heard, that day and the next, asking all over the house, "Where the devil is Clyde?" He was furious.

"He left me with half a wall of unfinished shelves and tools all over the floor. Irresponsible," he kept saying when, after two weeks, Clyde had not come back.

"I always told you," Julia declared over the telephone, "you can't depend on any of them. And you always said in another time and place he'd be a scholar."

"Well, I still think he would. What has that got to do with this?"

A terrible heat seared the earth for the rest of the month. Then storms came, thunder, lightning, and torrents of rain.

"What queer, unseasonable weather we are having," Père remarked. "Is it the weather that's making you so silent, Tee?"

"No," she said.

I only want to feel the way I felt before, when Clyde and I were friends. I hate the anger that's in me! Why did he do that? He's spoiled all the goodness we had. He knew how stupid and ignorant I was, yet he did that to me. And now there's no one to talk to anymore, not about anything and certainly not about this. I have so many questions. Whom can I ask? No one. No one.

Inside the house, the walls crushed down. Outside, the dark Morne towered and threatened. The sea glittered harshly. And there was no place in which to hide from loneliness, none, anywhere.

When the storms ceased, the heat came back to punish the land all that long, long summer. Tee woke in the mornings with her hair wet on the pillow, although she had pinned the mass of it to the top of her head. She sat up and, feeling dizzy, lay back again. Things buzzed in her head, buzzed and throbbed like crickets, like frogs. Saliva gathered in her mouth.

"I feel like vomiting," she said when Agnes came in.

"Again! It's pork. I tell them and tell them not to serve pork in this weather, but nobody listens to me."

A strong scent came from the vetiver mats on the floor. "No, it's these mats. . . . They're sickening."

"They never bothered you before! Why, they've a sweet smell! Tee!" Agnes cried sharply, for Tee's nightgown had fallen off her shoulders, revealing breasts grown noticeably larger. Tee retched in the basin and fell back weakly, the mound of her belly stretching a nightgown grown too tight.

"Let me see!" commanded Agnes. "Don't be silly, you've got nothing the rest of us haven't got! Oh, my God!" Her mouth opened in an enormous O. She pressed her hand against her lips, swallowed, and then, after a moment, spoke very quietly, very deliberately. "Listen to me, I'm asking you: When did you last have—you know— when was it last?"

"I'm not sure. Well, May, probably."

"Oh, my God! Not since May?"

"I think so."

"You think? You don't know? You don't know what's the matter with you? You haven't looked at yourself?"

"What is it? What, Agnes, what?"

"Jesus and all the saints, what is it, she asks! You're going to have a baby! You don't know that? Who was it? Where have you been?" Agnes screamed, shaking at Tee so that the gold earhoops swung. "Why, you've hardly been off this place since we came here!"

Tee could not speak for terror, and Agnes's eyes spread wide, searching the girl's face. "It's not—it couldn't be—it's not that devil Clyde? Talk! Talk!"

Tee stood up, swaying.

"Oh, my God, I told you, Tee, I told you—" And putting her arms out, the woman took the girl in, offering strong shoulders, soft breasts, incoherent comfort.

"You guessed this, didn't you? You must have. And were afraid to think it. Oh, you fool, you poor baby, poor child . . . that devil . . . what are we to do with you?"

She heard herself wail, "I didn't know. . . . Nobody ever told me."

And Agnes keened, "Oh, what are we to do with you? Dear God in heaven, what?"

The woman's terror infected the girl, so that gooseflesh rose on her arms and her teeth chattered.

"You're freezing, look at you!" Agnes drew the blanket over Tee.

"In all this heat you're freezing." She rubbed Tee's back. She swayed and lamented. "Men! I told you—"

"You didn't tell me—"

"You're right, I didn't tell you enough. Men! You can't trust them, not the best of them, not any one of them. And the sooner a girl's taught that, the better for her. Oh, but this world's a rotten hard place for women, yes, yes—"

"What's going to happen to me, Agnes?"

"I don't know, but I know one thing, I'm going to take care of you, don't you fret a minute about that. Agnes will take care of you."

There, in the flowered room, in the ordinary morning, with the ordinary morning sounds of voices, mowers, and birds beyond the windows, the two cried themselves out, the girl weeping fear, the woman, wrath.

Like an animal afraid to leave its cage, Tee cowered in the room all week. Agnes brought food on a tray, but she could not eat.

"What does Père say?" she kept asking.

"What is there to say? His heart is broken."

"Will he ever talk to me again?"

"He will, he will."

She had to know what was going on, what was going to happen. Standing behind her door when it was ajar she could barely hear Père and Agnes talking in his study across the hall.

"At least our girls are taught how to be careful," Agnes lamented. "We teach them to carry scissors and hatpins in their dresses." Then she laughed. "It doesn't always work, but at least when something happens they know what's happening! Young white ladies—this poor child—stupid as babies until the day they marry!"

There came more inaudible talk, and at last Père said, "Well, be that as it may, Agnes, this is the situation. . . . We love her, and we'll help her. If her mother were ever to find out—"

"Oh, God and all the saints, she'd kill her!"

"Not quite that," Père said somberly. "But her life wouldn't be worth living. Not around here, anyway."

No, nor Père's life either, Tee thought. She rested her head against the door. If I would just die and get it over with. . . . But I don't believe it, really. . . . There's a mistake. Something has got to happen to make it all right again. . . . Something . . .

"They found Clyde over on the other side of the island," Agnes said. "In Lime Rock. I think he's got family there."

"They have, have they? I want you to get word to him, Agnes. Tell him—tell him I want to see him. I need him to take me fishing. He knows how to handle my boat."

On the sixth evening Père came at last to Tee's room. She was just sitting at the window looking out into the dusk when she felt him standing in the doorway.

"May I?" he asked softly. He came in and sat in the opposite corner. "I've something to tell you, before I say anything else. I went fishing today. Clyde took me. There was—an accident. The ocean was unusually rough. He fell overboard and I wasn't able to reach him in time. . . . He never could swim very well."

She didn't answer.

"I thought you might want to know."

She looked at her grandfather, who was waiting for a response. His tired eyes held questions and concern. Her answering look was dull. She could feel the weight of the dullness within her. Clyde was dead and Père had caused his death. That was a simple fact, but her mind worked so slowly that it took some minutes to assimilate the fact.

Père stood above and behind her, stroking her hair. "A complicated business. Justice and mercy. Yes," he murmured, talking to himself. "Hard. Very hard."

So he was dead. Dead, too, were the Brownings, the imperial parrot, and Gaudi's stone flowers in Barcelona. Dreams. A boy's dreams. Why did you spoil it all, not only for me, but for yourself? You had so much to live for; even if none of the dreams were ever to come true, you still had so much inside yourself.

Strange, she thought, I don't feel the same anger I've been feeling. Some of it's there yet, but it's changed. Père's glad he's dead. But I'm sad, it's all so terribly sad.

Père said, "Tee, little girl, I've made my plans. You'll go to France.

I have an old friend in Paris, an artist. He would do anything for me, and so for you. I trust him."

"France," she repeated.

"The French don't care about things like this as much as we do."

Scandals, he meant. Despite all his proud French blood, he always said they had no morals.

"And afterwards?"

"We'll see. One thing at a time. Agnes will go with you. On the ship she will dine separately, of course, but in France she can appear to be a friend. You can live together and eat together."

"At the same table with Agnes?"

"Yes, in France it can be done. They don't have the same ideas about color as other people do. She will take good care of you. She knows what to do. Shall we go and have something to eat? Agnes says you've been starving."

"I'm never hungry."

"Come, Adela is still in the kitchen. She can fix you some biscuits and fruit, at least. Come. They think you've been ill with a fever, that's all."

"Père," she whispered, "I don't know how brave I can be."

"You'll be brave. This family is tough."

"But I'm not." She was the timid and bookish one; hadn't they always told her so?

"Yes, you are. Tough inside. It's the slender tree that stands up in a hurricane, you know."

He put his arm around her shoulder. In the soft dusk, dark as it was, she could see the shine of his tears.

She was to leave from Fort-de-France in Martinique at the end of the month.

"But she's too old to be sent away to school now!" Julia protested, meaning, She's fifteen and it's almost time to start meeting young men. She had already said this a dozen times and now, on Tee's last Sunday before departure, was saying it again.

Tee moved the soup spoon around the bowl of black crab pepper pot. This was a soup reserved for feasts, as were the turtle and goose waiting now on the gadroon-edged silver platters where the servants stood at the sideboard.

"In France you'll see snow," Virgil observed, making neutral conversation.

"It's like sand, in a way," Uncle Herbert explained energetically. "If you can think of sand coming out of the sky and being cold and white."

"You're not eating anything at all!" Julia cried.

"She's excited," Père rebuked Julia. "It's only natural before such a journey, isn't it?" But his eyes begged Tee.

For his sake she took another spoonful of soup. What shall I do without you, Père? I'm so afraid of going—and more afraid of staying.

So the dinner was got through and, two days later, the sailing.

High as the deck rose above the quay, Tee could still see the faces: Julia's tears and Père's persistent smile. They had been fueling the ship since first light, the women, bearing the coal on their heads, weaving a long line from the sheds to the hold. Now they were finished and the gangplank was taken down. *Compagnie Générale Transatlantique* was printed on its side. The ship trembled and backed away. From the fort the farewell gun boomed, sending a flock of gulls and boobies into frantic loops above the harbor. The ship turned in a great arc toward the open sea.

"I'm never coming back," Tee said.

"You will! Of course you will!" Agnes cried.

"No, never. Except perhaps to be buried. Yes, they'll bury me at home."

"What kind of talk is that at your age? Come below for coffee. There's a box of almond cookies and a cake."

"No, not yet."

Staring, staring, I stand at the rail. I'm leaving you, Père. I'm leaving you, Mama, and I'm sad about that, for in your way you love me, too. So many thoughts go round in my head! Who will ride Princess when the morning's still cool and bring sugar to the stable? Who'll sail the *Lively Lady* past the headland to Covetown? Will anyone ask about me when the new term starts at school, or wonder why I've gone? All my books—I suppose they'll give them away, like Papa's things when he died. And then there'll be nothing left of me on St. Felice, nothing at all.

So, now, good-bye. Good-bye to the Morne and the little Spratt River, to the wind and the sun and the girl I was. I'm not sure where I'm going, but I know I have to go.

By midafternoon they had doubled back northwest, passing St. Felice. It was too far away to be more than a curve against the windy sky. Or a turtle, Tee thought, as she had done when she was a child, a domed and sleeping turtle, resting in the sea.

Two

A burst of wind rattled the north window of the attic studio.

"It's too bad we had to be so gray and gloomy on your first day in Paris. It must seem terribly forbidding after St. Felice," said Anatole Da Cunha.

Tee raised her eyes from where she had been looking at the tips of her dusty shoes and saw that he was studying her. His own eyes were mild and reddish brown, like his hair and the tips of his paint-stained fingers.

"Here, you may read the letter," he said.

Père's script was black and vertical, his signature like dark trees in a grove: Virgil Horace Francis.

"I don't need to. I know what it says."

"In that case, let's get rid of it. Watch me."

Torn paper fluttered into the fireplace, flamed at the edges, and was eaten up.

"So, Teresa, no one here knows anything at all about you except your maid, whom you trust, and myself, whom your grandfather trusts."

"Why does he?"

"Because I owe him something and he knows I won't forget it. When I was eighteen—I'm forty now—he befriended me. No need to go into details. He befriended me, I a Jew of no importance on the island—"

"You, a Jew? The Da Cunha family—"

"Is Jewish. Or was. They came from Portugal via Brazil in sixteen hundred and something. Traders, merchants, all over the islands. Of course, they're all Anglican now, except for my branch. I'm the last twig of a thin branch that hung on, for some reason or other. I haven't seen your grandfather in twenty years, the last time he was in Europe."

Everything overwhelmed, this day in which she had entered for the first time a great, pressing city, such as she could not have imagined: the incredible traffic, miles of houses, and this house on a street of walls so high that one saw only the roofs behind the walls. One felt trapped. Here in this chilly room pictures were stacked everywhere one looked; on an easel in the corner stood a portrait of a woman entirely naked, brazenly naked, no concealing shadow anywhere. Yet Père liked this odd man, so it must be all right.

"Marcelle!" Anatole raised his voice. "Come in now, Marcelle. Teresa, this is my friend, my lady. She lives here with me."

Tee put her hand out. Marcelle's long, pointed nails pricked her palm. She kissed Tee's cheek. Her sharp, intelligent face was unmistakably the face of the naked woman on the easel.

"Ah, yes," said Anatole. "Marcelle is the only other who knows why you're here. But don't worry. She has arranged everything for you in her village, a little house where you can be comfortable and you will not run into anyone who knows your family. No one will question you. Country people don't bother with strangers except to gossip behind their backs and why should you care about that? Tomorrow we'll be taking you there."

At the end of the single village street lay the house, the last in a row of ancient houses between the church and the *mairie.* It consisted of a simple kitchen and two sleeping rooms.

Agnes sniffed haughtily. She had taken an immediate dislike to Anatole and Marcelle. "I must tell you, monsieur, Miss Teresa isn't used to places like this."

"I'm sure she isn't," Anatole said calmly. "But in the circumstances, first things first. You'll be warm and cared for, Teresa. In a few months —it's easy to say, I know—but in a few months it will all be over."

The season deepened into an icy winter. Darkness settled in the old trees, and the lamps were lit early. At home now they would be having tea with chocolate cake, or at Drummond Hall, those wonderful crisp elephants' ears that Uncle Herbert brought from the patisserie in town. The four o'clock rain would have left a bright drop on the lip of a scarlet canna and the air would be cool on the back of your neck. In the stable yard Princess would be drinking from the trough, raising her aristocratic head to snort her pleasure, then dipping it again to drink. And Mama, with Baby Julia and Lionel—Tee blinked.

She had been reading the same sentence for the last five minutes. Her mind was three thousand miles away—or maybe it was four thousand? Sighing, she put the book away and folded her cold hands together.

Agnes was reading a newspaper. It was strange to see her thus at leisure. It occurred to Tee that she had never seen Agnes when she was not hurrying about at work. Up until now, she had never even seen Agnes eat! The business of eating, when you came to think about it—and in this time of waiting and isolation Tee had come to think of many curious things—was a very personal and serious business. Agnes ate delicately, reflectively, without sound. One wondered about her thoughts. Julia had once remarked that Agnes was surprisingly refined, *élevé au chapeau:* brought up to wear a hat, to have manners like a white girl. In the dusk now the gold beads, her *collier-choux,* gleamed against her brown neck.

"You're looking at my beads, you admire them? My lover gave them to me when I was fifteen, a little younger than you. It took him three years to pay for them." She laughed. "A good thing they were paid for by the time he got tired of me."

"You—lived with him—your lover?"

"Well, certainly I did! Naturally!"

"But you call Marcelle a bad woman because she lives with Anatole."

"Well, naturally. Because that's different. You shouldn't mix with people like Marcelle. You're not like me, you're a young white lady of good family. You're not like me," Agnes repeated. Her mouth twisted, as if in anger, or perhaps in sorrow.

I don't know her at all, Tee thought suddenly, aware of confusion in the other. I've never seen her except as a person who was there to do things for me.

Gloom crowded the room as cold seeped through the walls. The weight beneath the folds of her woolen skirt grew heavier. She wanted time to hurry; she wanted it to stand still so that the thing which was about to happen would never happen. But the clock rattled steadily, deepening both the silence and the dread.

When a bird whistled in a barren thicket at the window, Agnes looked up.

"Listen! *Siffleur-de-montagne!*" She sighed. "My God, I didn't know they had birds in this place. It's not fit to live in, even for birds."

Tee made an effort. "Oh, yes, in the spring they come back, thousands of them, Anatole says. And everything is green again."

"So then, we'll see. By spring your troubles will be past, anyway. That's one good thing."

Her troubles past! If they would just stop telling her that! Tears leaked, slid under closed eyelids and rolled over the trembling mouth from which no cry came. Her fists clenched as if to control her panic that those tears would never cease, that she would never end in a corner of some dim room shut away, curled knee to chin on a cot or sitting upright in a chair, just staring, staring with the useless tears brimming, like that poor cousin of the Berkeley family over at Belleclaire, the one it wasn't polite to mention.

"I'm sorry. I'm sorry, Agnes. I don't want to be such a nuisance, it's only that—that we're so alone here in this silence, it's like the end of the world."

"Ah, don't! You don't have to hide your wet eyes from me!"

"I really try—"

"Yes, yes you always did. You'd come in the house with a bloody knee, biting your lips so you wouldn't cry, poor baby! Listen, it's good to cry things out, then the lump in your throat won't choke you."

Agnes stood, letting the newspaper fall to the floor. "What a crazy world! Poor Tee, poor little Tee! If I could take what's in your belly and put it in mine! Forty-eight years I am and nothing to show for it! Can you imagine that? And how I wanted it, while here you are—"

"I hope I die."

"You're not going to. You're young and strong. You'll be walking around the next day."

Tee plucked at her swollen waist. "I hate this thing. And I'm sorry for it because I hate it. Can you understand that?"

"Yes. Yes. I'm sorry, too."

Agnes mourned. The little room was filled with mourning. Unbearable. Tee stood up, went in to the bedroom, and lay down. In the dimness she could barely see Anatole's half-completed painting propped on the dresser.

"Will you do something for me?" he had asked. "I should like to paint you as you are. I've never had a pregnant model."

Compliant, indifferent, she had sat for him, or rather, reclined, close to dozing, while he worked and talked.

"The fruitful body. It's beautiful, you know. Don't shake your head! Some day you'll feel what I mean, you'll have wanted children, you'll be proud. You don't think so now, but you will."

He rambled, musing, thinking aloud, as if he did not care whether she heard him or not, and indeed she had not cared, either, whether she heard him or not. Yet now there were echoes in her head.

". . . a strange history, our bloody little island. All the islands. At one time they used to fine a planter who fathered a mulatto child. Two thousand pounds of sugar, I think the fine was. And the woman, with the child, was confiscated and given as a slave to the monks. That was when the French were in control. Well, there was always a shortage of white women, you know. Back in the seventeen hundreds they even sent a shipload from Paris. Poor wretches, gathered up from God knows where, their only qualifications that they weren't pock-marked and were young enough to bear children! Talk of your island aristocracy, your first families! Yet there came a time when a touch of dark had a certain *style*. Like Alexandre Dumas. And they say even the empress Josephine, although I'm not sure—"

Now Tee rocked her head from side to side on the pillow. It was all too much, too much thinking. Two Clydes, the gentle, feeling, comprehending—and then that other. Two Pères, the generous, the tender—and the one who had killed. For her. He had killed for her. And all this horror had come out of those few minutes, only an inch's worth of clock ticks; all this dread, because of a caged bird and a drowsy afternoon, and—and a stupid, ignorant girl who hadn't even understood her own feelings!

With cold hands she covered her burning face. In the kitchen the clock struck, sounding distant and faint, so that with part of her mind she knew that sleep must be on the way. Oh, the comfort of sleep and the long nights of escape! If only they could be twice as long, to envelop the days and blot them out! Past, present, and future, all blotted out!

There are those who cannot sleep when they are beset, but Tee was able to, and perhaps it was that which saved her.

When the incredible pain was past, she heard low talking in the kitchen. Then the voices grew louder.

". . . a strong boy. Could pass for Syrian or Greek." That was Marcelle.

There came a rich sound, part cooing, part singing. That was Agnes.

Presently Anatole spoke. "Wrap him up and take him to the nurse. Just till we can get her up in a couple of days and back to Paris."

Three voices rose together, with a certain agitation in their mingling. Raising her head, Tee could see, through the partly open door, long shadows moving on the kitchen wall.

"Listen," Anatole said. "We arranged it all before and there's nothing more to discuss. She's not to see him! It's humane, it's sensible, it's what's done in cases like this. She can't keep him, so why start up? Take him away, Agnes. Right now."

"But shouldn't I?" Tee murmured. "Mustn't I?"

"Shouldn't you what, my dear?" Marcelle had come in and was standing by the bed.

"Look at the—"

"No." Marcelle spoke firmly, her lips snapping shut on the word. "No."

Now came the infant's first cry. Quavering and long it held, then broke for the intake of breath, quavered into a strong wail and ended in a sob. The sound tore at something in Tee's chest. Here he is, after the long months; unsought for, unwanted, already he weeps—

"I want to see him," she whispered.

"No, I said. There's nothing to be gained by doing that, and much to lose. Now lie back and rest, there's a good girl, and leave everything to us, will you?"

Conscience, guilt, relief, all clamored in Tee's tired head. Still she protested. "But isn't it monstrous of a mother"—and stopped at the word *mother*, so incongruous, so impossible, applied to herself.

"Monstrous!" Marcelle was indignant. "Yes, that a girl—a child— like you should be in a fix like this, that's what's monstrous! Listen here, Teresa, you've got to look out for yourself from now on. Self-preservation, that's the main thing, always, and don't you ever forget it."

"You listen to her, she's right." Agnes came in and bent over the bed. "Better you don't look at this baby. He go his way, you go yours. No way you can walk the same road together. Not in this world, the way it is. Here, let me fix your ribbon, lift all that hair off your neck."

Yellow ribbons, pink ribbons, taffeta and velvet; blue shadows from the Morne leaping from the window to the mirror; Agnes tying the bow—

"Don't cry, Tee. You've cried enough. Now get your strength back. You're all worn out."

"Stop torturing yourself, stop worrying," Marcelle admonished. "Haven't I been telling you Anatole would see to things? You're not to bother your head. Anatole has got instructions and plenty of money, and Agnes is going to keep the child. Tell her, Agnes."

"Well, you know me, you know what I always wanted. So now I can have what I want, can't I?" Two warm, wiry hands held Tee's between them.

"Yes, it's a fine solution all the way around, don't you think?" Marcelle spoke cheerfully. "Agnes'll pass him off as her own. Probably they'll stay in Marseilles. It's a polyglot place with all kinds of people always coming and going, so she won't feel strange there. Don't you agree it's a good idea?"

"A good idea," Tee repeated. So the need to think and decide had been taken away from her. Better so. She wasn't thinking clearly and hadn't been able to for a long, long time.

"Your lips are cracked. Take some water. So," Marcelle said briskly, "it's all over. All over, Teresa."

Tee looked up into the alert, strong face. Such faces belonged to people who solved things, who knew their way in the world.

"Where am I going to go?" she asked softly. "What am I going to do now?"

"Well, do you want to go back home?"

Home to Père and the silent knowledge that would forever lie between them. Home to Julia. Home to Morne Bleue. You could scarcely go anywhere on the island without looking up at Morne Bleue, unless you stared straight out to sea.

"No. I'm not going back. I'll never go back again."

"Never is a long time. Still, it's understandable. So you'll stay with us, that's all. Anatole will think of something," Marcelle said with pride. "He always does."

The room on the top floor of Anatole's house had a balcony on which stood three pots of geraniums. From it one could look out and watch the city wake up, that city of which Père had so often told, city of flowers and delights. But there was no temptation in it.

Tee shivered, although the late spring sun was warm. She passed her hand over her waist, which was flat and firm again.

"That comes of being young," Marcelle said cheerfully. "The muscles snap back like rubber."

Tee thought again, I should at least have looked at it—the words *he* or *him* being impossible to form in her mind. Yet she knew that if "it" had been brought to her, she would have been too terrified to look. So of course she had done right. Where would you go with it? What would you do with it? Marcelle and Anatole had said, over and over.

"When will you get this girl some clothes?" Anatole inquired one day.

"Whenever she's ready. I've asked you often enough, haven't I, Teresa? I want to teach you how to dress, so you won't look like a provincial when you go places."

"What places am I going to? I've nowhere to go."

"No, only the entire city of Paris. Or do you expect it to come to you on your balcony?"

Tee was growing used to Marcelle's sharp tongue and able to smile a little.

"Do you know you're very, very pretty when you smile? Do you know that?" Anatole demanded.

"I'm not pretty."

"Who told you?"

"No one. I've just always known it."

"Well, you've known all wrong."

"I'm awkward, too serious, too shy. I—"

"Awkward? You have extraordinary grace! You are too serious and shy, that's true."

"Leave her alone, Anatole. Will you go out with me tomorrow, Teresa? The first thing we ought to do is get your hair cut."

"Oh, what a shame!" Anatole protested. "That hair—it's positively aphrodisiac."

"Yes, but nobody wears it like that anymore. This is 1938."

So now in the mornings they would descend the steep flight before

Sacré Coeur and go down into the streets, Marcelle guiding Tee as though she had been ill or were blind, and talking, always talking, at the hairdresser's, the shoe store, and the milliner's.

"Watch that young girl, Teresa."

"Who? Where?"

"That one, in the blue dress with the fortune in pearls around her neck. That old man, in case you want to know, is certainly not her father. Pay attention, Teresa my dear, you're always dreaming. What were you thinking of, you were so far away?"

"Thinking how odd it is never to see a dark face."

"I shouldn't think you'd miss them."

"I miss Agnes. I think of her."

"Well, she was good to you, I must say, although she got paid for it. But she's well provided for and content. What we have to do now is to provide for you."

They walked on silently for a little time until Marcelle spoke again.

"Anatole and I have been talking it over. You will have to get married soon, Teresa. It will be the best thing for you. There's really nothing else for a woman, anyway. Yes, you're thinking, 'She's a fine one to talk about marriage!' But you're not me. You saw where I came from. I'm better off with Anatole than I ever was, even though he won't marry me. Yes, I'd like to be a respectable married lady, only I can't be, and that's that. But it's different for you."

"Strange. That's what Agnes always said."

"Of course. She's a realist. Negroes have to be. They know what the world is, how the machinery works."

A young couple passed and entered a park. The father carried a young child astride his shoulders.

Looking after them, Tee said bitterly, "Who would marry me? Who would want me?"

Marcelle stopped still. "My God, what kind of ten dozen fools are you? You don't actually mean you would tell a man what happened?" Then, more softly, she went on, "Listen, Teresa, you've had bad luck, a bad deal, and the sooner you put it behind you the better for you. Lock it up at the back of your head. Do you think every girl who marries a duke brings a notarized personal history along? Women have to be very smart, Teresa. Never be fooled into thinking you can bare your whole soul to a man. Any man who knew the truth about you would throw you away like a paper handkerchief after he'd blown his nose in it. That's the injustice of being a woman. A man may tell you he loves your soul, but what he really loves is your body, fresh and unused, your hair, your breasts, and the ribbons on your charming hat. Remember that."

"It's so terribly sad," Tee said. And she understood that if Julia had been one to speak her true mind, she would have spoken like Marcelle.

"Well, yes, if you want to think so, but that's the way it is, all the same."

"You're beginning to feel better," Anatole remarked that evening and, without waiting for an answer, "Come, I want to show you something. I've finished it. I've put you in a grape arbor, you notice."

Already framed, beneath a splendor of leafage and clustered grapes, sat a girl, a stark and simple shape in a brown woolen dress, her face half concealed by the fall of her rich hair; her thin, cold, blue-white hands were folded over the huge curve of her belly in an attitude of patience which she had not felt.

"The grapes are ready to harvest. A nice parallel, don't you think?"

"It doesn't seem as if I could ever have looked like that."

"Perhaps I shouldn't have shown it to you?"

"It's all right. I can't hide from myself forever, can I?"

Anatole's red-brown eyes puckered in a smile. "You're growing up. A few months ago you were sixteen, with the mind of a twelve-year-old; now you're even a little older than your age. You really have changed, Teresa."

Well, changing anyway, she thought, if not changed.

"I think you're ready now," Anatole said next.

"Ready for what?"

"There's a young man I want you to meet. An American. He's a stockbroker and an art collector. That's how I know him. He's been coming here for the last few summers."

She waited a moment or two before replying, "I know why you're doing this."

"Of course. I'm thinking he would be a good man for you to marry, if it should work out that way."

"No, I mean I know *why*. You really don't believe in this sort of thing."

Tee surprised herself with her own words. Only a few months before, she had not known enough to "size up" anyone, nor would she have spoken so candidly if she had. But a bold instinct for survival was now rising within her.

"You have two sides," she said. "One for yourself, the artist who lives the way you do and believes what you believe, but the other is practical, like the rest of the world. You're doing this because it's what Père would want you to do for me."

"Not bad!" Anatole laughed. "Then you'll meet him? He's healthy, decent, and has enough money of his own not to be attracted to you for yours. His name is Richard Luther."

At first sight of him, so finely dressed and out of place in Anatole's studio, she thought that Anatole had made a foolish mistake. This blond, assured young man with the easy smile and the air of always getting what he wanted could not be for her, nor she for him. The world, and Paris most certainly, was full of lively, confident girls who knew where they were and where they were going. What would he want with Tee Francis? So she gave him her hand and avoided his eyes.

But later in the room upstairs Marcelle said, "Anatole was right. Frankly, I didn't think you'd be his type. He likes you, though. He wants to take you to the theater tomorrow."

They went to a play and afterwards to supper, at which he ordered oysters, raspberries, and champagne. From a vendor on the corner he bought an extravagant sheaf of gladioli for Tee to bring home.

"Tell me about St. Felice," he urged. "It sounds so strange to me, like Patagonia or Katmandu. Who lives there? Is it all sugarcane? Do they have pineapple? Telephones? Do you have great parties on the estates? Tell me about it."

She laughed and was pleased at this curiosity, pleased at having been given something to say. And while saying it she understood that St. Felice had been the cause of attraction, that St. Felice—and therefore she herself—was exotic to Richard Luther, something new. He was a person who would want the different and the new: the latest fashion, the artist about to be discovered, the master chef in the tiny restaurant at the end of the hidden street. Having taken from all these what he wanted, then he would be off to something newer. So it would be with her, she saw.

Meanwhile, though, Richard gave her what she needed that summer, what she had not even been aware of needing. He gave cheer. Life was to be enjoyed. He was kindly (sugar lumps for the drayhorse at the end of Anatole's street); generous (a pocketful of francs for the flower vendor and an admonition to go home out of the rain). They were constantly on the move: a picnic in the country, a boat ride, the races, the art exhibits, the auctions, where he bought beautiful, expensive objects, which did not surprise Tee, for had not her mother also been a buyer of extravagant objects?

She went with him, then, a quiet presence, an observer, almost, of his enthusiasms, carried along, bemused and soothed.

Anatole asked no questions, but Marcelle probed for him. "What do you think of Richard, Teresa?"

"I don't know."

"You are the strangest girl! What do you mean, 'you don't know'?"

Actually, Tee was thinking, Is he, or is he not, just a little conceited? Is his face, so handsomely symmetrical, a little weak? And puzzled, she answered with a question.

"I have no means of comparison, have I?"

Marcelle softened. "True, true. I keep forgetting how young you are. Well, take it from me, he's ready for marriage, it's the right time for him. He's twenty-five, he's done all the sampling he wants. And you're different from anyone he can have known. Only sixteen! There's charm in that."

"I suppose I am different." What did he call her? Dark child, aloof—

"Your family would be pleased. He'll make a good husband."

"He hasn't asked me." In fear her heart accelerated, partly because he might not ask her (for what was she to do then?), and partly because he might.

Late in the summer, when it was almost time for him to go home, Richard Luther did ask her. They had left the bookstalls, where he had bought two old volumes, when he stopped and took a flat box out of his pocket.

"Open it," he said.

On gray velvet lay a triple strand of tenderly shining pearls.

"For you, Teresa. Pearls for the young and innocent. Diamonds for a little later."

"But I can't accept a present like this!"

"I know you can't, not from a stranger. This is just my way of asking you to marry me."

"You hardly know me!" she cried.

"I know enough. Teresa—it's a gentle name, like you. I'd be very good to you. You know that, don't you?"

"Yes," she whispered.

"I've lived in New York with my mother since my father died. My mother would be enchanted with you," he said confidently. "But of course we'd have our own place. We could have a country house, too. I've been thinking about New Jersey; there are miles of soft hills; they might even remind you a little of your mountains at home."

Still she hesitated.

"Are you thinking that you want to go back to St. Felice? Is that it?"

Her hands went unconsciously to her throat. "Oh no, oh no, I don't want to go back, ever!"

"Yes, now that you've started to see the world, I can understand that. Well, then? I do love you, Teresa."

They were standing at the river where the bridges, in both directions, arched like loops in stone, time-stained, yellowing and streaked.

For minutes Tee looked down. So long ago, in another age, she had stood watching a river twist to the sea, watching the same slow flow of water, the little froth and bubble, the water, like time, maybe, carrying things away, the self with the flow.

Oh, I can, it can be, I want—she thought, as she turned to him. He's a good man, so lively and kind. He's a happy man. You feel happy yourself when you're with him! You feel as if nothing would ever hurt you. You'd never be alone anymore.

He put his arms around her. Smiling, he stroked her cheeks and her hair. His face glowed with his smile, making a glad hope surge in her. Perhaps this, after all, was love, the real and true, and it would keep on growing forever. Oh, she would return his kindness, his goodness, ten times over, be everything he wanted, surprise him beyond his expectations.

And at the same time she was thinking, We have nothing to talk about, and I don't know if we ever will have. . . .

They were to be married quite simply in Anatole's small, unkempt garden. There were, in the preceding weeks, moments that stabbed her.

"Will I ever make this work?" she cried to Marcelle. "Tell me, how can it possibly work?"

"Why not? Why shouldn't it? Listen, you'll be a good wife, you couldn't be anything else, and he's crazy about you. Have many children, that's what will be best for you. You're the type for it and it'll keep both of you busy and happy. Above all, no guilt, no looking back! Never. Do you hear?"

So, on a gilded autumn day, just one year after she had arrived in France, Teresa Francis married Richard Luther. The very next morning they sailed for New York.

Richard's mother was indeed enchanted by the bride. "How young! How shy and young!" she said, and everyone marveled, "Born on an island in the West Indies, imagine!" And someone whispered, "There's no end to the wealth those people have there. . . ."

Well, anyway, they gathered her to themselves, and even in a New York winter, they warmed her. Richard went back to the brokerage office and was gone all day while Tee furnished a house. This world now was so different from St. Felice that one could forget its very existence. Besides, she was already pregnant. . . .

Eleven months after the marriage, she gave birth to a fine, large boy, fair like his father. Sitting up in her flower-filled hospital room, Tee held the child close, laying her cheek on his head. Here, here was repayment for everything! Hers now, her own! Never to love anyone as much as him; never to be loved by anyone as much as by him. She would be such a mother to this child! Nothing would ever hurt him, not the rough sleeve of his father's coat, nor the faintest draft from the door to the hall. There was something special between the two of them.

And indeed it was to be so, although she could not really have known it then.

On the day of his christening the baby wore the lace robe that had been in the Luther family for five generations. Afterwards they brought him home and took his picture with his parents on the velvet sofa in front of the fireplace, then laid him lovingly to sleep in his nursery upstairs.

His name was Francis Virgil Luther.

Book Two

COMING HOME

Three

HE knew he had been born far across the sea, but he had no recollection of the long voyage back to St. Felice, eighteen days from Marseilles. His mother said, "I didn't like it over there, Patrick. Too many strangers and too cold. So I brought you home."

His mother was Agnes, pronounced, as he later learned, with the accent on the second syllable, in the soft French way. She was strong. Her tongue could be sharp. When she gave him an order, she wanted immediate obedience. Yet, from her dark hands with their pink palms, he received, it would seem to him when he was old enough to think about it, daily and continual blessing: food, bandages for the bruised knees of childhood, and comfort when he was afraid. Sometimes he was very much afraid: of what? Of nameless things, of spirits among sighing trees, of being lost and losing her.

He was never very far away from her. As soon as he learned to walk, he followed her everywhere, from early morning, when they woke in the cabin, through the day in the big house, where she worked, and back to the little room again, where she gave him his supper and put him to bed.

The big house was vast and open, with tall doors, verandas, and wide halls through which breezes blew. The house had a shine to it; he had an impression of silver and shine. Even the dark tables and chairs had a silver shine when Maman polished them. It seemed to him that that was what she did all day, rubbing things to a glow: floors, teapots, and mirrors.

From the first he understood that this was not Maman's house. She was different there. *Shush*, she would say when he spoke too loud. In their own room she never said that. There she was loud herself, singing and rocking him. When other women came by in the evenings, they laughed together in high, shrill voices, talking fast, clapping each other on the back, swaying with laughter. And he would stand wondering at their laughter, not understanding it, yet in some nameless way enjoying it.

Little by little he learned to place himself in the world. The big house belonged to Mr. Kimbrough, a quiet man with a dry, white face and a white linen suit. Mrs. Kimbrough was white too; her hair was like chicken feathers.

In the kitchen of that house the faces were dark. The kitchen people were not nice. Tia, the cook, sat at the head of the lunch table; Loulou, who did the laundry, and Cicero, who served the Kimbroughs' meals on that other table in the dining room, sat across from Patrick and Maman.

"He certainly doesn't look like you, with that complexion," Tia would start slyly. She would shake her head while Patrick lowered his face to his rice and peas, away from her stare. "No, he certainly does not."

And Maman would answer, "How many times I tell you he is the son of a Frenchman? Born in France, you know that as well as I."

"A Frenchman, hey? And rich too, I suppose?"

"Rich enough, anyway, so I don't need to worry too much about this boy here."

"Why you working in this place then? You have so much money, why don't you quit?"

"I just might. I just might open a little shop somewhere, when I find the right place. Not in Covetown, though. The price is too dear."

Now would come Loulou's turn. "You boast too much, Agnes. Why didn't you stay in France, you had it so good there?"

"Because"—spoken scornfully—"because I came home to show off my boy, my baby you all thought I couldn't have."

Laughter, then. Years later he would recall it, only then comprehending the cruelty of such laughter, the sting of pleasure at someone else's expense, someone else's weakness or humiliation.

"Well, good you had him at last," Loulou would say. "If a woman never have child she bound to have troubles up here," and would tap her head significantly.

Then Tia: "Let's see how many more you can have, old as you are." Tia herself has nine children whom she talks about freely and rarely sees; they are cared for by her mother on the other side of the island.

Then Maman firmly: "I don't want any more. This one is precious enough. I want to bring him up right. Can't do that with too many pulling at your skirt."

He would remember a feeling which later he understood was confidence and safety. *This one is precious enough. I want to bring him up right.*

And he would remember old, disconnected moments, probably not in the right order or in rank of importance, though what was important was not always easy to know.

There was a house on a hill at the end of a long drive. They had been riding in cars and busses, riding and walking all day, looking for a shop to buy, Maman said. His legs ached.

"What place is this now?" he wanted to know.

"It's called Eleuthera."

"What does that mean?"

"I don't know. It's a name, that's all."

Eleuthera. He liked the sound of it. Words were pretty. On Sundays the preacher talked too long with a kind of dull roaring, so that he usually fell asleep, but sometimes proud words woke him up: celestial, eternity, paradise. Now: Eleuthera.

A tall thin man stood on the veranda.

"I was passing," Maman said. "I thought you might want to have a look at this boy."

The man didn't speak. He was silent for so long that Patrick looked up at him, questioning.

After a while the man said softly, "You shouldn't have brought him, Agnes."

"You've nothing to worry about, you know that," Maman said. "I won't bring him again."

The man put his hand on Patrick's head. "You'd like some cake and milk, wouldn't you?"

"No," Maman said, "he doesn't want any." But he did want some.

"Well then, some money for toys when you get back to town?"

He would remember of that day that she did buy him some toys, but he forgot what they were.

One day she said, "I'm going to open the shop now, at last."

"Like Da Cunha's, will it be?" For he had already remarked on the shops along Wharf Street: the bakery where you bought sweet rolls; the candy shop with whistles and balloons; then, at the far end near the hotel, Da Cunha's, where, peering in, you saw in the cool dimness, under the slowly whirling fans, tall shelves of bottles, clocks, glass, and china, all the gleaming things that reminded him of the Kimbroughs' house.

Maman laughed. "No, of course not. Those things are not for us. No, I mean to sell shirts and dresses to our own folks. And I can alter free of charge. That's one thing I learned when I was growing up. I can handle a needle."

"Will it be on Wharf Street?"

"No, not in Covetown. In Sweet Apple. It's a fishing village, and we'll be living right across from the beach where they pull the boats in. You'll like it there."

She had bought a good house, the best in the village. The owner had labored in America, had come home to build it and there died. It had a foundation, not stilts like the other houses; it had two bedrooms, its own well in the yard and running water inside. In the front room Maman put a counter and shelves. This was to be the store, their livelihood, the place where she was to spend her years.

Now he could venture out into the life surrounding. On certain days he saw the farmers bring their mangoes and bananas from the hills to market. He stood at the green to watch the older boys play cricket with palm-branch bats. Down on the beach he saw how nets were mended, how a circle of boats was drawn to trap a school of lobsters. Schooners came and went from Grenada and St. Lucia; he wondered what those places were like, whether the trees were the same there or the sky the same. . . . Sometimes a new boat was launched and that was a whole day's excitement, the men tugging the boat inch by inch on great logs across the sand, while a steel band played and somebody got to break a bottle of rum and people danced.

Sometimes, when his mother gave him a penny, he liked to go to Ah Sing's grocery store, the Chinaman's store. There were rows of canned goods with bright labels and a shelf of candy in jars. Soon he was aware that Ah Sing gave him more than his penny's worth. He had a nice smile and sometimes took a walk far up the beach with Patrick, talking with an accent that made Patrick miss every other word. Ah Sing taught him how to open a conch shell, how to watch out for the claw that can be hiding there even though you think the creature's dead; how to pull the body out of the shell, cut off the sickle, and clean it.

"Take it home to your mother and remind her to mix half sea water with the fresh when she makes the stew."

He remembered that. And Ah Sing taught him to swim and how to raise a pig, which he kept with the chickens in the yard behind the house.

But mostly, as befitted his age, he played, and his days passed sweetly, circling through unchanging seasons without aim, except as a plant stretches toward the sun or butterflies circle in the afternoon.

Then one day he was no longer a baby. He started school. Not everybody started school; you didn't have to go if you didn't want to, if your mother complained that she didn't have the money for uniforms, or if you were needed to help on the sugar estate in crop time. But Patrick had a supply of dark blue shorts and white shirts; his mother wanted him to go.

"Learn," she commanded, with her hands on his shoulders. "Learn,

so you won't grow up and have to work on a sugar estate. Listen to
the teacher and behave yourself, hear?"

That was strange, because sometimes she said, "You won't have to
work on a sugar estate, thank God for that." Anyway, he didn't know
what was so wrong about working there. The men in the village, those
who didn't fish for a living, all worked on Estate Sweet Apple, the
plantation from which the village took its name. So he left for school
with a certain confusion, a feeling that he was being sent off to do
something hard, that he would naturally hate.

Instead, it turned out to be delight. The whistle of the schoolmis-
tress, bringing the class to attention, became in those first years a
summons to a new kind of pleasure. On the long bench under the
trees he plowed obediently through arithmetic so as to get it over with
quickly, waiting for the big books with their stories of knights who
fought with swords and rode their horses in places with strange names.
All those things happened a long time ago, he wasn't sure when,
probably before he had been born.

Sometimes the teacher held up pictures. There was a stone church
much bigger than the one in Covetown.

"An abbey," she said. "Westminster Abbey."

"What is an abbey?" Patrick asked, but she didn't answer.

Then there was a long car called a railroad and this, too, was in
England. There was a picture of a man with a pointed long face and
large, pale, bulging eyes; he was the king, George the Sixth, and you
were his subject, you belonged to him.

"That means you are English," said Mistress Ogilvie.

"We are English, did you know?" he asked his mother.

"Why, who told you that?"

"The mistress."

"Ah, well. We were slaves of the English. Did she tell you that
too?"

"I don't know."

"You didn't know we were slaves?"

"I think somebody told me. But there aren't any more now, are
there?"

"No slaves? *They* make the laws, *they've* got the jails! And so, what are *we*? I ask you, what are *we*?"

He stood there, feeling the knotted frown on his forehead, uncomfortable in the face of her strange anger.

"Ah," she said abruptly. "I shouldn't talk like that! There's nothing I can do about it, and it only gives me a headache, anyway."

She could say such odd things, things to make you think she hated the people who owned the estates; then, at other times, she would admire some white lady they might see on a trip to Covetown.

"Ah, but there's quality! So well dressed, such fine manners!"

It was confusing. So much, it seemed, depended upon skin: what people thought of you and said about you. He knew, for instance, that people whispered in the village about his mother and about their house. She never told him, and he understood that she never would, yet here and there he overheard enough to bring him some vague understanding that her little money had come from a white man, the man who had fathered him.

Over the dresser in his mother's room there was a mirror. Standing on a chair, he could see how light he was compared with the people he knew, excepting, of course, people like the Kimbroughs. None of the children in school was as light.

So he wondered about color and faces, Ah Sing's, for instance, with his peculiar, narrow eyes.

"That's because he's Chinese," Maman said, which was no explanation at all. It was confusing.

One evening she told him a story. He had been lying, for hours, it seemed, too hot to sleep. Lightning flared; the air was heavy and he felt the melancholy of oncoming storm. At the window where his bed stood he could see the yellow, flashing sky. Yellow is always angry, he thought. It was not the sort of thought he would express aloud; it would seem a stupid thing to say. Still, he always thought that colors were saying something: orange, for instance, looked surprised, as though something nice had happened unexpectedly. It was amazing what you could do with words.

Thunder rolled and cracked; rain pounded the tin roof; a terrible crash shook the house. Maman came over and sat on Patrick's bed. He moved nearer to her, ashamed of being scared.

"You think a storm like this is anything? I remember when Mount Pelée blew up. That was in 1902, the eighth of May, and that boom was bigger than any thunder you'll ever hear! People thought it was Judgment Day. They even felt the ground shake here on St. Felice, can you imagine that? No, you can't, nobody could imagine what it was like. A cloud came out of the mountain; first it looked like smoke from a burning house, but it kept on coming, until it filled the sky" —in the three-quarter dark Patrick could see that she was leaning forward and gesturing with her arm—"filled the sky all purple and red as blood, a fearful, ugly thing. It made you think of hell. . . . Then the ash came, falling hard as rain. It smelled like rotten eggs. Sulfur, they said. We closed the shutters tight, but the ash got in anyway and covered the floors. And centipedes got into the house, a foot long some of them, trying to get away from the ash upriver. We poured boiling water on them. I was a maid at the Mauriers' then, my first position. I was hardly more than a child, but it was good working there, better than being a porteuse, I can tell you."

"What's a porteuse?"

"You know, the girls who load the ships, carrying the coal or rum or sugar on their heads. They worked twelve hours a day, then, got four dollars a month. . . . So I was well off at the Mauriers'. We kept right on working, everyone did in St. Pierre. The mountain stopped rumbling after a few more days and so we thought the ash would soon stop falling. But the country people kept coming in. They thought St. Pierre would be safe. Farther up the mountain, they said, the hot mud was rolling still, choking the rivers, and the ash so thick on everything that the birds were dying in the trees. Then suddenly in our yard the birds began to die, too."

"Why didn't you go away?" He sat up now, so interested that he had forgotten the storm.

"Well, Mr. Maurier took his wife to Fort-de-France, but the servants had to stay and guard the house. The city was full of thieves, people sleeping in the streets, stealing from the shops and fighting. It was terrible, terrible." She paused. "Then came La Veretta, the smallpox. So many died, they ran out of coffins. It's funny," Agnes reflected, "how people think that nothing can ever happen to them. Not brave, I think, only stupid. Leon, the butler, had such a nice room in the Mauriers' house, he didn't want to leave! Just sat there with a bottle of the best wine from the cellar. 'Sit tight,' he said. 'It'll pass.' But I wasn't so sure. Fires were breaking out all over town. Leon sent me in to buy things; *he* wouldn't go on account of La Veretta! It's good he sent me, otherwise I wouldn't have seen the mud coming. I saw it sliding down the mountain and I knew as well as I know my name that that was the end of St. Pierre. So I found a man with a fishing boat and I gave him the five dollars Leon had given me. I told him to get me away, anyplace, I didn't care where, but get away.

"We were just out of the harbor when the mud wall hit the sugar factory. You would have to see it to believe it, Patrick! It covered the factory—and that was a big place, let me tell you—covered it up. It was gone in a minute, gone with all the people in it. Oh, God! And the mud kept rolling into the harbor, driving the sea away. When the water came rushing back, it lifted the ships in the harbor like chips of wood and drowned them, drowned the whole city before it pulled back into the bay. Behind the city the cane fields burned and I knew the Mauriers' house was gone, too, with Leon drinking wine in his nice room. The sky was black as night. I never saw St. Pierre again," she finished, very quietly.

"Don't you ever want to?"

"I could go. I've got a piece of land there, family land that was given to us when the slaves were freed. My cousins live on it, but I've got the right to go back any time I want, of course—I'm family. I don't want to, though."

"Why? Was it a bad place?" Patrick liked this talk. It was grown-up talk and he wished it would go on.

"Oh, they say it was a wicked city, the theater and dancing and all that. They say it was like Paris. But that's not true. I've been in both places and I know. Ah, but it was a grand life! Sundays when the family went calling, Madame Maurier wore her diamond bracelets over her kid gloves, and they'd ride in the coach with their fine horses and the coachman with his gilt buttons—"

"Did you ride in the coach, too?"

"Who, I!" She laughed. "Of course not! I worked my feet off for the Mauriers! I had the job because my maman had been parlor maid there and when she died, they gave me a position. My maman died with her fifth baby, you know."

"And your daddy?" (He half expected the answer.)

"He went away."

Patrick nodded. Daddies usually did. His mind sped on. "Tell me what happened on the boat?"

"Well, then, we landed here on St. Felice and found everyone spoke English! I stood on the wharf and wanted to cry. But I wouldn't, because a crowd was there waiting to hear what was happening in Martinique and I was too proud to cry in front of them all. I didn't know where to go. Then a white man came and leaned out of his carriage and spoke to me in French, queer French, though he told me later that was the way they spoke it in France. I didn't believe that but I found out it was so. . . . Well anyway, that's how I came to work for the Francis family."

"At Eleuthera?"

"What? What do you know about Eleuthera?"

"You took me there once."

"Lord, you're ten now. You couldn't have been a day over three!"

"Well," he said proudly, "I remember it. Mr. Virgil Francis died at Eleuthera. I read it in the paper a while ago."

"Yes, I know."

"It was a beautiful house, wasn't it?"

"Beautiful? Falling apart! That house hasn't been fixed up properly since Lord knows when."

"It was beautiful," Patrick insisted. "On top of a hill. Were they nice to you?"

"Oh yes. . . . Young Mr. Francis, so gentle he was, reading all day till his eyes hurt. He fell sick soon after he married. I helped nurse him till he died and then I—"

"He died?" Death interested him.

"Yes. Oh, that's enough, I'm running off at the mouth. Listen! The storm's over."

It had passed and crickets had started their music.

"Tell me about France," he said suddenly.

"I don't remember much about that. It was a long time ago."

"The volcano was much longer!" he cried.

"Anyway, I don't remember."

"You don't want to! And I like to hear about true things that happened—you know I do!"

She ruffled his hair. "Sometimes you're like an old man." And as if she were not talking to him at all, but into the air, she said, "I hope things will be easy for you."

"That I won't be caught in a volcano, you mean?"

"A human being is so small," she said, still talking to the air. "You can squash him like a bug."

He persisted. "The volcano, you mean?"

She looked at him now. "No. Life is what I mean. So go to sleep."

Those were the years of his childhood.

Four

At thirteen or fourteen a boy became a man. Then it was that he might earn his first wage, cutting fodder for the animals on the sugar estate. He would become aware of the ways that were open to him. The most frequented led through the estate, first doing odd jobs on a day-work gang, planting and weeding. If he did well he would probably be hired permanently. By his early twenties he would have learned enough and his arms would be strong enough to cut cane. There would be, then, years of that, the larger portion of his life. When he grew too old to cut cane he would go back among the young boys to care for the animals. All this, of course, depended upon whether he was "taken on" by one of the local estates; if not, he might sail away to try his luck on some other island.

The other path was narrower by far. If a boy was ambitious and smart at his lessons, and if the money could be found somehow, he might go on to Boys' Secondary School in Covetown. Then someday, wearing a suit and tie, he would go to work in a shop or bank or perhaps in the customs office or the courthouse. Boys' Secondary was a white building set among tended lawns, with a Church of England chapel and a fine cricket field in back. The headmaster wore an impressive black gown and a clerical collar. The masters were of the white race, but since planters usually sent their sons overseas to school, few of the students were. Yet the atmosphere was loftily British and a bookish boy from Sweet Apple, passing by and staring within, could not be sure whether his heart was beating with prideful hope or apprehension.

Oh, it would be foolish to set one's sights so high! One might not, probably would not, even pass the entrance examinations! So Patrick told himself and told his mother too, who did not want to hear.

"I've saved the money, and you'll go," she said.

Yet, on that first morning while she waited with him for the bus, the bright pink "Jamboree" loaded with laborers and women taking their produce to town, there were tears in her eyes.

Suddenly it became clear that a human being can be of two minds. Much as she had wanted it for him, so much did she fear the step that he was taking into the larger world, among people who would make him different from the boy she knew. This awareness touched him with brief melancholy, even on so triumphant a morning. Here was a passage, a passing out.

Yet it had already begun a long time before. Ever since his first day at the village school he had been changing, leaving her. This now was only a further step, toward what he did not know.

At thirteen one often does as much thinking and inner growing after school hours as in school. If the school stimulates, so much the better—the two parts of the day can complement each other.

Patrick did well. The masters were serious, disciplined men. Some of them even had some humane comprehension of how a boy from a village shack would need to struggle for survival amid unfamiliar order and decorum. For Patrick it was easier than for many: Agnes had already taught him the social graces.

In the sciences and mathematics he held his head above water. But in the Latin class, in history and literature, the realms of words, he swam with the best. His favorite class was history, taught by Father Albert Baker, a celibate, overweight Anglican priest with tobacco-stained teeth and keen, kindly eyes.

It was through Father Baker that his friendship with Nicholas Mebane came about.

"You boys should get to know one another," he said one day after class. "You'd like each other, I believe."

Patrick stood awkwardly. Nicholas, he knew, was the son of a doctor and had his own group of Covetown friends among the light-brown aristocracy. The school—the world, he was already able to surmise—was tightly partitioned; here, in addition to Nicholas's group, were the clustered whites, sons of bankers and middlemen not in a class with planters, who did not necessarily go abroad to school; here, lastly, was Patrick's group, most of them quite black, these the brightest boys from the villages. Patrick, except for his color, did not fit with Nicholas.

But the latter put his hand out. He had a frank manner.

"Glad to," he said. "I know you don't live in town, but maybe you'll stay in later some afternoon?"

So easily did it happen, so easily can two people surmount all differences when the chemistry is right. Certainly Patrick had never had a friend like Nicholas, and it soon appeared that Nicholas had never had one like Patrick. It was not just because they were both good-looking, capable at sports, and clever at their studies, for these things were mostly true of all the other boys; they would not have been accepted at the school otherwise. It was a sharing, a point of view, a mutual admiration, an indefinable.

Through the eyes of Nicholas, Patrick saw Covetown as though it were entirely new to him. At the wharf Nicholas pointed out the moored yachts and identified their owners.

"There aren't many here now, but before the war the bar of Cade's Hotel used to be filled with planters and millionaire yachtsmen, my father says. And of course the Crocus Club." He grinned. "Funny, our country club has everything they have; in fact, our tennis courts are supposed to be better." He looked at Patrick. "You know what? I bet you could get into any white man's club." He put his head on one side. "Well, maybe not. You *almost* could fool them, though."

"As if I would consider trying!" Patrick was indignant.

"I didn't mean you would."

They stood looking out over the harbor. Sugar lay on the quay ready for shipment. Square-sailed fishing boats had drawn up to unload.

"I used to see destroyers here during the war," Nicholas said. "Painted in zigzags. Camouflaged."

For Patrick the war had been so far away that it seemed unreal, except when his mother's newspaper ran a picture of wreckage in London, of houses blown apart, and then he would wonder what had happened to the people in the houses.

"It's funny," Nicholas said. "There was all that modern stuff here, planes and bombs and submarines like the one that came to Grenada. My father was there when it came." A German submarine had sunk a Canadian passenger ship near shore, and then quite coolly had moved out again into the ocean. "Then you think how, on this island, the quickest way to get from Covetown to the other side is still by sailboat! And some of our roads are so bad that it's easier to travel by mule than by car. We're not much changed from what we were two hundred years ago."

He's only quoting his father, Patrick thought, liking his friend none the less for that.

Turning back to Wharf Street, they paused to peer in at Da Cunha's glitter.

"You think they've got a lot of stuff in there? I was in their cellar storeroom once. Loaded from floor to ceiling with things from all over the world! A lot of these merchants—I don't say Da Cunha—but a lot of them make a fortune in smuggled goods, especially whiskey; did you know that?"

"Even today? I thought all that ended with the pirates."

"You'd be surprised," Nicholas said wisely.

They went on up the hill past the government buildings. Patrick had never thought about government before. It had only taken shape for him in the form of a mailbox or the sight of a policeman in his white, tropical hat and his red stripes, standing in front of the court-house. Once when the king had sent a new governor from overseas, he had watched the crowd at Government House, the dignitaries in their fancy clothes passing through the gates. That was government.

"My father goes there all the time. He's a member of the Legislative Council." Nicholas made a pyramid of his hands, wiggling his fingertips. "At the top you have the governor. We're a crown colony, which means we're responsible to Parliament in London. We've got a legislature with two houses, just like Parliament. There's the elected House of Assembly—my father started out there—and then there's the Legislative Council, which is higher. Half of its members are selected by the governor. My father was selected by the governor," he added with simple pride.

Such matters of election and appointment were of little interest to Patrick. Regarding the union jack as it floated above the great white mansion, he had a physical sensation of awe, that was all. Councils and assemblies were too complicated to master, and somewhat dry; it was enough now to master Covetown, let alone London.

"The British Empire won't last much longer." Nicholas said then, solemnly.

"What do you mean? There won't be any more king?"

"It's more complicated than that. My father says there will be what he calls a loosening. It won't happen all at once. But people aren't going to work for half nothing anymore. Look at the riots they've had in Barbados and Jamaica."

Patrick hadn't heard of the riots but, nodding, pretended that he had.

"There've been more labor laws passed since the war than they'd passed in a century. They know in London that they've got to do something about conditions. . . . Why else do you think they sent Lord Moyne's royal commission to look into things? They haven't made the report public yet, but I'll bet you—my father says—it will favor federation of all the islands. Naturally, the business people and the planters will fight it, but it will come. Anyway, my father says independence will come one day, too, and the English know it. It's only a question of time. When it comes we'll need educated men to run things. That's why I'm going to be sent to England to study law."

The school taught to the Cambridge O level, and a sizable group of boys, working toward the overseas certificate, were planning careers in medicine and law. Patrick felt the allure of such a future but very little envy. There was in his nature an element of fatalism, of acceptance. He was not a Mebane and that was that.

The Mebanes lived on Library Hill, just under the pinnacle on which stood Government House. Here, in a row of stucco houses, each with its fenced-in yard, its boisdiable trees and its porch with a fine view of the harbor, lived the leaders of the black upper class: Dr. Sprague, the dentist, for example, and lawyer Malcolm Fort, and the Cox brothers, undertakers.

Dr. and Mrs. Mebane were handsome coffee-colored people. Their quiet clothes and the furnishings of their house were refined, Patrick knew, although his experience of refinement had been limited to the headmaster's rooms at school, where he had been asked to tea, his oddly vivid memory of the Kimbrough house, and his mother's nostalgic descriptions. All of these had been "white" homes. He was astonished, therefore, to see what he saw in his friend's house: so many pictures and books, elegant china, and the supper brought in by a servant.

They made him welcome. Dr. Mebane had a positive manner of speech, as though he were trying to convince the listeners of something important.

"My father was a doctor before me. I don't know whether you boys can realize how exceptional that was in those times. The only other two doctors on this island were white men, come out here from England. Both of them were alcoholic. My father, with half the training, was the one you'd want if you were really sick. He'd go way up into the hills at night anytime he was called, riding his horse, carrying a lantern.

"He worked like two men to educate me and my brother; I don't know how he did it. My late brother Edgar became a barrister and was one of the leaders of the Pan-African Congress in Paris right after the war. Nineteen nineteen, that was. They had a brave agenda, most of which didn't come to pass, although some of it did. Well, things move slowly. One learns patience. Anyway, it's men like him, educated men, who bring about the changes, never forget it." The doctor knocked his pipe out. "Am I talking too much, boring you?"

"No, sir," Patrick said.

He was honored at being included in serious conversation, even though he did not understand all of it. He felt great respect; he felt himself in the presence of a new way of living.

"What do they talk about?" Agnes wanted to know. She was pleased and curious whenever Patrick was asked to stay overnight at the Mebane house. Also he was aware of a certain resentment that she was trying to conceal.

"I don't know. Everything." He never meant to make his answer come out irritably. But it was hard, impossible, to explain to Sweet Apple what Library Hill was like. Oh, he could answer to her satisfaction what color the curtains were, and to please her he took care to remember—but the ideas and attitudes were something else.

There was a vague and growing disturbance in his mind. How little he himself knew compared, for instance, with Nicholas, who was his own age! It was as if he had been living in a cocoon.

"They say he sees white patients in town after office hours," Agnes remarked. "People who don't want to discuss anything too personal with their regular doctor."

"I don't know."

"I wouldn't expect you to know that. Haughty people, though, aren't they? All that kind are."

"They aren't haughty to me."

Yet there were things he would have been ashamed to let them see. Not his poverty, his simple house, for there was none of that particular kind of falsity in him, but other things: the ignorance.

Agnes kept the windows tightly shut at night. On each window she had painted a red cross. From earliest childhood he had known that this was to keep a loup-garou from getting into the house and sucking the blood from people's throats as they lay asleep.

"Sometimes it flies over the trees," Agnes had warned him. "You can easily mistake it for a bat. It's especially dangerous to babies."

When Patrick was about nine years old it had become clear that this was absolute nonsense. They had had a quarrel about it.

"You think you're too smart to listen to what I tell you, hah?" Agnes had berated him. "Getting too big for your boots, you are."

Afterwards, as always when she had been short-tempered, she had come to stroke his head. "Well, all right, maybe it isn't true. But suppose it is? How can one be sure?" That was the sort of thing it would have been embarrassing for the Mebanes to know.

But it worked the other way, too, an odd reversal. Dr. Mebane said things he would not dare to repeat before Agnes.

"My great-great-grandmother was a slave for the Francis family," he told the boys one day. "There's an old estate on the other side of this island—you may have seen it—Eleuthera. Well, the details are vague, 'lost in the mist of time,' I believe the poet says. All I know is, her name was Cupid and her father was a son, or maybe a nephew, of the Francis family. This was toward the end of the seventeen hundreds. She must have been a beautiful girl. White women were scarce on the plantations, you know, and life was very dull. So the white master went to the slave woman and naturally he chose the best-looking, the healthiest. Sometimes there was a lasting love between them. He'd buy jewels for the woman, dress her in satin and lace. When there were children, the father freed them, manumitted them. It would have been scandalous not to do so. Some of these fathers were generous with money, with land or an education. So after a century or more, what have you got? You have a brown class. Brown, less brown, least brown." The doctor smiled ironically. " 'Least brown' even acquired the dignity of being addressed as Mr. or Mrs. Well, anyway, that's the explanation of why the people who work on the sugar estate today are coal black and why," he said, with a certain mocking tone, "why I am invited to teas at Government House. Not to private little dinner parties, mind you, certainly not. But when you're in government you're as good as anyone. Yes, it all goes back to the bed, when you think about it."

Patrick was silent. Grown people didn't talk about "beds" in front of boys. At least, Agnes didn't. She would have washed his mouth out with soap if he had done so. "Dirty talk," she would have called it.

"Color," the doctor resumed. "We think about it all the time, don't we? Even when we don't want to admit it."

"I don't think about it," Patrick said untruthfully.

"I don't believe it."

"We never talk about it at home," Patrick said.

"Don't tell me you don't think about it, though. You're lighter than any of us here."

Of course he thought about it even more than he realized. It was just always there. When he looked around the class and saw that his features were exactly those of the white boys, only the skin betraying the difference . . . How easy life would be, he thought, if one could remove the last trace of that *other* from the skin. And on the other hand, he could recall how it had thrilled him when Nicholas won the debate from a boy just out from England, a freckled red-haired boy with a haughty accent barely understandable. The triumph had thrilled him, not just because Nicholas was his friend, but because it had been a victory for color.

"You are lighter than any of us here," Dr. Mebane said again. "How do you suppose that happened?"

Patrick felt a flush of shame. Whose shame? Not his own, surely. What had he to do with it?

The doctor leaned forward. "You're embarrassed. You shouldn't be. There is a proper way to talk about these things. They are a part of life. And anyway, we are all men in this room. You shouldn't be embarrassed," he repeated kindly.

But the doctor could not have known the full reach of his thoughts. He was thinking of his mother. That business about the white man and the mistress . . . She had been in France; the man who had fathered him had deserted her. And he was filled with anger toward his unknown father.

Now color was becoming totally confused with sex. Yet they were two different things. His mother ought to have hated whiteness, after that. But there was a contradiction in her, that contradiction of which he had so long been aware. She was proud that estate workers coming into her shop called her Miss. He had asked her once why she was more polite to customers who were brown like herself, and so often curt with those who were very black. He had received not only a denial but such a lashing of her tongue that he never mentioned the subject again.

But it was all around, in the very air. It came to him, lying awake one night, that even Dr. Mebane, for all his talk and insight, had betrayed his secret pride in his own light skin. A certain satisfaction had revealed itself in his smile and voice, belying the righteous indignation in his words. He is proud of those invitations to Government House, Patrick thought, and he felt an odd compassion, which would no doubt have astonished the doctor if he had known of it.

Also, he saw that this pride was really shame. It was like despising oneself.

The few years of schooling passed, flashing as they always do, so that when a long time later one looks back over them, only a few bright areas stand out in a sometimes serene, sometimes dull, sometimes fretful expanse of routine. In Patrick's case, the particular brightness, in spite of anything, was Nicholas and his father's cheerful house. Secondly it was Father Baker, who could always find time for a boy after school, who gave him hard things to do, long lists of books "to stretch the mind," he said. "Read Gibbon's Decline and Fall; hard going, but without it you won't understand how we came to be where we are."

Father Baker supplied the lists, but Nicholas supplied the books, a glorious boxful each Christmas. ("Patrick, don't be shy about accepting a gift. Don't let's be self-conscious with each other. I happen to have more money, no credit to me; it's not important and don't let it be.")

So he grew, in those vital years between thirteen and seventeen when it is said the best learning is done. Wandering about the island, he began to connect the things his eyes saw with the things he read or was being taught, all of these weaving and interlocking with each other into something that as yet had no design, but seemed to point toward one.

During the long holidays before his final year, Father Baker gave an assignment: Write something about St. Felice, anything old or new, geological, commercial, anything. Father Baker gave difficult assignments.

Patrick had at first no idea what to write about. He worried over it. Then one day it came to him. At home in Sweet Apple he had wandered down to the beach and there encountered his old friend Ah Sing. And for no reason he could explain, regarding the stone-black eyes slanted above the Chinaman's cheekbones, it came to him that Ah Sing could just as well be taken for one of the Caribs who lived in their reservation on the far remote slope of Morne Bleue. But they have always been here! he thought, astonished. And Ah Sing comes from the other side of the world! How could that be?

He resolved to learn more. Father Baker liked to talk about "intellectual excitement." Patrick had probably never experienced what the teacher had meant, yet now, walking on the hard wet sand near the water's edge, he thought he might be feeling it. "It is a kind of fire," Father Baker had said. Yes. Yes. I want to say something about this place where I live, a strange place, when you think about it. All these so various and different people, living here, each in his layer, like those bottles of colored sand that is laid in stripes, apart! First there had been the Indians. This place had been all theirs, yet there was only a remnant of them left. You never heard much about them, other than the comment made by blacks that they had "good hair." Sometimes you saw them fishing at night by torchlight at the river. Now and then you saw the men on the roads with their loads lashed onto their backs, it being beneath the dignity—that much he knew—of an Indian man to carry anything on his head. It was all right for women, but not for men. You saw them bringing their baskets to the market for sale, or more rarely, carrying bananas down the mountainside to Covetown. They didn't go in for hired labor very much, and almost never worked on the estates. They gave an impression of silence and independence; a superior reserve was on their faces.

Once he had made his way on foot to the place where they lived. He had expected no profound revelations, so he had not been disappointed to find merely what he had seen in any other inland village: two rows of shingled huts with tin roofs, some goats and some chickens scratching in a little garden plot behind each house. Some things were different: women pounding cassava in gourds and men hacking a canoe out of a cedar trunk. He had observed all these things, both the resemblances to and the differences from the life around them, and having done so, had not felt any further curiosity. Yet now he did.

He went to the public library in Covetown. It was a fair-sized room, dusty in shafted sunbeams, up the stairs from the tax office which had once been the courthouse from which buccaneers were sent to the gallows. Happily, it contained an encyclopedia and a moderate collection of history books. On the shady side of the room Patrick sat down with a pile of books and began to take notes.

The original inhabitants of the Leewards and the Windwards were the Arawaks, who came in canoes from what is now Guiana. They were a pacific people, farmers and fishermen. After many centuries—no one knows how many or how remote—they were followed by the Caribs, coming possibly from what is now Brazil. These were a very different people, warlike and ferocious. Indeed, the word *cannibal* is said to be derived from their name.

It has been fairly well established that many thousands of years ago, when a land bridge between Asia and America existed in the region of the Bering Sea, the ancestors of both these tribes had wandered across and slowly, gradually dispersed themselves . . .

So it was true, then! These people and the Chinaman Ah Sing! He had observed it! And it was true!

He read on.

The Caribs slaughtered the Arawak men and married their women. . . . For many generations the men continued to speak the Carib language among themselves; although they understood the Arawak tongue, which the women continued to speak, they would never use it themselves. *Hammock* is an Arawak word. *Hurricane* is another.

With a feeling of recognition, Patrick paused a moment. What pleasure in words! Written, the word *hurricane* even looked like the haste and ruin of the real thing which he had seen once, a few years before: whole villages blown to pieces and great palms uprooted like weeds, as the wind came roaring at 160 miles an hour from the east.

He went back to the book and picked up the pen.

> With whiskey and some cheap ornaments, the European bought island after island from the Caribs. Not satisfied with ownership of the land, he pressed on for ownership of the native, but totally without success. The Carib would not be enslaved. Through mass and individual suicide, he defied the conqueror.

Glorious courage, proud courage! Patrick was youthfully and deeply moved.

After a week of diligence, he completed his notes, went home and began to write. He worked all day; when darkness came he set an oil lamp on the counter of the store and kept on.

His mother complained. "You've been up half the night for three nights now!"

"I have to," he answered patiently.

He had set it all in orderly mental sequence, so that his pen ran easily: history, adaptation to change, daily ways . . .

> At the top of the palm is a bush which looks like cabbage. Used as a shelter or a garment, it will keep a man dry in the heaviest rain.
>
> . . . know how to hypnotize an iguana by whistling to it so it can be tied up.
>
> . . . can shoot fish with a bow and arrow. Their bowstrings were made of liana vines, and the poison for their arrowtips, in warfare, was made of the sap from manchineel trees. . . .

Early explorers report on their swimming feats. It is said that they were fast enough to knife sharks undersea.

. . . can still weave reed baskets fine enough to hold water.

And their inner life:

Long before Christianity, they had a belief in one central spirit of good, commanding the universe. Also, they had a concept of evil not unlike the early Christian belief in the devil. . . .

To sum up, I admire most their love of liberty. This is the reason, I think, why even now they will not work *for* anyone. They have no concept of rank, either. Again, even today, their chief lives in a house no better than anyone else's. They never understood the European's sense of hierarchy. . . .

When he had finished, it was the last night of the holidays. Having made a careful copy of his work, with no erasures, he went to bed, feeling tired, exhilarated, and also worried about the worth of what he had done.

Two days later Father Baker summoned Patrick to his office.

"Who helped you with this?" he asked.

"No one."

"Are you sure of that?"

"Who could have?" Patrick questioned simply.

"This is a scholarly piece of work," Father Baker said. Thoughtfully, he riffled Patrick's neat pages. "I never expected anything as thorough as this. You must have spent days on the research. What made you do it? Can you tell me?"

Patrick hesitated. "It started because of the Chinaman Ah Sing. I've known him since I was four or five"—and he went on to tell about his first puzzlement over the Chinaman's resemblance to the Indian. "Then I've been thinking, I guess I've always been thinking, about my own ancestors. You imagine Africa, you know—I suppose very inaccurately—but still you do. You think of cathedrals and those little English villages in picturebooks. All of that is in you. St. Felice makes pictures in your mind." He was ashamed to say how he still thought in colors, so he said merely, "People like the Da Cunhas—Nicholas said the first ones here were Jews, the wanderers, the Bible people. What could have brought them here, too?"

He gained confidence. "This island where we live is so small! Yet there are so many different kinds of people living here, come from all over, living together, and yet apart, not knowing one another. I was thinking: Can the whole world be like this, too? With people wandering from one place to the other, really all part of each other, but not wanting to be?"

Father Baker was looking at him so intently that Patrick stopped. Had he been making an idiot of himself?

Then Father Baker looked away. Patrick observed the ropy veins at the man's temples, the soiled and shabby gown, then followed his gaze out the window to where voices were competing on the playing fields.

Soon I shall be gone, he thought, and felt a painful emotion. Gone from friends and books, gone from the civility of this crowded little office and the man, the sort of men, who sat here.

Father Baker turned back to his desk, picked up a pencil, and made a little circular design. Then he spoke.

"What do you plan to do with your life, Patrick?"

"Well, get a job . . ." He had thought, or his mother had thought, he might apply at Barclay's Bank. The tellers were mostly light blacks, which would be, of course, anybody's definition of Patrick. "Maybe in a bank," he said.

"Is that what you want to do?"

Suddenly a new thought came. It was so powerful that it must have been in him for longer than he knew. "What I'd really like is to teach. To read a lot and teach. Like you—not the priest part, though," he finished awkwardly, and was ashamed that he had perhaps been tactless.

"I understand. You'd have no difficulty getting a certificate to teach grade school when you graduate from here. But a boy like you should really go to England, to university. It would be a nice thing if you could go with your friend Nicholas, wouldn't it?"

Yes, it would. But maybe Father didn't know how little he had. Maybe he thought Patrick was another Nicholas.

But no. "You surely would be able to get a partial scholarship."

That wouldn't be enough. His thoughts flew, then stopped. No matter. Whatever he would need, it would be more than he could afford.

"Well, think about it," Father Baker said as he stood up.

The new idea burned within Patrick in spite of himself. He did not speak of it to Nicholas, partly because he was a private person, even with his best friend, and partly because he was realistic and it made no sense to waste time talking of impossibilities. But he walked down to the wharf and watched the ships, even the interisland schooners, with a kind of longing that he had never felt before.

One evening at home something compelled him to speak. "My teacher said my paper about the Caribs was excellent."

Agnes nodded. "Very fine. Very fine."

"He thinks I ought to go to England. To university."

"He does? Maybe he'll give you the money for it?"

"I could get a partial scholarship."

"And the rest?"

"I don't know."

"Well, I don't know either. I think you'll stay here and get yourself a nice job and be grateful. Get foolish ideas out of your head."

Patrick flushed. Yes, it was only a fancy, a thing to be dismissed. But it clung to him. And he thought of Mistress Ogilvie, herself barely educated, teaching by rote the kings and generals of Europe—nothing, incidentally, of that great "dark continent" on which her pupils had originated; he compared her with the masters at Boys' Secondary and was shocked by the comparison. But if you were to set those masters beside the great scholars at Cambridge? What then? All the knowledge in the world, just bottled up in a few small places, uncorked for the few to drink! He thought of the laborers in the cane fields, who knew nothing. He wondered whether the folk in the great houses, men like old Mr. Kimbrough or—or the Tarboxes of Drummond Hall, for instance—might not, in their way, be as ignorant, knowing nothing much beyond the walls of their fine houses.

He felt a restless, cold discouragement.

"You want to go, don't you?" Agnes asked abruptly one night.

"Go?" he repeated.

"To England! To university! What are we talking about?"

"We aren't talking at all," he said angrily, "because it's not possible and I know it isn't."

"Maybe you're right," she said, a few days later.

"Right about what?" he asked, raising his head from his homework.

"Nothing. I was thinking out loud." Then she resumed, "What I meant was, right not to talk about your going overseas."

"I am right. And I don't want to hear it again!"

"Don't talk to me like that. I don't like your sassy voice."

He didn't look up and she went out of the room.

But a week or two afterwards she said to him, "I'm going away for a while, closing the shop. There won't be much to see to, but whatever there is you can see to it while I'm gone."

His first thought was, She must suddenly be homesick for Martinique. "Where are you going, Maman?"

"To New York."

"New York!" he cried, in astonishment.

He saw by her familiar sly smile that, in spite of her brusqueness, she was enjoying his surprise.

"Yes. I've business there."

"Business in New York? How will you get there?"

"On a freighter."

"Are you coming back, then?"

"Well, naturally I am! I have a little personal business, that's all! Do I have to tell you everything?" she complained. Then she touched his head. "There's nothing to worry about. You just stay here and do your work properly. I'll come home in a few weeks. And when I do, things will be different."

Five

TERESA, long afterward, was to remember the day by its colors: dim greens blurred through an intermittent, melancholy rain over the low New Jersey hills. It was her habit to see places and persons in color: her husband a troubled, cloudy gray and her children rosy, tender as petals. Eleuthera had once been a blue luster, but was no more.

Now a scattering of amateurish, poorly focused snapshots lay on the desk next to the window where she stood with her back to the room. Having been forced to glance at them, having touched them with her eyes, she had pulled away, as one pulls the hand from a hot surface.

"You don't even want to look at him properly." Agnes spoke quietly, yet Teresa felt challenge. "I'd like to know what you're thinking right now. Yes, I'd like to know."

Somewhere below, around the corner of the house, came the flute-like call of a child. Teresa trembled.

"I feel—I want to sink into a hole where no one could see me. Or get on a ship and go as far as it sails."

"As far as it sailed it couldn't take you far enough."

Teresa turned around. "How did you find me here?"

"Easy enough. In the New York telephone book. And somebody said you were in the country for vacation week."

"You always did know how to manage things."

"I had to learn. I never had anyone to manage them for me."

Delicately, without sound, Agnes placed the teacup in the saucer. Her feet, in their neat black shoes, were crossed at the ankles. Unobtrusively, she had already examined the room: the pale carpet, the marigolds in the dark-blue ginger jars and the photographs, these of an intimacy that belongs in an upstairs sitting room. Plainly she approved of what she saw. *Élevé au chapeau,* Teresa remembered suddenly, irrelevantly.

Agnes raised her eyes. "Don't be afraid of me," she said gently.

Afraid? No, terrorized. This must be the true experience of terror: the second before the fall through empty air . . . the strange footstep coming up the stairs at night . . .

"I'm not here to harm you. I could have talked long ago when I went back to the island, couldn't I? But I'm not cruel, I'm a decent woman. Besides, I want to protect my son, my Patrick. You don't think I want him to know the truth, do you?"

"Patrick," Teresa repeated.

"Well, you never gave him a name. So that's it, Patrick Courzon."

"I didn't know you had gone back home. Père never mentioned in his letters."

"He saw the boy once. I took him there when he was three, then never again. . . . You've broken your necklace."

Her cold, sweating hands had been twisting and twisting. Now blue beads rolled across the floor.

Agnes bent to pick them up. "Your nerves. But I keep telling you, I haven't come to ruin you. What good would that do anyone? I only need help for him, for his education. He wants to go to Cambridge."

Something throbbed and stabbed in Teresa's head. That figure printed on film. That quick impression of tallness and thinness, of teeth, of a white shirt—all of it lived and had been taken out of her, was of her. And if someone had asked—but Agnes had just asked a moment ago! *What do you feel?*—she could have answered only, I feel ruin. I taste the poison. Nothing left: no children, no home, no *name.* Richard would—it did not bear thinking of, what Richard would do.

"Seventeen years!" she cried out. "After seventeen years you come to me with this! My God, do you know what you're doing to me?"

Agnes said evenly, "Give me what I ask for, then, and I'll never come near you again."

Could one believe her?

"You do want to know what he looks like, don't you? Only it's hard for you to say so. All right, I'll tell you. He has the Francis nose, like you and your grandfather. And he's light. I've seen Italian sailors in Covetown not much lighter. I think really it's only his hair that gives him away."

Agnes had not oiled her hair that day; it coiled and crimped—one sensed the primitive, looking at that hair. Such curious and devious tracks does memory follow: one thought of drums, looking at that hair. Of drums? Years ago on the plantations, so Père had said, you could hear them all day Sunday, and once the child Tee herself had seen the African dance, the heat and stamp of the calinda, powerful and hot.

She wiped her forehead, pulling herself back into the present. "I can get you the money. I will."

Richard took charge of the investments and the bank accounts. But she could always sell a bracelet. There were so many of them. He bought too many expensive, unnecessary things.

"Yes, I'll get it for you. Then you'll leave me alone? After all, he's yours, isn't he, yours?" *It's only his hair that gives him away.* "I have four children of my own, my husband's and mine. Three girls." *Long, silvery hair like limp silk on their shoulders.* "And my son, my first." *My lovely boy, my strong and gentle boy; I have never said so and never will, but he knows and I know, he is my heart.* "I can't let anything happen to them!" she cried harshly.

"Of course you can't."

"If—he—were ever to find out, it would all be over." She flung her arms out. "He would pull this house down! He's not the kind of man who would even try to understand . . . forgive . . ."

"What man is?" Agnes regarded her with grave, sad eyes. "I tell you, put this out of your mind. I was a mother to you, do you forget? More than Miss Julia ever was."

"That's true." There was no real memory of Julia, other than a pastel presence. No joy, nor conflict, either. And Teresa thought, Is that, perhaps, why I am what I am? I suppose, if I cared enough, I could be analyzed—goodness knows it's the fashionable thing to do these days—and then I would know; know, too, why I can be repelled by the Negro-ness of Agnes and a moment later find warmth and comfort in her.

"My little girl, Margaret, is retarded," she said suddenly, not having intended to. "Not a normal child. She will never grow up."

"I'm very sorry, Miss Tee."

"You know, sometimes I've had the craziest idea—that she might be a punishment."

Agnes nodded. "Not crazy. I've seen things like that."

But of course it was crazy, absurd. Only a peasant from a place like St. Felice could believe it: a lingering atavism out of centuries long past, flitting through the mind in moments of gloom.

Agnes touched a photograph on a table. "Is this your husband? A handsome man."

"Yes." When she was angry, she thought of him with contempt. An advertisement for hand-tailored suits. A male flirt, a chaser.

She was not in a position to complain.

"You're happy enough? He's good to you?"

These were less questions than statements; the fine polish of the room, the long fields and graceful trees beyond the windows would, for someone like Agnes, who had nothing, very likely be compensation for almost anything.

"He's good to me. I'm happy."

For in his way, Richard was fond of her. The strange allure of the "different" young girl from the foreign island had long ago, and predictably, worn off, but he was basically kind and had, moreover, grown up among people who seldom divorced their wives. He had no reason—none that he knew of!—to desert her.

With their children he was good-natured, patient even with poor Margaret's sticky hands and silly laughter; proud of the other daughters and of Francis, the precocious, lively boy. How had they begot such a boy? There was nothing of Richard in him except for fair hair and a certain way of smiling.

And she thought, sitting across from Agnes's soft, penetrating gaze, *We never talk about anything true except the children. We have never entered together into the heart of anything.* But it didn't matter. Even the "other women" really didn't matter. She had given her life to the rearing of children, much as a botanist concentrates on his experiments, the temperature of the greenhouse, and the chemistry of the soil.

She wanted, suddenly, to talk about Francis. "My son, my son Francis reminds me of my father."

"You can remember him?"

"A little, I think. I remember the stories he read to me. His voice was beautiful."

He was a long, tired shape under white bedclothes, lying in a room where the shutters were always closed against the glare of light. A black hearse, pulled by two sweating horses with black plumes on their heads, carried him away.

"He died bravely. He suffered and never complained."

"Père always said the Francises were tough. He said I was, too, even though I didn't think I was. He said it makes life bearable, that toughness."

"Your grandfather certainly had it," Agnes said grimly. "You know what he did to Clyde. Not that it wasn't to be expected, a colored boy—"

"You think that was the reason? That he wouldn't have done the same to anyone?"

Agnes smiled. "No. He had hatred, Miss Tee. He only thought he hadn't."

Tee was silent. Clyde, his life and his death, but most of all his death, must be stifled and buried under layers of secrecy and trembling.

"Still," Agnes reflected, "I don't curse him for what he did. There's murder in every one of us. I know I would kill for Patrick if I had to."

The silence thrummed and hummed.

"Tell me, Miss Tee, do you ever see your mother?"

She wet her dry lips. "They've been here twice to visit."

"But you? You never want to go there?"

"No, never." Again the silence hummed. In a moment the humming would burst in Tee's head, would roar and crash into a scream. And laying her fingers on her quivering mouth, she looked past Agnes's head into the mirror that minutes ago had reflected only a pastel mosaic of flowers and books, but now thrust back into the room a fearful face, collapsed in a repression of tears.

She ran to Agnes. A shoulder received her; a hand soothed her back. She spoke, muffled, into the shoulder.

"I can't afford to cry."

"I know. Otherwise, I'd say 'cry it out, you'll feel better.' But you can't dare to."

Tee raised her head. "I've been lying to you. No, not lying, either. It's just—I don't know how I feel. I never do. I don't really know what the truth about myself is. Oh, I do want to know what he's like, I do! And still I'm afraid to know. Afraid because—because of what he is. Forgive me, Agnes."

"You don't have to say that. You think I've lived all these years in the world without knowing a few things about it?" There was grieving in the voice, voice of an old woman who has seen too much. "All right, I'll tell you more. He's a quiet boy, gentle, thinks about things. Half the time I can't figure out what he's thinking. Ambitious, too, only it's not money he wants. And proud. Light as he is, he's proud of being black. Prouder than some who're coal black. Queer, isn't it?"

"Oh, yes." Sad and queer.

"And is he happy, Agnes?"

"He has friends. People like him. Yes, I'd say he's as happy as anyone. . . . I don't know what else to tell you. It's hard to describe all these years in a few words. But he's been the best part of my life, he has."

"I remember the day you took him. I wanted to look at him—and I didn't want to. And I've been ashamed of the not wanting to, ever since."

"There wasn't anything to be ashamed of! You were barely sixteen and frightened to death. You had plenty of courage, though, never think you didn't."

"I often think there are two kinds of courage. There's the kind that holds on, just quietly endures, has a plan and clings to it. That's my kind, that's what my life is. But the greater courage is being able to risk, just plunge off the path into the unknown. And that I'm not able to do."

"Come out with the truth, you mean."

Tee nodded. Suddenly she was aware that she was breathing hard, winded as though she had been running.

"You'd be a fool to do that. And I'd say it even if I didn't want Patrick for my own. You'd be exchanging him for all this." Agnes waved her arm at the room.

"You know I don't care about things that much. I can get along with much less than all this, Agnes!"

"The four children? The husband?"

"The children," Tee said, very low.

"I see. That's how it is! You should have had more. You should have had a man to love all your life."

Tee's smile was faint. "So should you."

"I don't need it as much as you do. I never did. You had a heap of loving in you from the time you could walk. You were born like that."

"I loved you, didn't I, Agnes? You and Père. And now I've got Francis. I wish you could see him. Everything you said about—Patrick —I could say about him. He's quiet, gentle, curious . . ."

From below stairs came sounds of doors and feet. Agnes stood and put on her hat.

"I'd better leave before somebody comes and gives you questions to answer. But you will take care of that?"

"I will. And I hope—I wish everything that's good for him. I'll think, somewhere, making his way in the world, there's this boy who—" She stopped.

Agnes took Tee's hand between both of hers. It was an old gesture, long forgotten, now suddenly recalled.

"Agnes? After you've left I'll think of so much more I should have said. About everything you've done for me and what you are and how I love you."

"You don't have to tell me all that. I know."

They went downstairs to the door. On the threshold Agnes turned back, her gaze directed past Teresa into the hall, dim now in the fading afternoon.

"I see things. You remember how I could always see things."

"What things? What do you mean?"

"He'll come back into your life, Patrick will. Not through me, no, never through me! And maybe not into your life, I'm not sure. But into your children's. Yes. I see that clearly."

Teresa made no answer. Again the primitive, she thought, reassuring herself. Superstition, out of Africa. That, too, was part of Agnes. But her hands shook so that she could barely close the door and slide the bolt.

Later Francis asked, "Who was that colored woman with you this afternoon? I passed your room when I came upstairs."

"My old nursemaid. I guess that's what you'd call her."

"From St. Felice? What was she doing here?"

"She has a cousin working somewhere nearby, I think."

"I'm writing about St. Felice for economics, did I tell you? All about sugar prices and the competition of European beet sugar. People are always curious—even my teacher was—when I tell them my mother grew up on St. Felice."

"There's nothing so strange about it," Teresa said patiently.

"Well, they think it's all pirates and volcanoes, I suppose. But you know, when I read that diary of the first François, it was thrilling, actually."

Actually was the fad word this season at school. The youthfulness

of this, the innocent boast of the basketball letter on his sweater, these
as well as the two parallel lines across a forehead only sixteen years
old—touched her sharply. She wanted to respond to his enthusiasms.

"I suppose, too, they think we're all sugar millionaires?"

"Oh, of course! And," Francis added, somewhat shyly, "they've got
a lot of ideas about interracial sex. But I tell them"—he laughed—
"I tell them we're all white, there's none of that in our family."

She was aware that her hands flew to knot themselves in her lap,
then moved to twine on the dressing table among the combs and
powder boxes.

"I mean to go there someday, even if you won't go."

"It's not as romantic as you think it is. You'd be disappointed.
And"—prodding gently—"you'd do better to concentrate on getting
into Amherst year after next, since that's where you want to go."

"I'll do that, don't worry," Francis said with his father's stubborn,
charming smile.

Of course he would. He was a scholar. And Agnes's voice sounded
in her head: *A scholar. Never a minute's trouble . . .*

"You're frowning," Francis said.

"Am I? I didn't mean to."

"Things go hard with Margaret today?"

"No harder than usual."

Francis thrust his hands into his pockets, jingling coins, as mascu-
line a gesture, she thought, as girls' fishing for their shoulder straps
was a feminine one.

"Want me to help you get her to bed?"

"That would be nice. I am a little tired tonight, really. And she does
behave better for you than for any of us."

He looked thoughtfully at his mother. "People say you're wearing
yourself out."

"Who says?"

"Oh, friends and Dad's family and even the maids. Just about
everybody."

"They think I ought to put Margaret away someplace."

"Just a special school," he said gently, lowering his eyes.

"I wish they would all leave me alone!" she cried.

The boy was troubled. "Some people say you seem to be punishing yourself."

"Punishing myself! For what, I ask you?"

"I don't know, Mother."

A punishment, she had said to Agnes.

"Dad asked me to talk to you about it again, because you won't listen to him." Now Francis raised his eyes. Clear, beautiful, candid eyes they were, the only ones in all the world that could *speak* to her. "I said I would, but it wouldn't be any use. I told him you couldn't just desert a child like that. It's not her fault that she was born the way she was."

"You think that, too," she murmured.

"I think it would be easier for you to send her away. Most people would, but you wouldn't. You wouldn't do that to your own child."

There was such hell in her heart! And she turned away, so that he should not see its reflection in her face.

"Shall I go bring Margaret upstairs?"

"Yes, do, please."

Desperately she looked around the room, a room to which, as to the whole house, she had given her love, expressing it in the homely shapes of dear, familiar things: Francis' old, stuffed bear on top of a cabinet, a photo of the girls in party dresses, a framed snapshot of their first beloved Airedale, a row of garden books. There was no comfort tonight. Shadowed, alien, the room drew back from her, the walls receding, vanishing, so that the world's chill swept in. . . .

Margaret shuffled at the door. "Mama?"

"Yes, darling?"

"I don't want to go to bed." The loose, helpless mouth puckered toward tears.

"I'll read you a story first. I'll read you *Peter Rabbit.*"

"No, Francis read!" And the great girl, taller than her brother's shoulder, stamped her foot.

With enormous effort Tee summoned energy. At least the tussle would be easier tonight with Francis helping.

"Come, Margaret darling." And taking the girl's hand, she gave a grateful smile to her son. "Sometimes I don't know what I'd do without you."

When the house was quiet, she lay down. Richard would be coming home late, but she was thankful to be alone. She was often alone, he having an independent life in the brokerage house and the galleries. A faintly bitter smile touched her lips. He saw himself as a fascinating man, a financial wizard and a connoisseur of art. Yet, to be fair, he really did understand paintings.

"Anatole Da Cunha is one of the greats," he had told her. "Wait and see, his work will be priceless after his death." Acting upon this conviction, he had bought four of Anatole's landscapes. "His best work comes from his memory of the Indies. But you should be able to judge, Teresa: Does it have the living spirit of home for you?"

Yes. Oh, yes! Now, between the windows, in the path of the lamplight, hung Morne Bleue; in the foreground, under an oyster-colored sky opaque with heat, lay a stretch of familiar rippling cane, twice a man's height, and weaving through the cane a line of cutters, their black arms curved in the sway of labor like dancers on a stone frieze.

Richard had put it there for her pleasure, but she had not wanted it, had not wanted anything of St. Felice, not even Père's books when he died, although they had sent them to her anyway, sending too, without knowing that they had—how could they know?—the click of croquet balls on the lawn, the twinkle of candles in the Catholic cemetery, and the smell of rain.

Now too, outside on the New Jersey hills, it had begun to rain, an even, pattering, all-night fall. In St. Felice the rain comes plunging, pounding the earth and ceasing as suddenly as it begins, leaving a vapor to rise from the steaming ground.

Down at the wharf when the banana ship is moored, through the steaming wet come lines of barefoot women, bearing their loads on their heads.

"See," Mama says, "how gracefully they walk! It's the same as the nuns teaching you to walk with a book on your head."

But it is not the same; the child Tee sees that clearly. It puzzles her that certain things should be so, that the heavy work is always done by blacks and that they live as they do. She goes to town with Agnes to bring some medicine to the cook's old aunt; the hot street stinks, the gutters run foul; the house holds merely a cot and a table. Why? No one tells her. Perhaps no one can.

Père talks with pride of Cambridge, of boats on a quiet river, of choirs and Gothic arches, of *gentlemen.* How can all that merge with Covetown?

Agnes says, "This boy needs the best. He deserves it."

Père says, "Three generations of our people have gone to Cambridge."

Now comes the fourth, and he doesn't know he is.

Teresa's head tossed on the pillow. Oh Francis, Francis my son, is this the real reason why I love you so much? Too much, maybe? That I want everything for you? Is it because I need to expunge, to *wipe* that other away, to wipe all the pain away, so that I might say, Here, you are my son, my only son; I have no other and there never was another? Is that why?

Oh, hell, hell in the heart.

She balled her fists at her sides. She firmed her lips. Listen, Teresa, this is the way it is. You just keep on doing what needs to be done, you hear me? And close your mind. You can do that. You've been doing it for a long, long time now.

Strong words, strong resolution. And yet you know—how well you know!—the days and the years when fear will flood again in gray afternoons, and the mouth will go dry and you will close your book to get up and walk around the room.

Agnes asked, "Are you happy enough?" Was that deliberate discernment or only the chance use of a word, that difference between "happy" and "happy enough"? For what is "enough"? For that matter, what is "happy"?

Oh, you can recognize happiness in other people! My mother is happy because she's not touchable, not breakable. When Papa died, her tears gushed and the wound healed. Richard? Yes, surely, Richard is happy. He has all he requires out of our marriage. I don't think he can even imagine what it is to be lonely.

As for me? When I walk in the rain I feel contentment. Books keep me company. My house is warm and safe on a windy night. There are two or three friends who are dear to me and I to them. Thankful that I can, I help the sick and the poor. And Francis—ah, Francis is my joy of joys! Without him, there would be no one under this roof to talk to. Poor, mindless Margaret. Two other girls who are like Richard, such glossy surface: good girls, just different from me, that's all.

I remember once I wanted to die; they say most people do at some time or other. Yet they get over it, as I did. You fall, but then you struggle up again. At least if you're worth your salt, you do.

Besides, "The Francis family is tough. Remember that," Père said.

Francis, too, lay listening to the rain. Tonight was one of his "anxious" nights, when he had trouble falling asleep. Often he had been told that he was oversensitive, and he supposed he was, if by that was meant a sharp awareness of other people's moods.

His thoughts kept circling. His mother had been troubled. Of course there was always Margaret, but somehow or other he didn't think it was Margaret who had been the reason. Ordinarily he would have asked her for the reason; they had between them a frankness that was both serious and humorous. There were certain times, though, when something held him back—and this was one of them—when a darkness crept over her, as when a cloud moves on clear water. These times came oddly, unexpectedly; she might be standing with the other mothers at some school function where he could be so proud of her, smiling quietly among the fashionables with their nasal twitterings— and suddenly the darkness would sweep over her. And he would know that for those few minutes she had withdrawn, that she had not been *there* at all.

Once, when he was very young, he had heard two maids talking about her.

"She's kind of a queer sort, but nice enough," they'd said.

And he had asked them, "Why is she a queer sort?"

"Oh," they had answered him, "we only meant, she is so far from home. She must be homesick."

He had pressed her, then, with questions. "Why don't we go to St. Felice? Why can't we visit?"

"It's too far . . . your sisters are too little . . . I get seasick . . . maybe someday."

She would never tell him anything important about the place, just odd little facts about, for instance, "mountain chickens," which are really enormous frogs that people cook like chicken. He wasn't sure what it was exactly that he wanted to know, only that it was more than she was willing to tell, which was strange because his father always talked so freely about his childhood.

Two times his grandmother Julia had come to visit. She was an important-sounding woman who kept complaining of the cold, although it was June. The child Francis hadn't liked her, even though she smelled like flowers and had brought wonderful presents.

"Your mother despises us," she had told him. "Our backward little island."

It was untrue. Francis had known that even then, for his mother was not a person who despised anyone. On the contrary, she was always excusing people, even when they were wrong.

Last week the gardener had smashed up the station wagon.

"There was no possible excuse," Richard said. "Woolgathering, not paying attention to the road."

"It's easy to condemn," Teresa said. "One never knows what is *behind* anyone." She hadn't said it to be pious or for the sound of it, but Richard had been annoyed. And Francis had been sorry for her.

He wondered whether, in spite of all concealment, she might be aware of his father's "escapades." He was old enough now to understand that there must have been, must still be, others like the one that had so disgusted him when he was fifteen. At dinner with a friend and the friend's parents in a restaurant he had encountered his father with a woman, a common, gaudy young woman, at the next table.

Richard had pleaded. "Don't tell your mother, son. It would only make everybody miserable. There's no harm in it, you know; I wouldn't hurt your mother for the world."

Why did people make these foolish marriages? Couldn't they tell beforehand that they wouldn't work? You had only to be with Richard and Teresa Luther for a couple of minutes to know how different they were.

Richard was extravagant and fond of himself. Packages kept arriving at the door although the closets were already overflowing. Money poured.

"Like French wine," said Teresa, who tended to be frugal. "Wanton waste."

Richard liked hunting and the parties that went with it.

"Wanton killing," Teresa said fiercely when he came home with a bleeding, limp deer hung over the car. "I can't bear to see it." She rescued stray animals.

Much of this had been barely overheard. There was never any overt quarreling. But children know these things. There is a coolness in the air of a house where the marriage is faltering.

In some vague way he felt a need to make up to his mother for all this. That, when he thought about it, was the real reason for his particular patience with poor Margaret, so that, unlike his other sisters, he didn't allow himself even to feel exasperated when she wet her pants or upset her plate.

His mother was grateful. "You're so kind to her, Francis," she would tell him, with a look of astonishment.

"You have a Presbyterian conscience," his father said, laughing, but not unkindly. "And the soul of a poet. A strange combination."

He did sometimes feel removed from other people, that was so. It was a kind of shyness that he had, inherited, he was sure, from Teresa. He knew that this shyness would have deprived him of his peers' approval if he had not luckily been given also a strong, tall body and the ability to excel at sports. In such random fashion does fate play with us!

Lately he wondered more often what, indeed, fate might be preparing for him. At seventeen you had to look toward the future. Richard naturally assumed that his son would work in the firm when the time came. His was one of the more prestigious firms on Wall Street; a young man might consider himself fortunate to start there at the top. But the prospect was already distressing to Francis: a lifetime under electric lights on a shelf in a vertical box counting money—for that's what it all came to, really, counting money. And no air, no sun!

Yet he had no alternative in mind. How simple it was when you were possessed by some passionate talent for music or medicine or— or anything! To be just a "bright student" who did well at everything, yet to be without distinction or direction, was burdensome, a somber prospect to a young man who was too serious, anyway.

He had thoughts, sometimes, of going off to be a rancher in the West—he'd been there once on a vacation trip—or of being a forest ranger or a dairy farmer, or just of writing a book in some quiet, leafy spot, although he had no idea what he would write about. Perhaps some sort of history? The past allured him. Before that, though, he'd like to see some more of the world, the places with fantastic names: Bora-Bora, Patagonia. And St. Felice. Yes, certainly, St. Felice, he thought in that last lucid moment before sleep. And he turned on the pillow, finding a comfortable hollow. Let sleep come now, softly. There were, after all, a few years left before he must decide what to do with his life!

The rain died and in its place the night wind rushed. Wind of the world! It shifts and rises, it drives, it goes where it will.

Six

Four years. As always, there had been periods when time sped away like a bright bird; at other moments it plodded heavily and Patrick couldn't wait to get home. Years afterwards, he liked to say that it was England's cold fog that had brought him back to St. Felice, and perhaps there was a kernel of truth in his little joke.

The ship rose and sank with the swells. Standing at the rail, feeling the spray on his face, he realized that he had forgotten how soft the air could be. Overhead, the stars were blue; they looked warm enough to hold in the hand. In the north their glitter was hard and one could believe that they were millions of miles away.

The man beside him, a white man, a civil servant on his way back to Jamaica after a leave, resumed conversation.

"And so you're glad to be home again."

"Yes, as glad as I was to leave four years ago."

"Were you not—comfortable—in England, then?"

The man was middle-class English, reserved and courteous. If they had been anywhere but on board ship, he would not have permitted himself so much curiosity. But then, on land they would not have been conversing at all.

"I was quite comfortable. It was a new world. That is, you can read about a place, but it's never the same when you come to it, is it?"

How describe the richness, the splendor, the confusion, the strangeness, and the disappointments of four years, when he was still organizing the memories of them in his own head? "I met South Africans, Hindus, Arabs, Japanese—"

The man laughed slightly. "And Englishmen?"

"Yes, yes, of course. My first friend was a miner's son from Yorkshire. He had the room next to mine." Now Patrick laughed. "My first winter they had the worst snow and cold they'd had in thirty years. It was inhuman. I didn't go out for two weeks. He brought me sandwiches and coffee."

He had been a short, ruddy fellow, Alfie Jones, with the congenital indignation of a rooster. The education of the poor, or lack of it, outraged him.

"We had a lot in common, it developed. We're both going home to teach in the poorest district we can find. That won't be difficult on St. Felice, at any rate."

"I should have thought, don't most of—your people—study medicine or law when they go abroad?"

"Well, they do. My best friend from home, Nicholas Mebane, is reading law in London. He plans to go into politics. You'll be hearing of him throughout the West Indies, I expect."

The man didn't answer that. Probably took it as a challenge, Patrick thought, although he had not intended it as such. But everyone, especially a civil servant like this one, knew that drastic changes and upheavals were coming.

Now clouds closed over, wiping out the stars in minutes. The sky turned deep gray; the moving water shone like jet. There would be a squall before morning. The contrast between humanity's scrambling and scrapping and the powerful rhythms of indifferent nature could make humanity appear ridiculous, Patrick thought, and then as quickly: But that is ridiculous, too; there are some things you can only get by scrambling for them.

"I have no desire to be political, though," he heard himself say.

"You could go far. In Jamaica there are many good posts for—"
The man stopped, having been suddenly afraid, no doubt, that his
remarks might be too personal, or even taken as an insult.

"Because I am almost white, you mean?"

"Well, yes, no offense, only facing the reality of the situation. Fair
or not."

In England he had been taken for Syrian, for Greek or Hindu. Only
here, here at home, there would be no mistaking what he was, or what
was his place.

"But in the kind of government that is coming, not what you are
running now, such things will not matter," he said evenly.

That silenced the man, who now reached into his pocket for a
cigarette and had a time trying to light it between cupped hands
against the rising wind. And Patrick felt a contradiction within himself: pleasure at having countered a smug attitude and regret at having
embarrassed someone who had intended no hurt.

This contradiction was nothing new. He wished he could get rid
of it. Because of it, many an otherwise congenial occasion had been
spoiled, at least in part. There had, for instance, been that sumptuous
wedding reception to which an English fellow classman had invited
Nicholas and him. The bride had lived in a lordly house—three
thousand acres of forest and lawn, lofty halls, splendid terraces—built
by her eighteenth-century forebears with the proceeds of a West
Indian sugar fortune. Standing beside Nicholas on the lawn, he had
thought of his mother, come to serve in the Mauriers' house and
dazzled by its wealth.

"I feel so black here," he had told Nicholas.

Nicholas had been amused. "Black? You? How should I feel, then?
No, it's not race that is bothering you, it's economics. How do you
think Alfie Jones, or ninety-nine whites out of a hundred, would feel
in this place? You're too self-conscious, Patrick. You ought to get over
it."

The man beside him now flung his cigarette into the water. "I'll
be turning in. If I don't see you tomorrow—you'll be leaving at
Martinique, you said?"

"Yes, I change there to a schooner."

"Well, then, good luck. You're almost home."

"Yes, thank you. Almost home."

Agnes wept. "Let me look at you! Let me look at you!"

She was much older than he had remembered. White threaded her hair. She had shrunk. Patrick kept looking at her, searching. They kept looking at each other all day, across the table where they ate and afterwards on the porch, where she rocked in the wicker rocker and people passed in their Sunday clothes with the Methodist Hymn Book under their arms.

They talked and they talked.

"You'll be glad to know it wasn't wasted," he said. "I worked hard. My ideas have jelled. I feel more strongly than ever that education is the answer. We have to build a generation with a whole new system of values. Get rid of stupid learning by rote and total bias toward things European or English. We need imaginative, gifted teachers. When I think of my own poor, ignorant Mistress Ogilvie—"

"You mean you're going to take a place like hers, nursing"—Agnes was scornful— "a pack of babies all day?"

"It can't be news to you that I want to teach, Maman."

"Yes, but I thought in Jamaica, maybe, since they've opened the University College. Certainly not *here* on St. Felice!"

He smiled. "You're sorry I came home, then?"

"You know I'm not! I'm thinking of you; you're too educated now for this measly little place. I prepared you for the world, I didn't think you'd come back here!"

"You came back, didn't you?"

"I'm different. I'm an ignorant woman."

"I'll be fine. Don't you worry about me, Maman."

In the morning he took the bus into Covetown, seated between a pregnant woman with two young ones on her lap and another woman with two crated hens on her lap. The rickety-rackety bus careened dangerously over the abominable road, past cane fields and villages of daub-and-wattle houses where the privy stood at the back of the yam patch and naked babies crawled among tethered goats. He regarded it all in partial amazement, as though he had never really looked at it before, and partially with plain acceptance, because it was just the old familiar way of things.

The bus halted in the market square. He got out and walked down Wharf Street past the banks, the sugar brokers, and Da Cunha's, before whose windows tourists stood pricing cameras and watches. The undertaker still advertised coffins made to measure. Climbing the hill toward Government House, he passed the library, smiling at the memory of that far-off boy who had sat there writing his "master-work" about the Carib Indians. Boys' Secondary came next. Father Baker's office was in the left-hand wing. He went up the path and almost collided with Father Baker.

The priest's round face wrinkled with surprise and pleasure. "Patrick! Don't tell me you're back already! How are you? How are you? Come on and talk to me, let me introduce you to an old friend, Clarence Porter; but of course you know who he is, everybody does."

Patrick looked into the face of a sturdy black man in late middle age. "Forgive me, but I'm afraid—" he said, and was interrupted.

"No need to apologize, young man. My work came long before your time, and if you'd known about it when you were at school you probably wouldn't have cared, anyway." And Porter took Patrick's hand, giving it a rough shake.

The teakettle was on the electric burner in the study; the cups were the same blue and white, stained tan on the inside, from which Patrick had drunk only four years earlier. Father Baker's gown was still spotted. Cries floated from the playing fields beyond the windows as he questioned and Patrick replied. One might never have been away.

While he was giving his account of himself, the big dark man— shades darker than a walnut—sat quietly. He wore a workman's cloth-ing; his hair was gray; his eyes were watchful. When at last there came a lull in the questions and answers, he spoke.

"I was in England myself, many years ago. I could have stayed there, but I chose to come back. I'm glad you did, too."

"Clarence won't tell you much about himself," Father Baker began.

"Who says I won't? There's no virtue in false modesty. I've done my share and I'm not shy about it!"

"No more you should be. But let me tell it. Clarence has lived all over the world, Patrick. He's been a chef's helper in Europe, a travel agent's clerk in New York, a carpenter in Jamaica—"

"And an inmate of five separate jails," Clarence interposed. "Don't forget to put that in."

"I won't forget," Father Baker said quietly. He turned to Patrick. "They were honorable incarcerations. Clarence was jailed for leading strikes against inhuman conditions. He organized the first island-wide union here on St. Felice forty years ago."

Patrick wondered, "How is it I never knew about a thing like that?"

"To our shame," Father Baker said, "we never taught and still don't teach them in our schools. Not even at ours, which is supposed to be, and is, superior."

"Well," Porter said, "it's all ancient history. I'm taking it easy now. Just do a little carpentering when I feel like it, and go to union meetings, but leave the heavy business to the young." He tipped his chair back on two legs. "Oh, if I could write, I could tell—but you'd need a lot of skill to get down on paper all the courage, the fear, and the bloody brutality of those first years. I can remember the deportations and the all-white vigilantes. I can remember when they brought the Royal Wessex Regiment out from England to calm the countryside— But enough of that. Tell us what you're going to do with yourself now," he concluded.

The alert, remarkable eyes now fixed upon Patrick made him self-conscious. But he answered simply, "I'm looking for a teaching post in a country district. Somewhere over beyond Morne Bleue in some little place like, well say like Gully, or Hog Run or Delicia."

Porter looked surprised. "You really want to rough it, don't you? I grew up on that side till I was twelve and left home. They still went whaling over there in those days. Used to put lookouts on the hills; when they saw a whale spout they'd signal to the boats and the harpooners would give chase. But all that's changed. Suppose you'll have any trouble getting a post?"

"Jobs are scarce, I know. But I'm well qualified. And I feel sure I can do some good. That's why I want it so much, because I really believe I can."

"You're an idealist, then," Porter said.

Patrick ignored that. "I have a friend—he's my best friend's father —Dr. Mebane. He'll help me. He knows a lot of people."

"Oh, he knows a lot of people! The right people, too." Porter's irony was unmistakable. Nevertheless, he shook hands as Patrick stood to depart. "And if I can ever help you, in some other way, remember me. Or if you just feel like having a talk. My place is on Pine Hill, other side of the harbor, where the working class lives. Name's on the gate: Clarence Porter, carpentry, it says."

"I should think," Dr. Mebane observed, "that Father Baker or one of the other masters might take you on as an assistant. Or something. Teaching in a country school seems rather a step down for you."

"I don't see it as such. 'Give me the child before he is six'—don't the Jesuits say that?"

"You could do more to mold the mind in secondary school."

"How many of our children ever get to secondary school?"

Dr. Mebane looked out over the harbor where two white yachts rode gleaming in the sun.

"The pay is much less," he said.

"I don't require much to live."

"You're an idealist!"

Patrick laughed. "That's what Clarence Porter said yesterday."

"How do you know him?"

"He was with Father Baker when I went to call."

"That figures. The good father is a sympathizer."

"Sympathizer?"

"With labor."

"Isn't that a good thing?"

"Of course. But there are ways and ways. Porter has always been an angry man. Too angry."

"There's much to be angry about, isn't there? Or sad. You know what, Doctor? There are times when I am so sad, when I think of our history, our long history in this place—"

"I hope you're not affected that way too often. You're very young. If you can't enjoy some lighthearted selfishness now, when can you? I detect a tendency in you to be too emotional, Patrick."

The clock struck the half hour. Its delicate *ping!* befitted the fussy room, the tasseled pillows heaped on the sofa and the dyed feathers in a glass vase on the bookcase. Once he had thought this house was the zenith of elegance; now he had learned better. It merely yearned toward elegance.

"Besides," Dr. Mebane resumed with vigor, "you have another history on this island. An English history, a French, or both. Their blood runs in our veins, too. And it's proud blood: explorers, aristocrats, Huguenots fleeing the Terror."

Patrick was silent.

"I keep that in mind whenever I sit in the Council or in any official capacity."

It is the pomposity of old age, Patrick thought. Even Nicholas had remarked it once, not unkindly, of his father.

"Things are improving all the time and further than I thought possible. Federation is almost upon us. I was a delegate to the Representative Government Association at Roseau in Dominica in 1932 when all we hoped for was popular representation in the legislatures, an expansion of the suffrage. I have stuck with the movement ever since. Three years ago I was in Montego Bay—that was in February 1956—at the invitation of London to discuss the Moyne Commission report and to draft a federal constitution. So far have we come in these few years! I'm an optimist, Patrick, it's the only way to survive. . . . You don't want to go into politics with Nicholas? You'd make a fine team, the two of you."

"Politics don't interest me in that way. I'm a teacher."

"Well, then, we'll just have to get you a job, won't we? But you'll need some recreation, too; would you like me to put you up at the Crocus Club? We've just bought a boat for deep-sea fishing and—"

"It's too expensive for me, I'm afraid," Patrick murmured.

"It isn't; you'd be surprised. Of course, the social business can get silly; it's the tennis that really attracts me. Still, you do meet interesting people. The movers and doers."

"Thanks very much, but if I could be settled first at work, then—"

"I'll do everything I can, Patrick. I miss my son—you can take his place this next year. Then, when he comes back, I'll have the two of you."

I am too critical, Patrick thought, going home. Mebane had his quirks, as who of us had not? That particular quirk about ancestry was one that Patrick had remarked in him a long time before. He ought to be grateful for the man's friendship. And he was grateful. Yet, the doctor was a small man. Like his house, he seemed to have grown smaller since Patrick had grown up. He had remembered them both, the house and the man, as large and impressive. They were neither.

He had been teaching for three months, living at Gully, a village hung halfway between a mountaintop and the sea, in a meager one-room house on stilts no better than the homes of his pupils. Sometimes, preparing the next day's lessons by the light of a kerosene lamp, he was flooded with a sensation of virtue which he immediately stifled as being ugly, unjustified, and smug. For the most part he was still exhilarated; the minds of his appealing little children were the emptiest possible slates, and as his were to be the first marks upon them, he felt like a great experimenter, a messenger, literally, from abroad.

One Saturday he went down into Covetown to do some shopping, stopped for a beer, looked for Father Baker, who was out, thought how pleasant it would be when Nicholas was back again, roamed some more streets, and found himself on the far side of the harbor in the section called Pine Hill.

At one time, obviously, the hillside must have been covered with pines; now it was covered with flat-roofed bungalows, each with its fenced-in cement square that passed for a yard, some bougainvillaea vines, and some sort of vehicle in a shed—a Ford car, a light truck, or a Honda. It was a wage-earner's neighborhood, in which the prosperity of an owner could be gauged by the tidiness of his possessions and the freshness of his paint.

Suddenly Patrick remembered Clarence Porter. He walked on, searching among the names on the gateposts. Porter's house, no more costly than those surrounding it, had a grass yard, bright blue shutters, and tubs of flowers on the front porch. Porter himself was sitting on the porch.

"Remember me?" Patrick asked. "You said I might drop in for a talk sometime."

"Sure, sure! Come in. Draw up a chair. Anything special you wanted to talk about?"

"To tell the truth, no. I guess I was just feeling a little lonesome. Wanted some adult conversation."

"That's right, you're with kids all the time now, aren't you? Have a beer."

"Thanks, I just had one downtown."

"Have another."

Porter fetched the beer. Patrick began the conversation in the conventional fashion.

"You've a nice house here."

"Built it myself. Built two, as a matter of fact. That yellow one up at the end of the street is mine, too. I rent it out. You get a good view from here, good breeze, same as they get on Library Hill, only it costs half as much."

Patrick acknowledged that that was so. Far below, the boats were dots in the harbor and Covetown's business section was a cluster of white rooftops. He had not realized he had climbed so far.

"My wife loved it, being up this high. She's dead now. I live here with my daughter Dezzy. Name's Désirée, but I call her Dezzy, which she hates." Porter chuckled. "She works at Da Cunha's selling things she can't afford to buy. Maybe you've seen her—very tall, almost as tall as you, long hair."

"I don't go to Da Cunha's. I can't afford it, either."

"Guess not!" Porter chuckled again. He struck a match, lit his pipe, and lounged back. "So! Dr. Mebane got you what you wanted, I see."

"Yes. I appreciate it."

"Aside from that, what do you think of him?"

The blunt question was discomfiting. "Well, I've known him since I was thirteen. I was always welcome in their house. I was from Sweet Apple, you know; my mother had a little store there, still has; Dr. Mebane was very kind to me—"

"Of course he was! Look at yourself! Your color, I mean. Has he invited you to join the country club?"

"Yes. I'm not going to, though."

"My daughter couldn't join his club. She's too dark."

There was a silence. The man's sense of injury was palpable. And Patrick said gently, "Perhaps she doesn't want to, anyway."

"The funny thing is, she would love it. Just as she would love to buy the stuff on Da Cunha's shelves. But that's natural. Women always want things. I myself couldn't care less." He tipped forward and knocked his pipe out on the porch railing. "It all stems from the white man and his concubines! These light-brown people like to think about how they've descended from the aristocracy of Europe. They don't want to remember Africa. A seat in the legislature, a collar and tie, being invited to a reception at Government House—that's all it took to buy them off. And the British Colonial Office has done just that!"

"Surely—" Patrick began, but Porter was not to be stopped.

"Do you know how many of these so-called upper-class browns owned slaves themselves? They were cruel masters, most of them, as cruel as the whites. They had learned well, let me tell you. Why, even as recently as the nineteen twenties— Listen. I remember there was a white man, an Englishman who came out here with a company that was to put streetlights downtown, a socialist he was, serious red-haired fellow; he went around making friends among the blacks here, the working class; made a few speeches, harmless enough. One night a gang beat him up. After that, they got rid of him, shipped him back to England, and who do you think applauded, who was behind it?"

"The planters, naturally?"

"Of course, the planters, the powerful families, men like old Virgil Francis. But never think the Mebanes and their kind didn't go right along. They've got their little vested interests, too, and the lower wages are, the more stays in their pockets."

Patrick said doubtfully, "But this is nineteen fifty-nine. People think differently now. I know that Nicholas Mebane isn't like his father, if his father is altogether what you say he is."

Porter stared at him a moment. "I hope you're right. I don't know. I get heated up. I'm not very tactful, am I?"

"Not very." Patrick laughed. Porter's vehemence was interesting, anyway.

"I shoot my mouth off. I'm self-educated. I read everything. Father Baker helped me. He's a man, a real man."

"Even though he's white?"

"Even though he's white. He thinks a good deal of you, by the way. He tells me—"

"I'd rather hear about you. About the early unions. I know almost nothing about them."

Porter looked pleased. He cleared his throat. "It's a long story. But in a nutshell, this is it. We had small unions as far back as the eighteen nineties, mostly in the construction trades. They didn't get far then because picketing was against the law. Also, a union could be sued for damages resulting from a strike. It took a world war, the first, and then a world depression to change things. You're too young to recall the bloodshed in the thirties. Strikes and riots from Trinidad to St. Lucia, from coal bearers to sugar workers. Slow, slow progress. But it's only the labor movement that's put another meal on the table, remember that."

The man's voice swayed Patrick, drew pictures in his mind. Sweet Apple, years ago, and the eight-year-olds working in the cane. Gully now, the children walking shoeless in the rain, bringing a lunch of lard on bread to school.

"But," he said, "when federation comes, economic progress will come with it. You condemn Dr. Mebane—and I do understand some of what you mean—but still, it is men like him who are bringing this great change about. With the end of colonial rule will come wider social justice. It's bound to come."

"Perhaps. Perhaps. Oh, I don't want you to think I'm an embittered man, prejudiced against people because they have more money than I have or their skin is lighter than mine—I wouldn't be talking like this to you if that were the case, now would I? But what I fear is this: We'll get our political independence only to have a new class step into the Englishman's shoes, and the workman will be no better off. Or not much."

The gate clanged. Against the glare of five o'clock sunlight Patrick could see only a tall, thin figure, obviously female, coming up the walk.

"Got the soapbox out again, Pa? I could hear you halfway to the corner."

"Come in out of the dazzle, it hurts my eyes. This is Patrick Courzon, a friend of Father Baker's. My daughter Dezzy. I told you, she hates being called Dezzy. She likes to be called Désirée."

"Why not? It's my name."

The girl set her packages down on the table.

"What have you got there, now?" Porter wanted to know.

"Dishes. A set of Spode."

"Good God! You hand them back all your wages on gewgaws!" It was a reproach, but a tender one.

"We needed dishes. The old ones are a disgrace. And these are seconds. You'd never know the difference, though."

"Well, I certainly wouldn't!"

She reached into the box and held up a cup. "There! Isn't that a lovely pattern?"

Patrick was not looking at the cup. He was looking at the pleasure in her face, the most beautiful he had ever seen. It was a classic face with narrow, sculptured lips, large, round-lidded eyes, and a thin, patrician nose—all of these cast in ebony. She wore a red blouse and a white skirt. She had a silver chain on her wrist. Something profound and powerful stirred in Patrick's chest. Afterwards he thought it must have been fear that she would vanish as easily and quickly as she had appeared.

In those few seconds he was changed.

She addressed him. "Has my father been bending your ear?"

"Oh, no, not at all. I've been enjoying myself." A stilted answer, schoolmasterish and dull, when he was capable of doing so much better! Her beauty had quenched his flow, silenced his wit.

Porter asked, "Why don't you invite Mr. Courzon to supper?"

"Patrick. Please, my name is Patrick."

"Patrick, then. You're invited," said Désirée. "I'll have it ready in half an hour."

The table, at one end of the front room, had been set with the new dishes. Hibiscus flowers, cerise and yellow, floated in a crystal bowl. He saw that the bowl was very fine.

Clarence Porter followed Patrick's gaze. "Another Da Cunha special. Out of place in this house."

"Beauty is never out of place," Désirée said.

Patrick ate silently, while a pleasant banter crossed and recrossed the table. The girl got up to fetch the next course. From where he sat he could see into the large, clean kitchen. He watched her moving about, watched as she lifted her hair and twisted it into a coil on top of her head. That long, straight hair, heavy as rope—from where had she got it? From some Arab traders wandering south and west into Africa two centuries ago? Or from some Spanish buccaneer who had wandered into the slave cabins on this very island?

"It gets so hot on my neck," she complained, with a little petulant sigh.

"Désirée is part Indian," Clarence Porter said, as though he had read Patrick's thought. "My wife's great-grandmother was a pure Carib, off the reservation."

This time the father had given her the name that belonged to her. The name had a caressing sound, apart from its meaning. If you didn't know the meaning of *desire*, those syllables alone would tell you.

"And what do you think of the land settlement they are pressing for on St. Vincent?" Porter asked.

"Pa, don't!" Désirée turned to Patrick. "My father is too serious. Sometimes I simply have to close my ears."

Porter was amused. "All right, I'll be quiet."

"Too much heavy talk," she said. "Taste the ice cream. Look out at the evening."

Patrick followed her gesture. The sun was an orange ball, tipped on the long, even line where the sky met the sea. Covetown lay in cobalt shadow.

"How wonderful it is!" she said softly.

Her perfume smelled like sugar. Flowers and sugar.

"The time is today," she said, as if to herself.

Patrick looked up at her then. "You know, you're right," he said.

Too much heavy talk. Everything has grown too heavy. Ever since I was six years old, when Maman sent me off to school, it's been a competition. Work. Strive. Be earnest. But what of laughter? It's true. The time is today.

His courtship was short. He needed only a few weeks to learn what he wanted to know about her.

He took her to dinner at a place he couldn't afford, Cade's Hotel at the end of Wharf Street. It was a fine, square stone house with a high-walled garden and, if one didn't count boarding houses, the only place on the island where travelers could stay. In a quiet dining room, dominated by a loud tall clock and gilt-framed portraits of the royal family, one dined alongside English tourists and traveling salesmen on expense accounts. Locals, the whites and the near-whites, came occasionally for a change from their clubs.

Désirée had never been inside. Her pleasure was infectious.

"Look at that, Patrick, will you!"

"That" was a colored print of Queen Victoria at Balmoral, a scene replete with enormous yardages of plaid, fuzzy little dogs and a view of cold, foggy mountains.

"Scotland," he said. "I've been there."

Her eyes widened. "Oh, I would like to see it! I would like to see everything, anything. I've never been anywhere. Only once to Martinique and once to Barbados."

So, over drinks, he retold his English years as best he could, bringing color and drama to the telling, enjoying her attention. With a flourish of expertise he ordered the dinner: calalu soup and crab farci.

"I've never had crab cooked this way," she said.

"It's the French style. These are land crabs. They're fed for a few days on pepper leaves. Then they're baked."

"How do you know so much about cooking?"

"I don't. I only happen to know about a few French dishes because my mother is from Martinique and she's a wonderful cook."

Désirée was silent for a moment. Then, hesitating, she inquired, "Your mother—she came to Martinique from France?"

"No, she was born there and so were her people before her." And aware that this was not the answer that the girl was seeking, he said quietly, "What you're really asking is whether my mother is colored or white."

"I'm sorry! I didn't mean—"

"It's all right. My mother is dark, quite dark."

"As dark as I am?"

"No. Nor as beautiful, either."

He thought he saw her frown. Her face was lowered and he couldn't be sure.

"Is there anything wrong, Désirée?"

She raised her head. "You understand, I—we—don't go to places like this. Without you, I wouldn't be here. They wouldn't put us out, but they would make us so unwelcome that we wouldn't want to come."

"Of course, I understand."

An ant, crawling up the side of the water bowl in which the sugar bowl had been set, fell struggling into the water. Patrick shoved the whole contrivance to the other side of the table.

He laughed. "Look, it's not so fancy—you needn't be overawed. For me, in fact, the ants remind me of home."

She laughed, too. "You make me feel good."

"I don't think *you* need anybody to make you feel good. It's the other way around when I'm with you."

"Is it? Then I'm glad."

"You're a glad person."

"Well, I am most of the time. Or I try to be. The trouble with me is, I want things so badly."

"What things, for instance?"

"Oh, I don't know. Just a vague kind of wanting inside." She made a fist at the hollow of her throat. "When I see something beautiful . . . The Da Cunha brothers have pictures in their houses. There was one I loved, a ruined building, all columns and moonlight, you could feel you were there. Rome, Mr. Da Cunha said. He gave me a print of it for Christmas. I have it in my room."

The simple, childish recital touched him, reminding him of himself at age fourteen or so, reminding him, too, of the "blank slates" on which from Monday through Friday he struggled to write something that might inspire and endure.

"Désirée," he said softly. "I'll always call you that." Then realizing the implication of that "always," he added, "I'm going to know you for a long, long time."

In the evening they walked, carrying their shoes, on the long beach beyond the harbor. Between the ocean and the pine hills lay the salt pond, rose pink in the faltering light.

"This one has been here since the time of the Caribs," Patrick said.

"What makes it pink?"

"The algae. Red algae."

"You know so much. You know everything."

He glanced at her. For a second it flashed through his mind that such praise might be a mere feminine trick, the flattery that is supposed to ensnare a man; but no, her honesty was total. The quick-talking girl with the tossing hair who had subdued him at first meeting was, under the surface of a touching worldliness, only a naïve and tender child. And he knew that he had won her.

A pair of black-necked stilts came running through the shallow water.

"Hush," she said. "Watch them."

But he was watching her. In the still, unmoving air, her perfume was strong again: sugar and flowers. He touched her arm.

"Come," he said.

In a pine hollow, perfectly hidden, dark and soft, they lay down. He removed her white blouse and skirt. How many women had he known? As many as any man his age and as many varieties: the eager and lustful, the indifferently accommodating, those who had to be coaxed or pretended that they had. This one was different.

It was her first time. He felt an excess of tenderness on discovery, but no guilt or remorse, because he knew himself; knew, as his hands thrust the heavy hair from her shoulders, smoothed her firm breasts and long thighs, that he would never leave her. And he felt as they lay there together, both of them too overcome or perhaps too shy as yet for words, that she knew it, too.

When at last they stood up, it was quite dark.

"Shall we come here again tomorrow?" he asked.

"But it's a working day, isn't it? You have to travel so far."

He trembled. "Why? Don't you want to? Are you afraid?"

She laid her head on his shoulder. "No. I was only thinking of you."

So they will merge to make a whole. A serious man will respond to a sensual woman and to her delights, whether they be in a bauble or the music of rain or—or in himself. She grasps life with both hands and will teach him her way. While he, born earnest, will draw her up to form, out of her young, captivating spirit, new tenderness and new strength.

Agnes was angry. He had taken Désirée to meet her in Sweet Apple one Sunday afternoon.

"You're not going to marry that girl?"

"I haven't asked her yet, but I'm sure she will."

"My God, but the older you get, the more stupid you get!"

"I can't think what you mean!"

"You can't think? Well, look at her! A dark girl like that! A smart man marries up! He marries light, to improve himself and his children, don't you at least know that?"

He controlled himself. "I don't understand you, Maman. After all you have told me about the years of slavery, you can still talk like this?"

"What has that got to do with it? You have a way of twisting what I say, you always do."

"It's you who are twisting, you who're so confused that—"

But she had gone out, slamming the door.

He took a sheet of paper and wrote out something he had seen once in a history book about the slavery era.

> White plus black equals mulatto.
> Mulatto plus black equals sambo.
> Mulatto plus white equals quadroon.
> Quadroon plus white equals mustee.
> Mustee plus white equals mustafina.

He shouted, "What the hell am I?"

He looked in the mirror. Quadroon? Mustee? God damn! Who was the man who had fathered him? Three generations away from slavery, Agnes was, and still the confusion was entrenched, the pride and the shame intertwined like a nest of snakes. A stubborn woman who would not, simply would not, talk.

And yet, what difference would it make if she did talk?

In a burst of rage he threw his hairbrush across the room, splitting the handle of the brush and making a dent on the door.

Agnes opened the door. "I'm sorry," she said.

She stood there, breathing hard, holding on to the wall. For the first time he noticed her knobby, arthritic fingers. A lonely old woman, nearing the end of a lonely and limited existence. What could she know? His anger dissolved.

"I'm wrong," she said. "Go ahead and do what you want. Whatever makes you happy."

He knew she only meant it in part. Her feelings would not change. So this would have to do.

"You're marrying Clarence Porter's daughter? A beautiful girl," said Dr. Mebane. "Not radical like her father, I hope? No offense meant."

"No. She isn't interested in public affairs."

"That's good. A man's woman. When will it be?"

"As soon as she will." He had to have her. Suppose someone else were to come along one afternoon while he was away in Gully? He went cold at the thought.

"Why don't you wait a little? Nicholas will be home in a year and the two of you could have a little fun together. Spend a week in Barbados. Jamaica, even. Enjoy yourself. There's time before you need to tie yourself down."

"It's not being tied down when you want it," Patrick said gently.

"I just hope you're sure of your own mind. There are a lot of girls around."

He meant, You could do better.

"I'm sure," Patrick said.

Clarence Porter was happy. "I knew it all along. I could tell the first day you laid eyes on her. And she on you."

They were to live in Clarence's other house at the top of the street. The present tenants were to move and Clarence would paint the place fresh for them.

"I'm so relieved we'll live in town," Désirée said. "I never liked the country."

"You couldn't live where I am now, anyway. I'll just get up an hour earlier each day and drive." He had bought a wheezing car, third or fourth hand. "We'll have to get a ring for you at Da Cunha's."

"Da Cunha's, Patrick? Where are you going to get enough money for that?"

"Don't worry, it won't be anything very large! But my mother sold a piece of land she had in Martinique and gave me some money a few years ago. Enough for my education and a bit left over."

"Then maybe we can have a better house of our own sometime."

"I don't know. Teachers don't earn much."

"Perhaps you won't always be a teacher."

He scarcely heard her.

They were married at the Anglican Church of the Heavenly Rest on the ocean side of St. Felice. It was a small Gothic building that might well have stood at a crossroads in the Cotswolds, except for the coconut palms along the edge of the graveyard and the breaking surf on the shore two hundred feet below the cliff. For fifty years now it had been more or less abandoned by the planter families who had built it, the advent of the automobile having made it easy to attend cathedral services in Covetown.

"But I would like to be married there," Patrick had told Father Baker. "I love the age of it, the way it has rooted itself like a tree."

The little group—the bride and groom, with Clarence Porter and Agnes—arrived ahead of Father Baker. They wandered along the nave. The filtered light of stained-glass colors, amber, rose, and lavender, lay on ancient, pale memorials, on florid script chiseled into stone.

> In holy Remembrance of Eliza Walker Loomis, devoted Wife and Mother, a charitable and pious Example to her Relations.
>
> Alexander Walker Francis, born in the Parish of Charlotte in the year of Our Lord seventeen hundred and fifty-two. Died in the service of His Majesty, King George the Third in the year of Our Lord seventeen hundred and seventy-eight. Valiant and honourable in the performance of his sacred Duty to God, King and Country.

In the dampness of the unused building lichen had begun to creep, obliterating the old words.

> Borne aloft on Angel Wings. Here lie interred the Remains of Pierre and Eleuthère François, infant sons of Eleuthère and Angélique François, died and entered into Paradise on August the fourth in the Year of Our Lord seventeen hundred and two at the Age of eight Months. Our Tears shall water their Grave.

"Francis," mused Désirée. "And François. The same family, do you suppose?"

"It is the same," Agnes said.

Father Baker came. Patrick took Désirée's hand and they went to the altar. Through the poetry of the marriage service scraps of thought went in and out of his head: I wish Nicholas were here today with us. . . . It's not really Gothic, those are Corinthian pilasters. . . . I don't want to forget what he is saying.

He did remember kissing Désirée and shaking Father Baker's hand. He remembered the creak of the old door as they went out from dimness into light and drove away.

They circled the island, making a slow trip back to Covetown. On a hill where a little river curved to the sea he stopped the car to look at the view.

"See over there," said Désirée.

A columned house stood alone on the slope. Not large, it still had a simple grandeur.

"Imagine the view from those windows!" she cried.

"Perfect, I should say."

"It's called Eleuthera. It's empty now. I don't know why."

"Eleuthera! It seems to me I was there once."

"What would you have been doing there?" she asked him curiously.

"I don't know. Perhaps I only imagine I was."

"Oh, I should love to live in a house like that. Wouldn't you?"

He laughed. "I assure you I never give it a thought, my darling."

"Perhaps you could have lived in a place like that someday if you hadn't married me."

"Why, what on earth do you mean?"

"Who knows how far you could go? Without me you could join the Crocus Club, for instance."

He leaned over and kissed her. "I have absolutely no desire to join the Crocus Club. And this is no talk for a wedding day, or ever."

The sweet night fell in a jalousied room above the garden of Cade's Hotel.

She woke once from half sleep. "Have you ever had a white girl?" she asked him.

"No," he said, astonished.

"Why not?"

"I never wanted to." He could have had them, prostitutes, near-prostitutes, and once the sister of a Cambridge Fellow. Piqued by curiosity about him, no doubt. A novelty, he'd have been.

EDEN BURNING

"Funny," Désirée said.

"Not funny at all. Anyway, I don't want you to talk like that."

He drew her to him. The dark, dark beauty of her! Warm perfume of windblown grass and sun, fragrance of night, of woman and earth! He had it all, all he would ever want, this one only, no other. Flowers, moist on a ledge in the unexpected corner of a desert. The blue eye of a lake on a towering mountain. Landfall after a long, long voyage.

Seven

Ruin, on the day it descends, is actually no more sudden than is disease. The rot that is cancer was not created in the instant of discovery; slowly, unrecognized or only unacknowledged, it has long been making its secret way. And so it is with the secret disappointment in a marriage or with a financial collapse.

For some time Francis had been aware of trouble behind the closed door of the inner office. With hints, frowns, questions, and long silences, his father had revealed that something of consequence was happening within the company. It had to do with an enormous, risky loan, a grandiose project and unreliable people—in short, a gamble. Canneries and food processing were involved; as news leaked out and auditors, hastily summoned, moved in and out of the rooms pulling papers from file drawers, it came to be spoken of by some sardonic underlings (although never where they thought Francis could hear, for after all, he was a partner's son) as the Tomato Scandal.

It was as the Tomato Scandal that it burst at last onto the front page of the morning papers. In his newly furnished dining room above Central Park, Francis read: RESPECTED FIRM TO GO UNDER, S.E.C. INVESTIGATORS REVEAL.

My God! How had his father allowed this to happen? And did it really merit a two-column headline? At the same moment he knew it was naïve of him not to understand that the failure of such a house as Luther, Baines and Company was front page news, indeed. He broke out into a sweat.

"What is it, Francis? You look as if you'd been struck by lightning," Marjorie said.

"I have been." He handed the paper to his wife.

While she read, he watched her. They had been married for only eight months, and he was still not over his surprise at having won her, who was so smooth and assured, so different from himself. He was still not accustomed to the sight of her, fresh and animated as she was even in the mornings, wearing her silk robe and with her short dark hair perfectly in place. Her lips moved as she read—he always teased her about lip reading—and he wondered what she could be thinking about this failure of the family which she had so recently joined. She had very high concepts about duty and honor and status. Her own family was not rich, but it had distinction, and she was, he knew, very proud of that. He had met her at a cousin's party. Funny, he hadn't even wanted to go that night, either. But his father had been distressed when he had mentioned that he might not go, so he had gone, and there she had been.

His father had been distressed about him for more important reasons, too. He was thirty years old and he still hadn't done what was expected of him, namely, joining the firm. Instead, he had gone to South America with the Peace Corps; he'd taught school on an Indian reservation in New Mexico; he'd worked as supervisor on a dairy farm in upstate New York. He'd embarked on a master's degree in history. That's what he'd been doing when he met Marjorie.

A tall girl with magnificent dark eyes, she had a cool, quiet manner that said "quality." But it had been her voice that drew him. Funny, to be so moved by a simple thing like a voice, so that you kept coming back and back and couldn't stay away. It was like listening to the rush of water or staring into flames. Even her laughter soothed him, registering somewhere, he estimated, in the middle strings of a harp—he knew little about musical instruments—it soothed him, giving promise of tender and exquisite delights.

He had almost come to blows with his cousin.

"She's a cold fish, Francis. Not your sort. Can't you see she's not your sort?"

His cousin hadn't understood! He had common tastes; naturally, Marjorie's classic calm, her classic reserve, would baffle him. As for himself, he was entranced. She was like no girl he had ever known.

It had been only sensible, upon marrying her, to go into his father's firm. After all, he'd had his years of leafy wilderness and exotic places; having Marjorie meant, of course, supporting her. So he had been well aware of his good fortune in being able to embark so easily on the new life; to have this dining room with a view of the park where on Sundays they went bicycling or skating together, this bedroom where they lived their lovely nights.

Marjorie laid the paper down. "We ought to go over there," she said.

"Over where?"

"To your parents. It's only right that we should be with them."

Yes, of course it was. Marjorie would see that.

The scene in the dining room of his parents' house was the same as the one they had left. Coffee cups had been shoved aside to make room for the spread newspaper. His mother was reading it; Margaret was dribbling the milk from her cereal spoon. His father, who was standing at the window, turned around when Francis and Marjorie came in.

"Why didn't you tell me it was this bad?" Francis asked gently.

"You couldn't have done anything."

That was true enough. More to the point, he wondered what he could do now. He sat down beside his mother and put his hand on her arm.

Richard observed the gesture. "It's your mother I feel for," he said. "I thought we could get out of it quietly. But the damn newspapers—"

Teresa looked up. A familiar vein twitched in her cheek and her lips were tight, as if her hand had been pressing them shut so that whatever passion or rage was within might not be allowed to escape. Francis had seen that, often enough. It was nothing new.

After a moment or two she spoke.

"Richard, I don't care about that. Today's scandal will be forgotten next week. All I care about is that my children don't suffer because of this."

"I suppose," Richard said, in a shaky voice, "I suppose what I should do is commit suicide. Like Wayne Chapman. You remember when Chapman, Searls and Fitler crashed twelve years back and Wayne went out the window?"

"What would that solve?" Teresa asked.

Prattling, Francis thought. His father's appalling offer, which he intended to be so tragic, was only foolish melodrama. His mind turned and turned.

"There's the property on St. Felice. It's Mother's, so it won't be touched by all this."

Teresa spoke again. Her voice was flat, without accusation, and this very flatness made it all the more accusatory. "The property on St. Felice is gone and has been for a long time, Francis, except for one piece, my grandfather's run-down place in the north. I learned that this morning."

"Gone?" Francis echoed. "I don't understand." He looked from one to the other of his parents.

"Tell them, Richard," Teresa said.

"Well, you see, expenses were high and with so much tied up in securities—" Richard faltered.

Fool, Francis thought.

"I had to raise cash from time to time. So I disposed of the properties. Oh, I got a fair price for them, I didn't throw them away! Herbert Tarbox bought them for his son, for Lionel. I always got a very fair price—I can show you all the documents."

Francis ignored him. "So your brother, your half-brother, has it all," he said to his mother.

"Not everything," Richard corrected. "There's the place your mother mentioned—"

"Eleuthera," Teresa said, sighing.

Francis demanded scornfully, "Why didn't he buy that, too?"

"He didn't want it."

"And you did all this without Mother's knowledge? Just like that?"

"Not just like that. From time to time, over the years. I had power of attorney. She never knew anything about business, anyway."

Richard turned back to the window. Francis followed his gaze to the back yard, where a late, wet snow was falling on what in a month's time would be a showy bed of imported tulips.

And suddenly, the incredulous outrage in Francis melted into pity. His father was totally gray: his hair, his face, his flannel suit. His wrists, with the fine watch—"the most expensive watch in the world," he had boasted—were helpless as the hands of the dead. Poor, proud fool. The world, his particular world, would judge him with contempt; it had small patience with failure. Almost, Francis could feel more sadness for him than for his mother, who would, as always, weather what she had to.

Someone had to take charge. "So Eleuthera is left," Francis said. "We'll sell it and put the money in trust for Mother. Let's see what we can get for it."

Richard took up the idea. "Yes, yes, I can write to Lionel to put it into the hands of a local agent."

Francis made a swift determination. "No Lionel. No local agent. I want to take care of it myself."

His mother started. "What do you mean? Go there in person? Go down to St. Felice?"

"Why not? It's the only way to get anything done. Do it yourself."

"That's ridiculous! You don't know anything about the area! You'd be wasting time and energy. What do you know about property values down there? It's ridiculous!"

"Not at all," Francis said. Excitement mounted in him, the adrenaline of anger, adventure, and action. "How energetically will Lionel pursue your interests? Maybe he would and maybe he wouldn't. No, I'm the one to go."

"I don't want you to, I said." The pulses in Teresa's neck were visible. Her cheeks were dark red. "That long trip—it'll come to nothing—"

"I can't understand your objection," Richard spoke timidly. "Unless you'd prefer to have me go. One of us really should."

"You have enough to handle here," Francis told him.

"No one listens to me!" Teresa cried shrilly, pathetically. Her calm, that air of being able to stand up under any amount of pressure, was suddenly shattered. Certainly, she had had enough of a blow this morning to shatter it. Yet strangely, or so it seemed to Francis, she was more distressed by the prospect of his journey than by the crumbling of their fortunes. And why?

But he laid his hand on her shoulder. "Leave it to me, please, Mother," he said gently. "I'll work things out." Firmly he added, "Marjorie and I will leave next week for St. Felice. And you're not to worry, hear?"

The light crashed down from the sky, stunning the senses like a bugle call in the morning.

"My God, how marvelous!" Marjorie cried.

They had been standing among bundles and crated chickens on the schooner's deck since dawn, watching the landscape emerge from the sea in a haze of lavender and gray where day encroached on night. A Turner, thought Francis, who like his father frequently conceived of reality copying art, rather than the other way around. Now, in one instant in this shower of light, everything clarified itself: a clump of roots, a line of surf, a steeple.

The man beside them at the rail, a seedy fellow of uncertain age with a wry mouth, had been talking for the last half hour. He was "in dry goods, shoes, overalls, nigger wares." Francis had started at the ugly word.

"Been coming here since before the Depression. Missed the war, naturally, but now I'm back on the old route. Things are no different.

The nigger is still the nigger. A lazy animal. Give him rum and a woman, that's all he wants."

There was no place to move, or Francis would have moved away.

"You folks putting up at Cade's Hotel, are you? It's the only place in town except for some dirty boarding houses. You'll see some funny types at Cade's. Salesmen like me, of course, but mostly English tourists. Retired army people and professors. They come to hike around and study birds. You folks putting up at Cade's?" he repeated.

"No. We have relatives here. We're visiting."

"Now, I'll bet, I'll just bet, you folks have come for the wedding!"

"Wedding?"

"Some planter's daughter. Tarbox, one of the big owners, is marrying the governor's son."

Francis wished he were more adept at lies and evasions.

"We're related to the Tarboxes. And there is to be a wedding, but not until next month."

"Oh. It was in the papers, anyway. So you're related," the man said, with sudden respect.

Ah, well, poor guy, Francis thought, making the swift change from disapproval to forbearance which was so typical of him, poor guy. Now we have become important.

"You planning to stay long?"

"Not very."

"You wouldn't want to. It's a dull place. Hasn't changed in three hundred years. Why, there are parts here without roads, just trails into the mountains! Nobody comes here much, as I told you, except millionaires on their yachts. They like out-of-the-way places. They drop anchor in the harbor, go ashore for a drink with the planters at the country club or the men's club in town, no women allowed. Some of these planters, boiled-shirt types, are worth their weight in gold, but some of them are dirt poor, up to their ears in debt. I wouldn't take the whole island as a gift."

They were well into the bay. At one side stood the remains of a fort, surmounted by cannon, which even now pointed at the schooner as it approached.

"Used to take potshots at pirate ships," the salesman said, showing off for Marjorie. "Cannon like those look small, but they can do a lot of damage. Some of the planters used to keep one on the roof for when the niggers went killing on the rampage. It could happen again today, too; it's not farfetched, let me tell you. And when they do, it'll be bloody. You'd better hope you won't be here when it happens."

The words fell like a shadow on the morning.

"Yes, these islands have seen a lot of blood."

Francis shaded his eyes. The streets were steep, for the town had grown up the side of the hill. The center was a three-sided square, the street along the waterfront marking its fourth side. He could see arcades and wrought-iron balconies: the French had left their mark.

Someone was throwing coins into the harbor. Two black boys dove off the dock and retrieved them. The salesman, laughing, dug in his pocket.

"Nigger kids sure can swim! Well, I'll bid you good-bye. Enjoy your stay. One thing, you've got to hand it to the climate here. Always a breeze. And it won't start raining till June, but you folks'll be gone by then."

"He didn't paint a very good picture," Marjorie said.

At the foot of the gangplank a colored man tipped his straw hat.

"Mr. Luther, suh? Mr. Herbert sent the station wagon. He say welcome to St. F'lice and excuse him, please, it being banana day. They waiting lunch for you at home."

A fragrance, half-sharp, half-sweet, struck Francis in the face. There was languor in it, the perfume of blooming things, mingled with the sea smell of salt and tar. His heart accelerated.

How many generations since the first François had set his foot down in this place? "In the year of Our Lord sixteen hundred and seventy-three—"

He was embarrassed by his own emotion.

"But surely," said Julia Tarbox, for the third time since their arrival, "you knew young Julia's wedding was tonight."

"We thought it was next month," Marjorie said. She was flustered, which was unusual; Marjorie didn't fluster easily. But Julia had authority.

"I thought I had written Tee that we'd advanced the date. Not that it mattered, since she wasn't coming anyway. Of course it's marvelous that you're here. Shall we?" She pushed back her chair and everyone rose from the lunch table. "We'll have our drinks on the veranda. There's a breeze."

The long veranda faced a lawn so brilliantly green as to seem unreal. Beyond the flower borders and a low white fence five or six horses grazed in rich pangola grass.

"Oh, how lovely," Marjorie said.

"Yes, isn't it? Lionel's place is, too, in a different way. They've a view of the water. He and Kate were so sorry to have missed your wedding, but the trip would have been too much for her after her miscarriage." Plaintiveness crept into Julia's voice. "I never could understand how Tee could have stayed away all these years! And not to come for her sister's wedding! We managed to come up for yours! And yet, you know I wasn't even there when she herself was married. I don't know—her grandfather sent her abroad and the next thing I knew she was married. She was scarcely grown. I don't know." No one said anything. And Julia brightened, clasping her still youthful hands. "At least it will be festive tonight! You know, here in the privacy of the family I can admit there's something dreamlike about it all. Julia marrying the son of Lord Frame!" She sighed, then turning to Francis, said abruptly, "So your father has managed to lose everything, has he? To tell you the truth, I'm surprised it didn't happen long before this."

Herbert Tarbox coughed. "Isn't that putting it too strongly, Julia?"

"The truth is the truth."

"The truth is not always easy to know." Herbert's firm voice surprised Francis; all during the lunch he had deferred to Julia. "I've known struggle in my lifetime. Women don't know what it is. It's not just getting money, it's holding on to it. You've got to have luck with you." His big red hand clutched the glass of rum on the armrest of his chair; his big red knees bulged from his khaki shorts. "I want to say something to you, Francis. You must be having some thoughts about the sale of all this property. I'd like you to look at the papers, so you'll know that I paid your father top price for every acre."

"I have no doubts on that score, Uncle Herbert."

"I don't understand why I never knew anything about it," Julia complained.

"Because Richard asked me to keep the transactions between ourselves. What his reasons were, I never asked. Had no right to ask." Herbert addressed Francis. "I bought it all for my son, for Lionel. I plan to retire. I've raised sugar and bananas for a quarter of a century, and that's long enough. Now let sugar and bananas support me. Next year this time, maybe before that, Julia and I will have a little place in Surrey. We'll raise a few roses, have a flat in London near young Julia, and maybe spend a winter in Cannes. Who knows?"

"You've worked hard and you deserve it," Francis said. It seemed to be what he was expected to say.

"You don't know how hard. The worldwide Depression began early in the West Indies. In 1923 sugar brought over twenty-three pounds a ton. By 1934 it brought five pounds. We had hunger and riots here. Fire and blood. Then the unions came. Can't blame the workers, it was inevitable. But they've grown too powerful, on your back, clawing at you. The last ten years or so—" He shook his head. "And you've got nature to fight. Floods. Hurricanes." He ticked off on his fingers. "Dampness. Spoilage. The trick is to diversify on export crops. I've put in a lot of cocoa. Lionel's put in sea island cotton and arrowroot. He's a better businessman than I am, and I've not been too bad, I think I can say that without being immodest. So I'll leave it all to my son. He was born here and he knows this life like the back of his hand. His wife does, too."

"Kate is like a man," Julia said sharply.

Herbert laughed. "Hardly! What you mean is, Kate knows agriculture. She gets along with the workers, which is a great help to Lionel."

"It's a good thing he keeps a rein on her," Julia said, "or she'd give everything away to the workers."

"You know, she always reminds me a little bit of your Tee."

"Of Tee? Nonsense! Tee was always quiet. Kate's got opinions about everything."

Herbert was chastened for the moment. "I meant, the way they both care so much about animals and growing things. I remember Tee was like that."

"You don't know a thing about Tee! What do you know about her? Come to think of it, I know very little about her myself."

Marjorie and Francis looked at one another. Herbert changed the subject.

"So you want to sell Eleuthera, Francis?"

"My parents need the money."

"I should have thought," Julia remarked, "that your father would have made a fortune with all the money from these properties. Investing in growing industries."

"Apparently," Francis said dryly, "he invested in ones that didn't grow."

Poor Father! Fortunate for him that he did not have to confront Julia face to face!

"It won't be easy to dispose of," Herbert said. "It's on the wrong side of the island, you have to go over and around Morne Bleue. As the executor when old Virgil died, I had the devil's own time knowing what to do. For a while I had it rented to a fellow who thought he could make it pay, but he gave up and went back to England. It's been lying fallow ever since." He stood up and walked to the other end of the veranda. "Come here, Francis. Look over this way. Thirty-three tons of sugarcane per acre every year. Machinery, that's what makes it possible. Eleuthera's mills, in Virgil's time, still used cogs of the lignum vitae that had come over in sailing ships. The old man never put ten cents into modernizing. That's why it'll be hard to sell."

Francis sighed. "I'll get what I can, that's all I can do. I want to put something aside for my mother and Margaret. You've seen Margaret, so you know what the need is."

Herbert laid a hand on Francis' shoulder. "You're a good son. Talk to Lionel after the wedding. He's got a head for business."

"If you haven't brought anything to wear, Marjorie, I can lend you something for tonight," Julia said. "We're practically the same size."

"Thank you, but I think I'm equipped."

"I thought you would be. I can tell the minute I lay eyes on someone. I like your wife, Francis. She's our kind. Life on this island," Julia continued, as they went upstairs, "has changed just dreadfully since the war. Before then you'd never go to Government House in the evening without black tie. Or to dinner at each other's houses, for that matter. Oh, but my grandmother used to tell me about real elegance! Why, the thermal baths on Nevis were more fashionable for Londoners than anything in Europe! They'd spend the whole winter at the Bath Hotel. That was a hundred years ago, of course. Well, things change and we must change with them. Tonight, though, you'll be meeting some of the oldest families on the island. I do wish Julia would come home, it's four o'clock, she'll be frazzled for the wedding—"

Her voice was still ringing in the upstairs hall when Marjorie and Francis closed their door.

"Well!" Marjorie said. "She's quite a character, your grand-mother!"

"Is that all you'd call her?"

"But Herbert is rather sweet, I think."

"He's a decent sort. I don't know how he stands her, but he doesn't seem to mind."

"I'm curious about the daughter-in-law. Obviously, she isn't Julia's favorite person."

"If she's like my mother, as Herbert said, I can see why. They'd be oil and water."

Marjorie sat down to take off her shoes. "Funny that your mother never talks about all this, when it's so spectacular. It really is spectacular, don't you think? All these servants! I haven't counted, but we've certainly seen five since lunch. I love the way the chambermaid walks around in bare feet, don't you? Your grandmother showed me the original kitchen, detached so it wouldn't heat up the house. The paneling downstairs is perfect Adam. You wouldn't see anything finer in England." She flipped a brush through her short hair. Her face sparkled. "This house was a wedding present to a bride in 1778, did you know? Her father had the marble for the floors brought from Italy, and all the silver, the Crown Derby porcelain, came from—"

Francis was amused by her enthusiasm. "You'd like a house like this, wouldn't you?"

"Yes, if you could transplant it to Connecticut or someplace. This is a million miles from nowhere. I should hate it." She took a dress from the closet and held it up. "Darling, does this look all right for a wedding? Thank goodness I threw it in at the last minute. Will I do for tonight?"

He looked at her. She was perfection. He would never get used to having her, never believe the marvel of it.

"Oh yes, you'll do, you certainly will." His voice was thick in his throat. "Pull the spread off the bed, will you?"

"Francis! Whatever—there's no time!"

He looked at his watch. "We've an hour and a half. Pull the spread down."

Eight

In the lofty rooms of Government House, above the bride and groom, above Lord Derek Frame and Lady Laura, above the diamonds and the silks, hung the stern portraits of the regime: Victoria, wearing stomacher and diadem; Elizabeth the Second, youthful and grave; generals and admirals and judges in white perukes. An orchestra played "Tales from the Vienna Woods." The champagne was presented in fluted glasses on silver trays.

"What a pleasure to see champagne served properly," Julia exclaimed. "I hate those flat things. They're only fit for sherbets."

"This is absolutely fantastic," Marjorie whispered. "Could you ever have imagined a place like this, Francis?"

"You must be Francis and Marjorie," someone said. A hand in a long kid glove touched theirs. "I'm Kate."

Francis looked down, far down, at a small girl with a freckled face. Red-brown hair lay on her shoulders, too much hair for such a little person. Her wide eyes, with very clear whites, were alert and amused.

Lionel stood behind her. "I've been hunting for you everywhere in this crush. You're Marjorie. I always knew you'd find yourself a stunning wife, Francis." His gaze encompassed Marjorie from slippers to earrings.

"No more than you did," Francis answered with proper gallantry.

Marjorie said, "I can't believe we only arrived this morning! It's dazzling. Another world."

"My wife thrives on excitement," Francis remarked tenderly.

"I wish I had six pairs of eyes." Marjorie's own were brilliant. "That wedding dress! I thought mine was something—but this!"

"It belonged to me," Kate said. "Mother—my mother-in-law—had it altered for Julia. My father had no money, so Mother Tarbox bought it for me in Paris. It weighs a ton and the satin sticks to your back. Lucky for Julia it's a cool night."

"But I am sweating," Lionel announced. A large man, not much younger looking than his own father, he ran to early fat. "Shall we find a table outside before they're all taken?"

Fountains of flowers gushed out of stone jardinieres along the steps into the gardens. Flowers ringed the silver candelabra on the tables. Lionel led them to a table where two or three people were already seated and made the introductions.

"Mrs. Lawrence and Miss Lawrence, Mr. and Mrs. Prentice, from London. Father Baker. My nephew, Francis Luther, and his wife, Marjorie Luther."

The British ladies chirped. Father Baker remarked, "You seem more like brothers than uncle and nephew. Not that you resemble one another."

"There are only four years between us."

"So you've come all this way for the wedding," one of the ladies said, making conversation.

"Actually we didn't know the wedding was tonight. Francis came on business," Marjorie explained.

She was literal, Marjorie was. For some reason her reply irked Francis; he was not in the humor for explanations. Lionel leaned across his wife toward Francis.

"Father tells me you want to sell Eleuthera."

"Yes. Do you want to buy it by any chance?"

"I? No, no! I've got all I can handle. But someone will, if you let it go cheap enough. I wouldn't be discouraged," he added kindly.

"I'm not. At least not yet," which was not quite the truth.

"Virgil was fifty years behind the times. But Eleuthera was a poor choice for sugar in the first place. The family's first ancestor picked it out, I can't imagine why. Colonial plantations were usually situated near a harbor, or at least with good road connections to one. But it must have had some meaning for that old pirate," he said almost affectionately. "It certainly had for Virgil. He loved the place."

"It is beautiful," Kate said. "It is like a poem. A dream."

"A dream!" cried Lionel. "Good Lord!"

"There is an engraving of Eleuthera, made in the eighteenth century," Kate said, ignoring him. "The house is in the background. In the foreground it shows a sugar wain drawn by sixteen oxen, eight before and eight behind, to hold the weight going downhill."

"Kate is a history buff," Lionel explained.

"So am I, after a fashion," Francis admitted.

"Then you ought to see those engravings," Kate said. "There is another one, showing some imported deer in a fancy enclosure. There was a lot of extravagant living on these places once."

"A lot of heavy eating, drinking, and other things," Lionel added.

Kate smiled. A separation of two front teeth gave a certain good humor to the smile. Not really pretty, though, Francis thought.

"Kate is a music buff, too," Lionel said. "She plays the piano like mad. And that's not all. She rides a horse like the wind, can handle a sailboat, and on top of all that, she plays Lady Bountiful to the Negro."

The girl's smile left her face as though a rough hand had wiped it away.

Why is he doing this to her? Francis wondered and looked to Marjorie, who was always tactful in awkward situations. (She had, for instance, known how to "handle" Margaret at some difficult moments.) But Marjorie was involved now with the British lady and an elderly gentleman who had joined the group and was pressing a diagram of some sort into the tablecloth with his fork.

Father Baker spoke up. "Kate has a working conscience. She has been a great help to me in many ways."

"With all respect, Father," Lionel said, "I can only agree up to a point." A fine spray of saliva came through his loose, wet lips. "It is all a matter of how much and how far. Back in the eighteen seventies, I'm told, my own grandfather predicted most of the troubles we're having today. He always said"—Lionel looked around and lowered his voice— "said that the trouble would start with the mixed race. They have the intelligence of the white man and the temper of the Negro. With a little more encouragement of the kind some people give them, they will steam up the lowest elements and dispossess us."

"I believe you exaggerate," Father Baker answered.

"I believe not. Oh, I don't think we're going to have communism here, at least not for a long time. They're too busy organizing in more important places than this, like Jamaica and Trinidad. But look, they want one man one vote now, and that'll be the worst mistake ever made, letting people without property have a say in spending public monies. But we're going to have it, no doubt about that, and it's something to worry about. Why even the middle-class, educated browns are worried! You can't tell me they aren't, although they may not always admit it. Take a man like Dr. Mebane, he's a fairly wealthy man. . . . There he is, by the way, coming down the stairs."

Francis saw a dignified brown-skinned man descending the stairs with a brown-skinned woman in an elegant dress.

Father Baker observed wryly, "Quite true. You need not fear confiscation by Dr. Mebane."

"No, fortunately not. His son," Lionel told Francis, "his son is supposed to be brilliant."

"He is," Father Baker said. "He was my pupil."

"He's got a law degree and will run for office, they say. God knows what's going to happen. Maybe it will turn out all right. It's all confusing, to say the least."

"You are a colonialist," Kate said deliberately. "You are living in the wrong century and I'm sorry for you. You would have been so much happier in the eighteenth."

Lionel, laughing, patted his wife's cheek and stood up. "If you all will excuse me, I've people I ought to be talking to. A little politicking.

See you later." He leaned over, whispering to Francis, "Don't take the priest too seriously. He's a fuzzy thinker. Bit of a rabble-rouser."

"I'm afraid," Father Baker remarked when Lionel had gone, "that we are boring you with our affairs, Mr. Luther. We island people tend to think we're so important and all the time we're so small."

"No." Kate was stubborn. "We are important. We're a microcosm of the entire world and what is happening to it." Abruptly, then, she changed her tone. "But if you'd rather hear of romance on such a romantic night, I can tell you the tales my great-grandmother told me. She lived until I was ten and she loved to talk about her youth, about quadrilles and mazurkas and traveling theatrical companies from France. In those days many of the older families still spoke French at home. I could tell you about the staircases—there still are a few on the island—built so wide that three ladies in hoopskirts could walk down side by side."

She puzzled Francis with her sarcasm and her passion. He didn't know whether he liked her or was sorry for her.

Marjorie had freed herself from the elderly British pair. "Oh, that's delicious, Kate! And do you live in an old house, too?"

"Very old. It's called Georgina's Fancy."

"There has positively got to be a story to a place with a name like that."

"There is, quite a story. The builder was a rich man, of course. He sent his sons to England to be educated, as they all did. One of the sons brought back a bride, Georgina. She was very young, and it's said she never wanted to come here to this far, lonely place. She was terrified of the slaves and with good reason, as it turned out, because she was raped and murdered in a slave revolt. Ten houses were burnt that night and their owners massacred before the revolt was put down."

"Good God!" Marjorie cried, shivering.

"There's a portrait at our house which we think is hers, a kind of imitation Gainsborough of a young girl in an ankle-length dress and black laced slippers, carrying a little dog."

"You're giving me goose bumps," Marjorie said.

"Yes, can you picture it? The sultry darkness, everybody sleeping, she in a great four-poster bed, and then the slaves creeping in at the windows, carrying machetes, no doubt. And they must have had torches, to fire the house."

"Savages!" Marjorie breathed.

"Yes. And yet one can understand. She must have been an ancestor of yours, Francis. Of course! Georgina's Fancy was a Francis estate! She might have been your great-great—I don't know how many greats —grandmother. Or aunt, anyway."

It had grown quite dark, a violet evening. From a pond somewhere not far off frogs began to throb and trill. Two boys drew up chairs to Father Baker's side and talked about cricket. A young woman across from Marjorie started a conversation about auctioning the contents of a French manor house. Francis glanced at his watch. It was not yet time to leave. But it had been a long day and he was suddenly tired. Marjorie and the other woman changed to the subject of cars, or maybe it was cigars. The frogs and the orchestra drowned the words.

Kate Tarbox lit a cigarette. He ought probably to talk to her, since the man on her other side was busy with somebody else.

"Do you have children?" he asked, and was immediately shocked at himself for having forgotten about the miscarriage that had prevented her attendance at his own wedding.

She replied quietly, "No."

Then he said, "Well, you certainly seem to keep busy with public affairs, don't you?" Oh, Lord, worse and worse! He was saying all the wrong things.

She answered with a blunt question. "What do you do?"

"I've been in the securities business with my father."

"Oh, yes, surely, I remember. Do you like it?"

"Not particularly." He surprised himself with his reply, for he had thought, during this past year, that he did, after all, like it well enough.

"Why do you do it, then?"

"I don't know. I drifted into it. I guess that's the best answer I can give."

"It's an honest answer, anyway."

He tried to think of something else to say. "What is this tree we're sitting under? The roots are extraordinary, I've never seen one like it."

"It's a banyan. From India. Practically everything on this island is from somewhere else, you know. The parrot and the sugarcane, coffee, bananas—"

"Bananas are not native?"

"No, Alexander the Great saw them first when he went to India. Europeans brought them to the New World. Carried by long tides from other places to take root here. Like me, and like us all."

"You speak poetry," Francis said. Imagining that he saw a small frown between her eyebrows, he added quickly, "I don't mean you're affected. I meant your imagery. Maybe you're not even aware of it."

"Oh, yes, Lionel always tells me my imagination runs away with me."

"What are you saying about me?" Lionel inquired, coming back to the table.

"Well, you do always say I'm unrealistic, don't you?"

"Lord, yes, you haven't the foggiest notion. But then, that's the charm of the feminine, isn't it? Right, Francis?"

"I'll let you know when I've been married four years, like you," Francis replied, giving Lionel the "social" smile which, since he had married and entered the social world, he had at last had to learn. Then, catching Marjorie's glance, the smile turned genuine. He was uncomfortable in this cloudy atmosphere of antagonism, and suddenly grateful for the harmony in his own marriage, he reached over to take his wife's hand.

"I've a complication," Lionel said. "The fellow I was just speaking to has to leave tomorrow afternoon, so I'll need to spend the morning with him on business. And I had planned to drive you to Eleuthera. I know you're anxious to get it over with and go home yourselves."

"No problem," Francis said quickly. "If you can get us a car and give us directions, we'll make it on our own."

"You'd never find your way around the place after you got there, never know what you were looking at. Two thousand acres, rank as a jungle."

"I'll drive you," Kate offered.

Marjorie protested, "That would be taking up your whole day!"

"I don't mind that. I'll pick you up at half past eight."

She came bouncing down the drive in a canvas-topped Jeep. "A Jeep is what you need for these roads." She looked at Marjorie's white sandals. "You'll ruin those, or break your ankle. Haven't you anything else?"

"Only sneakers for tennis. But they'll look so silly with this dress."

"Put them on, then. No one's going to look at you." And as if aware that she had been brusque, Kate added honestly, "Not that you don't deserve to be looked at."

For the first few miles the road ran close to the sea. Fishermen were hauling in their nets. Laundry was drying on the rocks beside coves where salt water met fresh. Bare-bottomed children played in front of dilapidated, moldy cabins. Soon the road turned inland and began to climb as cane fields gave way to banana groves. Through the tattered leafage one caught here and there a glimpse of the sea below, calm and gilded in the morning sun. Laden donkeys plodded downhill. Women stood aside as the car passed, their faces without expression under the heavy baskets of produce that rested on coiled pads on their heads.

"How delightful! How quaint!" Marjorie cried.

"You think so?" Kate responded, somewhat dryly.

Here and there, among the notches and furrows of the rising hills, a lane ran to a grand white house.

"Estate Anne," Kate said of one. "Friends of Herbert's and Julia's. They race horses. Or rather, he races horses and she plays bridge. Not that I've anything against bridge, I don't play too badly myself, but it seems to me one ought to do something else, too, with one's life."

From the rear seat behind the two women, Francis had a three-quarter view of Kate's face. Changing its expression from moment to moment, it reflected, he saw, what was going on in her head. There was no deception in that face. Just now a cloud was passing across it, as though she had been reprimanded or were recalling a reprimand, some loneliness, some exclusion.

Then, in the next instant, as if remembering an obligation to be entertaining, she said, "Look at those mountain palms, over there, the smooth stems with the puff on top; don't they remind you of a Gay Nineties hat? Feathers and Lily Langtry, with the long neck?" And she went on brightly, "There are gorges high up here where you can actually see fossils and shells from coral reefs. All this was under the ocean once."

Mahogany and bamboo arched above the narrow way. Great ferns of the rain forest dripped and glistened where, in the proliferation of leaf and vine, no light could penetrate.

Kate expressed Francis' thought. "This place swarms with life. Crawling, walking, swimming, and flying."

"I shouldn't think anything could move through here," Marjorie said with a shudder. "Not that I'd want to. It's eerie."

"There are trails. People come up to poach. The most marvelous parrots breed here and it's illegal to steal them, but people do. They smuggle them out of the country in suitcases, and most of them die on the way. It's brutal. I get furious when I think about it," Kate said passionately.

Now began a gradual descent from the summit. The road wound and twisted. They passed a village, a handful of cabins, a patch of coconut and banana trees, then tilted fields and sunshine on the great mountain's flank, with sheep and cattle grazing in deep grass.

"Oh, what are those?" cried Marjorie, observing everything. Out of the distance she had picked what appeared to be white birds, standing on cows' backs.

"Cattle egrets. They eat insects off the cow's back."

"Well," Marjorie said, "curiouser and curiouser, as Alice remarked."

Suddenly Kate stopped the car. "There it is. Eleuthera."

Beneath them on a spacious tableland stood a long white house. At its back the mountain soared; before it, in enormous silence, lay the shimmering sea.

Kate spoke softly. "The end of the world, isn't it? A dropping-off place."

She released the brake and the car descended. Rusted gates were flung back against stone posts. The long lane between royal palms was overgrown. The aristocratic arch above the door had broken off; tall windows were shuttered; weeds were knee-high on the paths. Ruin, like a disfiguring disease, had eaten away.

They stared for a moment. Marjorie asked, "This is the house, isn't it, where your mother grew up?"

Francis nodded, unable, for the moment, to speak. He had not expected to be so moved, to feel such pain. People had sat and talked on this veranda; people had come up this driveway to the sight of flowers and the welcome of a barking dog. All of this had been alive.

His eyes went moist and he got out of the car to squint into the sun so that no one would see.

They went inside. In the great hall every surface was chiseled and adorned. The stair rails were elaborate twisted spirals; the newel posts were pineapples; the walls were paneled and carved. Through the open door the sun came shafting and a fine golden wood dust stirred in the warm air.

"It's like Drummond Hall, on a smaller scale," Marjorie observed.

"These great houses are cut pretty much to the same pattern," Kate answered. "Here's the library. That's mahoe, cabinetmaker's wood, and very precious. It's beautiful when it's polished."

"There are no shelves on this side!" Marjorie exclaimed. "It's only half finished! Isn't that odd?"

Francis felt that a man should assert practicality. "The roof's been leaking, look." He added doubtfully, "I wonder whether a thing like that ought to be repaired before we put the place on the market?"

"I don't think you ought to put a cent into it," Marjorie declared. "To begin with, we haven't got any money, have we? No, just mark it down and sell 'as is.' Clearance sale. That's that."

"Strange that the place hasn't been vandalized," Francis remarked. "It hasn't been, you can see that."

"People here are afraid it's haunted," Kate said. "The village people believe in spirits and witches, you know. You've heard about Anancy tales?"

"Yes," Francis said. "Old tales from Africa."

"Incredible ignorance in this day and age!" Marjorie commented.

"Not incredible, considering the way they live," Kate answered. There was a trace of impatience in her voice.

She really is too impatient, Francis thought. Yet it's true, the villages are miserable places. What can those people know?

"Shall we walk around the grounds now?" Kate asked. "There used to be roads to drive on, but they're too overgrown for the car."

"How do you know your way around?" Marjorie asked.

"I used to visit here sometimes when I was a child. My grandfather knew Virgil Francis."

"You knew my great-grandfather?" Francis was astonished.

"Not well. But everybody on St. Felice knows who everybody else is. You know, I think you must be like him. He was tall as a reed, and the one thing I do remember is his sort of beaky nose, like yours," she said, regarding Francis. "It's funny the things one can remember about people, unimportant things from years ago."

Marjorie had discovered a sugar mill, or rather, the ruins of one. The top layers of tile had broken off to a third of the original height. Their rubble lay in the long grass. An enormous rusty cauldron lay there, too.

"They used to bake cassava flour in that to feed the slaves," Kate said. "And here, look, here's the keystone of the mill. T.F. F for Francis, naturally. I don't know who T was. . . . The date's 1727."

Marjorie had gone on ahead, grasping things swiftly, as was her way, and passing on to the next. Francis, on the other hand, liked to linger, to savor and speculate. *Flour for the slaves.* Vividly, he could feel this place as it must have been, not silent as now, but busy with running feet and voices, tension and commotion, in the buzzing heat.

"There must have been a house here," Marjorie called back. "There's a foundation."

Kate called, "The overseer's house. He would have lived there with the bookkeepers. And past them were the slave quarters, the bar-racoons. There would have been about fifty huts on a place this size. And then the factory compound, with the boiling house and the mill."

There was a sudden movement in the tall grass. A small flock of goats clattered into view, stared for a moment at the strangers, and went back to feeding.

"Gone wild," Kate observed.

"That stuff they're eating looks like cactus, for heaven's sake," Marjorie said.

"It is. It's called Turk's head, and goats are the only creatures who'll eat it."

Francis stood still. Let me feel this, he thought. Bee hum. Wind rush. Goats rip the grass.

A soft languor and longing, a peace that was part sadness, lay upon him. And he spoke it aloud. "Sad. Sad."

"Nonsense! It was based on slavery," Marjorie said briskly.

"I don't mean that, of course. I mean—" His voice fell away.

Marjorie's voice rang clearly. "They deserved what they got. In addition to owning other human beings, they were disgracefully in-competent. They exhausted the soil, spent more than they had, and let everything fall apart. Shall we go back to the house?"

They sat down on the veranda steps. Far below them, the river was a silver trickle. Around the point of the little bay one saw a fringe of cliffside trees bent inland by the ocean wind.

"That's where the Atlantic rolls, meeting the Caribbean. If you're the kind who gets seasick," Kate warned, "it's no place to go sailing."

Marjorie screamed and jumped. A small snake had slithered across what remained of the garden path and disappeared in the under-growth.

"It won't hurt you," Kate said. "It's harmless."

"No poisonous snakes on the island? I've heard there are some who kill in a minute."

"The fer-de-lance. About five feet long. They'd hide in a bunch of bananas, and you would die in minutes if one struck you. There still were a few when I was a child, but there are no more now."

"I feel creepy here all the same," Marjorie said. "Let's go, shall we? Unless there's anything more you need to know, Francis?"

He considered. "What I need to know is, what persuasion can I use to sell this place? What are its assets?"

Kate made a sweep with her arm. "Its assets are all around you, aren't they?"

He looked at her. She was very serious. "Yes," he said gently, "the beauty. The beauty on this hill."

"You're not going to sell beauty," Marjorie said. "Here, I've got pencil and paper in my bag, let's make notes. Now," she told Kate, "it's obvious you know how to run an estate. What would you do with this if it belonged to you?"

Kate spoke promptly. "I'd begin by planting trees. On the higher slopes you have deforestation. That's pretty true all over the island, the result of improvident usage. From it you get soil erosion, droughts, and floods. As a matter of fact, we have been trying to educate the small farmer along those lines."

"Without much success, I'll bet," Marjorie said.

"Education takes time," Kate replied.

Francis was uncomfortable. Plainly, the two women disliked each other. He had no idea why or what to do about it.

And Kate continued, "After that, I'd plant bananas. Very little sugar, since you'd need too much new machinery for it. I would diversify with cattle, sheep, and fruit. And not just for export. There's tremendous need right here. Do you know that this fertile island doesn't even feed itself? It's a disgrace! Children, when they drink it at all, drink canned, imported milk. The people are terribly under-nourished. A disgrace!" Kate struck her fist into her palm.

Marjorie regarded her coolly. "Go on, please. I'm making notes."

"I'd plant cocoa. This is the rainy side of the island, and it will do well here. Use the bananas as temporary shade when you set out new cocoa plants. And coconuts. We've a copra mill in town. The women here make cooking oil out of the milk and the dried remains you keep for cattle fodder. Then there's mace, which is the cloak on the nutmeg. You can raise that for export. See, there's some over there by the bamboo fence. Have I given you a few ideas?"

Marjorie had been writing rapidly. "Yes, thanks. Although it occurs to me, anybody who'd even consider a place like this would know something about how to run it, wouldn't he? These notes are probably unnecessary."

"You can't tell."

Francis stood up. "You're convincing, Kate. I should let you convince a buyer for me. By the way, have you any idea how I might go about finding one?"

"It won't be easy. But you could try Atterbury and Shaw in Covetown. They deal in properties. Shall we go?"

He stood for a moment with his hand on the door of the car. Great cumulus clouds had wrapped the peak of Morne Bleue in cotton and washed the house in pearl-gray shadow.

Kate looked at him curiously. "It's got to you, hasn't it?"

"It's a poem, as you said."

She smiled without answering, showing the gap between her two front teeth. He thought irrelevantly, I don't know why a gap between two teeth should be so charming.

Upstairs in their room at Drummond Hall, Marjorie said, "You liked her."

"Liked who?"

"Don't play dumb," she said pleasantly. "Kate, of course. Who else?"

"Well, she's a very nice person. She went out of her way to be helpful."

"I don't mean that. You really liked her. You were attracted to her. You desire her."

"You're out of your head," he said fondly.

"She's your sort. Lusty and sexy," Marjorie said, undoing her bra. Above her white breasts the tan made a heart-shaped curve.

"Sexy? She's not even pretty. Well, not very."

"She's older than you are."

"Half a year!"

"They're not happy, couldn't you see that?"

"I know. I'm sorry for them."

"Yes, she's your sort. Outdoors. Animals. Spiritual, too. And she undressed you with her eyes."

"What!" he shouted.

"Yes, when she said that about how you look like your grandfather."

"I don't remember."

"Yes, you do! She said you had your grandfather's beaky nose."

"Great-grandfather."

"You see, you do remember!"

"Quit it, Marjorie."

"It's true, you desire her."

She was settling her breasts into a fresh brassiere, two lace cups on black ribbons.

"Listen," he said, "just wait till we get this damn dinner over and get back up here, I'll show you something about desire."

The pier glass reflected a supple girl with a quick, mobile mouth and clever eyes; the man beside her, although exactly her age, wore the soft look of a boy who is eager to please.

"Well, now that you've seen decay at Eleuthera, let me show you a thriving enterprise," Lionel offered one morning a week later. "Georgina's Fancy is half again as large as when I took it over, I want you to know. I've added a lot of acreage."

A tractor was loading cane stalks into carts, and some dark little boys, no older than eight or nine, were sweeping up the droppings.

"Shouldn't they be in school?" Francis asked.

"They leave in crop time to help out. They need the money." And as Francis made no comment, Lionel added, "Trouble is, these people have too many kids; they can't possibly support them all.

"We've got a central mill in town now, a big change from the days when each estate had its own mill. If the island were large enough, we could have a railway to get the stuff there faster. You can't let the stalks lie in the sun a minute too long or the juice will ferment, and then it's no good."

At the farthest boundary of the property lay the village, like all of them that Francis had seen. He had a quick impression of rotting wood, bare dirt, chickens and goats, before they moved on.

"I've got a tip-top manager, but even so, it's not the same as when you're on the job. Oh, I could get myself a house in town or on the beach and drive out here every couple of days, but I like to keep an eye on the ball myself. And my dad does the same. That's why he survived when so many others went under. You've got to know business, too, dealing with commission merchants; they take options on your crop and then at the last minute decide they've overbought and turn you down. It's tough." Lionel sighed.

I don't see him married to Kate, Francis thought, surprised that this intrusive thought should have come into his head, when actually he had been listening with real interest to all this information, so new and different from anything he had ever known.

They trudged on. "Yes, that's why you have to have at least two export crops to make it pay. Bananas are the best. They require very little care except pruning. Of course, nothing's perfect! There's a pesky little animal, the taltuza, something like a rat, that eats the roots. And we've had Panama disease—that's a fungus—but for once the government acted promptly and we wiped it out with lime."

They had walked uphill away from the cane toward the Great House. Two fawn-colored horses whinnied delicately behind a fence.

"Kate's pets. She's an expert horsewoman, but she treats those two like lap dogs. Comes of having no children, I suppose."

Francis was silent.

"The doctor says she can't have any. Took her ovaries out after the last miscarriage."

"I'm sorry," Francis said.

"Yes. Well. So, we were talking about bananas. It looks easier than it is, let me tell you. You're at the mercy of world markets, depressions, and wars. During the war you couldn't ship, at all, naturally. Now sometimes the ship is overloaded; you've got your load on the dock and they won't take it on. So you leave it there for the goats. And sometimes the inspectors reject your stuff—when there's nothing wrong with it, mind you; it's just that they've got too much and they want to keep the price up on the other side. Tough. Yes, we've had some hard times here. And now there's all this talk of independence. I tell you, your head can swim. Still, it's home, it gets under your skin. I wouldn't leave. At least, I don't think I ever would."

"You'll be managing Drummond Hall for your father when he goes?"

"Yes, Kate will help me. She'll keep the books, ride over and look around. Another pair of eyes." They reached the steps. "I'll drive you back to Father's. I'd ask you to stay to lunch but Kate's in town. I'm to meet her at half past twelve."

Francis felt the sinking of slight disappointment. Ridiculous! "That's all right. You've given us a lot of your busy time. It was especially nice of Kate to take us to Eleuthera that day."

"Oh, she loved it! She loves traveling around, showing things to visitors. She's a good girl, Kate is. You know," Lionel said, with embarrassment sitting oddly on his bulk, "the other night at the wedding, maybe you thought I was a little hard on her. . . . You don't have to say whether you did or not. We get along fairly well, she and I, only her problem is she's a bleeding heart and it's going to get her into trouble some day. That's the fact of it, and it makes me sore as hell."

He did not want to see Kate exposed. And he repeated, awkwardly, "Well, you've all been very good to us."

"Anything we can do, just ask. Anything worrying you, just speak up."

"Nothing worrying us, except Marjorie's being afraid she hasn't brought enough clothes for all the hospitality!"

"That's no problem. Try Da Cunha's. They've got French dresses and what-all stuck away in the back. Marjorie could outfit herself for two years to come."

"We shan't be here that long, I'm afraid."

"You'll be here longer than you think. Unless you just want to go and leave things in the hands of Atterbury and Shaw."

"I may have to do that. But what I'd really like is to have a nibble before I leave. And I think—it's nothing short of miraculous—but I think we may possibly have one. I don't know whether he's a land speculator or what. Fellow from Puerto Rico. Well, we've cut the price to the bone, that's probably the reason."

Lionel nodded. "It's the only way."

And they drove back to Drummond Hall.

Mr. Atterbury saw Francis to the door. "My man expects to hear pretty quickly from his lawyers in Puerto Rico. I think it's fairly safe to say we've got a sale, Mr. Luther."

Francis, thanking him, held up two crossed fingers. He had left the borrowed car parked in the back of the building, but for some reason he did not feel like returning yet to the tennis-and-lunch regime at Drummond Hall, and he went on down Wharf Street, past the classic Georgian facade of Barclay's Bank to the square.

It was market day, and the town bustled with real life: he had already drawn a distinction between the "real" life of the island and the suave amenities of his relatives' homes. Busses from the country were still bringing people in, barefoot women wearing home-woven straw hats and cotton dresses in every imaginable electric color. Children of every age darted among mounds of bananas, breadfruit, fish, and coconuts. Yellow dogs—all the dogs here seemed to be of one variety so that, although they were mongrels, they had almost evolved into a breed—prowled in the shade and scratched at their mange.

Francis stood for a while observing this animation, then walked around the corner. At the orphanage he stopped to listen to a rehearsal of the children's choir; he had heard them sing on the previous Sunday at the cathedral service. The orphanage was opposite a cemetery. He walked across the street and leaned over the railing, thinking that this would be, after all, an agreeable place in which to spend eternity! Date palms and palmettos framed the space; the graves were elaborately trimmed with conch shells. In the cool, fragrant morning air, the pure child voices sang "Now Thank We All Our God." And feeling a pleasure serene as a beatitude, he waited until the hymn had ended.

Now quite familiar with the map of the little town, he turned into the arcades. The leaning houses with their narrow windows and crumbling iron lace balustrades might, were it not for the deep black shade of the fig trees in the yards, have been standing on the Place des Vosges in Paris. At the next small square he paused before a round bronze plaque set in the middle of the pavement. It was still legible: "In this place on the eleventh of July in the year 1802 Samuel Vernon, late a member of His Majesty's Council, died by hanging for the murder of his Negro slave Plato."

"Gruesome, isn't it?"

Kate Tarbox smiled from under a large native straw hat. "This one went a little too far. It amused him to watch men being beaten to death. Even his peers got disgusted with him, finally. So they tried him and hanged him."

Francis shook his head. "A very complex society!"

"Oh, yes! And it still is. What are you doing in town?"

"Just ambling about. And you?"

"I have a little office over there. The Family Counseling Service. Yes, I know it's like trying to empty the ocean with a soup spoon. I saw your raised eyebrow."

"Did I raise it? I didn't mean to."

There followed then that moment of indecision during which one can either speak the few graceful words necessary to terminate the meeting or else take up another subject which will prolong it.

Francis said, "I was thinking, as long as I'm here, I might pick up a few presents to bring home. I thought maybe, do you—would you make a suggestion?"

"There's always Da Cunha's. I don't know what you want to spend."

"Something middling, let's say. A pin or some beads, maybe."

"Da Cunha's, then."

They walked back through the market square. Francis felt conspicuous; he was so tall beside her, and he was used to walking next to
Marjorie, who was almost his height. In high heels she was even with
him; they were known as a handsome couple.

He needed to say something. "I don't recognize half these vegetables. Those are beets and cabbage, of course, but what's that stuff?"

"Akee. That's cassava. Those are pomegranates next to the mel-
ons."

"Pomegranates? Like the Bible?"

"Like the Bible. Those are tamarinds, that's sour sop. And plan-
tains, they taste like bananas, but we serve them hot. And there's
breadfruit."

"As in *Mutiny on the Bounty.*"

"Right! Captain Bligh brought it from Tahiti. Easy feeding for the
slaves. You can practically live on it. Here's Da Cunha's."

An exotic black girl with waist-length hair came forward.

"Désirée," Kate said, "this is my friend—no, my nephew. I'm his
aunt by marriage, isn't that ridiculous? Anyway, this is Mr. Luther.
He needs to buy some presents."

The thick, arched walls were of the eighteenth century. The ceiling
fans, placidly whirring, were of the nineteenth. Singapore and Somer-
set Maugham, Francis thought. Liquor and crystal, porcelain and
silver, made a lavish sparkle. In a glass-covered case lay a discreet
selection of diamond watches.

His negotiations were few. Having quickly made his purchases, a
doll for Margaret (who was twenty-four), three silver pins for his
mother and remaining sisters, and some cigars for his father, they left
the shop.

"Isn't she a beautiful girl?" Kate asked. "I always feel so insignificant beside her. An African princess."

"She is beautiful, but you don't have to feel insignificant beside
anyone," he said, with automatic gallantry.

"She's married to a schoolteacher. Her father's a labor leader,
Clarence Porter. A friend of mine."

"Of yours and Lionel's?" Francis inquired cautiously.

Kate laughed without mirth. "No, certainly not of Lionel's."

And he remembered having had, on the ride to Eleuthera some days before, an impression of melancholy, of loneliness and exclusion.

"How about lunch?" He spoke abruptly.

"I'd like that."

"You name the place, then."

"There is only one place outside of the country club. Cade's Hotel, on the other side of the harbor."

From light they entered into the dimness of mahogany. A few men were seated at lunch among the dark portraits. They went out again into light and took a table in the shade of the garden wall.

Kate took her hat off. Her bright hair, released, curved about her freckled cheeks, grazing her chin. He had a sudden memory of Marjorie in the bedroom, of her clear pronouncement: *Oh, yes, she undressed you with her eyes.* He went warm with embarrassment.

But Kate's eyes now were on the menu. "The fish is always good. It's deep-sea, mostly. Abrecca, ballahou, salmon, grunt—"

"I'll have salmon. It's the only one I recognize."

They settled back. Her hand, resting on the table, displayed a large, square emerald ring which he had not noticed before. It was in perfectly good taste—son of a flamboyant father, he was critical of excessive display—yet it did not seem to belong to this particular woman, with her simple dress and sandals, her simple manner. Marjorie would have worn it with flair and style. Too bad, because he could not afford, and probably never would afford, to buy one for her.

"You've really got rid of Eleuthera? A lot quicker than we expected."

"I think so. Of course, the lawyers have all sorts of papers to go over, still."

"So then you'll be leaving."

"I should go home now, but if it's only a matter of another week or two before we get everything signed up, it's probably wiser for me to stay and see it through."

"You'll come back."

"It's not around the corner. What makes you think so?"

Her face crinkled in a smile. "Oh, those long tides will bring you. And the wind and the clouds on Morne Bleue."

"The clouds on Morne Bleue. I said you talk poetry, didn't I?"

"Seriously though, there's a lot you haven't seen. Christmas and Old Year's Night, what you call New Year's Eve. Do you like calypso? Steel bands?"

He nodded.

"You ought to hear the real thing at carnival time, not what they give you in tourist hotels on the big islands. Everybody 'runs mask.' The costumes are marvelous, and the singers make up original songs; they'll make one up about you if you ask. The streets are jammed. It's a circus, a revel. You have to see it to believe it. Then on Ash Wednesday it's all over." She snapped her fingers. "All over, like that."

"Well, maybe I will see it sometime."

"How odd that your mother, who grew up here, never told you about it! But perhaps," Kate reflected, "she might have had unhappy memories. Not getting along with a difficult mother—"

"If I have heard that once," Francis interrupted, "I have heard it a dozen times: 'How odd that your mother never talked about St. Felice!' "

Kate was astonished. "I'm sorry. I really didn't mean to pry."

He was ashamed, then, of his irritability. "No, *I'm* sorry—"

She shook her head. "I do say things that are too personal, I know I do. It's a terrible fault. I should bite my tongue for saying that about your grandmother."

"Don't bite it. I haven't been fond of her either, the few times in my life that we've been together. I don't suppose it's easy being her daughter-in-law."

"She tolerates me, barely. That's because of my ancestry. I have excellent ancestry." She chuckled.

"Tell me!"

"Well, we were planter families on both sides, who lost everything when the slaves were freed. By the time I came along there was no money at all. My father had been beautifully educated, in England, naturally. He was a clergyman, a good friend of Father Baker's, who's sort of kept an eye on me since my parents died. He's a wonderful person, not one of those clergymen who *mouth forth*. He believes in works."

He wanted to ask, How ever did you come to marry Lionel? but of course did not.

And just then she said, as if he had actually asked the question, "Lionel wanted to marry a girl with colored blood. He's still in love with her. Naturally, that was impossible, so he married me."

"I see!"

"She won't admit it, which is shameful, although it's not her fault that she won't. It's the world's."

"Then how do people know?"

"Everybody knows everybody else's ancestry. And most people are related to each other if you go back far enough. For instance, I'm related to the Da Cunhas about six generations ago. One Jew, back there, and the rest Scottish and French since then."

He wanted to know more, but she said merely, "I used to go in for genealogy when I was young. I've more important things to do now."

"When you were young!" he mocked.

"I'm thirty. I've told you."

"So am I."

"You look older. I imagine you always have. You feel responsible for things, for people."

"As a matter of fact, I do," Francis said thoughtfully.

Noontime stillness lay like a warm hand on the little garden. When they had first sat down, birds had been flickering, but now they had gone to rest and there was no sound except the drip and splash of water from the mouth of a stone cherub set into the wall.

. . . *but of course that was impossible, so he married me.* The words kept repeating themselves in his head.

"Have I bored you with all my talk?"

Francis started. "Bored? No, keep on, please."

"Lionel says I'm a walking storehouse of useless information."

"Not useless to me," he said graciously. "Tell me, those odd trees on the other side of the wall, what are they?"

"*Sabliers*. Sandbox trees in English. They used to fill the seedpods with sand and use them to sprinkle parchment. Feel better, now that you know that?"

"Oh, much! Now another: What, exactly, is Creole?"

"It means someone born here who is purely European, that is, purely white. Anything else you want to know?"

"Dozens of things, but right now I'm enjoying the fish."

. . . of course that was impossible, so he married me.

"I suppose you do some traveling?" he asked.

"We went abroad on our honeymoon. Lionel is serious about work, though. So we don't go very far very often."

"Do you feel you're missing anything, do you feel that an island is confining?"

"Not really. People in large cities like to talk about all the things going on there—six orchestras, four ballet companies, a dozen theaters—but when you pin them down, actually most people don't do very much of all that. I have a record collection—it's my chief extravagance—and a good piano. Books are a problem, though. Our bookstore is small and things have to be ordered. It takes forever."

"I'd be glad to send you stuff when I get home. Or," he corrected himself, "Marjorie will, if you send a list."

"That's very good of you."

"Tell me what else you do besides reading and playing the piano and riding your horses and the—Family Counsel, is it?"

"You're not laughing at me?"

"Why ever should I do that?"

"Some people do, you know. I'm thought to be eccentric. Not practical." She folded her hands under her chin. Her nails were unvarnished; only the emerald glistened. "But I see myself as very practical. You've seen how people live here; aside from its not being morally right, it isn't wise to allow it to go on, because the day will come when they won't accept these conditions anymore. People like

Lionel want things to stay exactly the way they are, but even a child can see that they won't."

"What do you propose to do?"

"Make the changes peacefully and fairly. We need schooling. Light industry and jobs. Housing. A decent hospital. I've tried to persuade Lionel to head a drive. He's got money enough, investments in hotels in Jamaica and Barbados. He could do it."

"But he won't?"

"He makes halfhearted promises and does nothing. Like the government."

"So you feel frustrated."

"Yes, I do. That's why I've got involved with family welfare. I feel I'm doing *something*. Teaching people how to feed their children. Handling problem children. They call them 'bad,' but it's really that they have no fathers to lead them."

Her eyes were prisms. As the light shifted through the leaves, they turned from violet to brown, then to a dark and austere blue.

"We also," she said, looking directly at Francis, "we also show them how not to have more children."

"Birth control?"

"Yes. You don't approve?"

"If people don't want children, they shouldn't have them. For the children's sake, if nothing else."

"Some people, black and white both, are outraged. They say I do this because I can't have children of my own."

"That's not only malicious, it's stupid."

"It's a terrible thing to want a child and not have one," she said softly, "but worse to have six you can't clothe or feed." She stood up. "You're finished? You've got things to do and so have I."

He walked with her to his car.

"Do you know," he said, with his hand already on the door, "do you know I have been having the strangest feeling? As if I had been here before."

"Déjà vu. It's common."

"I've always been sensitive to place: rooms, houses, streets. And not because they have beauty or grandeur or status. I've been in beautiful places that were cold to me, in which I've known I would be miserable. And I've walked down a street in some ordinary little town and thought I would be happy there."

"You feel that way here? That you would be happy?"

"Yes. Absurd, isn't it, considering that I don't know anything about it? And yet I feel like Brigham Young coming to Salt Lake City. There's a monument there where he halted the wagon train, looked over the valley, and said, 'This is the place.' "

"This particular place can be ignorant and cruel. You have to love it a lot to put up with all that."

"That's not what you said when you were telling about carnival and music and the rest."

"Every coin has two sides," she countered.

Yes, it is absurd of me, he was thinking.

"I don't believe Marjorie would like it," Kate said. "I see her as completely urban."

He came to. "Of course. I'm only fantasizing. Thank you for having lunch with me."

He did not say *Remember me to Lionel.* She gave him a little wave as he drove away.

That was impossible, so he married me. He would have given anything to know more.

Damn! So much stupid, unnecessary waste in the world!

Two weeks went by as they waited for word from the prospective buyer. Marjorie played tennis and went swimming. Francis, although there was no necessity to do so, went back to Eleuthera. Alone, he sat on the veranda steps, watching green lizards scurry up the columns. His eyes wandered out over fields and hills. Bananas on the hill, Kate Tarbox said. Fruit orchards. Cattle in the meadows by the river.

"I have founded a kingdom of my own," the first François had written in that diary which had so enthralled the child Francis, "where a pure river runs and the air is salubrious, far removed from the noisome crowding of towns."

A kingdom of my own! The old peasant, turned pirate, turned planter, had possessed a streak of poetry as well.

He leaned his head against the railing. Let's not get foolish, Francis, with that "streak of poetry." Poetry doesn't feed anyone. Yet he could feel again that old dread of the city, of the office on a shelf, the telephones and ledgers, counting money. It was all right if you were made for it, but he was not.

What, then, was he made for?

He thought, There's nothing to go back to. I should have to make a new start. Why not make it here? Why not?

And he sat up, excitement pouring like wine. Take charge. Create something. As a painter stands before a vacant canvas, or a sculptor contemplates a lump of stone, so might a man feel here before this wasted land. He would have been ashamed, reserved as was his nature, to put these feelings into words; they would seem puerile, vague, without value in the telling, although he felt, he knew, they were neither puerile nor vague.

So he marshaled arguments. Surely it could not be *all* that difficult! Surely he could learn as well as Herbert or Lionel had learned, enough to make this pay and enough for his parents while they needed it. He would do more; he would provide a better living for the people who worked the soil, build that hospital, show what intelligence and good will can create. . . .

So his mind ran, all that week and the next.

"You can't be serious," Marjorie said. "You can't be."

They were getting ready for bed. She sank back against the pillows.

"I really am. At first it seemed a wild idea, but I've been thinking it over for days. I've spoken to the bank about a mortgage, for cash to get started. They think, with hard work, I can do it. They've even put me in touch with a good manager, a fellow named Osborne, who managed a large estate in Jamaica."

Sweat came out on Marjorie's forehead.

"To my amazement, Julia has agreed to cosign a note so my parents will be taken care of until my father can get on his feet. Shows you never know about people."

"No, you don't," she said bitterly.

"Let me try, Marjorie. Please? I can make it work. I believe in my bones I can."

"It's that Kate who's talked you into this! All that stuff about fruit and cattle! If it's so easy, why hasn't someone else done it?"

"I didn't say it was easy. I said it was possible. And Kate had nothing to do with it."

He had not mentioned the lunch in town. It had seemed to him that would be giving it too much importance. Marjorie might not see it as the chance encounter it had been. When, on the following day, he had decided there was after all no reason why he should not have mentioned it, then it had seemed too late; she would think it odd that he had not mentioned it before.

She began to cry. He felt deeply sorry for her and put an arm around her shoulders.

"You know," he said gently, "you know, I never really liked what I was doing. I realize now how little I liked it."

"You never told me you didn't!"

"I guess I didn't really know it until now."

"That's ridiculous! You know how many young men would give their eyeteeth to have that job?"

"But they're not me and I'm not them." He looked out past the window; he could hear a rustle of leaves. "It was like being in prison, with good food and all the comforts, but still a prison."

"That's ridiculous!" Marjorie said again.

She wept and he put his arms around her.

"You're forgetting, I haven't got the job anymore."

"You could get another. Don't tell me you couldn't."

"Marjorie, darling, here's something I think I can do well. Call it an emotional decision, but aren't all big decisions emotional, when you think about them? The really big ones, like marrying you, for instance? Listen, Marjorie, listen, it's a challenge, an adventure.

EDEN BURNING

We're young enough to try anything. If we don't like it, we can always sell out. What difference if we sell now or a year from now?"

The argument went on for most of the night and the next day and the next. In the end, by dint of his promise that the experiment would be just that, an experiment and no commitment, by dint of that, with combined reluctance and valiant sportsmanship, Marjorie gave in, and Francis won.

Nine

THE fragrance of raw wood was strong and sweet under a sultry sky. The heat in the lumberyard was stifling.

"Likely to pour any minute," Francis said.

The other man looked up. Clouds were speeding in over the roiling bay; the clouds were iron gray, rimmed with silver.

"October. We'll have had our two hundred inches of rain before the year's out. No hurricane warning yet, anyway."

"You'll deliver that stuff by the end of the week? I particularly want to finish the post-and-rail fence so we can let the horses out."

"You'll have it. We were saying, Mr. Luther, what a change! It's not much more than a year since you took the place over."

"Almost two."

"Well, if anybody had asked me, I'd have said it couldn't be done."

He felt gay as he headed out of town. The man's praise had been earned. No one had believed, neither Lionel nor he himself, how fast he would be able to pull shape and order out of chaos.

What a bombshell he had dropped! His father, at the time, had been numbly accepting of any new blow, but his mother had been shocked. When he and Marjorie had gone back to New York to arrange their move, she had implored, Why, why, when his future was before him, settle for a backwater? Was it fair to Marjorie? Did he want to rear a family on that speck of an island? Yes, he really did want to; was she not herself a product of the island? In the end he had temporized, as he had done with his wife: It need not, after all, be permanent; few things in life were, and he would very likely come back home eventually.

Ultimately his father's affairs had been straightened out. Friends had found a place for him at another brokerage house, and as his mother had declared, last week's scandal faded for some other to take its place in the news.

They had sold the country place and sent its furnishings on to Eleuthera, to Marjorie's great joy.

"We could never have hoped to collect all these things, wouldn't have had time or money enough," she said, as one after the other the cargo containers were opened upon carved beds and Oriental runners, Hepplewhite chairs, and Queen Anne silver.

Richard had not wanted to part with the Anatole Da Cunha island paintings, but Teresa had insisted that they rightly belonged in the setting of Eleuthera, and he had had to agree. So now, when Francis sat at his dining table, he could look behind him and see Morne Bleue in a gilded frame; when he looked before him, Morne Bleue itself, framed by the windows, rose into an arch of cloud.

Eleuthera being a large house, Marjorie had found it necessary to add to the furnishings. She was extravagant. The porcelain lamps, ordered through Da Cunha's, were the finest, as were the draperies and the old Venetian mirrors.

"You can't put cheap things next to what we already have," she argued, which was doubtless aesthetically sound, but costly. They were skating on thin ice, very thin, Francis told her, with debts to the bank, a banana crop barely taking hold, and some yearling beef sold at a profit, nothing more as yet. "Very thin ice," he kept repeating.

But in the main she had accepted the enormous change in her life, a change which she could never have anticipated, with great dignity. She liked to say that thoroughbreds didn't complain.

"Mrs. Luther has a head for practical affairs," said Osborne, who was himself a capable man, honest, respectful, and cold.

Francis had wanted to get busy at once on good living quarters for the full-time help, some sturdy cottages with proper sanitation. Going with Osborne into the villages to recruit labor, he had been horrified by what he saw. Some of the worst dwellings were made of beaten kerosene tins. Parents and children slept together in one bed, and sometimes on the floor.

"They don't know any better. They don't look at it the way you do, Mr. Luther," Osborne said.

"If they don't know any better, which I doubt, they ought to be taught. When they can afford it, they do live better."

"You can't do it now," Marjorie argued, as they went over figures with Osborne, who agreed.

"When you get on your feet financially, then you can think about indulging other people. Until then let them stay in their villages as they are."

He supposed that this made sense, but only for the present. He had made a mental list of the things he wanted to do, and housing had high priority on it.

To the left now lay the country club, deserted, for the sky had just released a drenching rain. He could see the turquoise pool ringed with white umbrellas. Marjorie spent a good deal of time at the club, as did most of the planter wives. Right after breakfast she'd get into the car and drive three quarters of an hour to spend the day at golf or tennis. Happily, she had been making friends here, more than he had made, and that not only because she had more time, but because she possessed qualities which he did not, an independence which attracted people, which they respected. She knew when to talk and what to say. Even her silences were confident.

He swung the car onto the mountain road and let his mind roam. It was not often these days that he had a solitary hour in which to do just that.

It will be better when we have a child, he thought. Children. Surely something must happen soon? And then: What did I mean by "better"? Just as surely, there is nothing wrong! Oh, Marjorie. Lovely, loyal Marjorie.

He ought to spend more time with her. But he was out at dawn, when the workers came trudging up the lane. With them he made the rounds from cattle barns to chicken pens, uphill to the new banana groves and back down to oversee new fences for the fodder corn. Later in the day there were the books to be gone over. A constant round.

He thought suddenly, We never see much of Lionel and Kate. Lionel is a good sort in his way, at least as far as I'm concerned. He's been cordial and helpful with advice. Sometimes in the evenings he would drive alone over the beastly mountain road to visit. "Kate's busy," he would say, although naturally no one had asked where she was. When he had gone, Marjorie would talk about Kate.

"Everyone knows she married him for his money. She didn't have a cent. You remember, she said the Tarboxes even bought her wedding dress."

"That's nasty gossip!"

"Don't be so holy, Francis."

He wondered what chemistry had produced such dislike between the two women. Marjorie was usually fair-minded. Yet a little thing like a voice, for instance, could set your teeth on edge, couldn't it? Or it could draw you near, as it had drawn him to Marjorie. Nor was jealousy a part of Marjorie. She wouldn't stoop to it, she always said; it was humiliating to be that insecure.

"She's really very odd. Not that the projects aren't well intentioned, but they won't work and she overdoes them. No wonder he's impatient with her."

He didn't want to talk about Kate. Well, she is a bit "odd," he thought, different from the mold, and probably that's why the women pick on her. He hadn't had a word alone with her since their lunch. There had been a Christmas party for the family, a farewell when Julia and Herbert left for England, and four, no six—he depressed his fingers for the count—other parties where they had met. Eight times in all. It would have been interesting to see her more often, just because she *was* different. Sitting there with her farmer's hat and her emerald, talking about music and tractors and clinics! Sitting there with the pluck and the spirit on the surface, the melancholy underneath. There was a lot more to her story than she had told, he was certain.

He had never repeated a word about Lionel's other woman, although Kate had made no secret of it. But it was no business of his. He wondered whether there was someone else in her own life. Again, it was no business of his.

The rain was coming so furiously that the wiper was unable to clear the windshield, and he bent forward to peer. Deep ditches flanked the road on either side, making it impossible to turn and go back to town. He had never seen such savage rain. It assaulted the car. He was afraid and ashamed of his fear.

After a while he knew that he had somewhere taken a wrong turn. The road didn't feel right; it was climbing more steeply than it did on the way home, and there were great boulders in its middle. This must be one of those branches that come to a dead end in some mountain village before trailing off into a mule track. The rain was as solid now as a curtain; the world reeled beneath the awesome power of the wind.

Then through the side window he caught sight of life: a banana station, a thatched shed about the size of a city bus shelter, where bananas were piled to await the pickup trucks. Two men were huddled in it.

He stopped the car and leaned from the window, calling over the roar of wind and rain, "Can you tell me where I am?"

A man answered, but Francis did not understand him. "I'm sorry, I didn't hear you! Can you tell me what place this is? Is there a village here?"

The man answered, and again he did not understand. The language was not English.

"Can you speak English?" he called.

The answer was a shake of the head, so he rolled the window up and went on, the car laboring now through a river of red mud. A few minutes later he came to a village, a short double row of huts with a schoolhouse at the far end. It was the usual rough board building on stilts, with a wide roof overhang that kept the rain from coming through the unglassed windows. With enormous relief he stopped the car and raced up the path.

The benches were empty, since it was already late afternoon. At his desk the teacher sat before a pile of papers.

"May I?" Francis called. "I've lost my way." He was out of breath and soaked. "I have no idea where I am."

"Come in, surely. Hang your wet jacket on a peg." He was an extraordinarily pale Negro with a thin aquiline face. "I've some papers to correct, if you'll excuse me."

Francis, with his usual sensitivity to voices, noted the cultivated accent. He took a seat, observing discreetly and alternately the man (pensive eyes, fine hands) and the rising fury out of doors (trees bent to earth, tossing and roar).

The teacher stood up and came close to Francis, making his voice heard above the gusting storm.

"I'm Patrick Courzon. You're in the village of Gully."

Francis extended his hand. "Francis Luther. I live up near Point Angélique. I seem to have strayed."

"You'll have to go back the way you came and take the next fork left, about two miles down from here. It'll bring you straight into Eleuthera."

"Oh? How did you know?"

"That you own Eleuthera? Everyone knows everything about everyone on this island. No, that's not quite true. But people are naturally interested in the revival of such an old, neglected place. It's somewhat romantic, isn't it?"

"I don't know about that. Mostly it's digging and grubbing or consulting books to learn how to dig and grub."

The young man put some books on a shelf and Francis asked, "Am I keeping you from your work? I'll just sit here until the storm ends, if it ever does."

"It will, in an hour or two." Courzon sat down. Apparently he wanted to talk. "It can't be easy for you, coming from the city, to start this sort of life."

"Fortunately, I've got a very good manager to teach me about bananas and fences and sheep and hiring—just about everything."

"Hiring? I don't suppose you've had trouble with that. We've a deal of unemployment." The face was bland.

"I know. I feel bad about that, and about the wages, too. As a matter of fact, I'm offering thirty cents a day over the standard, which hasn't," he added frankly, "exactly endeared me to the other planters." And added hurriedly to that: "Not that I'm trying to be holier-than-thou. It's just—" He did not finish.

"That's a substantial increase, considering that the farm wage is eighty cents a day in the cultivating season."

He could not tell whether the man was being hostile or merely straightforward.

Then Courzon asked, "What are you planning for your vacant land, if I'm not too inquisitive? But I, like others, am curious about you."

Francis decided that he was straightforward. "I understand what you're driving at. Estate owners leaving a tract out of cultivation so they won't have to pay taxes on it. That's a regulation which surely needs to be changed. No, I will cultivate and plant wherever the cane has gone wild, which it has done for what looks like generations. It should be a matter of conscience, when the need for food is so great."

"You astonish me, Mr. Luther."

There was a silence. Then Francis said, "On the way here just now I stopped some people to ask directions. They spoke no English, which surprised me."

"They speak patois in these places. A mixture of Carib and African words added to French."

"Yet the island has been out of French hands for a hundred and fifty years!"

"Longer. But these villages are removed from the world. Many of my children speak patois at home and are hearing English for the first time in my classroom."

"British English?" Francis asked with a smile.

"Well, I was educated by Englishmen in Covetown and after that I was at Cambridge, so I suppose a bit of the accent has worn off on me."

"You were born here on St. Felice, then."

"No, oddly enough, I was born in France. I was brought here when I was not yet two years old."

A French father? Francis wondered. Yes, probably. God knew what passions, heartaches, and shame had combined to produce this refined, this obviously sensitive human being! But then, that was probably true of us all in one way or another.

"My mother was born on the island," he said, "but she left it. And I came back to it. I sometimes wonder why. A wish to escape something else? The pull of history? I'm a type, Mr. Courzon, the kind of man who becomes an antiquarian, who putters about restoring old houses. I'm in love with the past, with roots. I've even made a start at writing the story of St. Felice, of all the people who came here and what brought them."

Courzon nodded. "If it's history you're looking for, we have it. Your own Morne Bleue—how the French and English fought over that mountain! Four times it changed hands in some of the bloodiest battles of the eighteenth century. There were the remains of a fort on the flank when I was a little boy, but that's gone now. People took the stone and bricks for use. The French built with stone—did you know?—and the British with brick."

"I didn't know."

Courzon stopped abruptly. "Sorry. I just overheard myself talking like a schoolmaster."

"Well, you are one, aren't you?"

At that moment the front door, forced open by the wind, slammed violently against the wall. Courzon got up and closed it firmly.

Francis was anxious. "Is this by any chance a hurricane? I haven't been here long enough to see one."

"You'll know one when you do, don't worry. When I was fourteen we had one that wrecked St. Felice. Our windows were smashed, a tree stove in the roof, and the floor was three inches deep in water. The island's entire cocoa crop was lost that year."

"A perilous dependence on weather," Francis said, shaking his head. "My uncle, Lionel Tarbox, tells me floods and droughts have come close to wiping him out a dozen times."

The other man said nothing to that, and in sudden comprehension, Francis flushed. "Of course, I know it is much harder for the poor," he said.

He looked around at the schoolroom with its shabby desks and meager shelf of worn-out books. There was a little blackboard on an easel and that was all.

"Yet you came back, too," he said, thinking aloud.

"Pardon?"

"I meant, it's a hard life here and yet you came back to it. You could, I suppose, have stayed in England."

"You mentioned conscience a while ago. I had to come home. Most of the children on this island stop their schooling after five years. Most adults are functionally illiterate."

"So now you are doing something about it."

Courzon looked out to where the rain had begun perceptibly to slacken. "Sometimes, lately, I have had my doubts. What sense does it make to teach Browning to children like these? 'Oh, to be in England now that April's there—' " His voice mocked the wholesome words.

Yet mockery, Francis thought, his interest growing, mockery would not be this man's typical mode or mood. His was a fundamental simplicity.

"I try to give them as much as they can absorb of their own history, the African and the West Indian. That at least has relevance to their lives."

Strange that he did not hesitate to speak this way to Francis, certainly he would not do it with—well, with Lionel, for instance, or with anyone else Francis knew.

"Are you thinking of politics, then?"

"I'm not sure. I'm not a man of action, that's my trouble. I am really not. But I have a friend, Nicholas Mebane, who has come back from England, too, and is starting a new party. He's working on programs to be ready when independence comes, and he wants me to work with him. So I'm thinking about it. Only thinking."

"I've heard mention of Nicholas Mebane. There was something in the paper, wasn't there? And it seems to me that a priest was talking about him the night I first came here."

"That must have been Father Baker."

"Perhaps. I don't usually remember names, and it was a while ago, but for some reason that one stuck in my head. The priest said he was brilliant, if I recall correctly."

"That's true, he is. He's a thinker and an orator. The two don't always go together, but when they do, it can be an unbeatable combination. Nicholas will achieve things. His achievements will spread outward from this one island like ripples in a lake."

Thrusting his hands into his pockets, Courzon walked the length of the room and back.

"Independence will give us initiative. From initiative comes character, a national character, with which to build democracy. But you have to begin with a strong leader, who can show the way. And Nicholas is strong—strong and large-minded. He will fight." He was exhilarated. "You've picked a time when great changes are about to happen, Mr. Luther."

"That's exactly what my Uncle Herbert told me." *Warned me.*

"From a different point of view, I imagine." Courzon smiled. "Do I offend you? I hope not."

"No," Francis said soberly, "if I'm to live here, I should know every point of view, shouldn't I?"

"It would be wise. That always has been part of the trouble, the ownership of the great estates by individual absentee owners—or worse, by foreign companies. They can't know, hence don't care, what is happening here."

"Well, I do care. My head is full of projects for cooperatives and—" Francis' voice trailed off, as he recalled a rush of ideas, Kate's ideas. "For one thing," he resumed, "I want to build some decent housing on my place for my permanent employees."

"I heard you did."

"You heard?"

"I told you, news travels on St. Felice. Well, if you can do that, just make a start at it, and if others will follow suit—which is to be doubted, I'm sorry to say—you'll be doing a great deal. Poor housing is certainly one of the reasons why the family structure is what it is. But we could talk all day"—Courzon threw his hands up—"I should end by discouraging you with all my talk! You'll want to clear out tomorrow and go home."

Francis shook his head. "No. Home is here now."

He was intensely curious about this man. Cambridge, nearly white, he had yet appeared to identify completely with the Negro peasant. He took a chance on a blunt request.

"Tell me something real about *yourself*, Mr. Courzon."

"Something real?"

"Yes," Francis said boldly. "What it's like for you, living here— as you are."

"Not being white, you mean?"

"I suppose I do mean that, partly. What is it you want most?"

"To begin with, I'd like to lift the restrictions on the franchise. One man, one vote. I don't own property, I'm a renter, so I can't vote. Listen, Mr. Luther, on this island as throughout the Caribbean, ninety-five to ninety-eight percent of the people are black, or some shade of it. Very few own property, so they have nothing to say about the way they are to be governed. Nothing at all."

"That's outrageous, of course it is. I'm told, though, that it's about to be changed. This year, even. What I meant was yourself, your personal life. You're married?"

"I have a wife, Désirée. We live in town."

"Désirée? Not the one who works at Da Cunha's?"

"Yes. You know her?"

"She waited on me for Christmas presents and for my wife's birthday. But I haven't seen her in a while, not that I do so much shopping."

"She's stopped working there. We have two children and they need her."

The rain had ceased entirely. Heavy drops splashed from the roof and the trees. The sun shone through a steamy haze. The two men walked to the doorway.

"I like to think the world will be better for my two children—and for all the others," Courzon said. "And I'm an optimist, I have to believe it will be. When you look back over history, making allowances for some bloody backsliding, the general trend, although you can barely discern it, the general trend, I believe, is upward."

"I hope so," Francis murmured.

A strange man, this, and a very strange encounter. And he had a sudden thought about history: it was power, history was, and that's all it was. Winning it and losing it. Power for good, but more often for ill. He could use power here, not with the greed which had brought the downfall of his poor foolish father, but with justice. Lionel and his kind would say he was as great a fool as his father had been! Yet he felt secure enough, this moment, to refute them.

He had begun his good-bye when something held him back. "A magnificent tree," he said, pointing to the sumptuous green bower beneath which he had parked his car.

"A flaming royal poinciana. Red flowers in June. You must have them on your place."

"None that large. They remind me of flamingos when they bloom."

"Speaking of flamingos, they used to be plentiful on this island. Not so long ago, either, when I was a child. You'll pass Flamingo Pond on your way home; they used to feed there on shrimp. There were fifty or sixty in a flock, a gorgeous sight. Bonaire's the only place you'll see them nowadays. Hunted to death."

"Change isn't always to the good, is it?"

"Not always. The whole world could be Eden if it weren't for the waste and destruction."

Francis folded his wet jacket over his arm. "I must say you've told me more about this place in half an afternoon than anyone has done yet except"—he didn't know for the life of him what made him say it—"except my relative, Kate Tarbox."

Courzon said simply, "She has heart."

"I forgot, you know her! Or your wife does."

"We both do. I got to know her through my father-in-law, Clarence Porter. They're involved in a good many projects, mostly through the Family Counseling. Clarence is helping raise money in the unions for a decent clinic, and Kate, of course, knows all the important families. It's hard, though. The people who could give don't want to, at least not more than tokens. But Kate's a rare woman, don't you agree?"

"I imagine so, although I don't see her that much."

Courzon shook hands. "It was nice to meet you, Mr. Luther. Good luck with all your projects."

"I'll tell you," Francis said, "I'll tell you—you ought to come visit," he blurted.

"Do you mean that? Or is it just 'drop in some time,' which I would never do?"

"I don't say things I don't mean." Marjorie would hardly be overjoyed, but no matter. He liked this man so much.

A smile spread from Courzon's quiet mouth. It was the first true smile of the afternoon, a smile without irony or melancholy.

"I shall call you. You're in the book in Covetown? Patrick Courzon?"

"I'm in the book."

He was still standing with arm upraised in a wave when Francis turned out of sight around the curve, downhill.

Book Three

LOVERS AND FRIENDS

Ten

"Have I shown you this? I must have," said Francis Luther, offering a leather-bound volume. "It's the diary of my first ancestor on St. Felice."

"I've seen it, but Nicholas hasn't." Patrick glanced at a page before handing it over. " 'I mean to buy land and live on my property like a gentleman, to marry well.' This is original history, Nicholas."

"Fascinating," Nicholas murmured.

He occupied the seat on the window ledge with particular grace. His slim feet in their English shoes were crossed at the ankles; his patrician head was sculptured against the afternoon light. And Patrick felt some simple pride in having brought him for the first time to this house, even though the suggestion had come from Kate Tarbox. He saw himself as a link between the gentleman planter who owned the house and the brilliant black politician whose rise to prominence was unmistakably beginning.

"Books," Francis was saying, "are my one extravagance." He gestured toward a pile of new ones in bright jackets. "I keep having them sent down from New York. If there's anything you want to borrow, you're welcome as always."

"This is fascinating," Nicholas repeated, replacing the diary.

"If you want to borrow that, Mr. Mebane, you're welcome to. I've had several copies made besides that one. It's a curiosity, isn't it?"

"I'd like to, very much. Incidentally, I wish you'd call me Nicholas."

"Nicholas, then. Shall we have a drink before dinner? Or, I should say, supper, since that's all it is on Sunday evening."

With a pleasure almost physical, Patrick observed the glimmering, small ritual of the drinks, the shimmer of ice and spurt of soda, the bubbles rising in the glasses. In the dozen or more evenings he had spent here in this library during the year just past, a sense of belonging had won out over a first suspicious sense of apartness. Not since that early boyish affection between himself and Nicholas had he felt so easily drawn to another man as to Francis Luther, come out of a world so different from his own and yet so like himself in mind and tastes and in that indefinable quality called heart.

None of this was true of Marjorie Luther. I am an invader in her house, he thought, and she despises my skin, although she'd be ashamed to admit it even to herself. It was in her face behind the proper greeting. One knew these things. But no matter. His own Désirée had her resentments, too.

Through the tall windows at his elbow he could see the little group on the lawn, the women in the shade with Father Baker, who had preferred to stay outdoors. It was an Impressionist scene, or a good imitation of one, with the willow drapery arranged so airily and the women in petunia colors. Laurine, Patrick's ten-year-old, was sitting on the grass at her mother's feet. Kate Tarbox held Maisie, big as she was, on her lap. Marjorie Luther held a small white dog on hers. Impressionism, except for black skin, he thought now wryly.

"What a handsome room this is!" Nicholas exclaimed.

"Funny, it was only half completed when we moved in. I had it finished myself, which cost too much, but it was worth it. I practically live in here." And Francis nodded toward the large desk, which was covered with papers.

"Francis is writing a history of the Caribbean world," Patrick told Nicholas. "A great work, starting with the Arawaks."

"Judging by the progress I'm not making, I shall never finish it."

Nicholas asked curiously, "What is your inspiration? Your family history?"

"Oh, I should imagine so. I've been learning more about them since I came here. One, who'd been taken prisoner in the Battle of Worcester, came in Cromwell's transports. Another was a poor soul from a debtor's prison. And one was a governor. A mixed bag, as you see." Francis laughed.

"So you have really come back to stay, have you?"

"Yes, I've been in New York a few times to visit my parents, and each time the sight of the city did me in. Eleuthera! It's well named. It's my freedom."

"I wish," Nicholas said, "you'd finish what you were saying a while earlier, Mr. Luther."

"Francis, please, if you're to be Nicholas."

Nicholas inclined his head. "Francis. You were telling us about some of your plans for this place of yours. Of course you must know that your model village is already being talked about."

Francis interrupted. "Please! I've got ten houses up for my permanent workers, that's all I've done. Nothing for the seasonals. Nothing even worth talking about yet."

"Don't underestimate it. That's a fine beginning, an example to others."

"I'm not sure how much of an example it will be. I'm afraid, in my short time here, I am already thought of as a troublesome disturber of things as they are." Francis tapped the table thoughtfully. "However, it's my money, what little of it there is, and I can tell you there's little enough! Luckily I don't crave enormous wealth. I'd just like to pay off my mortgage one day, that's all."

"You see," Patrick said, "you see, Nicholas, why I wanted you to meet each each other. It's a basic attitude, men of good will—" In his eagerness he floundered, feeling himself naïve, his emotion overflowing too visibly.

Nicholas leaned toward Francis. "Our good friends, Patrick and Kate Tarbox, brought me here out of the goodness of their hearts. Let me put things in a nutshell. Now that we've at last got universal suffrage, independence is only a few years away. Huge tasks await us. After political autonomy must come economic stabilization. Huge tasks! My party wants to come to power on this island. It's a democratic party, the New Day Progressives, young men with plans. But —and let me make this clear—we are not radicals. We don't want to confiscate. On the contrary, we want the support of the planter class, of those more enlightened members of it who will cooperate with us toward greater prosperity for all. And frankly, I need your help."

"My heart and conscience are with reform, but I'm not a political man," Francis objected.

"On the contrary, you are. A man who can see a need and take steps, even take one step toward alleviating it, is political. And as Patrick has just said, it's an attitude. An open-minded attitude. Oh, don't worry, I'm not asking you to make any immediate public declarations which would embarrass you! I understand your position very well," Nicholas said astutely. "All I want is to get acquainted with you and to feel that in you I have a mind and an ear to consult with. It's a gradual process, this building of a sympathetic understanding. May I, then, from time to time, have your ear?"

"That surely! I'm always glad to listen. I enjoy an evening visitor anytime. Patrick knows that. I believe I hear the supper bell."

Patrick's sense of ease evaporated in the dining room. Now, at this formal table, with Negro servants passing silver platters, he felt acute discomfort. And he wondered what the servants were thinking or would say out in the kitchen.

He looked around. An ill-assorted group, as the world saw it: the whites in their patrician home; the two black children—quiet and well behaved, or they could not have been brought here—with their tight braids; Désirée, silent in her pride and so vivid that the other two women faded by comparison. Marjorie Luther is frosted, he thought. A frosted woman, with fine skin, white as paper. Her silk was pale, her pearls were milky. He embarrassed himself with a flashing image of her in bed with Francis. She would be cool, he imagined, surely not like Désirée! Still, one never knew. And Francis had such great heart! He hadn't been ready for marriage. He was only now waking up out of ignorance. All this went through Patrick's mind while he unfolded the napkin and picked up the spoon.

Silence fell over the table. The incongruity of the gathering must have occurred to them all. And needing to break the silence, he addressed the hostess.

"Your cook, I would wager, is from Martinique."

"How did you know? Is the soup too spicy?"

"No, no, it's perfect. My mother came from there, and she's a wonderful cook. You must ask yours to make some of their recipes. Turkey with curry sauce—ah, that's something to remember!"

"Tell me some I should ask for, then." Marjorie Luther bent into the candlelight, pretending interest.

"Well, there are steamed *palourdes,* for instance. Clams with lime." He sought for something exotic to make interesting conversation. Actually, he had little interest in food. *"Acra de morue,* that's codfish fritters with green peppers. A typical dish."

"I shall certainly try that," Marjorie Luther said politely.

Silver clinked on china. Father Baker ate with an old man's greed, attentive to his plate, while Désirée fussed over the little girl and the others were apparently mesmerized by Morne Bleue, which filled the tall windows at the end of the room. This time it was Nicholas who rescued them from silence.

"Do I hear rightly that your mother has thoughts of going home to Martinique?" he asked Patrick.

"She talks about it. I don't want her to go, but she's getting older and seems to be feeling some pull toward her family land, or what's left of it."

"Do you all know about 'family land' ?" And Nicholas explained. "It's a concept that has nothing to do with the legal code. It's custom, out of Africa. You can move away from the land for years, for a lifetime, but if it belonged to one of your ancestors, you have the right to come back and live on it and to eat the fruit that grows on it."

"And to be buried there," said Kate, turning away from the twilight on the Morne.

"You know that!" Nicholas remarked in some surprise.

"I've learned a few things in my time," she retorted with a smile.

"In the West Indies," Nicholas continued, "this land is almost always what was granted to a slave when he was freed."

"I should be making notes," Francis said, "for my history."

"That you'll never write," Marjorie added.

"Your husband," Nicholas said graciously, "has many irons in the fire. The day must not be long enough for him."

"I hope not too many irons," Marjorie replied.

"My wife is always afraid I work too hard," Francis said, apologizing for whatever it was that was going wrong at his fine table in the benign and mellow evening.

Kate threw out a question. "Speaking of irons in the fire, what about the new party? You men relegated us to the lawn, even though that's what I came to hear about."

"Oh," Nicholas said, "we talked a bit. No decisions yet."

"I'm sorry to hear that," Kate said, "because that's the reason Patrick and I wanted to get you together. Of course, I am always in too much of a hurry, I know."

Marjorie drank water, picking the glass up and replacing it with a harsh thump.

Kate went on speaking softly and rapidly. "We shall never get anything good done in this place without government. You all know that. Volunteer efforts just can't do what needs doing. That's something I never could get across to my husband. Not that he'd work with you people anyway, if I could get it across. He wouldn't even come tonight and sit at table with blacks, you know that."

Marjorie picked up her glass again and set it down so decisively that the water, tipping over, made a little puddle on the polished wood. It was as though she had drawn an audible gasp, although she had not.

"Don't be shocked, Marjorie," Kate said. "These are my friends. They know the facts of life. I speak openly with them."

"That you do," Father Baker agreed. "From the first words you ever spoke." He looked around the table with fond pride. "I knew Kate before she was born. With all her faults, I love her and I usually agree with her, too, although not always."

"Not on birth control," Kate said quickly. "Family planning, I should say. It sounds better and is more accurate, besides."

"It's a curious thing," Nicholas remarked, "how population has become the number-one issue in Central America. It wasn't always so. Most people, I think, don't know that during the slavery period there were more deaths than births. The difference was made up for by importation from Africa." His finely modulated voice took command. Everyone moved to face him. "I suppose to some extent it was undernourishment and overwork, but chiefly it was disease. Now medicine has rid us of yaws and cholera, of yellow fever and typhus. So as a result, we are crowding ourselves off the island. Off the planet, for that matter."

"Then would you be willing to include the subject in your platform?" Kate spoke earnestly.

Nicholas smiled. "With the usual ten-foot pole, I would," he said candidly. "After all, you have to get elected before you can accomplish anything. Isn't that so, Mrs. Luther?"

"Oh, of course," Marjorie acknowledged.

A consummate tactician, Patrick thought, as Nicholas continued, "It's a fortunate thing, I always say, when a community has citizens like you ladies. Active, educated women. . . . Women always have so much more concern for the basics, for the quality of life. I believe your husband said you're a graduate of Pembroke, Mrs. Luther? My fiancée went to Smith. Doris Lester, from Ohio. I should be honored if you would meet her after we're married."

Marjorie took interest. "When will that be, Mr. Mebane?"

"A Christmas wedding." And he added, Patrick knew, so that there would be no misunderstanding, "Her father is a minister of the African Methodist Church."

The atmosphere, thanks to Nicholas, had grown lighter. "And have you found many changes here after your time abroad?" Marjorie asked, addressing him but not Patrick, who had also come home from abroad. It is his charm, Patrick thought, not minding.

"Not really. We've been asleep here for centuries. But"—and as if to warn, Nicholas raised his hand—"but let me tell you, change is on the way. We already have daily flights to the main cities of the Caribbean, with connecting flights to here. Eventually we'll have a jetport of our own, connecting us directly with Europe. All this will affect the way we live and the way we must be governed."

"It quite makes one's head swim, doesn't it?" Marjorie said smoothly. "Unfortunately, I am not at all political."

"That's what I said a while ago," Francis said.

"Everyone is political, or becomes so," Kate corrected.

"A profound statement," Nicholas observed pleasantly, as they left the table.

In the car, Désirée complained, "I'm exhausted! All that heavy talk! It's like carrying bundles till one's arms want to drop off. If you notice, I barely said a word."

"It was intelligent conversation," Patrick objected. "Your father would have enjoyed it."

"Oh, you and Pop! Tell the truth, weren't you feeling uncomfortable in there?"

"Maybe a little, but only because of her. Francis is an honest man, an independent. He didn't have to ask us. He wanted to. There's surely no advantage to him in having people like us in his house."

"No? You don't think he's counting on Nicholas coming into power? Maybe he's smarter than the rest of them. Looking out for the future."

Patrick said loyally, "Even so. There's more to it than that. Francis Luther likes me and I like him."

"It's a queer friendship," Désirée argued. "Your mother thinks it is. She keeps asking me. It bothers her."

"Probably," Nicholas suggested tactfully, "what's really upsetting her is that she's leaving."

"She doesn't have to," Patrick replied.

He didn't say that he had invited Agnes to live with them, now that she was too old to tend the store. No, she had told him, there was no room for two women in one house. Yet she was going back to live with a cousin. And he knew that neither time nor two babies had eased her resentment of Désirée. Indeed, he had once caught her comparing the skin of her arm with his babies' arms, which were many shades darker than hers. There lay the crux and cause of her anger! Yet in a curious way, and unjust as it was, he could understand and forgive her. Like so many, she was only a victim of universal prejudices. He felt a wave of sadness at losing her; he remembered her long-ago tale of Mount Pelée and how, only a child herself, she had fled to St. Felice.

Désirée spoke from the back seat. "Francis Luther made her have us there today. You can be sure she won't let any of her friends know she entertained us at her dinner table! Personally, Patrick, I feel humiliated in that house."

"Forget her," Patrick said impatiently. "What about Father Baker? Your father can tell you a few things about him. And what about Kate Tarbox? The few services we have, the little we have in the way of hospital care, are mostly her doing. Your father can tell you that, too."

"All right, Kate Tarbox. I'll agree," said Désirée. "But she's one in a hundred thousand." She laughed, reflecting, "Did you see Marjorie Luther's face when Kate said that about her husband not wanting to eat with us? I thought she would go through the floor, not that she doesn't agree with Kate's husband herself, Lord knows."

Nicholas chuckled. "She speaks her mind, that Kate. An interesting character. I have an idea she can be trusted, too."

"Trust Kate?" Patrick repeated. "Take my word for it, you can do that."

"The Luther woman is the much better looking of the two, though. She has height, for one thing," said Désirée, out of satisfaction with her own height. "And she knows how to wear clothes. That dress cost a fortune."

Patrick objected again. "You don't know what you're talking about.

Kate has life! She has fire! Take a good look at her the next time."

"Listen to the man! Anybody'd think you were in love with her," Désirée told him good-naturedly.

Patrick was stubborn. For some reason it was important to defend Kate Tarbox. "She's *real*. One isn't used to a human being like her. Most people wear a mask. She doesn't."

"Well, if she doesn't wear one, she'd better do it soon, or the whole world will see she's in love with Francis Luther."

"That's ridiculous! Women!" Patrick said, shaking his head at Nicholas.

"Marjorie Luther knows it, too. That's why she hates her."

"Oh, women!" Patrick repeated, in mock despair.

Nicholas said quietly, "Désirée is right, you know. I sensed it, too. That's why I made an effort to draw Mrs. Luther out. The art of politics, my friend. You have to have keen perceptions or you won't survive."

"I'm not keen at all," Patrick said, feeling some wistfulness.

"You're not fair to yourself," Nicholas admonished him kindly.

They topped the last hill before the descent into Covetown. Pink and silver gilt and rose touched the rooftops, as the great red ball had begun to lower itself into the sea, and this final splendor rekindled some memory of the day's contradictions.

"Eleuthera," Nicholas said softly. "Freedom. A beautiful name."

"Yes," Désirée said. "You could certainly feel free in a place like that, couldn't you?"

"Freedom is relative," Patrick admonished. "You can live in a palace and have a mind so narrow that you might as well be in prison."

Nicholas teased, "You haven't changed since we were at school, my friend. I told you then and I tell you now, you should have been a philosopher."

"Oh, I never know what he's thinking," Désirée said affectionately. And as the car drew up in front of their narrow little house, "What I do know is, I could sit on that lawn forever, looking out at the ocean. Do you think people like them have any idea how lucky they are?"

*　　*　　*

Long stripes of pink and silver gilt and rose lay over the sea as the horizon tilted upward to consume the sun. The four, when the others had departed, sat out on the lawn with their faces turned to the radiance.

Marjorie was the first to speak, underscoring the nouns. "I don't know about all of you, but I found that exhausting! So much effort to manufacture *conversation,* especially with that *woman.* What on *earth* was there to talk about? That Nicholas was the best of the lot, a *gentleman.* He seems more like one of us, although of course he isn't really, either."

"That doesn't sound like you," Francis chided. And somewhat disturbed before the others, he explained, "Marjorie is too kind to have meant that the way it sounded. She's not a bigot."

"No," Marjorie insisted, "no. I did mean it just as I said it. I don't like having my house used for a political meeting. To me it was a false occasion. Artificial. What can we have in common with those people, or they with us?"

Father Baker answered calmly, "We may have to have—apart from any moral considerations—we may have to have much in common before we're through. They are going to be running the government here sooner than you think. The British Empire is being chipped away. India is already gone, and the rest of us are going, make no mistake about it."

Marjorie was in a mildly argumentative mood. "I don't see why you people are so ready to give up, to humor all these agitators! These people don't have such a bad life, you know. The climate couldn't be easier. You go down into the markets and see all those piles of marvelous vegetables and fish and—"

Father Baker interrupted. "Surely you must have learned by now that there's not nearly enough food to go around and not enough money to buy what there is."

"Well, there would be," Marjorie persisted, "if they didn't have such enormous families. It's really disgusting. All these children and no husbands. But of course there was no wedlock in Africa, so I suppose—"

"There are no jobs for the men, haven't you heard?" Kate put in. "That's why so many of them leave."

The women are sharpening their knives, Francis thought.

Marjorie digressed. "They're a childish people. One of the maids almost scared me to death last week. Shrieking that spirits were making her baby sick and spirits were throwing the furniture around in her house. I thought she was going insane till Osborne told me it was just obeah. What can you do with people like that? And they want to run the government!"

"You sound like Lionel," Kate said. Her jaw was set.

They despised each other. Francis moved restlessly in his chair, wishing the guests would go home. It was only seven thirty; in an hour they could decently take their leave. He felt annoyed with Marjorie and also defensive of her.

"Is it so bad to sound like your husband?" Marjorie asked. *Your husband* was accusatory. "I happen to admire him."

"Oh, he is admirable in many ways," Kate replied.

"I admire the way he enjoys life. He works hard and spends his money without all this heavy guilt about having it, which gets so tiresome."

The conversation went in waves. After each crash came a lull, in which the force of the wave withdrew to gather itself for the next collision. And he wished again that they would go home, and his wife go to bed, and leave him alone. They were upsetting him, which was a pity, for he had truly enjoyed the afternoon and the interaction between minds so different in experience from his own.

"They were both in my classes," Father Baker was saying. "I suppose I feel involved with their future because I always took special interest in bright boys of the other race. A mixture of compassion and, I'm afraid, some plain curiosity."

"Nicholas is obviously the smart one," Marjorie said.

The old man contradicted her. "Smart, yes. Clever, yes. But Patrick is the thinker. Slower and far less ambitious, almost without ambition, but— Well, time will tell."

"There is something very fine about him," Francis said. "I always have a sense of depth, of much unspoken. There is something in his eyes"—and, looking over, caught Kate's own eyes.

"Yes," she said, turning away.

"Do you hear from Julia and Herbert?" Marjorie inquired now of Kate. She was remembering her obligation as a hostess, in spite of all.

"We had a letter two or three months ago."

"Yes, she says it's a good thing Herbert was brought up in England, otherwise they'd be just another pair of colonials. Colonials are never top-drawer, you know. It's all so funny really, these silly people sticking labels on themselves! 'I'm better than you; he's better than she.' Like those women at the club in town—especially the foreigners—acting so grand toward the help. They're almost worse than those of us who were born here."

"I haven't found them so," Marjorie said stiffly. "I've made good friends at the club. I wish we lived closer in. I wish Francis would buy a house in town, one of those lovely old ones with a walled garden in an alley."

"You know I have to be here," Francis said.

"You have Osborne. You always say he's so trustworthy."

"Yes, but not to wear my shoes."

Marjorie sighed and Francis thought again, She ought to have a child. The thought was always with him and no doubt always with her. Her nerves were going bad. During their visit to New York they had both had tests and the doctors had found no reason why she had not conceived. Everyone they knew had children, sturdy children with sun-bleached hair and rosy tans. Their joys and their tribulations were the inevitable subject of adult conversation. Sometimes he thought, although probably it was unfair of him, that Marjorie suffered more from a feeling of failure and deficiency in not having given birth than from the fact itself.

Yet he felt his wife's pain.

"It's getting damp," she said now. "Let's have our coffee in the house."

"Will you play for us, Kate?" asked Father Baker. "I remember when you were a little girl, practicing the *Liebeslieder* waltzes."

"I don't play very well anymore."

"But will you, anyway?"

She sat down at the piano. From his "own" chair near the window, Francis had an oblique view of her cheek and the curving hair which swayed like a curtain as she moved. He supposed she played with skill, but he was no judge; he only knew when music moved him, and Brahms always did. He had not worked, because it was Sunday, and had no reason to be so tired, yet he felt a need to soothe fatigue, and putting the coffee cup aside, he laid his head against the back of the chair and closed his eyes. The music rippled, telling of simple, country things, of May and streams, of gardens and first love. And the scents of frangipani and wet grass blew in with drenching sweetness.

Then, abruptly, the music changed. It paused and slid into a minor key. It was as though the shadow of some sorrow had darkened the spirit of the player. Just so, two or three times in the past, he remembered, had a visible shadow passed across her face.

. . . but he married me instead. He could still hear the cadence of the words, could see the sudden gravity and then the determined cheerful toss of the head. Funny, plucky little soul! A scrapper, he thought, afraid of nothing, and yet—

He had been thinking of her ever since. No, not thinking, exactly, just aware, as of a hovering presence at the back of thought, so that on an errand in town it would cross his mind that he might perhaps encounter her again on the street. It had never happened. Or entering a room at one of those crowded gatherings where you stand all evening holding a drink, it would cross his mind—oh, idly, very idly—that she might be there among the crowd. She never was.

All of this was meaningless, of course—aberration and whim! It came to all men at some time or other. It came and passed. And opening his eyes, he met Marjorie's rather thoughtful gaze, just as the music stopped and Kate closed the lid of the piano with a final thump.

"It's late," she said. "Come, Father."

It had grown quite dark. At the car Kate paused and looked up at the sky, where there was no moon and blue stars quivered.

"No wind up there. No sound," she said. "It seems so strange. Turning and turning, millions of stars in total silence."

He thought he saw tears in her eyes, but it might have been only their natural shine.

"We don't know anything, do we?" she said, and got into the car.

He went back up the walk to where Marjorie was waiting. Braced against the doorpost, she, too, was looking up into the sky.

"A depressing night," she said.

"Depressing?"

"Yes. Yes. Tell me, do you really think we'll ever have a child?"

With his arm around her, he could feel the rigid muscles under the soft silk.

"I don't know," he began. "Still—"

"But how stupid of me to ask! How can you know?" She began to cry. "I'm sick of myself, Francis! What excuse is there for a woman without a uterus that works? What am I to do with my life? Keep putting a good face on things with my friends? Run around like Kate Tarbox, making an idiot of myself?"

His fingers, which had half-consciously been soothing her shoulders, withdrew.

"What have you got against Kate? She's never harmed you."

"I don't trust her."

He spoke quietly. "Can't women have compassion toward each other? You know she's not happy at home."

"That doesn't give her a license to poach."

"Poach, Marjorie! That's total nonsense!"

Was it? Hesitating and denying, tentatively reaching and withdrawing, with their silences and their eyes, they had been communicating, he and the other woman. Yes, they had.

And, very troubled, very afraid, his arms went out again to his wife, but she had pressed herself against the door and shrank away.

"I've done you an injustice," he said, "keeping you here." When she did not deny it, he continued, "I suppose we ought to quit and go home."

"You know you're not going to do that, you're too committed here."

It was so. Now, would he have gone willingly with her if it were she who had committed herself to a labor and a way of life that fulfilled her need? With painful honesty he tried to answer Yes, he thought he would. True, this was a man's world, but there was in him a sense of fairness, and he thought he would. Then, was he asking too much of *her*, after all? He thought he was not.

As if she knew there was nothing more to be said on the subject, she sighed again. "I'm going in. Are you coming?"

"In a minute," he answered.

She wanted sex tonight, he understood. It was not only because of her now-frantic need to become pregnant. It was her need to receive her due, proof that she was desirable and that their marriage was successful, according to the books. He couldn't prove that this was so, but when he lay with her, his body knew it.

Something had happened, something had changed. And it was not just because they were living here; for here, as there or anywhere, one throve if all else were right. Neither was it her twinge of jealousy; he would give her, he vowed, no cause. He'd seen enough of that sort of thing with his father. Was it, then, simply because they had no children?

He became aware of an agitation in his chest, an altered heartbeat.

Far below, a sliver of sea gleam shone through the wilderness of leaves. A wind rose, moving through the high acomas. And Francis' memory, drifting without direction, plucked through some association with this sound of wind, a picture of Marjorie, standing with her arm in his, laughing, struggling as a gust blew the wedding veil across her mouth.

When had it changed, and why? He didn't know, he couldn't say, only that it had. It occurred to him that such must be the regret you know when you are old. He felt a lonely, chilling sadness. And he stood quite still, waiting, willing it to pass.

Ah, well, only a fool expects to keep forever all those first, mysterious raptures!

EDEN BURNING

Then, then, there was always this, which alone would never change: he flung his arms out to the breathing night. All blue it was: the far pale stars were blue and the trees threw blue-black shadows on the grass. A bird, not yet sunk into sleep, called one clear, genial note and, falling still, stilled also some portion of the agitation in the young man's heart.

And he, too, sighed as Marjorie had done and went in and closed the door.

Eleven

"THERE'S so much to be done," Nicholas urged, tipping back from a spacious desk on which papers were ordered with soldierly precision, "while you're holed up in a village school, wasting yourself."

Around him the office walls held shelves of law books and well-framed diplomas. Above the windows hung a long green-and-yellow banner which proclaimed with spirit, NEW DAY PROGRESSIVES FOR A BRIGHT TOMORROW.

Nicholas followed Patrick's glance. "Like it?"

"It certainly catches the eye."

"Well, have you thought any more about our last talk?"

Now Patrick had to play devil's advocate. "No honest work is ever wasted. And I've always wanted to teach, you know that."

"You also understand what I mean. We've discussed more than once your sense of futility at teaching children what they'll never use."

"Still, if you can reach just one, light a fire in just one—"

"I know, I know. Pious hopes. But someone else could do what you're doing now. What I'm asking of you is far more demanding. You want to improve conditions? Then consider the power of the press! You write well, and our party needs a paper that will express

— 194 —

its point of view. The island needs a paper, as a matter of fact. Here, listen to this." Nicholas picked up a copy of the *Clarion.* "Here's the front page: 'Miss Emmy Lou Grace was guest of honor at a party in celebration of her eighty-fifth birthday last Wednesday at the home of Mrs. Clara Pitt.' And here's what passes for an editorial: 'We must deplore the condition of the square on market day . . . fish heads attracting stray cats!' " Laughing, he flung the paper down. "Pap like this! And nothing about schooling, nothing about housing, nothing even about independence, which can't be more than two years away! Pap! Patrick, I've got money enough to start a paper and keep it going until it can support itself. When my father died last year he left much more than I knew he had. Look, I'm supporting this whole office, all this extra space I've taken for the party! I want you to take charge of a paper for me. I want to build a constituency before any of the other parties get ahead of us."

"They don't amount to anything. They've no real leadership, no programs except muttering discontent."

"Exactly. But you can't count on that forever. When independence comes—before it comes—we want to be in first place. You're an idealist, but what good are ideals if all you do is talk about them? Here's your chance to bring some of them to life."

Patrick looked out the window, away from that pair of searching, vivid eyes. Across the cove an outboard skimmed, its wake a triangle drawn upon a clean page. Cathedral bells made a brief alto clatter and ceased. Sunday calm lay over the town, touching his ears and eyes with its languor, beguiling him away from the coiled energy of Nicholas and the decisions he was urging.

I am not a man of action, he thought again.

"Have you talked about me to your father-in-law?"

"Oh, yes." Patrick smiled mischievously. "He says to tell you he doesn't resent you because you wear fine suits and speak with an Englishman's accent."

Nicholas laughed. "So he approves?"

"Well, you know he wants a government that will represent labor. He says if you can do that he will certainly support you."

"Good. And what about the paper?"

"Obviously, it's important to have access to the press. The planters will no doubt fight all the way."

"Except Francis Luther and maybe a couple of other mavericks."

Patrick said slowly, "Clarence isn't even sure he trusts Francis. Needless to say, I don't agree!"

"Not trust him!" Nicholas exclaimed.

"Well, Clarence is getting older and has seen too much. He admits he's probably too cynical."

"He certainly is. Listen, it's our job to point out conditions that are insupportable, that can't go on. We need to persuade. It's stupid to assume that because a man is a planter and has white skin he's unteachable, or a natural enemy. And now there's something I haven't told you. I just found it out yesterday. Kate Tarbox wants to join you."

"How so?"

"She's left her husband. Finally. Should have done it long ago, or so the gossip goes." Nicholas shrugged. "Anyway, she's moved back into a house she had from her father. It's an unpretentious place, down that alley at the foot of Library Hill. And she wants to earn some money. She'd like to work on the paper, maybe even write something, under a pseudonym, if necessary."

Patrick whistled softly. Could this move of hers have anything to do with Francis? At once he decided not.

"Well, what do you think? It would be pleasant, I should imagine, to work with her." Nicholas looked at his watch.

Patrick stood at once. "Let me mull it over some more."

He went downstairs and got into his car, feeling the weight of Nicholas's pressure. The offer was complimentary, to be sure. Also, it had its temptations—chiefly, more money. Désirée would be pleased with that! A small knot gathered on his forehead. Deliberately, he smoothed it. No use fretting! She had a strong taste for luxury, and this taste had been encouraged since Doris had married Nicholas and come here to live. Doris, by Désirée's standards, perhaps by anyone's, was a sophisticate, a connoisseur of good things to wear and eat and be surrounded by. Doris and Nicholas were living in the house that had been his father's, but there was talk now, so Désirée reported wistfully, of their building a waterfront house on a hill about two miles from town. Very modern, it was to be, with much glass and open space. In the style of Le Corbusier, she had explained. She had very likely never heard of Le Corbusier until now, but she was an apt student.

His mind slid back to the paper and Kate Tarbox, who had walked away from a splendor which would have dazzled Désirée. . . . And his mind slid back to Agnes. She had sold the store and was ready to leave. He'd worried: What sort of place was it where she was going? What sort of house?

"Wattle and daub," she'd told him. "One of my cousins' husbands built it."

"But you've had running water here, you aren't used to that," he'd objected.

Her earrings had swung. "Why not? I was born under wattle and daub. I'm not too high and mighty to live under it again."

Funny how some people wanted things and wanted so badly, while others didn't care!

As for himself, he was comfortable, cleanly housed, and well fed. He was, for the most part, doing what he liked. And with a twinge he thought of "his" children, certain faces appearing to mind according to the bench they occupied. There was Rafael, restless and cunning as a monkey; just lately Patrick had begun to see some settling of his mood. Then Tabitha, a stammerer who, he was certain, had been beaten since infancy. And Charlotte, with a head for numbers more competent than Patrick's own by far. No, he was not about to abandon them! He could not! They challenged him and held his sympathies in their bare hands; they angered him, they tried his patience, and they loved him. Well, some of them did, anyway!

What Nicholas wanted was, moreover, a step into the dark. If it didn't work out, he would have forfeited his place in the school system. And if it did work out, he had no illusions about what it would lead to. Involvement in a tough political struggle, that's what. He had no taste for it, none at all.

And yet perhaps it was a grown man's duty to involve himself?

He thought, I really need to talk to someone. Almost at once, his car turned off the shore road, back up through the foothills, curving leftward toward Eleuthera. He wouldn't mind, Francis wouldn't; he might even be pleased to know that someone felt the need of his counsel.

In a state of heightened emotion, he was so intent upon himself that, as he was later to remark, it was a miracle he had observed anything beyond that self and the few feet of road ahead of the car. Indeed, he had actually driven some way past what his eyes had seen before the sight registered in his brain, so that he was not really sure he had seen it; something caused him to stop the car, to back it up over the narrow, twisting road, to find out whether he had imagined what he had seen.

No. It was quite real. Some feet back from the road, a child, a boy of nine or ten years, was standing, slumped and standing, tied by wrists and ankles to a tree. Patrick rubbed his eyes and shook his head. He got out of the car.

"What is it? What happened?" he cried. The boy must long ago have stopped crying. His eyes were dry. His lips were bleeding; he had been trying to gnaw through the coarse, frayed ropes that bound him.

Patrick knelt and, with his pocketknife, cut the ropes. He took the child in his arms. The boy had wet his pants; his tight black curls were sweaty; Patrick held him close.

"Who are you? Where do you live? Who did this?"

The boy struggled, not wanting to be held, perhaps in terror of being held, and Patrick released him.

"Tell me, tell me," he whispered. "What's your name?"

"Will. And I'm thirsty. I'm hungry." Still he did not cry.

"Get in the car there, Will. We'll find a place down the road and get you something to eat right away."

The boy climbed in beside Patrick. He sat quite erect and still, with two fists clenched on his knees. It would have seemed more natural if he had been hysterical, Patrick thought, but then, he was no psychologist.

"Who did this to you, Will?" he asked, very quietly.

"Bert did."

"Who's Bert?"

"Where I live. Bert."

"With your mother and"—he hesitated—"father?"

"I got no mother and father."

"Grandmother, then?" For that, of course, was a normal family pattern.

"No. She died."

"Brothers? Sisters? Who?"

"I had an uncle, but he went away. Took all my stuff with him, too."

"He did? What stuff?"

"I had pots. And I had two donkeys my grandma gave me. He stole them. Sold them and went away."

"I see," said Patrick. This tale of the abandoned child was not unfamiliar, only a more horrendous version of it than was usual.

"I want to eat, mister."

"You can call me Mr. Courzon. No," he said, looking down sideways at the dirty little fists so strangely knotted, as if to challenge the unfeeling world, "no, I'll tell you what: call me Uncle Patrick. I'll be your uncle, your good uncle, for today. Here's a store. I'll see what I can find to eat."

The store, actually the front room of a sagging house, had a few shelves of canned goods, some bags of rice and flour and sundries. He bought a chocolate bar, bananas, and a can of soda.

"Not the best lunch in the world," he said, with a cheerfulness he did not feel, "but it will hold you till we can get something better."

Will stuffed the food down. When he had finished, Patrick began again.

"Now tell me where you live, Will. I'm going to take you back. I'm going to ask a few questions, too, when we get there," he said grimly.

"Delicia. That's the place."

"Delicia! I ought to have asked before, oughtn't I?"

They had been traveling in the wrong direction. He wouldn't get to Eleuthera today, but first things first. He turned the car about and off onto a rutted track, not far from where he had found Will on the main road. I might have figured that out, he thought, irritated with himself.

"We'll have to put some salve on your arms and legs," he said. "Does it hurt very badly?"

"Some," Will said.

He was either too frightened to talk or too tired. My God, Patrick thought, swallowing outrage and pity, quite literally lumped together in his throat.

Delicia, he recalled now, having been there once when he'd got lost, was a remote and meager cluster of shacks in a humid wilderness of bananas. He could have written its history, he thought, stopping now at the place Will pointed out. There would be a core of strong and faithful women who remained to grow old on the estate, caring for the scattered children of the young who went off-island to work and seldom came back to claim them, or perhaps claimed two or three and left the rest or gave them away. There would be the men, the itinerants who stayed just long enough to father a brood and leave it; there would be those who, staying, had only cruel discipline or, at best, neglect for the children whom they or other men had fathered. A beggarly place, this, far removed from a village like Sweet Apple, for poverty, like wealth, had layers and levels: poor, poorer, poorest. Delicia was poorest.

Children, in shirts that left them bare from the belly button down, shared a dusty common yard with dogs and tethered goats. Sitting on the ground around a stone firepit, five or six women were eating breadfruit and salt pork out of a pot. Their heads turned to Patrick as he strode toward them, his footsteps angry on the ground.

"Whose boy is this?" he demanded.

Will had got out to lean, as if for protection, against the fender.

A woman answered, evading the question. "His mother dead. Estelle. She died birthing him."

"Well, who takes care of him now?"

"He had an uncle. Gone off-island. New York, I think."

"No, London," another corrected, "and never coming back."

"I don't care about that. Who takes care of him now, I asked?"

"We all do. I feed him sometimes with my kids," one said.

"Who tied him to a tree?"

No one answered.

Will spoke up himself. "You know. Bert did."

Patrick raised his voice. "Who's Bert? Where is he?"

"He not here."

"I see he isn't. Where is he?"

"Gone for the day."

A woman cried out defensively, some vague thought of lurking, imminent punishment having flitted through her head, "That boy there, he dig up yams! He dug up three yams. That why he got beat and tied!"

Will's roar startled the group. "I was hungry! Damn you, I was hungry!"

Patrick would have liked to cry outrage himself. Instead he put a hand on the boy's shoulder.

Then a young, pregnant woman went up to Patrick. "You want to take this boy? If he do misbehave again, Bert going to beat him, tie him up again. Bert or somebody."

She was telling him, asking him, to take the child away! Given her own dire wants, one could not have blamed her if she had simply turned her back indifferently; but no, concern and pity were alive in her, so that she cared enough to plead for this miserable, unwanted boy. As a naked bulb flares white in a dark room, comprehension flashed in Patrick.

Oh, if he had stopped to think further, to consider his own household, or measure the responsibility and problems that might ensue, then surely it would have made more sense to refuse, to drive away with a weary heart and in time to forget little Will Whatever-His-Name! But he did not stop to measure or weigh.

"Has he got any clothes? Anything to take?"

The woman nodded. "I'll show you."

They went into a house. In the front room, on the bare earth floor, chickens roosted and coconut oil—from stolen coconuts, I'll wager,

Patrick thought—was boiling on a tin stove. In the other room were a bed and a pile of covers lying on the floor.

"This is his cover," the woman said. "Sometimes he sleeps in this house, sometimes anywhere, whoever has room that night. He can take these pants. And two shirts. One belongs to my boys, but he can have it."

"Just give me a pair of pants. He's wet the ones he's wearing."

They went outside. Suddenly it occurred to Patrick that he might be taking too much for granted.

"Tell me, Will, do you want to go with me?"

"Where you want to bring me?"

"Home to my house."

Will raised black unreadable eyes. They bored into Patrick's. "Do you beat your boys?"

"I have no boys. I have two little girls, and no, I don't beat them. I don't believe in beating children, or tying them up."

"Then I'll go with you," Will said.

So casually was the transfer made that, before the car had turned about, the women had gone back to their meal. The car bumped through the sultry shade of the banana forest and came out into the broad afternoon on the main road. It was like leaving some eerie landscape of surrealism—the clump of huts in that vast, dank jungle, the women squatting by the iron pot—to emerge again into such normal light. And Patrick shook himself, as if to make sure he was awake.

Will startled him. "Maybe Bert was hungry, too."

"What do you mean?"

"He wanted the yams himself. That's why he got mad and tied me up."

"You mean to say you're not angry at him?"

"I hate him. I'd like to kill him."

Patrick nodded. That was better, a decent rage. Still, what strange insight for a child to possess! *Maybe Bert was hungry, too.* How fathom the minds of men, or of a child?

"Put your head back," he said gently. "Or curl up on the seat and sleep a while. I'll wake you when we get there."

Oh, I've done a damn fool thing! he thought. Désirée will probably be frantic. And why not? Then, arguing with himself, came justification: I've wanted a boy, and Désirée won't have any more children. Her figure, I suppose. The girls are delightful, of course they are, but a man wants a son. Father and son. Do I want that so much because I never had a father? Anyway, a boy . . . And he glanced over at the sleeping child, a sturdy boy, tall for his age, Patrick guessed, and dark as Désirée. He had straight features, a nice-looking boy. Then the torn and welted skin on the thin, young arms removed the last of his doubts. He was prepared to do whatever battle might be necessary when he reached home.

Some hours later he was on his front porch rocking in the dusk. Clarence had given Will a bath, and he had been put to bed in the spare room. If it had not been for Clarence, who had come over from his house when the news was brought, why then, it would have been a much harder battle, Patrick thought, feeling grateful to the old man.

The screen door swung open and Désirée came out on the porch.

"Are you furious with me?" he asked.

"I was, but I've got over it. Anyhow, it wouldn't do any good. You'll do what you want to do."

"Am I such a tyrant, then?"

"Not really. But I hope you know what you're doing this time, I surely do."

"I know."

She said quietly, "I'm the one who'll have all the work."

"What work? He's no infant. It's another plate on the table and a bit of washing, that's all." He put his hand out, drawing her to himself. "I've wanted a boy. If I were pious, which I'm not, I could say the Lord sent him. As a matter of fact, I do seem to be feeling a touch of religion now and then. Old age coming on, I guess."

"You're shocking!"

"Why? Because I said that about being religious—or not being?"

"Yes, and that about old age, when you're only thirty-four. And there's nothing old about you. Especially in bed," she added.

So he knew he was forgiven. "Nor you. You'll be young when you're sixty." He kissed her hand. "I want to thank you for being so good about this."

"What did you think I'd do?"

"I was afraid you'd raise hell and I couldn't have blamed you. Bringing a strange child into the house without a word beforehand! Why, most men wouldn't bring a puppy home without talking about it first. Still, if you could have seen him there, tied up—by God, you'd have done the same, you know you would!"

"He won't talk to me."

"Nor to me, very much. But what do you expect? He must be torn to pieces inside."

"He took a liking to Pop. Told him this house is beautiful. Like a king's palace, he told him."

"Now, what can he have heard about a king's palace, poor little thing?"

"But Patrick, what are we going to do with him?"

"Do with him? Why raise him, love him. What else?"

He went upstairs to the little room at the end of the hall, passing his daughters' room without looking in, for they would be sleeping quietly under their pink blankets. It was the unwanted boy who drew him. Discarded, he thought, and but for a good mother, I, too, was discarded. Freshly washed and full of a good supper, Will had fallen asleep. His hands moved, twitching, as if he were dreaming. And Patrick, standing over him, could only hope that whatever dream he might be having was filled with peace and trust.

Suddenly he remembered the morning's meeting. Yes, he thought now, yes, Nicholas was right! If you wanted change, if a chance, however slight, were given you to change a world that could permit a life like this child's, then what right had you, what decent excuse, for refusal? Nicholas was right, and he would join him to do however little or much he could. He would call him now and tell him.

But at the telephone he thought first of someone else and called another number.

"I almost paid you a visit today," he said to Francis.

"Almost? What prevented you?"

"I've got a boy," he said. "We've got a boy in our family." And he went on jubilantly to tell about Will.

"I marvel at you!" Francis exclaimed, sounding glad.

"Yes, and there's something more. I'm quitting my job to go to work for Nicholas. He's going to start a newspaper and I'm to run it."

"Wonderful! We surely need a good paper around here."

Patrick hesitated. "Kate Tarbox is going to work on it with me."

"Is she?"

"Maybe you didn't know? She's moved back into town."

"When did that happen?"

"This week. Just now. She seems to have left her husband."

"Well," Francis said. "Well. It's been a day of news." His voice moved into a falling cadence. And Patrick understood that he wanted to get off the phone.

"I'll see you soon," he said at once. "Good night, then, Francis."

"Yes, yes, soon. And good luck, Patrick, in everything you do."

Twelve

"I_{T's} almost nine o'clock," Francis
said cheerfully. "Aren't you going to get up?"

He raised the shades. Lemon-colored light splattered the pillow
into which Marjorie's face was buried. Receiving no answer, he repeated the question, careful to keep the cheer in his voice.

"Aren't you going to get up? I've made my rounds, had breakfast,
and I'm ready to go."

"Then, go," she said, without moving.

The night before, when he had come home late from a meeting
of the Agricultural Association, Marjorie had already gone to bed and
they had exchanged only a few words, but those had been sufficient
for him to recognize one of her moods. Confident, though, that it
would pass as usual, that by morning the cloud would have lifted, he
had turned out the lamp without more ado and fallen asleep.

Apparently, now, the cloud had not lifted. Inaudibly, he sighed and
then, determined to proceed normally, went on, "I've a copy of the
Trumpet. Want to read it over breakfast in bed?"

"The *Trumpet* is a rag."

"Oh, but the editorials are strikingly good! There's one here—it
sounds like Kate's style, although it might be Patrick's—I'm not sure,
anyway, it's about taxing vacant land, and I thoroughly agree. Why

should anybody have the privilege of keeping land out of cultivation when there's a shortage of food and then be free of taxes on it to boot? It makes no sense, and I've said so myself many times."

Marjorie sat up abruptly. "Yes, you certainly have, haven't you?"

"What do you mean by that?"

"Oh, nothing, nothing at all. Except that you're being talked about as a troublemaker all over creation. Women were even talking about you at the club the other day after tennis. When they saw me they stopped."

"I can't help what a bunch of silly women who have nothing better to do decide to say about me."

"It's not just some 'silly women,' as you put it. You know very well they're quoting their husbands."

"You'd think I was a fire-eating bomb-thrower. All I care about is elementary decency, a tax structure that'll help clear up some of the mess you see around you." He tapped the paper. "These people are one hundred percent right."

"These people!" she mocked. "Kate Tarbox and your friend Courzon! A great pair! I shouldn't wonder if the two of them weren't—"

"Weren't what?" Francis asked, coldly now.

"Weren't sleeping together, for all I know."

"That's disgusting!"

"Why? Because it would be interracial? I shouldn't think you'd object to that, you're so broad-minded!"

"One can be 'broad-minded' without having sex with people. I meant that Patrick has a beautiful wife; he's an honorable man, and you've no right—"

"Yes, and Kate Tarbox is living alone in some miserable little house in town, having left her husband who always treated her well and would take her back in a minute. And you tell me there's nothing fishy there?"

"You can twist things around so I don't know which end is up! First you start in with editorials, and now we're on to Kate! Why don't you ask her, if you're so interested in her private life?"

"Why don't you?"

"I haven't seen her since the day she was here with Patrick and his family a year ago. Moreover, I don't care."

Marjorie lay back. "That makes two of us. Why should I give a damn? Why should I?" She put her hand over her eyes, shielding them from the light, murmuring to herself. It sounded like "in the last analysis one is always alone," but he wasn't sure.

"What did you say?"

"What difference does it make what I said?"

"What the hell is the matter with you, Marjorie? Would you mind telling me what you're angry about now?"

"Not a thing. Not a thing. Should I be angry about anything?"

"I hate that answer you give me! With that hint that I ought to be feeling guilty! No, I don't think you should be. So why are you?"

She took time to reply. Their eyes fastened upon each other's in a long, hard stare.

"Let's just say I'm tired, shall we?" she said at last.

"From what? With a house full of maids?" Normally one who avoided argument to a point where he sometimes accused himself of cowardice, Francis could also be prodded into rage. "I'm sick of this verbal fencing! If you've got a grievance, come out with it, or else shut up. I'm not going to waste a day trying to probe into your head, Marjorie." He looked at his watch. "Come on, we should get to town before the crowds block the streets if we want to see the parade."

"I don't want to see it."

"You had a good time at Mardi Gras last year!"

"That was last year. Besides, you don't care whether I go or not, so don't pretend you do."

He could have slapped her—an aberrant thought, of course. Exasperation tightened in his solar plexus, a maddening knot. There had been too much of this kind of thing lately!

"Then I'll go alone. I want to see it."

"Go. Enjoy yourself."

He went downstairs and out to the car. The tires squealed as he wrenched the wheel, speeding around the curve, easing his tensions, taking a small revenge on injustice. Juvenile, he thought then; slow down. Be reasonable. It's not all that bad, having a blowup every month or so. Maybe it was her monthly cycle, after all? Maybe I want too much, some sort of impossible perfection. How do I know what it's like in other marriages, other houses? Except that in other houses there are children. . . .

Yet, during his own childhood in a house filled with children, there had been long strained silences as well as jovial warmth. So perhaps this was just the way things went between two people living a lifetime together, with or without children. . . .

The drive eased him. With the top down the wind whirred about his head. Once he had climbed the shoulder of Morne Bleue and begun the long descent toward Covetown, his anger sloughed away. Maturity is acceptance, he told himself. By evening things would have fallen into place again, he told himself, assuring himself. A faint sadness settled now in his chest where the anger had been.

Funny, he thought then, funny about Lionel and Kate. A queer couple, mismatched from the start. Did people see just such a mismatch between himself and Marjorie? He puzzled over that for a moment and thought not. Surely they were not like Lionel and Kate! Lionel said only, "It didn't work out." How much that hurt, or whether it hurt at all, one couldn't tell, for being a gentleman, Francis thought ironically, he would surely never show it. A gentleman didn't reveal his emotions. Oh, well! Oh, hell!

Covetown blazed with color and brass. There were bands in the squares and other bands marching with the long parade that wound and twisted through the streets. Indians in feathers, skeletons, Chinese dragons, crowned kings and queens rode on floats or walked and danced and pranced. Everyone was drunk with music and some with stronger stuff. Wearing one's mask, it did not matter how one screeched or capered, or what stranger one seized and kissed. It was all pure, reckless joy. Perched on a railing, Francis sat for a long time, watching the color and dazzle. He felt like a child before a Christmas tree and a pile of presents, and was suddenly aware that he had been needing this reckless joy.

After a while he got up and bought a rum drink, content to drink it alone, just sitting in the shade with his thoughts. He wondered whether he could be classified as a loner. He didn't think so, for there were always people whose company gave him warmth and light. They were selected people, though, not the "social" crowd among whom one was expected to take one's pleasure. He did not want to feel superior to them or anyone; nevertheless, they bored him with the monotony of their interests and opinions; they repelled him with their inbred selfishness. Or most of them did, at any rate. There were a few whose minds were open enough so you could say what you thought without raising eyebrows, but only a few. Lionel was patient with him out of a firm sense of family loyalty and also because he was a good sort in his way. Francis always thought of him like that: Good-Sort Lionel. Yet even he found Francis odd and off-beat. Concern for the whole community was a thing you just did not talk about; as long as the dogs were quiet, you let them lie. The idea was to live your own life as peacefully as possible.

And looking about today at all this gaiety under the sun, one might well shrug and think, Let it be! After all, why should I upset the peace? Except that the peace won't last, he thought, finishing the drink.

And now a sense of loneliness, as powerful as his earlier joy, swept over him. He had nowhere to go. He didn't want to go home. He would have liked to see Patrick. Yes, they'd sit and talk about things they'd read, and speculate and argue and get nowhere except for the pleasure of argument. . . . There wasn't really anyone else he could think of, when you came down to it, with whom he could so comfortably do just that. He walked on up the hill toward Government House and the library, fine old buildings among fine old trees. At the foot of Library Hill he turned off into a narrow alley formed by a double row of houses. Probably built for civil servants, out from England in the seventeen hundreds, he thought, recognizing the Georgian doorways and the narrow windows with their sixteen lights. He hadn't been down this alley in a long time.

Kate lived in one of these, he recalled now. Patrick had described a house in an alley, at the very end, the only one with a view of the water. Well, no business of mine, he told himself.

At the end, where the hill, abruptly rising, made a natural wall of green, a little house stood sidewise to the street so that one could see the back door and the yard. He stopped.

She was feeding birds, dumping a pan of crumbs on the flagstones. The birds, who had no doubt been waiting for her in their hidden places, came swooping down, not minding her presence. She had been wearing a hat, the same straw farm hat—or another one just like it —that Francis remembered. Now she took it off. Her bright hair shone red-gold in the light.

Then she saw him. "You've been spying on me!"

"Only for a minute. May I come in?"

"Use the front door. There are stickers on those vines, you can't climb over the fence."

On the front step he barely missed a bowl of water.

"For stray cats," she said, opening the door. "The neighborhood's full of them. It's a pity."

He stepped into a cramped little hall. Confusion made him awkward.

"You run an S.P.C.A. of your own," he said, needing to say something.

"I'm a thwarted mother. I like to nourish."

This childless woman could say that without bitterness! As though, quite simply, she had accepted the fact and was determined to live with it. "Besides, I'm terribly frugal," she said. "I can't bear waste. I suppose it's from not having had anything when I was young."

"I'm frugal, too, but with me it's because when I was young I had too much, which we couldn't afford. Only I didn't find that out until much later."

"You're in time for lunch if you want any."

"I've only had tea this morning and a rum cola just now, so I think I do."

"Come into the kitchen, then."

"It smells good," he said, following her.

"*Tourtière de la famille,* or not to be fancy, meat pie. You put in everything you've got, all the leftovers. There's ham and chicken, some veal scraps and vegetables. Shall we have it outside?"

A table with two chairs stood near the back door under an oleander bush, where a large homely mongrel and a haughty white poodle dozed together.

"A funny combination, aren't they? The big one I picked up along the road. He was on his last legs. Lionel gave me the poodle when he was a puppy and of course I love him, although I really don't care about poodles, they're too fussy. But I couldn't have left him behind, it would have broken his heart. Wait, I'll just bring out the cheese and fruit and then I'll sit down."

Well! Rather different from Georgina's Fancy, Francis thought, remembering Lionel's great dining hall. Rather different from my own place, too, he thought almost ruefully. But then, this was a doll house. Yes, a doll house.

"I've been following your editorials," he began, "and I think you're doing a wonderful job. Everybody's buying the *Trumpet*. Most of the people I know are annoyed with it and some are pretty angry over it, but at least they're reading it!"

"The credit goes to Patrick Courzon. And I'm not being modest, it really does. I'd like," Kate said earnestly, "to see this place, the whole of Central America, for that matter, governed by people like him and Nicholas. They could set things straight—or at least they'd try—and ward off a lot of trouble."

"I wish I could see Patrick more often than I do. I'm always glad when he comes over for an evening."

"He's awfully busy now. Ever since they got the boy, Patrick's felt obliged to do things with him. Désirée's not too good with him. She's a sweet person, maybe not smart enough for Patrick, not like Nicholas's wife! She's a little childish, and in any case, a better mother for girls. Besides, the boy's difficult."

"He didn't have much of a start, Patrick tells me."

"That's why he wants to father him. He's a strange, serious child. It's hard to make him laugh."

"You don't laugh very much, either," Francis said, surprising himself. He hadn't intended to say it.

"It's true, I haven't in years. But I do now. In the office. Ask

Patrick. It's really quite gay there, and I love it. We've great young reporters, one bright black girl, two young cousins of mine, and then there's Robby Welch, the bank manager's son, home from England on vacation. His family had a fit at first about his working in an office with blacks, but they've come around. It's a good staff and I love it," she repeated. "It's really the best thing I've ever done for myself."

"I'm glad for you, Kate."

He wanted to ask about Lionel and her, but of course would not. One waited until one was told about private matters.

Grown of a sudden self-conscious, he avoided her eyes. His gaze fell upon her hands, from which the emerald ring was missing. His gaze fell upon a lizard, a quick green creature that, having slid up an unoccupied armchair, stood now a few feet away, staring with its jeweled eyes, while the pouch of its whitish neck throbbed in the heat.

"Gecko," Kate mused. "The name suits, doesn't it? Does one grow to suit one's name, or is it the other way around?"

"Well, let's think about that. Kate, for instance." And he forced himself to look at her. "Yes, Kate is the only possible name for you. Kate means freckles and bright hair. Someone small and lively and curious and earnest."

"Who talks too much and has too many opinions. While Francis —let's see—Francis has to be tall and rather quiet. His conscience commands him. He is also very, very kind."

"You're thinking of the saint, not me," he said with a lightness he didn't feel. "Here, let me help carry these inside."

Standing next to her, stacking dishes in the sink, once again words came from him that he had not intended to speak, perhaps not even thought. But they came, demanding and rushing.

"Do you realize that ever since that day we had lunch in town, the day you made me decide to stay at Eleuthera—yes, it was you who made up my mind—ever since that day we haven't spoken two words directly to each other? The few times we've been together, we've avoided each other. What are we hiding?"

"What?" she cried. "What are you saying?"

They stared at one another. She had the look of someone who is about to fall.

"You said I'm hiding something?" she whispered.

"I said you—" He faltered, murmuring something that blurred on his lips and in his ears; and then she did fall—fell toward him—and he caught her; he was drowned in an exploding surge of longing and immediate fulfillment, so that the longing and the fulfillment became one.

How long they stood in the kitchen, pressed and entwined, neither could have said, but when they drew apart the moment of astonishment had already passed and the blending, the merging, had been established. So it was, and neither spoke. She took his hand, guiding him lightly through the hall and up the narrow stairs. He felt himself floating, as if some great tide were bearing him forward.

After the sun glare her room was cool, a purity of gray and white. She pulled the shades, and in the shadow their bodies blanched. He was aware of a beautiful old bed, too large for the little room. He saw, as they fell back upon the quilt, red zinnias in a bowl on the dresser and, in the mirror above the dresser, the curving of her hips and thighs and the reach of his own rounding arms; then, closing his eyes, saw nothing.

They lit two cigarettes and lay against the pillows. Two smoke spirals drifted in a newly risen breeze. Now words came, thousands of words, questions and thoughts so long held back and denied, now to be admitted and released.

When had he first distinguished her at all from other women? And was it true that she'd felt something from the very beginning, on that first day at Eleuthera? And had he really not known the truth until now, this afternoon?

"What made you finally leave Lionel?" he wanted to know.

"You had better ask why I married him in the first place."

"Why did you?"

She put her head on his shoulder. "It's not a pretty story. It hurts. I told you once, I think, that we were very poor in my family. An old name, and so much damned dignity! Oh, you must have seen some of these fine, land-poor families, with the paint peeling off the walls and the refrigerator kept in the drawing room because the kitchen roof leaks. No money to spend, just sitting on the veranda drinking the evenings away. We have them still, but there were more of them even a few years ago, before the corporations started buying them out." Kate sighed. "When your last pair of stockings has a run you wear them anyway, and you pretend, oh so gaily, that it just happened this minute and you simply can't be bothered to run upstairs and change them. I was so sick of it! Lionel was slender then and good-looking. Anyhow, it happened so fast I had no time to think. He took me to Da Cunha's and bought me a ring worth more than my father's house, this house we're in now, that I love so much and despised then. Well, I was very young, if that's any excuse."

The breeze had turned into a wind and the sun had gone around the corner of the house. Kate shivered. Francis drew her nearer, pulling the quilt around them, making a warmth into which she crept, closer and closer.

"His parents were wonderful, even my mother-in-law, your grandmother, was. She can be a terror, but she welcomed me. I didn't know why until much later, when I learned about the girl Lionel was in love with. Remember? Of course he wouldn't have married her, she has colored blood, but they were afraid he might. She's very beautiful. She lives in Barbados now, in Bridgetown, and he goes there to be with her.

"He did wrong to marry me, but I don't blame him. I wronged him, too. Neither of us loved the other."

"So it's finished? For good?" Knowing that it was, he yet wanted to be told that it was.

"Oh, yes. And my doing, not Lionel's. He would have gone on as we were. He was quite comfortable, but I've grown up. I know who I am. I don't need his money anymore and I don't want his kind of life." She laughed. "The only thing I miss—well, I do miss the horses! Can't very well keep them here. I support myself, though. Lionel wants to give me things. He's very kind; kindness seems to run in your family, doesn't it? But Nicholas pays me well enough and I have this house and I don't need anything. By this time next year we shall be divorced."

"You're brave. You're lovely. You're very lovely, Kate."

"Is it all right if I ask about Marjorie? Or would you rather not?"

"I'd rather not," he said softly. "Not now."

And he thought again, as he had too often lately, of how everything had changed. Yet Marjorie had not really changed. Comely, reliable, intelligent and graceful, she was, in essence, what she had always been. And he, wasn't he also what he had always been? Only the allure between them was gone, the passion and allure. So it was the marriage itself which time had altered, time working away, as the sea builds dunes and shapes the cliffs.

"Oh, God," he said.

"Francis, dear, dear, what is it?"

"I love you. I love you, and I don't know what to do about it."

She put her hand over his mouth. "Listen to me. Things solve themselves. Sometimes, after the first few months with Lionel, I'd lie awake looking up at the gray ceiling and I'd think, I've wrecked my life. I had no one, no place to go. But see how it's all unfolded! We'll grow old together, Francis. I don't know how, but I know we will."

Against his chest he felt the thudding of her heart. She had closed her eyes; the dark lashes on her cheeks were gilt-tipped. Lovely, lovely! This little woman, so pert and brisk, and still so soft, so soft! Innocent in her conviction that the world could be, and must become, a better place where no man turned a cold cheek to another and no one hungered and no one kicked a dog! Innocent.

And I, too, feel her indignations; I think of myself as one who wants to give; yes, there is all that in me. But also there is the very private man who cherishes his own domain. A cut above the men at the bar in the club, Francis, with your poetry and history? Yes, yes, you know you feel you're superior to them, and yet you're terribly ashamed of yourself for that glimmer of superiority. You chose a wife, you were drawn to her, because she, too, has that very private pride. . . .

Light fingertips smoothed his forehead. "You're frowning," Kate whispered.

"I'm thinking."

"Thinking of what?"

"Oh, scoops and pieces of things. You playing Brahms once on a quiet evening at Eleuthera. Of us in this bed. I'd like to wake up every morning in this bed."

But he was actually thinking of other things, of himself, at home saying, "Listen, Marjorie, it's no good, no good at all anymore." She would protest; he could hear her weeping that it was still good, it was, it was! And truly, if there were no Kate, he would know no better and it would probably still be good enough—as good as most people ever have, at any rate.

His thoughts fluttered away. Softly they lay, half sleeping, as day cooled into evening and the room turned dusky blue. Kate roused.

"I have to get up. Patrick said he'd bring some papers over at seven."

"Patrick. The salt of the earth, as my father would say."

"Yes, he's very, very special."

A book of poems lay on the bedside table. Francis flipped the pages. "Emily Dickinson. A favorite of yours?"

"Yes, lately. I've gone back to reading her. A woman who lived alone. I thought I might learn how."

Something hurt in his throat. "You can't live alone. Don't you always say waste is sin?"

She smiled, not answering. He took a long look around the room, wanting to fix it in his mind: the wallpaper, arabesques within squares; the mat by the window where one of the dogs must sleep; her slippers, blue, with feather puffs on the toes.

Outside at ground level it was three-quarters dark, while at the top of the hill the great fireball still blazed in the sky.

"Look," Kate said. "The sun god! The Incas' priests used to throw kisses to him at dawn."

They stood on the step with their arms around each other.

"How can I leave you?" he asked.

"You aren't leaving me. You never will."

There was such an ache in him! They did not hear the creak of the gate, nor Patrick's footsteps on the path.

"I'm sorry to be early," Patrick said, not looking at them. He thrust out a sheaf of papers. "I'm in a hurry, I'll just leave these."

Francis said quickly, "I was just going."

The two men walked away down the alley, neither one speaking, until Francis said, "You saw. Well, now you know."

"I don't know anything you don't want me to. I'm an expert forgetter."

"Thank you for that."

They walked on. The parade was over, the streets had emptied. And the loneliness that had engulfed him in the morning came back to Francis now. He needed to talk and to hear another voice answer.

"You'll say it isn't any business of yours, but I want to tell you. Today was the first. It happened today, brand new."

"Not brand new," Patrick spoke gently. "It's been there for a long time, I suspect."

"You're right, of course, although I didn't know it, or want to admit it— The thing is, what happens now?"

"She's a special person, a beautiful person," Patrick said, meaning, Francis understood, "Be kind to her, be careful of her." And Patrick added, "There's no other man I can think of who's nearly good enough for her."

"I despise a cheat," Francis said suddenly, an unexpected memory of his father and the florid girl in the restaurant having flashed through his head. And as the other didn't answer, he went on, "I came here and fell in love with this place. There's nowhere else on earth I ever want to be. And now there's Kate and—I don't know how to explain it—Kate and this place are one in my mind. In my heart. My wife—" He stopped.

Patrick put a hand on his shoulder. "Sit down. You're shaking."

They sat on a stone wall at the side of the walk.

"Strange, isn't it," Francis mused, "that no one condemns, not really, a light 'affair,' a casual woman, but for this they'll throw stones?"

"Do you care if they do?"

"Not for myself. But for Marjorie—you don't like Marjorie."

"She doesn't approve of me," Patrick answered quietly.

"That's true. I don't think she can really help that, though. It's the way she's lived all her life. The shaping starts in the nursery."

"But you were shaped another way?"

"I can't tell. After all, you're the only one of your race I've known so well. So how can I tell what my shape is?"

"You're truthful, at least."

"I try to be. It's better, even when it causes pain. Anyhow, that's the way I see it. But I'm a coward, I dread having to look at Marjorie's pain."

"Listen," Patrick said gently, "you don't have to draw a map of your whole life tonight. Go home and try to sleep. Go to work tomorrow and let things turn over very slowly in your mind. They'll reach a level after a while."

Francis just looked at him.

"You think I'm speaking platitudes? Well, I am. Forgive me. It's because I don't know anything better to say."

Francis reached out and took his hand. "Believe it or not, I'm glad you found out. It would be awful to have to keep anything as tremendous as this locked up in myself. And there isn't anyone I'd rather have know, or could trust more." He stood up. "Now I'll go home."

Marjorie was sitting in the bedroom with a magazine at her feet when he came in. She had been crying, and her puffy eyelids were ugly. He was ashamed of himself for thinking of their ugliness before he thought of her self.

"Where were you all day?" she asked.

"You know I went to the parade."

"All day?"

"I met some people. We had lunch and a few drinks." He then realized that she was still wearing the robe she had worn that morning. "What have you been doing?"

"Sitting here, wondering why you didn't ask me what happened yesterday in town."

"I don't understand."

"You knew I went to the doctor."

"Yes, but—why, did anything happen?"

"Oh," she said with artificial calmness. "I would say it did. He told me I'm pregnant, that's all that happened."

Francis went cold. "In heaven's name, why didn't you tell me yesterday?"

"Why didn't you ask me? You came in the house talking about twin foals and never—" Again she wept.

"You knew it this morning and last night—"

"Yes, that's why I was what you called 'angry.' I wasn't angry! I was wounded—oh, my God, we've been waiting for years and you didn't even care enough to ask what the doctor said!"

He knelt on the floor beside her chair, putting his arms around her. "Marjorie, Marjorie, of course I care! But you'd been so many times before— How could I think it would be different this time? I thought it was another routine visit. Forgive me."

And at the same moment he was thinking: Kate.

"I can't believe it. I'm afraid I'll wake up and find it isn't true. People always say that, but that's just how I feel."

"I'm sure it's true. Wonderful and true."

"Do you care whether it's a girl or a boy?"

For so long he had been having fantasies about a son. But he gave the wise and decent answer.

"It doesn't matter. Just let it be well."

"You'd rather have a boy. Probably it's silly, but I have such a strong feeling that it is." Now she was chatting, comforted and exuberant. "What shall we name it? I don't like 'Junior' at all. If it's a girl, I'd like 'Megan,' I think. Or maybe 'Anne'—that was my favorite grandmother's name—"

Compassion struggled in him, not for Marjorie alone, but for the microscopic being in her body, the life so desperately desired, that he went weak with it.

Oh, Kate, what shall I do?

He was stunned. He was numb. They went downstairs and ate a late supper. Afterwards Marjorie wanted to walk outside and look at the sea. She was filled with a tremendous ecstasy. He had not seen her like that since the day of their wedding. It was far too soon for hormones to have done this to her; pure happiness had exalted her. Naturally, it would not last. No exalted state could. But he wondered how long the residue would last. Simple joy was not one of her qualities, as it was one of Kate's. . . .

He did not sleep. Marjorie, having cried her tears of relief, slept deeply with a hand folded under her cheek. Her face was tranquil, classic. How he had loved her, or believed he did! If only one could go back and undo! Or if one could simply go forward! But he was locked in. Too late. Too late.

And all night long a thousand tiny creatures throbbed and trilled in the trees, all that pulsing life going on, century after rolling century, under the heavens. Ignorant, happy creatures with nothing to do but grow and thrive and mate, into whose cycle no anguish crept, no agonies of loss or conscience! All night long they throbbed and trilled.

"Oh, my darling," Kate said. "You wanted a child."

"That's true."

"You're thinking that if it were yours and mine—"

"I am, I am."

"But I can't have any, Francis, not ever."

"I'm so sorry for us. So sorry for us all."

"Not grateful, even a little?"

He lay on the sofa in her parlor with his head on her lap.

"I don't know. I feel as if something had been given me by one hand and taken away by the other."

"We won't let anything be taken. We'll find a way to keep it all."

"How?"

"I'll always be here. We can always be here like this."

"Secret afternoons aren't what I want for you or what you ought to have."

"But far better than nothing, my darling."

In the den, between the humidor and the ship model, his father sat, beckoning. "Don't tell your mother, son. You know I wouldn't hurt her for the world."

But this was different. Here was no blowsy slut to be hidden away! Here was his heart's love, to be announced to the world.

"I guess I knew," he said, thinking aloud.

"Knew what?"

"That there'd be no turning back, once I had made the admission. I guess I really knew the day we had lunch in Cade's Hotel. But I wanted to spare you this."

"And spare Marjorie?"

"Yes, Marjorie, too. God knows I'm not noble! It's only that something in me wants things to be open and clean. I hate concealment."

"So do I. Sometimes, though, there is no other way."

"Patrick said I needn't decide the whole future in a minute. 'Go slowly,' he said, 'and it will unfold itself.' But he didn't know about the baby."

"He was right, all the same. You don't have to decide anything. We won't hurt anyone. Just loving each other won't hurt anyone."

She bent to kiss his forehead and he put his arms about her. Here, here were his refuge and his desire. His whole being was warmed and the sweetest peace enveloped him.

Thirteen

In the hour before dawn the sea glowed with phosphorus. The pirogue lurched and the torch in Will's hand wavered as Clarence pulled in the seine to lay it on the bottom between their feet.

"Not bad for a nonprofessional. A fine haul of ballyhoo! We'll sell some, give some to our friends, and have the rest for supper." He took up the oars. "Hard work if you have to do it every day for a living, but kind of a good time like this, wouldn't you say so, boy?"

Clarence seldom waited for an answer, but not being himself a talker, Will didn't mind. He felt closer to the old man than to anyone he had ever known. And he settled back now in the stern, watching the first faint rise of dawn on the horizon and the seabirds soaring.

"This boat's the kind the Caribs made, with the knife-edge bow. Made out of a gommier trunk. They used to fell the tree when the moon was new, thought that would keep it from rotting. Old magic. Well, I guess we all keep some kind of private magic to believe in, don't we?"

The light grew and the torches were put out. A crowd of little boats turned back toward Covetown as the night fishermen headed home. They had all come a long way, skirting the island. A scalloped line of treetops became distinct as the minutes passed and the sky grew white. Cattle were moving dots on hillside pastures. Village rooftops glittered when the sun reached them. A fine house with lawns like a great, swooping skirt emerged from shadow.

"Chris-Craft," Clarence said, waving toward the private dock. "Look at that beauty. Fifty thousand, if it's a dollar."

Low on a bluff stood the house, the familiar porticoed and columned home of the West Indian planter. Its shutters were still closed; it slept.

"Florissant," said Clarence. "Belongs to the Francis family. Right behind it there's Estate Margaretta. Belonged to the Drydens. One of them married a Francis when I was a boy. Pooling the wealth, sort of. Colonel Dryden was my colonel in the First World War."

Will sat up. This was the first really interesting piece of information that he'd heard on the outing.

"You were in the First World War! You never talk about it."

"Don't like to. It was a bad time to remember."

"Did you kill anybody?"

"Never ask anyone a thing like that," Clarence said seriously. "If a person did, it wouldn't have been his fault and he shouldn't be reminded of it. As it happens, though, I didn't. I worked in the mess."

"What was so bad about it, then?"

Clarence considered. "It was just—oh, the whole business, the way we had to live. For instance, a black could never hope to be an officer in the British army, never be more than a sergeant, no matter how well educated he might be. At Taranto—that's where I served in Italy —we weren't allowed in the movie theater or the Y canteens. It's things like that that make you so mad, they fester in you. Some of the men wouldn't take it anymore. There was a mutiny at Taranto. It's an ugly thing when men get so mad." His voice dropped to a murmur.

"I can't hear you," Will said impatiently, wanting to hear.

"I said it's awful to see men maddened that way! They do terrible things and terrible things are done to them. I lost a younger brother there."

"Dead?"

"Dead. Shot in a riot. Then I came home. I worked on the transport ship *Oriana,* which brought the mutineers back here to serve out their sentences."

"And that was the end of it?"

"Not really. The end never really comes. Every end gives birth to another beginning, doesn't it? Well, in 1919, in Honduras and Trinidad, there were more riots. As soon as the troops were demobilized, they went rampaging, burning the homes and businesses of the whites."

Will was excited. "What happened then?"

"Oh, the riots were put down. They always are. That's why violence solves nothing. All the hopes and the fine talk came to nothing at the war's end. You know," Clarence said reflectively, "there'd been a lot of talk—in fact the British Labour Party had endorsed Du Bois's idea about making an African state out of the former German colonies, the colonies that we helped win for Britain. Reparation for centuries of slavery, he said, giving us back our own land in Africa, where we were taken from. Some people in Barbados even had a scheme to repatriate West Indian Negroes—"

"What is 'repatriate'?"

"To send you back to your fatherland. But," Clarence said with emphasis, "I'm not sorry that part came to nothing. This is my home here. My people have been here six" —he frowned, counting on his fingers— "seven or eight generations, probably. Two centuries, as far as I can count. The same for you, too, I imagine. Has anybody ever mentioned it to you?"

"No," Will said. Stupid question! Who would have told him?

"Well, you were too young to care about all that, anyway. You hungry now? Désirée made sandwiches and cake."

Will noticed he had recently stopped saying "Dezzy" after Patrick said he hated it.

Clarence unwrapped the box. "Coconut cake, your favorite. She's awfully fond of you, Will. You know that, don't you?"

Will nodded, feeling a small quick pain which was part anger. She wasn't "fond" of him at all; she was good to him because Patrick wanted her to be, and because one was supposed to be kind to an orphan. Curious how you could sit back, not saying a word, just listening and watching, and figure people out! It was really easy, he thought now, eating the sandwich. Easy. Désirée was lazy, in a way. She didn't want to have to think too much, just wanted to enjoy her peace, being loved and loving Patrick and the girls. She spent too much on clothes and fancy knickknacks for the house. Patrick complained, but he never did anything about it. Maybe he couldn't. Mentally, Will shrugged.

"Look," Clarence said. "Remember, I mentioned Estate Margaretta a while back? You can see the roof from here. It's an interesting house with a rotunda. I always thought I'd have liked being an architect, if the circumstances had been different. *Margaretta,*" he mused. "They used to name their places after their wives or after their daughters when the house was given as a wedding present. Yes, it must have been a great life for a planter way back then! Plenty of servants to bring you the best food and drink on a silver tray, gardeners to keep the house filled up with flowers, black mistresses dressed up in gold lace." He chuckled. "Not bad, not bad at all. But it didn't last. That's one thing history teaches—nothing lasts, not the Roman Empire, not anything. Say, have you read that piece I gave you about Wilberforce, who brought the slave trade to an end in the British Empire?"

"Not yet. We haven't come to it in school, anyway."

"Yes, and you may never come to it, the way the schools are. Read it for yourself."

The old man was a nut about history. Again Will felt impatience, but because he liked the old man he wouldn't show it.

"Yes, and then came the hard times for the estates. Debts, mortgages, and bankruptcies."

"Served them right," Will interrupted.

"My grandfather told me you could ride around and see great houses gone back to jungle with trees growing out of the rotting rooftops." Clarence stopped abruptly. "You're bored with all this, aren't you?"

Will grinned.

"You may be only eleven, but that's not too young to start understanding the past."

"Why?" Will asked, arguing the question.

"Because that's the only way to make the future better."

"Have you made it any better?"

Clarence looked at him sternly. "Yes, I have. Listen here, my grandfather worked a full year on a sugar estate for wages of five pounds. He lived on the estate and paid rent for his house—his hovel —and could be evicted at the owner's pleasure. And you ask whether it's better now? Yes, I'll accept credit for my part in the labor movement that has made it better, although not nearly good enough, God knows." He pulled on the oars and they creaked. "Now I'm too old. It's in the hands of men like Nicholas Mebane and your father. They'll push us still farther along. I'm glad your father left teaching. He can use his powers in larger ways."

Something bursting in Will's chest came out in a harsh voice, in harsh words. "He's not my father! Why do you always call him that?"

"He is! He's fathered you more than anyone else ever did! Sometimes you puzzle me, Will. You seem so critical, so sullen. But you're much smarter than your age and I think by now you should be able to see yourself and see the people around you for what they are." And letting up on the oars, he placed a hand on Will's knee. "It hurts me to hear you shouting out 'he's not my father!' "

"All right, I'm sorry," Will said.

"Then why do you keep doing it?"

"Look at him! And look at me!"

"The color, you mean? That bothers you? Why? Do you think you're pure African or I am? It's only a matter of degree. Listen, it took years to work out the resentments between the browns and the blacks. The browns had the good jobs, the money, and the vote. You know when they started to get together and work together? After the blacks got ahead a little bit and sweated themselves enough to buy a scrap of land, why then they got the vote, too, and the browns wanted their votes to get elected to the legislature. So," and here Clarence, laughing, leaned back while the boat drifted toward shore, "well, a black man, knowing that, would simply not pay his taxes; so he wouldn't be able to vote, and then one of these upper-class light skins would pay his taxes for him in exchange for his vote! Clever, wasn't it?" he cried, wearing a frisky expression.

Will was not amused. "Tricks. That's all it still is. Tricks, instead of having their rights. He and Mr. Mebane, hanging around Mr. Luther, up there in that fancy house! 'Eleuthera means free,' he tells me every time we go there. Free for who? Not for people like us! You think we'll ever live in a place like that? He gives you a cold drink and a piece of cake and thinks he's so grand."

"Who does? Francis Luther? It happens you've picked on one of the most decent men on the island."

"I heard you say once you didn't trust him."

"I didn't mean it that way, exactly. I was being wary. Give him a chance to prove he means what he says, that's what I meant. And so far he has. He's built houses, he's opened a dispensary with a nurse on his place, and a doctor comes out once a month for checkups. Nobody else has done what he's been doing. A very decent man," Clarence repeated firmly.

Will snickered, remembering something. "He shacks up with Mrs. Tarbox in town."

"What! What kind of talk is that? Where'd you hear a thing like that?"

"I heard Désirée talking to Pat—to Dad—in the kitchen. He said it wasn't true, but she said people see him at her house."

"People get me sick! Nothing better to do but spread lies and dirty gossip. I'm surprised at Désirée. And don't you repeat it, hear?"

"Well, all right." The old man was really angry, you could see that. "Well, all right. But still, Uncle Clarence, everything you said, sure it's okay that he has a nurse there and all that stuff, but still—"

"Still what?"

"Still it's only crumbs, isn't it? Like the kids diving for money in the harbor when white tourists come. They think they're so kind, throwing money away. The other day in town a man and woman, American, I think, by the way they talked, they stopped me on the street and handed me some candy. I threw it on the ground and told them what they could do with it."

"Will, Will, that was mean! You shouldn't have done it. The people meant well, they meant to be kind. Don't you see that?"

The crinkled face was distressed, its lines reaching up to where the white hair receded from the temples like cotton tufts. He's old, Will thought. Too old.

"No, I don't understand you, Will. It's hard to remember what I was like when I was your age. But I don't believe I was like you. No, I wasn't. You're a very bright boy, much more than I was. You don't study hard enough, though. Sometimes"—Clarence spoke slyly—"I catch you sitting over your books, just sitting there looking at nothing. What are you thinking of?"

"I'm thinking that you people don't do anything! You sit and talk about committees and elections and independence coming and how you can hardly make ends meet and shoes are so expensive. But in the Da Cunha shop they're selling wine from France and diamonds worth more than your whole house. Talk, talk!"

"What would you have us do?"

"Get out in the streets! Get out and shoot! Burn their houses down and take what you need. That's what."

"That sort of thing gets nowhere! It's not civilized. One works through government, through the labor unions! Ah, well, you're a child. Come, here we are, let's get rid of this fish and go home."

A small crowd awaited the catch on the beach, where an impromptu fair and barter had been set up. Homemade brooms and hats and baskets, baked goods and flowered cotton aprons were set up on improvised tables and upended boxes. Will took the net of gleaming fish and laid it in a box while Clarence fastened the boat.

"Better not let anybody hear you talk about burning houses, son," he warned, as he tied up.

Will stood there watching the old man fuss with the rope. Fumble. Fumble. Fumble your life away. He felt a strange softness toward the old man. He wanted to reach out and stroke him on the shoulder. Then anger filled him again, and he did not.

Fourteen

ONE day Teresa Luther went back to St. Felice. Tee Francis resisted still, but Teresa Luther gave in at last.

"How can you refuse?" Richard urged. "He's asked us so many times, and now, with our first grandchild coming—"

"I have responsibilities," she began.

"Nonsense! You have grown daughters who'll look after Margaret. They'll all get along without you very well for a few weeks," he said gently.

Adversity had softened and weakened him. Oddly enough, she often thought, it had given him a greater dignity, as well.

"Look," he said. "I got out this old album. Here you are."

There she was, serious and pale under the dark fall of her hair. Here they all were, Père with his gold-knobbed cane on the lawn at Eleuthera and Julia, in flounces, standing with Tee in front of the twin staircase at Drummond Hall.

"That must have been taken not more than a year or so before we were married," Richard observed.

"It must have been."

He said unselfishly, "Francis would be so glad! I can see his face when you walk in."

"And when you walk in."

The album rested on the windowsill. A flurry of dead leaves, driven in gray, chilled air, blew past.

"It's too bad we had to be so gray and gloomy on your first day in Paris," Anatole Da Cunha had said on just such a day.

"You're a strong girl, stronger than you know." That was Marcelle, who had taught her to survive.

Strange, I haven't thought of her in years. Not strange, I have made every effort not to.

"You can do whatever you have to do," Marcelle had said.

That was true. A marriage without love, a secret like a box of dynamite in the closet—one could manage anything if one had to. Now, finally, I am called upon to go back. There can be no excuse this time, I have run out of them.

"Then you'll go?" asked Richard. "I can make arrangements?"

"Yes, I'll go," Teresa Luther said.

It was not very much changed. The public market, the cathedral close, the soft-drink stalls and the dusky, gray-green tamarinds were all the same. Raucous radios, more cars and horns, and a storefront movie advertising a cowboy picture, these were different.

And the house was different. They had built a new wing, with guest rooms and a nursery for the coming baby. Marjorie had renewed the house with a fitting and patrician charm that, in a way, resembled herself. It's not what it was when I lived in it, Tee thought, remembering crumbled plaster.

And she told her daughter-in-law, "It looks like you."

Marjorie was pleased with the comment. "Not, I hope, the way I look now," she said, touching her enormous belly, and pleased, Tee saw, with that, too.

Francis wanted them to tour outdoors with him. He walked ahead with his father, Tee following, up the slopes toward the banana groves.

"This is the major source of income," he explained. "Green gold, Father."

Richard was fascinated. He had never been in any part of the world like this one.

"The original tree is called the mother. New trunks grow out of the old roots. See this bunch? We call it a stem. See these? We call them hands. You get anywhere from seven to twelve hands in a cluster. The bananas are called fingers. You get over a hundred fingers to a stem."

The two men, framed by shaggy leafage, paused on the path, the one still wearing his dark city suit, the other in workman's khaki. Francis' hair had lightened and his skin been darkened in the sun; he shone. She wondered what Père would have thought about this young man of his blood. And with that extreme perceptiveness of him which she had always had, she recognized that something new, something vibrant and exciting, had come alive in him.

Richard, interested in finance, wanted to know how the crop was marketed.

"Well, Dad, I have to tell you I'm rather proud of something I've been able to do. We used to work on contract, you know, anywhere from one to five years with a big company; you'd give them a weekly estimate of what you'd deliver. Every planter, large or small, was on his own. But now we've got a cooperative. I had a hard time convincing people it would be a good thing, but now they admit it is, and we market through the cooperative, which gives us much greater bargaining power, naturally. Also, we help out in other ways, making loans for fertilizers, and disease control, and—there's a lot more to it, but that's the general idea, anyway."

Tee paused, letting the two men climb. Above, where the banana groves stopped and the jungle took over, one could see light playing in the upper branches of the dense acomas. Cathedral light, although one might very well put it the other way, remembering forest shadows in old churches at the place where the apse meets the nave. Mounting farther up the Morne, you would come to where the light, shafting straight as rulers, struck the ground and sifted up again into a mist, knee-deep. Yesterday. Yesterday.

And in the morning of childhood, yellowbirds with legs like two thin twigs came to the sugar bowl on the veranda. Each dark-gray wing bore a white mark, a beauty spot, she used to say. The afternoon drowsed in cicada hum until, at four, the rain came, leaving its sharp and bitter fragrance on the air. . . .

Returning, Richard and Francis roused her into the present moment and they walked back to the house. Humped Brahman cattle, grazing behind rail fences, raised their cream-colored faces toward the sound of voices, questioning with dark, languid eyes.

"First prize at the agricultural show," Francis said proudly. "Bananas are only what keep me solvent, you know. All the rest is what I really care about. I'm diversifying, trying to raise the island by its bootstraps. Lionel thinks I'm a fool to take risks and care so much. He'll probably tell you so. But he believes just in looking out for number one."

"There's something to be said for looking out for number one," Richard observed.

When Francis did not answer, Tee asked, "Don't you get along with Lionel?"

"We get along all right. Marjorie likes him more than I do, though. They think alike. He'll be here tonight at dinner."

"Marjorie said something in her last letter about Lionel's divorce. She didn't say why, just said it was 'civilized.' What sort of person is his wife? I mean, what was the reason?"

Francis looked away. "I don't know, really. A marriage fails: it comes down to that, whether there's one reason or a thousand, doesn't it? It failed." He stopped abruptly, then resumed, "I'm worried about Marjorie. The doctor says her pressure's too high. They may have to take the baby if it doesn't come soon by itself." He turned a troubled face toward his parents. "I'm glad you're here."

"We'll do anything we can, you know that," Richard said.

"And there's something else. A damned mess, just when you've come for your first visit! There's talk of a strike, a general strike. It could paralyze us. It could get very nasty." He squinted thoughtfully into the sun. "Still, maybe not. And I really don't think—in fact I'm sure they won't bother me personally. I've done so much and they know it. I've been on labor's side since the day I got here. No, I'm sure they won't bother me."

*   *   *

In the dining room, Richard sat opposite Anatole Da Cunha's painting of Morne Bleue.

"I have to admit it hurt to part with it," he said, "but it belongs here without question. Oh, he has the touch, hasn't he? Marvelous, marvelous! You can feel the sun on your skin! You know, I'm disgusted with some of the things the art critics write these days. Such as last week: 'A face representing a civilization in decline.' Now what the devil does that mean? Fuzzy personal impressions masquerading as analysis! When all that matters is whether you can feel the sun on your skin."

Marjorie got to the point. "It must be worth a good deal, mustn't it, now that Da Cunha's so old?"

"Oh, definitely. And when he's dead, the value will really shoot up. You know, Teresa, I should have had him paint you when we were in Paris. I wasn't thinking."

The mirror over the sideboard reflected Tee's face, very white in candlelight and dusk, a face still without lines, still sweetly curved, and yet not young anymore.

"Let's see," Lionel remarked, "you were fifteen, weren't you, when you left? So I must have been not quite three. Yet I always thought I remembered you, I suppose because Mother talked about you so much." He laughed. "You were a wild girl, she always said."

"I? Wild?"

"Oh, she only meant bareback riding and running around with animals—dogs and colts and parrots—all the things she never did, I suppose."

"Parrots!" As always, Richard was enthusiastic over anything new. "You have them wild here, don't you?"

"They nest way up the Morne toward the rain forest, and you don't always get to see them, but with luck we might. I've even seen the imperial parrot a couple of times. Sisseron. Amethyst and emerald, a glorious bird. If you're willing to climb," Francis offered, "we can go one morning."

"Oh, I'm willing!" Richard cried.

Tee thought, I should not have come. Her mouth went dry and she laid the fork down, then picked it up again and took some food, something without taste.

He could not possibly be here, could he? Patrick Courzon? The name made a sharp impact on her ear. And even if he were, she would never encounter him! The island was small, but not that small. And so stratified by color and caste into concentric circles which didn't touch. Surely, though, he was not even here! He would have stayed in England, or gone somewhere else to use his fine education. Not here.

But suppose he were? She tried to picture him: a year older than Francis, half of his blood, of her own blood, each of them alive and breathing at this very instant—now!—on this high, blue day; alike, so alike they must be, by the very law of averages! And still so different.

A maid poured wine for Francis, her thin, pretty arm, red-brown, dusky, stretched parallel to his pale one, making exactly the contrast that that other boy's would make, one supposed, if ever they should—Impossible! And yet, as fear trembled in Teresa for the thousandth time or more, something else trembled in her, too: pity, profound pity.

The young maid moved about the table, pouring the wine. There was proud grace in the poise of her narrow head; substitute for the blue cotton uniform a sweeping ballgown and you would have a princess, a dark princess. The girl, meeting Tee's gaze, smiled slightly.

Crazy world, with its strictures and classifications; all those gradations of mankind based on color and money, on legitimacy and class, when all we are is only—what? Protein, minerals, and water, mostly. Sea water. Yes, it's absurd, all of it, and still I haven't the courage to challenge it, or even to face it. If I could know what he is like, just quietly, secretly know, without anyone else's knowing, without ruining everything, facing rage. Sometimes I think I've been brave, but not brave enough. Sometimes I think I died here in this house when I was fifteen, and everything since has been a dream.

There came over her then an engulfing sense of unreality, of time so telescoped that the far past was only yesterday, and yet so long ago that it might never have happened. She gripped the edge of the table.

"Is anything the matter?" Marjorie asked. "You're feeling all right?"

"I? Just tired after the trip, that's all." And Tee smiled, forcing herself away, after long habit, from the ghost of a memory that had been keeping step with her since she was fifteen.

"You'll rest well tonight. Your room's in the new wing, very quiet, away from everyone."

"And you'll lunch with me tomorrow," Lionel said. "There'll be no hostess, but I'll give you a good lunch. I do all my own entertaining these days, now that I'm without a wife. But then, Kate never was very sociable anyway."

Richard, seeing that the subject was not taboo, inquired, "What did she do with herself, then?" He enjoyed gossip.

"Oh, good works. She was, and still is, on every blasted committee you can think of for the improvement of this, that, and the other. But to be fair, I shouldn't make light of it. She believes in what she does, and you have to give credit for that. In other words, she puts her money where her mouth is."

"She never liked people," Marjorie remarked.

Lionel contradicted her. "I wouldn't say that. She likes some of them too much. It all depends on what people you're talking about."

"Naturally, I mean our friends, the people we all know," Marjorie explained to Tee. "I've made wonderful friends here. They've been a saving grace for me, while Francis was busy with his bananas and cows and things." It seemed to Tee that she had bitten the words off.

Richard inquired, "Do you get many visitors from home during the winter?"

"Oh, yes, there are always a few yachts in the harbor. Last year the Crowes, friends of my mother's, the Standard Steel Crowes, dropped anchor and spent a day with us. And there are always a lot of chartered schooners in season. My cousins come every year and we have a marvelous time. They can't get over all the land we have and all the servants! They keep telling me you can scarcely find a decent cleaning woman at home anymore. So it's kind of fun, and I keep busy."

What does Francis talk about with her? Tee wondered. Marriage was a lifelong conversation, or it wasn't much of a marriage. And she wondered whether Richard would have noticed. No, he would not have noticed.

"So you're due any day now," Lionel said to Marjorie.

"I'm afraid I'm overdue. If the baby doesn't come in the next day or two, they'll have to take it."

Lionel frowned. "If I were you, Francis, I wouldn't wait that long. I'd take her in to town. You can't tell what will happen. If the strike comes, they're liable to block the roads."

"You really think so?" Francis was doubtful. "I rather think it will be settled quietly. I don't foresee violence, even if there should be a strike."

"You told us this afternoon," Richard reminded him quickly, "that it could be nasty."

"I meant verbal nastiness. Something unpleasant, not dangerous."

Lionel shook his head. "I'd feel more secure if Nicholas Mebane were in the country. He's one Negro with a white man's common sense. I've no love for him, mind you, or for any of them, but I have to admit he seems to be a man with the country's best interests at heart. However, he's at some sort of powwow just now, some meeting in Jamaica over federation or independence or some such. Without him, we could be in for a pack of trouble."

"These people aren't violent!" Francis argued. "It's simply a question of wages, a union affair."

"No? What happened right here last month?" Marjorie challenged.

"We had a little problem, nothing to do with what we're talking about. You see," Francis explained to his parents, "when you run a place like this, you're almost like the head of a family. Workers come to you with problems, when they want a loan, or have a quarrel with another worker. And it happened that one of the men lost his temper and slashed another with his machete, severing a finger. So I had to settle things down. It was disturbing, of course, but it has no bearing on the strike, none at all."

"I think it has," Lionel said. "These people are only one step removed from the savage."

Richard wanted to know what the unions were demanding.

"More money, naturally," Lionel answered. "They've a long list of grievances, wanting to be paid once a week instead of every other week—"

Richard interrupted. "That seems reasonable enough. Or am I wrong?"

"Very inconvenient and more expensive. Much more bookkeeping."

"Personally, I think they're entitled to most of what they're asking for," Francis said.

Lionel gave a sigh of exasperation. "Are you willing to raise wages?"

"I'll compromise. I'll meet them halfway. I've got good people, and if it costs a little more to keep them here in peace, I'll do it. I'm making a living."

"You would do better to be thinking of saving money for your own flesh and blood," Marjorie said quietly.

"My flesh and blood will be taken care of. No need to worry," Francis replied, as quietly.

There is nothing between them except the child in her belly, Tee thought. It was a sudden revelation. They had nothing! Quite possibly neither of them even knew it—and might never know it. That was the terrible thing: might never know it. If you were to ask Richard about his marriage, he would tell you it was good. He believed it was.

Too much, too much, she thought, feeling a great weariness. My son's marriage ought to be no affair of mine, but it will be, nevertheless; I shall go home with the burden of this, too.

Marjorie was pressing a question. "Will you drive me to Covetown tomorrow morning as Lionel advises?"

"I will, although I still don't believe there'll be any danger."

"When you've lived here as long as I have," Lionel said, "you'll know better. Good God, I remember when I was a child, there was an argument in a barbershop and a party of Negroes came in and cut the barber—he was a white man—cut him to pieces with his own razors. No one ever caught them, either. For all you know, they could be working for you here at Eleuthera." Lionel laughed. "Seriously, though, there's a lot of agitation out there, and don't think the fireburn went out with the end of slavery, because it didn't. Why, they burned half the estates on St. Croix back in my grandfather's time, and that's not so long ago! Burned them up because they weren't satisfied with their labor contracts. And things are more tense today than they were then, let me tell you."

Richard put his coffee cup down. "We're scaring the life out of these women. It's especially unfair to Marjorie. She's got enough to think about right now as it is."

Lionel apologized. "Sorry. You're absolutely right. So you'll have lunch with me Friday, if all goes well? Tee, do you remember the way? You won't get lost?"

"No, I won't get lost, and yes, I remember the way. I remember it very well."

As soon as he opened his eyes on Friday morning, Francis felt the unnatural stillness. Quietly, so as not to awaken Marjorie, he slid out of bed and pulled on his clothes. But she had heard him.

"Is anything the matter, Francis?"

"No. Go to sleep. You feel all right?" Her eyes, between heavy lids, had a bright sickly gloss.

"Dizzy, I think. I don't know how I feel, really."

Alarm jerked him more widely awake. "Stay there, then. I'll be back in a minute. We'll call Dr. Strand and drive you in to Covetown."

He went downstairs and outside. By half past six the milk cows should have been let out to graze; differing from many owners, he kept his cattle in at night to protect them from the damp. By half past six, in picking time, the men should have been in the groves. And hastening, he strode along the river gorge, up the steep path down which the stems were to be carried to the roadside for pickup. Except for the whistlings and twitterings of the forest, there was no sign of life. Thick as candles on an altar, the bananas stood on the trees, ready for picking. On the other side of the island the Geest refrigerator ship, like a great resting seabird, waited for the crop.

The strike had come then, with his own people in it! Betraying what he had liked to think of as a mutual trust! They had let him down, after all. The whole crop to be lost, all those months of steady bloom and growth! Anger clashed in his middle with his worry over Marjorie and still another urgent fear: he needed money. He needed it quite desperately, he owed the bank, another half-dozen cottages for the full-time hands were only partially completed, he—

Osborne was running between the barns.

"So it's begun," Francis said. "With our people in it, too."

"I'm afraid so. Don't worry about the stock, though. I've got my sons milking and feeding. My wife's seeing to the chickens. We're slow, but we can do the necessary."

"What about the crop?"

Osborne threw his hands up.

"What do you mean? Just forget about it? To hell with it?"

"What else can we do?"

Oh, Osborne could afford to be calm! It wasn't his money. He'd get his salary and his house, regardless.

"Haven't I treated my people decently?"

"Surely you have, but—"

"But what? When my foreman's wife wants a new stove, I don't question. She gets it. Merton's baby has an ear infection. What do I do? I get in the car and drive him to the hospital myself. I don't want thanks, I tell you, I only want— Listen, Osborne, I've got to talk to somebody. There has to be somebody who can be talked to. Where is everybody, anyway?"

"A lot of men have gone to a meeting in town. And there's a crowd with picket signs outside the gates. You can't see them from the house."

"I'm going down there. I'm going to put it to them fairly and squarely. Biting the hand that's fed them better than anybody else on this island's ever done just makes no sense, no sense at all, and I intend to tell them so."

"I wouldn't do that if I were you, Mr. Luther. They've made up their minds. You wouldn't get anyplace. And some of them are union people from higher up. They don't even know you, and they could get pretty mad. This is island-wide. No, don't go down there, Mr. Luther."

Francis stared at the other man. A cold fish, with his calm counsel, who, for all he could tell, might have known perfectly well what was going to happen this morning! At a time like this, one could suspect anybody. But he must keep his head and save whatever could be saved. Keep his head! With Marjorie's condition, and— He turned abruptly.

"I'm going in to telephone. I'll reach someone who can do something. Damned if I'll just sit here and let that crop rot on the trees."

Patrick, he thought. Patrick's the one. They hadn't spoken for the past week or two. Francis' head had been filled with Marjorie and with his parents' visit, while Patrick had, through the newspaper, been involved with the strike, writing exhortations to both sides to negotiate, to be patient, and to keep their tempers.

Having called the doctor and been advised to bring his wife in before noon, he telephoned Patrick. Would Patrick possibly be able to rush out to Eleuthera right now? He hated to ask, but it was so important, and would he please come to the office next to Osborne's house. Yes, surely Patrick would.

Francis swung in the swivel chair and drummed on the office desk. His nerves were singing like telegraph wires. He'd had a teacher once who was all gone on the subject of relationships, of how everything was hooked on to something else and nothing stood alone. He hadn't comprehended it then, had been bored as hell by such dry abstractions, but now suddenly he saw what had been meant. Here was his child about to be born—pray God it would be well—and it was up to him to protect that child's security; but then, the workers wanted their own security, too!

"They've much on their side, you know that," Kate always said, and it was true; Kate saw things fairly; Kate—

He rubbed his hand over his eyes. Everything, everything circled round him: Kate and Marjorie and the baby, and money and justice, racing and colliding. Yes, the strikers had much on their side, their demands being neither impossible nor outrageous. If the planters had any sense, they'd accede and choose peace. In the end, they'd have to give in; couldn't they see that?

And he said as much when Patrick came rushing in.

"I'm glad you see it that way, Francis."

"Well, I do. Everyone must know I do. Then why are they punishing me, too?"

"It's not punishment. It's not personal. It's just that once a thing like this starts, there's a momentum. It took a long time to build. Now you can't stop it."

"That doesn't answer me! Haven't I been fair, been generous? I've plowed money back into improvements when I could have used it to pay off what I owe. I've a grocery store on the premises and put its profits into a welfare fund, I've— Why are they doing this to me?" He heard himself pleading.

Patrick spoke gently. "What can I tell you? It's not fair, of course it isn't. But they don't make exceptions. That's the size of it."

"Won't, you mean."

"Even if some of them should want to break the strike for you, they couldn't do it, you surely understand that. A union is a union. Orders come from the organization, from the top."

"Well, then, let's get to the top!"

Patrick shook his head. "Francis, it can't be done."

The patience in his manner irritated Francis. This was the stubborn patience with which one "handled" children, denying without explaining why. He struck the desktop with his fist.

"I have got to get this crop to the ship! It's an outrage, a wanton waste for the entire island, those ships going back empty, with space for a thousand tons!"

Patrick sighed. "I know, I know."

"I'll pay what they're demanding. Let the other planters do what they want, or say about me whatever they want. I don't give a damn."

"You've got courage and you've got principles. But you see, it's not the money alone. It wouldn't be, even if they could make an exception of you, which I tell you again, they can't. They've got to stand together."

"If it's not the money alone, then what is it? What do they want?"

"I suppose," Patrick said slowly, reflectively, "it's wanting to direct one's own life. That's the feeling that's been gaining strength here on these islands. These people have grown up. They've migrated overseas and sent back reports. They've seen how people live in other places and what they have. And now they're sick of being directed from abroad by foreign companies—"

Francis interrupted. "I know all that. I'm not a foreign company. I'm here every day working where they can see me."

Patrick was silent. He looked tired.

"You just said I have principles. You admit I've been a good guy. Go out to my gate now and ask those men to come back and harvest my crop."

"Francis, they wouldn't listen to me! I'm not even a union man. I only write for a newspaper."

"Then ask your father-in-law. They'd listen to Clarence Porter."

"Clarence is old. He's been out of things for years."

"Don't tell me he has no more influence!"

"If he has, he won't use it to break a strike, I can tell you that. He'd have my head for even daring to suggest it."

It was almost as though a game were being played, some board game, chess perhaps, in which Francis moved and Patrick blocked him and Francis moved again and Patrick blocked him. Once during childhood, when he had been losing at checkers, Francis had gone into a rage of frustration and thrown the board over. He felt that way now.

"Well," he said, controlling himself, "well, maybe you have some other solution for me." And he waited.

"I wish I had."

"Then," Francis said coldly, "it comes down to the fact that you really don't care about helping me."

"That's not true! But you're asking me to do the impossible. This will only be solved when the Planters Association signs a contract with the union, when contractors sign with their unions—it's spread all over, Francis. It's a movement, don't you see?"

Patrick's chair creaked. Osborne's porch door banged. The noises shuddered along Francis' spine and in his teeth.

"Well? Well? What do you advise me to do then?"

For a moment Patrick was silent, examining his fingers. Then he said gravely, "I have no advice. Except to sit and wait."

"And take my losses."

"What else?"

Francis could have struck him.

"What else?" he mimicked. "You and Osborne, with your quiet resignation! Oh, you talk, you people who've got nothing to lose! Have you any idea what I've put into this place?" He twisted his cigarette into the ashtray. He shot up out of the chair. "Yes, just sit here, I must, while they shut my place down, this horde that depends on me for wages and wants to be the master of my life!"

Patrick smiled sadly. "They believe, you see, that people like you feel entitled to be the masters of their lives."

The black arm of the wall clock moved forward with a jerk and click both visible and audible. Half past nine. Marjorie. He had to get her in to town before noon. Leave all this mess. Everything falling apart. No one helps. It's all on me. Again the clock jerked and clicked.

Suddenly something happened. He struck his hands together. "Illumination!" he cried. "I've got the answer! The Carib reservation! They'll do it! I can get a gang for a few days' work and pay them anything they want to pick this crop. It'll be worth it."

Patrick whistled softly. "Blackleg labor?"

"You can call it whatever you like."

"Apart from the rightness or wrongness, you ought to consider the dangers. How will they get the crop past your gates? The roads will be blocked—they'll never reach the dock."

"We'll chance it."

"There'll be a battle."

"If it's battling they want, let them have it."

Patrick had risen. The two men, of equal height, stood as if in confrontation.

"Francis, you're making a mistake. I know you feel you're being treated unfairly, not appreciated, and that may be true, but as they say in the labor movement, you can't make an omelet without breaking eggs."

"So, I'll break eggs, too!" Words came which ordinarily would not have fitted in Francis' mouth. "They've gone too far this time. This is my land. I've treated them well, and if they can't acknowledge that I'm the master here, to hell with them! And that's all I have to say."

Patrick's face hardened, surprising Francis, who had never seen hardness in that quiet face.

"I don't like the word *master*, Francis. It's ugly and it's out of date."

"Listen here, I've got thirty-six hours to get those bananas onto the boat. I haven't time to quibble over words."

"You've surprised me this morning. I didn't expect this of you."

Francis moved impatiently. "I'm sorry I haven't lived up to your expectations. But tell me about it some other time, will you?"

"I can tell you in one sentence right now. You are acting too grand, too feudal for this century."

Anger turned to fury in Francis. This—this *unknown*, whom he had befriended and liked and treated with so much respect, to turn against him, to rebuke him now, like a teacher scolding a child!

"Grand! Feudal!" he shouted. "After all I've done! You ungrateful son—" And he bit off the word.

"Of a bitch, you wanted to say?"

"Yes, son of a bitch!"

"The same to you, then," Patrick answered. He swung about and the door crashed.

For a minute or two Francis didn't move. The explosion in the little room, the voices of anger, left shockwaves trembling behind. A door had been slammed shut, not the sheet of wood that hung on a frame before him, but an invisible door which up to this morning had been open onto a warm communion between two men. He became aware of his own heavy breathing. He wasn't used to being this angry. Well, so, that's the way it is, he thought; I've seen his true colors. And then, ironically: True color? No, that's nasty, I can't mean that.

He raced next door to Osborne's house, across the veranda into the untidy living room where toys and newspapers littered the floor. You'd think, he thought irrelevantly, with the wages I pay, they'd manage better than this.

"Osborne!" he called.

"Yes, Mr. Luther?" Osborne came out of the kitchen. "Any luck?"

"No. I spoke to my friend and got exactly nowhere." He heard the bitterness in his own voice. "Listen here, I want you to get hold of some Caribs to pick that fruit. You know the chief. He knows me, too. You can pay whatever they ask and damn the consequences. We've got just thirty-six hours to get that crop to the ship."

Osborne's eyes were blank. He's not on my side, Francis thought, but he'll do what I order; he wants to keep the job.

"They can come down the mountain, in through the back way," he said. "I'll leave it all to you. I've got to take my wife into town. They may have to do a cesarean. Everything seems to have clobbered me at once today."

Osborne nodded. "Yes, sir. I'm sorry," he said, with proper sympathy. His eyes were still blank.

"You shouldn't have come. I tried to reach you but you had already left," Lionel said, adding crossly, "Francis shouldn't have let you, he ought to know better."

Tee explained. "He'd already left for the hospital with Marjorie by the time we got up." She worried. "I'm sure he'll call home or here the minute anything—"

Richard interrupted. "Maybe we should start back right now. The last thing I want is to get caught in a riot."

"There's been some trouble in Covetown," Lionel said, "but nothing out in the countryside. Yet. And maybe there won't be. Still, I'd finish lunch and get going fast if I were you."

He rang, and the servant came at once with the dessert and coffee.

Conversation stopped as she moved around the table, her soft-soled shoes making the only sound in the noon stillness. The table was an island in the enormous, airy room. At the far end of the room glass doors opened to a terrace and a stretch of empty lawn. The house was an island, too, with no protection but a row of glass doors.

Tee rose abruptly. "I'm ready," she said.

They drove cross-island. "Looks peaceful enough," remarked Richard.

He didn't, naturally, know the difference. Not a soul was at work either on the roads or in the fields. The stillness was oppressive, like that ominous, waiting silence in the last sultry hour before storm strikes, when the wind dies and birds hide. And thinking this, Tee thought at the same time, It's my nerves, I am overreacting, as usual.

In a wide valley between the hills that roll toward Morne Bleue, only a mile or two beyond Eleuthera, they came, suddenly, upon a crowd. On foot, on muleback, in farm carts and battered cars, men, women, and children had converged upon a broad, mowed field. At its center a simple platform had been set up, from which a man was making a speech.

"I wonder what's going on," Richard said. "Let's have a look."

"I don't think we should. They might not like it."

"We can just sit in the car and leave in a hurry if we have to," he argued, curious as always.

Facing the sun as they were, it was difficult to see the speaker, but his voice carried clearly, for the crowd was remarkably quiet.

"For centuries the grandeur of England rested heavily upon these islands." The accent was faintly British and the tone reasonable, almost conversational. "The wealth that came from sugar was princely. Most of it went abroad. I saw great houses in England that make our grandest estates look like cottages, and they were built on sugar. People who had never laid eyes on St. Felice lived on the wealth drawn from its earth. And what was returned to St. Felice? Nothing. Nothing. And what did you, who produced this wealth, get out of it? You know the answer: Not very much.

"It's true that things are a lot better now than they were back then, or even a few years ago. Some of you are old enough to remember when an estate worker earned twenty cents a day. On average we've come a long way from that, and some planters, a very few, are doing better than average. That's all true.

"Yet it's still also true that you are the victims of a system which leaves two thirds of you unemployed from January to June, once the peak season in the cane fields is over. So out of crop season you have to scrounge for work. Your women take jobs breaking stones on the roads. Your men leave the island to look for work elsewhere. And they say you have no family structure! No family structure!"

With scarcely any change in pitch the voice revealed, nevertheless, a passionate intensity, so that Richard whispered, "My God, the fellow's an orator!"

"When I was a teacher, I listened to the children. From them I learned more than you can ever tell me about drunken husbands and frustrated youths and babies who cry all the time because the houses are so crowded, so noisy, that they can't sleep. These are the facts of daily living.

"So then, what do you want? You want higher wages, and it should be simple enough to understand why you must have them. They say they can't afford to pay more. Well, the way things are run here that may be so. What is needed here is investment, is planning. Why, take coffee alone! We raise the beans, then we send them to England to be processed, and we import our own coffee to drink! Could anything be more absurd? Take sugar: why can't we refine our own sugar, make our own bags, manufacture molasses, rum, and bottles for the rum? Our people are crying for jobs; the population is growing. Ah, well, let me sum it up. With some intelligence and will, things can be changed. Now that every adult has a vote at last, you must learn to use it wisely." Here the speaker flung his arms out. "It's funny, I was asked to come here to talk about the strike and I've done so, but I couldn't help making a pitch for a bigger thing, for the kind of government which will be so responsive to your needs that strikes won't be necessary. I didn't intend this to be a political speech. I'm not a politician. I'm not a labor leader either, for that matter. I'm just a citizen who wants to improve things, that's all. And that's why I'm putting in a word for Nicholas Mebane, who couldn't be here today. I was asked to stand in for him and that's what I'm trying to do. Nicholas Mebane—you all know him—and the New Day Party!"

Cheers came from the crowd.

"He's a white man!" Richard cried. "Look, Teresa! I think—no, no he isn't. Almost, though. I wonder who he is?"

The speaker raised his hand for silence. "What we want is a twenty percent raise. That sums things up for the moment. You'll refuse to work and you'll not give in until you get what you're entitled to. It's as simple as that."

He leaped down from the platform and was engulfed in the crowd. All was swirling movement, a pushing toward the center of the field, a streaming out and a noise of many voices.

Richard leaned from the window as he backed away, calling to a black man who was passing. "Who was the speaker? Who was that?"

For a moment the man in overalls regarded Richard in his linen jacket and Tee in her lilac summer dress. *Why do you want to know?* his silence challenged. Then he answered.

"He writes for the *Trumpet*. And he knows what he's talking about. Name's Courzon. Patrick Courzon."

For young Will the long night had begun at the supper table. Patrick worried. "I don't like the looks of things. On the way back from my speech I passed two police stations that somebody's smashed up. It looks as if some tough elements want to take over."

Désirée changed the subject, just when it was getting interesting. This habit of hers exasperated Will. She always steered away from anything the least bit ugly. Fear was ugly, as were poverty and dirt.

"I'm so sorry I didn't get to hear you," she said soothingly. "You didn't tell me you were going to speak."

"I didn't know it myself. I was on the way back after that fiasco with Francis Luther this morning when they got a message to me. They wanted me to pinch-hit around the island in support of the strike. 'The New Day Party supports you all the way'—that sort of thing. I wish Nicholas hadn't left just now, though," he added darkly.

"You're more upset about Francis Luther than anything," Désirée said. "It's really not worth you're being so upset, Patrick."

Patrick didn't reply to that.

Will was alert. "What happened? You have a fight with Mr. Luther?"

"Now Will, it's none of—" Désirée began, but was interrupted.

"It's all right, the boy can ask. I'm too tired right now to talk about it, Will, but when all this business is over, I'll tell you."

Laurine spoke up. "Pop-pop told me the police are thick all along Wharf Street. They must be expecting something to happen."

"I hope to God not," Patrick said. "A strike is supposed to be an orderly way of obtaining one's due, not a celebration for hoodlums." He got up from the table. "Anyway, it's a good night to stay indoors, just in case things do get out of hand. Where you going now, Will?"

"Just out to the shed to look over some stuff."

From the shed you could slip around the garage and down the hill without being seen. If there was anything going on in town, his friends would be there. Most of them didn't have fathers as strict as Patrick and could spend their evenings hanging around where they wanted to, anyway.

At the next corner he fell in with two of them going to town; by the time they reached the foot of the hill where several roads met, a stream of boys of every age from twelve to twenty was pouring toward the center. The stream grew wider and moved faster.

"What's up?" Will asked his neighbor.

"I don't know. Somebody said there was stuff going on downtown."

The boys began to trot, their shoes slapping the pavement. Evening was melting into night; lights went on and houses became alive. Doors opened; voices shot out into the streets. Excitement rang like radio waves in the air; it pulsed through Will's veins, tingled in his chest. He felt like laughing. He didn't know why, only that it was good to be running like this in the center of a crowd, all together, all one, running toward action!

Where Wharf Street cut across their path a line of police brought them sharply to a halt.

"Blocked off! Blocked off!"

"What for? What do you mean?"

"Order of the governor, that's what for."

From far down the street came a tumultuous shouting, car horns, the crash of glass, and the low whine of an ambulance.

"Da Cunha's!" someone cried. "Yeah, they've got the old man's diamonds! Da Cunha's, isn't it?"

The black faces under the proud white police helmets ignored all questions.

"Aw, let us through! Let's see!"

The uniformed line drew tighter. "Back, boys, get back. Nobody gets through."

Next to Will someone had an idea. "Round the square! We'll get in at the other end!"

The group swung about, raced past Nelson in his wrought-iron enclosure, whooped past the careenage, hurled a few stones gaily through the windows of Bata Shoes and World Travel, came out at the other end of Wharf Street, and once more were halted.

"Shit," Will said.

Another ambulance wailed by. Fire engines clanged; the street lights flickered over the jostling mob on Wharf Street. In his frustration Will's feet were dancing. For a minute or two the group stood undecided. Then, grumbling and frustrated, they began to disperse. With a couple of others Will walked back to the square. Out of the deepening darkness a fan of light from a streetlamp had spread open over Nelson. With what arrogance he stood on his pedestal, one hand on sword, chin lifted in surveyal as if he owned the place and everyone in it!

"Bastard," Will said.

His companion stared. "Who is?"

"Nelson. Nelson's a bastard."

The other boy shrugged, not understanding. "Where you going now, Will?"

Will didn't know. But he knew he wasn't ready to go home. Not tonight. He wouldn't be able to sleep, with so much happening or about to happen, in this place where nothing ever did happen.

A truck roared on the other side of the square. The driver leaned out.

"Hey, boys! Want a lift?"

Will and Tom Folsom ran across. "Yeah, where you going?"

"Home. St. Elizabeth's. You live out that way?"

"Yeah," Will said.

"Hop in back, then. I've got a crate of chickens on the front seat. Holler when you want to drop off."

"How'll we get back?" Tom whispered as they started out of town.

"I don't know. Get another lift, maybe. Or walk if I have to. Anyway, I'm in no hurry to get home."

The words were careless and grand. Tom looked at him with respect.

The truck, an open pickup, careened through the countryside, through tunnels of trees; the headlights, like two feelers, pierced the night ahead. Behind lay only darkness, dark sky over darker land. The wind raced through Will's hair; it seemed to him that he was flying, that he was powerful and could go anywhere, do anything.

At a crossroads, the driver slowed and craned his head around.

"Look there! Jesus, they sure broke that up!"

The police station had been smashed. The door had been kicked in and lay now on the grass along with a little pile of broken desks and chairs. Just beyond, where a row of cabins stretched on both sides, lights were on and people were gathered outside, far past the hour at which such villages were usually asleep. Will was wide awake.

"What's going on?" he called to the driver.

"Folks got mad, is all. You'll see two, three more like that along this road. And burned-out cane, probably too dark to see."

Tom wanted to know how far they were going. Scared, Will thought contemptuously.

Suddenly they stopped. "Hey, look there!"

At the edge of the road, half in the deep ditch, a truck lay on its side, its load of bananas flung into the road.

"I heard about that," the driver said. "Happened this morning. Fellow near here up at Eleuthera hired some Caribs off the reservation to carry his bananas to the boat." He laughed. "Straightened them out, all right."

Eleuthera. Lawns and flowers and pride.

"I turn off here, boys, road to Myrtle. You two didn't say how far you're going."

Something decided itself in Will. He could not have said why. Simply, it clicked. "I'll get off now. Got a friend lives just down the road."

"Let's go on to Myrtle," Tom said. "We can get a ride back from there. Come on with me, Will. It's late. I want to get home."

But Will had already swung down, so Tom followed. When the truck had turned out of sight, Will reversed his direction, toward Eleuthera. Plodding along through the empty night he struggled with his thoughts. Something had happened there today between Patrick and Mr. Luther; he wondered whether the overturned banana truck had anything to do with it. Patrick being the easygoing fool he was, most likely the argument was Luther's fault, he reflected. But however it had been, it was no concern of his.

"Where the heck you going, Will?" Tom complained. "I'm tired."

"Nobody asked you to come, did they? So put up or shut up, will you?"

The night was soft. The commotion in Covetown might have been taking place in another world. When Will's foot kicked a little stone, its clatter startled the silence. Alongside the road, behind a wire fence, he could make out the shapes of resting cattle. The air smelled sweetly of vanilla and hay. Stopping, he took a long, long breath. He walked on, with Tom padding silently behind. Still he did not know why he was walking, why he had come here.

A few minutes later he rounded a bend. And there it lay. To his right on a little knoll stood the house; for an instant, as the moon struck through dark and mounting clouds, its white columns glis-

tened. Once when Patrick had brought him, he'd been given lemonade on that veranda. He remembered the woman of the house; she'd
worn a lace collar and had been polite, but he had hated her. He stood
there now, remembering.

A wind rose suddenly, making a sea sound in the trees. Below on
his left the sea was making wind sounds; pale gray it gleamed; in a
shaft of moonlight he saw a wave shatter itself upon the distant rocks.
It was more beautiful than anything he had ever seen: beautiful, all
of it, the water, the wind, the fragrance, and the stillness. Beauty like
that could give you pain. And it could make you angry at yourself for
feeling so. Angry. Angry.

Now again, clouds covered all the silver. It is going to storm, Will
thought. In the house there were no lights. Yes, one, in an upstairs
window. Bastards getting ready for bed. He stood looking at the
window. Then he walked slowly up the path. He had no idea why,
or what he wanted except just to look. Between hibiscus hedges he
moved nearer.

A dog barked and another joined in. You could tell by the yapping
that they were little dogs, some sort of silly pets.

"Quiet!" he heard a man's voice say. It was so still that the voice
carried clearly over the rustling wind.

Will waited. For a moment or two a woman's shape appeared at
the window, too far away to be recognizable, if he had known her. All
he could sense was remoteness; beyond reach, in some long pale
garment, cloud-white, flower-white, she stood high. Perfumed, he
thought, cushioned like one of those jewels in a velvet box in Da
Cunha's window. And his brain, which was so keen tonight, so filled
with jumping images, brought him inexplicably the smell of kerosene
burning in a battered lamp on an oilcloth-covered table in a littered
hut. What would that woman up there know or care about that hut?

And he stood there, leaning against a tree, with his hands thrust
into his pockets, watching that window even after she had gone. One
pocket held a broken cigarette, left over from a secret smoking session
in the shed. Also, there was a full book of matches. These he took out,
turning them over in his hand. He fondled them. Then he had a queer

thought, which he pushed away. The thought came back. It jumped in his head. And the tingling began again, just as it had in Covetown earlier, when he'd been running and the ambulance had clanged and glass had shattered. Once more his feet danced; hot excitement poured; it was wild, it was joyous, it was angry. Why not? Oh, why not? Be damned to everything. Why not?

And laughing now, laughing silently from deep in his chest, keeping out of the path of light that beamed from the bedroom, he crept toward the house. There was here, unmistakably, the smell of fresh paint. Under a downstairs window, which was ajar, a couple of painters' cloths had been left lying on the grass. He picked them up to smell them. Yes, turpentine and paint.

It was so easy! Some of the biggest things you could do were sometimes so ridiculously easy! Just shove the cloths in at the windows where they would touch the blowing curtains, then strike the match. That's all you had to do.

Frightened and fascinated, Tom watched. "What are you doing, Will? What are you doing that for?"

"Because I want to, fool. And if you ever," he whispered fiercely, "if you ever open your mouth I'll say we planned this together and you'll be—"

"Will, Will! You can trust me! What do you think I am? I swear I'll never—"

The fire ran up the edge of the curtain. Too bad they couldn't stay to watch! They sped down the driveway. Three or four miles down the coast, past the junction to Moorhead, they could probably pick up a lift. If anyone should ask, it would be plausible to say they'd been at Moorhead. And that was all there was to it. The last thing they heard when they reached the end of the drive was the shrill commotion of the dogs.

"Useless little things, Pekingese," Richard says. "I wish they'd stop yapping downstairs." He waits for a comment.

"I suppose they miss Marjorie," Tee replies.

She has gone to bed early because of a headache. Richard offers aspirin, and thanking him, she takes it. But aspirin will not assuage this ache. This is a terrible, terrible pain. She does not recognize herself through the chaos of such pain.

She is wracked with shame. Shame because of having borne him or because of having denied him? Truly, she does not know. She is heavy with pity for his young pride, the pride of Patrick Courzon. But her mouth is dry with fear. She scourges herself for her fear. Yet it is there all the same.

He'll come back into your life, Agnes told me. *Someday,* she said. Wise and good. Honest and strong. Agnes, who saved me.

Cursed, she thinks, oh cursed, like the island itself that I loved so much, as Père loved it, as Francis does and as now, so it seems, does—he!

How tough he was this afternoon! Tough and solid as Père. Everything intensifies in this isolation, this extravagance of light and heat. Anger is harder, grief is sharper and desire more keen.

Strange it is, although one's heard it often enough, that nothing can ever be forgotten. One buries and covers over, layer upon layer, but in the end it is no use, there are all those secret cells in the brain which remember even when one doesn't want to. Now, not piece by gradual piece, but instantly, "as in a blinding light," one sees . . .

Rape, you say? Attack? Yes, and also no. The happiness of that summer! Sun and wind and poetry. The astonishment of discovering one's own mind reflected in another's. How ignorant, how wise, how daring, and how young!

She took his hand and held it. The parrot, flashing royal blue and emerald and gold, fled upward into noontime silence. "I'll never forget you for this," she said, or something like that. She took his hand, she looked with tenderness into his face.

Attack, you say?

And that is what happened when she was fifteen, knowing nothing, but feeling everything, feeling what she had never felt before, or since.

Richard comes in from the bathroom to ask again how she is.

"Better," she lies, for her head is hot, and under the blanket she is shivering. She turns and twists on the pillow, her cheek rubbing her spread hair. *Aphrodisiac, said Anatole.*

"A very attractive room," Richard remarks.

"Red and white," she says. "Cheerful." He expects an answer. Yet it is good to keep talking of easy, banal things; it is a way to keep rooted in reality, as, when someone is hideously dying in the house, it helps to make coffee and slice bread.

"Not red and white," Richard corrects. He has such a fine, critical eye! "It's far more subtle. Crimson and cream. Those are Chinese peonies, you know."

He picks up the telephone and shakes it. There is neither hum nor buzz. "Seems to have gone dead. I've been trying it downstairs for the last half hour. I suppose it has something to do with the strike."

"I suppose."

"I'd like to know what's happening at the hospital. Our first grandchild," he says, with marvel in his voice.

Gone domestic now, in middle age, she thinks, not unkindly. Reformed. All the zest gone out of him, just leaked away. I never knew him, really. Maybe there was never much to know. He was always thinking of something else, someplace else, when you tried to talk to him. Only art moves him. I never did. Maybe it was my fault. But maybe no one else ever moved him, either.

"Francis says the doctor's excellent, trained in London. The first child is the hardest, of course. Although yours took no time at all, did it? But then, you were so young."

Lived a whole life like two strangers, he and I, and had all those children. A pair of friendly strangers, living side by side, but separately. Yes, for a long time I tried to make a union of us two, something solid and warm. I wanted it. I needed it. Only it didn't happen. So we speak now of common, daily things and I have known quiet happiness of a sort, yet there is always the silence, the secret silence, which he is not even aware of.

What if he were to be told *who I am*?

"Survive," Marcelle said. Hers was a lesson of cunning and courage. It has served well. Yet there is another courage that goes not with cunning but with truth.

"Richard," I shall say, "Richard, listen to me, there is something I must tell you—"

He is taking off his shoes. The room has gone pink in the lamplight. If I should speak those words, the peonies would explode into shredded petals on the floor and the lamps would shatter.

"I was thinking about that speech this afternoon," Richard says, taking off his shoes. "The fellow was eloquent, wasn't he? Must have had a fine education. In England, I imagine, on account of the accent. He was practically white, too. Must be hard for a person like that."

She thinks, Surely he had Père's nose, as Agnes said? Surely he looks a little bit like Francis?

Something dares her. Maybe she is losing her mind. But she walks to the edge of the precipice.

"Did you think he looked something like our family? My family?"

"Good God, no! What kind of an idea is that?"

"I thought maybe he did." It is like playing Russian roulette. Shall I? Shall I wait till morning or shall I never at all?

"You need to have your eyes examined." Richard yawns. "What are those two ridiculous dogs yapping at again?"

"The barn cats' prowling, I guess."

He calls the dogs upstairs. He strokes them and quiets them, then he gets into bed.

"That wind!" he complains. "I didn't know it could blow like that here."

"It's a northeast trade. I'll lower the windows a bit."

She gets up and stands for a moment looking northward to the Big Dipper.

"Eerie," she says, thinking aloud.

"What did you say? Eerie?"

"Yes. The way the night just drops down."

She goes back to bed. By his breathing she knows that Richard has fallen asleep at once. She is sorry for him because of what she must —might?—do to him in the morning. To him and all of them. If only there were some way of knowing what was right to do! It is this island that is at fault; one can't even think straight here!

The sad wind cries in the trees. She remembers these nights, the croak and peep and shrill of forest life, the sudden squeal of a small wild creature seized in bloody terror by some larger creature; all these have stayed with her except the sadness of the wind. She has forgotten how it blows all night off the Morne.

This will be a night without sleep. She does not even try to coax it. When morning flickers on the ceiling and birds rustle, she will be still awake. Perhaps, by that time, an answer will have been given her. She prays mercy for all who lie awake hoping for an answer by morning.

Perhaps, though, she dozes after all, or is so drowned in her trouble that it seems a sort of sleep. She starts up, aware of a change in the texture of the night. There is a sound of swishing under the wind rush. It is like footsteps in tall grass or tissue paper crackling lightly in a box. She thinks maybe Richard is making the sound, but he is lying quite still on his side in the other bed. A storm must be rising. She sinks back into crowding thoughts.

After a while she hears the roar of surf. That's odd, because the house is too far from the beach for surf to be heard. It puzzles her, but not too much. She is too tired. She turns again into herself.

Suddenly then, unmistakably, there is the salty tang of smoke. There is a new sound, a sizzle and snap as of meat frying and jumping in a pan. She gets out of bed and stands unsurely, dizzily, in the center of the room, trying to orient herself. Something is burning somewhere. Then all at once she understands. Jolted to panic, she rushes to the bedroom door and tears it open. A gust of incredible heat, like an eruption of the sun, flings her backward into the room. The entire hall and the stairway are blazing! Smoke flames into her lungs. With frantic force she tries to push the door shut, but the strength of the roaring heat is like the strength of a hundred men. She fights to breathe. Now the flames catapult into the room. They are taller than soldiers; they are an army advancing with their fearful weapons drawn. They catch the sheer curtains and the carpet; they reach for the ruffled shoulders of her nightdress and her long black hair. Her lungs are agony.

"Richard!" she screams.

Barely awake, he stumbles to the window, pushes the screen out and her out after it. There is a terrible mingling of cries in her ears, his as the sweeping fire sets him ablaze, and her own as she escapes it, to fall in fainting terror onto the net of the ancient boxwood hedge beneath the window.

Fifteen

D_{R.} Strand's private clinic lay on the outskirts of Covetown, above Government House. For fourteen hours Francis had been there, waiting. He had paced, attempted to read, and briefly, lightly, dozed. Now at midnight he stood at the window, looking down upon the harbor and the moving lights of cars.

The doctor came from across the hall with another report. "We're monitoring her pressure, Mr. Luther, and it's holding. She's fairly comfortable right now. The medication, you know."

Francis, wondering whether his confidence in the doctor was justified, nodded. The man had a good reputation and gray hair, which always bred a certain amount of confidence in the beholder.

"We've time yet to make the decision. Naturally, I'll avoid a cesarean section if I can."

One must have seen hundreds of cartoons and jokes about young husbands waiting outside delivery rooms. For some reason people found humor in the situation, God knew why, when in reality a man's head was plagued with doubts and questions. Some men must be torn with love of their wives and fear for them, while some would be praying first for the safe arrival of the child, though that was wrong, wrong, wrong . . .

"A good patient, plenty of courage," Dr. Strand was saying. "She wants this baby. No complaints, not a murmur out of her. A woman of pride."

"Yes, great pride."

But suppose this were Kate's child? Guilt ran hot and cold down his spine; his spine was naked, all of him was naked and exposed.

He hadn't been with Kate that often, a dozen times perhaps since Marjorie's pregnancy, not counting the time they had flown to a hotel in Barbados together. All night long the wind had rattled lightly in the palms. He'd got her a bouquet of gardenias—they grew almost wild down here—whose musky sweetness, reminding him of something, had kept him awake. It had reminded him of his father. Yes, yes. *(Don't tell your mother, son; I wouldn't hurt her for the world.)* And he hadn't hurt her. He hadn't walked out on his children, either. But then, his woman had not been Kate.

What do we ever know about anyone? he wondered now. I'd given up believing that my mother would ever come to St. Felice. For what subtle reasons, out of what fears she stayed away so long surely I never knew; maybe she herself never knew. His thoughts spun, driving, hurling him from Marjorie to Kate, back to his parents and to the child now struggling to be born. Oh, let it be safe and well, let it be a son who will be to me what my father and I never could be to each other!

He hadn't realized he was holding his head in his hands until the doctor touched him on the shoulder.

"You need a drink. If it weren't worth one's life out in the streets I'd go get you one."

At once he became alert. "What's happening? Have you heard?"

"Riots and demonstrations all over the island. A big tax protest over in Princess Mary parish. Somebody fired on the police, they fired back, and there were three killed, some wounded. More over at the south end too, I think. Anyway, Lord Frame expected this a week ago, it seems. There's a cruiser on the way from Bermuda with a detachment of troops. That'll straighten things out, if," the doctor finished glumly, "if they get here in time. Why don't you stretch out on the couch? I'll be back."

Francis lay down again. He was deeply tired. Far easier to labor in a field than to endure such pressure in the head and spirit! This could be disaster night, he thought, recalling old tales of rebellion, the night of the sword. Attempting to console himself, he reasoned that that sort of thing didn't fit the twentieth century, and was immediately aware of his own absurdity. Not fit the century of Hitler and Stalin?

He woke to the sound of rustling. In the lamplight, on the other side of the room, Lionel was reading. He moved his lips and strained his neck over the newspaper as a man does who is not accustomed to reading.

"Hello. Have you been here long?" Francis asked.

"Only a few minutes. I ran the gauntlet. The governor's declared martial law. The town's full of rioting drunks and scared merchants and planters who've rushed in from the country, afraid to be out there alone. Cade's Hotel is jammed. How's Marjorie doing?"

"We don't know yet. They'll probably have to operate. It's awfully good of you to be here, Lionel."

"That's all right. Family, after all. Besides, I happen to be fond of Marjorie."

"Well, she likes you, too."

I must be better at dissembling than I knew, Francis thought. He felt—he felt sly, in the presence of this bluff, bumbling man, having to hide his sometimes furious jealousy that the man had lived with Kate and "had" her. "Had." An antique, yet still expressive, use of that simple verb. Had. Possessed. Her dear flesh.

He became aware that Lionel was looking at him quizzically.

"Damned hard for you, Francis. May I say something frankly?"

"Yes, of course."

"I know about you and Kate. Don't ask me how. People find out things."

"I won't ask."

"That's what I meant by 'hard for you.'"

"Yes." And hearing his own laconic voice, like that of a stage Englishman, Francis thought, I don't know what else to say.

"If you had seen her first instead of—" Lionel began and stopped.

Instead of Marjorie? Oh, if only—! But it might not have made any difference if he had. Too young, without experience and so in awe of beauty, he had not been half the man he was now. And so the lovely, brief enchantment had simply slid away as imperceptibly as the change of seasons in a northern country.

"She would have been right for you," Lionel resumed. Not meaning to, he was twisting the knife. "What are you going to do?"

"Oh, God," Francis said and murmured, "We've a child now."

Lionel nodded. "Of course. And you don't want to smash Marjorie's world. Well, you can have it both ways, can't you? The family at Eleuthera and the little place in town. It's done all the time."

Kate had already offered that. Better than nothing, she'd said. But she ought to have more.

And he said so. "Kate deserves more. For that matter, so does Marjorie."

Lionel smiled. There was kindness and a certain amusement in the smile.

"You're really in a moral bind, aren't you, old man? I'm sorry for you. You know, I always have felt a little sorry for you, anyway. You take everything too seriously, too hard and heavy. I suppose you can't help it."

"I guess not."

"We both know I'm a rougher sort than you. I don't seem to feel about a lot of things the way you do. You suffer. To me you're a little soft in the head. Oh, I like you in spite of it, make no mistake! It's just that I think you'd be a whole lot better off if you stopped worrying about other people so much and looked out for yourself."

"Maybe you're right."

Words, words! You are what you are, and Francis could no more be Lionel than Lionel could be Francis. Still, he had looked out for himself that morning, hadn't he? Or perhaps it had not been on his own behalf that he had issued that defiant order to get the crop out; perhaps really it had been because he was now thinking of the child, of money and safety for his child. Already it made a difference. He hadn't yet seen its face, but it made a difference.

Lionel returned to the newspaper. And Francis sat on, straining for sounds from across the hall which might have meaning, but there were only passing footsteps, conveying nothing. He studied a row of "arty" photographs on the wall: horses knee-deep in pangola grass, which made him think of Kate; veranda columns casting shadows, as at Eleuthera; black children in a schoolyard, as at Gully, where he had first met Patrick . . .

The lights went out.

"Must have struck the power station," Lionel said. "They've already struck the phones, you know."

A nurse came in with a pair of oil lamps.

"There are fires all over the parish," she reported. "Our handyman just came in the back way and he says they've attacked the wireless station with stones and bottles, broken every window, smashed all the equipment."

They won't attack Eleuthera! Francis thought. They won't go after private homes. Besides, it's so far out of the way. He said aloud, "I had a hassle this morning." And he told Lionel what had happened earlier in the day. "I wish there was a phone, though. I'd like to find out what happened, whether they got any of the crop out."

Lionel shook his head. "You took a chance. Not that I blame you. Damned radical devils! So much for your fine friend Patrick, hey?"

"I don't know. I was mad as a hornet, but I've cooled off some. It's possible he really couldn't do anything, although I still think he could have bestirred himself a little for me."

"There you go, making excuses for everybody! Matter of fact, on my way here tonight somebody told me Courzon was out your way this afternoon giving a very inflammatory speech. Egging the crowd on to pillage and burn, he said."

Francis shook his head. "No. Impossible. That I won't believe."

Lionel shrugged.

"You don't have to stay here with me," Francis said considerately.

"It's safer here. Wouldn't dare go down into the streets now. Besides, where would I go? The hotel's full and so's the club."

The two men waited, one sleeping with his head back on the chair, the other wide awake, watching the maddening, slow advance of the hours. It was the longest night. The oil lamp flickered weakly. The silence was expectant; one awaited gunfire, and the crashing-in of doors, sounds that must surely explode in the next moment or two; one imagined also dreadful, perhaps final, things occurring in the room across the hall.

In the last hour of the night when, in spite of darkness, some subtle alteration of the atmosphere predicts the dawn, the doctor came back. He looked both weary and pleased to bring an announcement of importance.

"A natural birth. Hard, but we didn't need to operate, thank goodness. Come in and see them now."

Not yet out of ether, Marjorie lay with a look of peace on her lips, as if, in spite of her pains, she had gone under with a smile. Her hair curled on her temples as it always did when it was damp. She must have been soaked with the sweat of her struggle.

"She wanted this baby," Dr. Strand said, "and she fought for it."

Francis felt his tears collecting. "I'm so glad," he murmured foolishly. Or perhaps not foolishly: what else was there to feel but simple gladness? He smiled, for once not ashamed—he knew he cried too easily for a man from a northern culture—to let another man see his tears. He reached down and touched Marjorie's limp hand. She would be a good mother, too fussy, no doubt, as she always was, but a good mother, all the same.

"I'm so glad," he repeated.

"Don't you want to see the baby? She's down the hall."

"She? I thought you said—"

"I didn't say anything. You must have imagined it. Why, were you expecting a boy?"

"Well, I thought—" He stopped. He was as disappointed as a child who has been expecting a bicycle for his birthday and has been given a book.

"Sorry, but you've got a girl. A pretty one, with a cleft in her chin. Big, too, which was part of the trouble. Here, have a look."

She had her mother's dark hair, a whole head of it.

"Enough to tie a ribbon on," the nurse said.

Francis stammered. "Aren't they usually bald?"

"Usually." The doctor laughed. "I told you she was pretty. You'll have your hands full when she's sixteen."

"A girl," Francis said.

"She'll mean more to you than ten sons. Take my word for it. You'll come back and tell me so."

Well, true or not, she can't help it, he thought. And he reached down to touch the baby's hand, as he had the mother's. The scrap of a hand was warm to his touch. The fingers grasped his finger. Only a few minutes out of the womb, where it had been hanging upside down, a feeble creature floating in warm water, and here it was already making a demand of life! The fingers clung. He had the strangest feeling in his chest, in his throat. And he would not have pulled his hand away if the nurse hadn't put the baby back in the crib. . . .

In the waiting room Lionel looked up with a question.

"A girl," Francis told him. "And both well."

"Are they, then? Well, good luck, old man! And here's another good omen for you. Come and behold."

In three-quarter darkness the cruiser rounded proudly to port, lights glittering and gleaming from stem to stern. It seemed to fill the harbor with its authority.

"So," Lionel said, "that settles that. It's been a long night on both counts."

"Yes, both counts. Mother and baby," said Dr. Strand, who was literal.

"I meant," Lionel corrected him, "I meant the birth *and* our small revolt. In a few more hours, now that the troops are here, we'll have peace and order again, thank God."

"No, my friend, you haven't seen the end of this by any means," the doctor cautioned.

"You think not?"

"Oh, yes, for now, but this was only a skirmish. I'm looking ahead a few years. Yes, I'm looking ahead."

But Lionel was concerned with the immediate. "You're not starting home yet, Francis? Things can't be calmed down this soon."

"I want to get home and sleep. I could sleep for a week."

"Well, just be careful. It's been a long night, that's sure. Just be careful."

The morning was almost still. In the mild breeze small ash puffs rose from a bed of cinders where the new wing had been. Only a few feet from the central portion of the house a miraculous and mighty rain had halted the fire.

"If only it had come sooner!" Osborne lamented. "We tried using the well, but the pump was too weak. And we couldn't stretch the hose from the river. We fought with buckets, we tried everything, Mr. Luther. My wife came out, and the maids and everybody. We almost killed ourselves trying."

"You did what you could," Francis said quietly.

"That fire went wild! I wouldn't believe it if I hadn't seen it myself. Of course, the wind was against us. That and the fresh paint. Thank God, though, the rain came, or we'd have lost the whole house."

Nothing, nothing was left of the new wing but some twists of metal —andirons or candelabra, perhaps.

"Terrible," Osborne said. "Terrible." He spoke with awe.

All that morning and all the day before people had been talking at Francis. Thinking to give comfort, they seemed compelled to talk.

"By God, I wish I knew how this happened, Mr. Luther! It was the only house on the island to be fired! Oh, some cane fields here and there went up, but that's to be expected at a time like this. We haven't seen a house burned, though, not since I was born and probably a time before that."

"No," Francis said. He had a pain in his chest. He wondered

whether anyone as young as he could have a heart attack from grief. He couldn't afford to have a heart attack, leaving Marjorie with an infant in this chaos.

Osborne lowered his voice. "I keep asking myself, to be frank with you, whether it wasn't on account of the bananas. We got one load through the gates before the crowd could stop us. They were pretty mad, let me tell you! Still, I'd swear it wasn't any of our own people. Sure, they'd overturn a truck, but they wouldn't do a thing like this. There were a lot of gangs in town setting fires, you know, kids no more than fourteen years old, they tell me. Wild kids, slippery as eels. They'll never catch them."

For the first time in hours thought took shape in Francis' numbed brain.

"Not kids from town. Why would they come way out here to pick just my house? It doesn't make sense! No, it has to have been the strikers, Osborne, maybe not Eleuthera people, but hotheads from other villages. My uncle told me they'd been steamed up to pillage and burn. Why, there was a radical meeting right here in this parish, not two miles from our gates! I didn't believe him when he told me, but I do now. Because—here's the result."

Osborne did not comment. Instead, he held out his hand to catch a flurry of drops that had suddenly fallen out of the calm, bright sky. "Sun-shower," he said.

A rag had blown from the fire onto the grass. Scorched at the edges, the center still disclosed an arabesque of buds. Recognizing the fabric that Marjorie had had sent from New York, Francis bent to pick it up. How she had labored over her choices! The decoration of these new rooms had been the gladdest thing in her life here until her pregnancy.

He rubbed the cloth between his fingers. His father had died while that cloth flamed. A living torch, he had been extinguished among red and white Chinese peonies. Gone now were all the gaiety and kindness, the generosity and the foolish weakness; no one need fret or worry about him ever again. Bound and bandaged, his mother lay stunned into silence as if she had not yet assimilated the disaster, or as if she were remembering her own reluctance to come back here. It was only because of me that she came, Francis thought, over and over.

The sun-shower sprinkled his shoulders. For a long time he stood there crying in the warm, quiet rain.

Sixteen

IN later years these events would
be described by someone with a gift for imaginative language, someone, for instance, like Kate Tarbox, as a series of shock waves come
and gone in a handful of days. There was, first, the shock of death,
death of the innocent at Eleuthera, and then those killed in confrontations between police and citizens, along with one lone soldier from
the cruiser, an ignorant lad shot by a wild bullet on his first trip out
of England. But the greatest shock came from realizing the extent of
anger, its depth, and the speed with which it could spread.

To be sure, the cruiser stood firm guard in the harbor. Order was
restored. Shattered glass was cleared away and people went back to
work. Passing on the roads and in the streets they gave greeting again
as before; yet one had to wonder what rages and resentments still
burned beneath the greeting.

All this passed outside of Francis' awareness. Beclouded, he moved
through required hours and places. From the memorial service—that
is to say, the funeral without the body of the dead—he went to the
hospital. There Marjorie, half hysterical with fear and horror, alternately trembled, wept, and consoled herself with her new baby.
There, down the hall, his mother, winning a valiant struggle for

acceptance and control, recovered from burn and shock. Most of the time he sat at home in the cocoon of his library, staring at grief, which seemed to hover just beyond the window like some threatening, faceless dervish in whirling robes, waiting to descend and clutch.

He was sitting there like that when Kate came in.

"Oh, my darling," she said.

He put his head on her breast. Her fingers moved in his hair.

"Oh, my darling, What can I do for you?"

"Just stay here. Be with me."

"Yes, yes. I am. I will."

Opening his eyes, he saw the little rise and fall of her breast. Her neck and upper arms were scarlet.

"You're sunburned," he murmured.

"I was weeding. I should have worn a jacket."

He raised his head, reproaching. "You're so tired. You don't take care of yourself."

"It's just that I haven't slept. How could I sleep when all this was happening to you?"

Her eyes were troubled. Darkened, they were almost violet, a morbid color, color of pain.

"You love me," he said, as if the discovery were new. "You love me."

She swallowed hard. He could see the small lump move in her throat.

He had never been so near to another human being in all his life, so near that the very blood in their veins seemed to run together. And suddenly desire, which had been the farthest from his mind during these last hours, tore him into its current.

He got up and drew the curtains shut, making a wall of rippling green. The room, now dimmed, assumed an aqueous coolness, a forest coolness.

"Lie down," he said. "Take your dress off."

"Now? In here?"

"It's all right. I can lock the door."

Elsewhere in the house he would not have taken her. Some subtlety of judgment, some refinement of choice, would not allow him to do this thing in any room that had been adorned by Marjorie, in which her presence remained as though she herself were standing in it. He could not have done that to Marjorie, to Kate—or to himself. But this room belonged to him alone and there was no one here except himself, with Kate.

In her now he found all comfort and all healing.

Afterwards they lay quietly, not speaking. Slowly, the ceiling turned from white to a luminous gray.

"It's getting late," she said. She sat up and put on her dress, then pulled the curtains back so that light slid across the floor.

Francis looked out the window. The whirling specter was gone; no threat was there, only the afternoon lying placidly among the trees.

"Did you know—could you have known—how I needed you?" he asked.

A smile began as a tender curving at the corners of her mouth and almost as quickly stopped. Her face fell into sadness.

"What is it?" he cried.

Her reply was so low that he barely heard her. "Suddenly I feel guilty. I don't know why. I've not felt that way before. It's this house, I suppose. Being here like this in her house."

It angered him that any shame should blight them, yet he didn't know what to say.

"Do you—don't you feel what I mean, Francis?"

"I don't know. I suppose I should. I don't know."

He unlocked the door and poured a drink from the bar in the cabinet.

"Have one? It'll steady you."

"No, thanks. Tell me about the baby, please." She had begun to steady herself.

At once laughter tingled in his throat. "She's pretty. . . . Funny how I wanted a boy. Maybe men always do? But now I don't mind at all. Her name's Megan. It's Welsh. Her mother's people were Welsh."

"I'd like to give her a wonderful present. May I?"

"Of course you may! Why do you ask? Why shouldn't you?"

"I don't know. I thought maybe, in the circumstances, it might not be—"

The laughter left him. "Oh Kate, Kate my love, why can't things ever be clean and clear and easy? Everything's such a goddamned tangle!"

"But we'll manage, won't we?"

"I've done this to you. I've complicated your life."

"No. You've brought life into my life. I'm sorry I felt grim there for a minute. I won't let it happen again. One has to—to take charge." And, jingling her car keys, she told him, "The first thing I'm going to do is buy Megan's present. The next thing—oh, I hate to pile another trouble on you, I wasn't even going to mention it, but I've no one else to ask, at least not until Nicholas Mebane gets back, and that won't be till tomorrow night, and it would be a shame to wait that long—"

"What are you talking about?"

Kate sat down again. "They arrested Patrick this morning."

Francis' heart jumped a beat.

"Can you imagine anything so idiotic, so criminal? Some utter ass must have decided to cast a net out for anyone and everyone who's ever opened his mouth to express an opinion! 'Incitement to riot!' Patrick of all people!"

He wet his lips. "What did you want of me?"

"Bail money. I'm awfully short or I'd never come bothering you with all you've got on your mind. I just hate to see a man like Patrick spend a night locked up, that's all."

He couldn't believe what he was hearing. And he tried to speak without betraying outrage.

"For my part they can hang him tonight," he said in a flat voice.

Kate stared. "You can't mean that?"

"My father was burned alive in my house, and my mother escaped by the grace of a miracle; you ask me whether I mean it?"

"It wasn't Patrick's doing, Francis! For God's sake, you don't think he crept out here that night and put a torch to your house, do you?"

"His were the brains behind the hands that did it. You can't tell me otherwise."

"I sure as hell can tell you! And I sure as hell will!" Kate's indignation crackled.

"He is not the man we thought he was. Open your eyes—"

"Maybe not the man *you* thought, but—"

"He could have helped me save my crop! At least he could have made an attempt. But he refused. And after that went about giving inflammatory speeches right at my doorstep. He knew the temper of the people, but instead of protecting me, his friend, he whipped them up—"

"Inflammatory speeches! He couldn't give one if he tried! He wouldn't know how to inflame anyone, he talks way over most people's heads, like a schoolteacher. If he ever wants to go into politics he'll have to learn to do better, let me tell you."

"He did well enough, apparently. Lionel told me—"

"Lionel!" Kate's scorn was hot. "Oh, *now* I see the connection! So it's Lionel who put his words in at Covetown, he's the one who's responsible! So he's turned out to be a rotten informer—I really never thought he'd stoop *that* low, no, I didn't!" She got up, snapping and unsnapping the clasp of her purse. "Francis, listen to me. Listen to me. To me; not Lionel!"

He didn't hear her. He was hearing, instead, Patrick Courzon's cool voice: "You're too feudal for these times." He was hearing Osborne's lament: "We did all we could, Mr. Luther." He was standing in mournful rain looking at cinders where his proud house had been.

"Bastard!" he cried. "Dirty, arrogant, ungrateful bastard! And you actually came here to plead for him! Is that why you came? Not to be with me, but because you were thinking of him?"

She was dismayed. "You don't mean that. You know I came for you! But I did think I could also ask you to help one of the best human beings you or I will ever know. I certainly didn't dream you had any crazy idea like this in your head."

"Crazy? It's one thing to have understanding, Kate, to be compassionate, to be"—in the turbulence of his anger he stammered—"to be *liberal*, but you carry it too far; you'll excuse anything in one of your underdog protégés. Arson. Murder. Anything!"

She put a hand on his arm. "Francis. Please. You're not talking sense. Don't fight with me. This is us, Francis and Kate."

"No, Kate. You can't get around me that way. I've had a blow between the eyes. Life doesn't hand out many blows like the one I've had this week," he said bitterly.

"Don't you suppose I know that? But we're talking about two different things."

"We're not. It's the same thing. You're making a hero out of someone who's partially responsible for what I've suffered. That hurts me, Kate. I can't forgive it."

She withdrew her hand. Neither of them spoke for a minute or two. Sounds of awakening activity, a slammed door and voices from the kitchen wing, announced that the afternoon was late and time was hurrying.

"I would like to talk reasonably to you," Kate said at last.

"I'll talk reasonably. But first you have to be loyal to me," he said quietly.

"Even if it means stabbing a friend in the back? An innocent friend?"

"He's not innocent. That's the whole point."

"But if I think he is?"

Her very stance was stubborn, her proud head and shoulders defied him. More now than in her first flaring anger he felt the force of her will.

"You've built a stone wall," he said, with a tired gesture. "I can't get through to you."

"There's a wide door in that wall. It's your narrow-minded prejudice that won't let you open it."

"Prejudice! What the hell are you talking about? You know very well I'm not prejudiced."

"You don't think you are, but you are, Francis. Suddenly I see it. You were enraged that Patrick Courzon, a mere native, could refuse you, when he ought to be so grateful for your attentions that he'd turn himself inside out for you. And that's the real reason why you're blaming him."

He was exhausted, wounded, and baffled. That she could turn on him like this! That she could fail to comprehend what was so plain! Enraged, he went to the attack.

"You're a blind fool, Kate. A fool and a fanatic. I hate to tell you, but maybe Lionel does see you clearly, after all. Certainly he's known you longer and better than I have."

"That's a filthy thing to say! Damn you, Francis!" Her eyes threatened rage. "If you can say a thing like that, we have nothing in common. I don't want to cheapen myself, or I'd slam my fist into your mouth for saying that."

"Perhaps," he said, "perhaps you'd better leave. We're not on the same side, are we?"

She went to the door. "God knows I'm not on your side! And God help me, I never want to be!"

He heard her heels clack furiously down the hall, heard the door close and then the sound of the car starting down the drive. The sofa pillows were disarranged where they had lain together. Thoughtfully, he put them back in place. Everything had happened so quickly, all that enthralling beauty, that sweet ravishment, turned into this sick churning in the pit of him!

The one time, the only time he'd needed her total devotion, in the greatest crisis of his life, she'd drawn back, withholding a part of herself to give to the very man who had hurt him the most! So he hadn't known her, after all, had he? Nor had she known him.

We are ensnared and beguiled.

You are singing to yourself in your car on a fair day; you are at the pinnacle of health, but around a curve, on the other side of a hill, a moment later you are crippled and ruined in a heap of crumpled metal. Or you are talking to a friendly stranger in some pleasant place; you are laughing, having a drink together, but a moment later his face turns mad and he points a gun at you. That's the way it happens.

He went inside and took a shower and then, because he still felt dirty, took another. A supper had been prepared for him, but he was unable to swallow it. Brandy went down more easily. He had never drunk very much, but he took the bottle into his bedroom, wanting numbness, wanting forgetfulness, and kept on drinking. There was a whirling in his head. Fire soared and glass crashed; black men hurled murderous rocks and Patrick Courzon sneered; Kate's mouth twisted with contempt; Marjorie writhed on a hospital bed; his parents screamed for help; his mother's bruised eyes grieved. All whirled as the walls spun, until at last came vicious nausea, then exhaustion, and finally, sleep.

Patrick Courzon was released, of course, along with all the union leaders. Only those who had committed violence were sentenced. The magistrate, an Englishman in a white wig, facing a series of black barristers in the same white wigs, made a graceful little speech about freedom of speech and the right to strike. The centuries-old system of justice, transplanted from the foggy north to the dripping heat and fly-buzz of the Covetown courtroom, worked.

The strike had not been altogether a failure, either. Some two weeks after it had been put down, the planters met and agreed to improve the wage scale by fifteen percent, which was almost, but not quite, what the workers had asked for in the first place.

Ironically, the two people who could most nearly relate themselves to Francis' emotions were Lionel and Marjorie.

Even Father Baker could offer only platitudes in the form of kindly counsel. "I know it's unspeakable for you, Francis. But hatred corrupts the soul. For your own sake you must try to conquer it. Especially since we don't really know who the guilty ones are."

Putting in a roundabout plea for Courzon! And Francis gave cold dismissal: "I know perfectly well who they are, Father."

Nicholas Mebane offered an alibi and self-exoneration with his condolences. Almost at once upon arriving back in St. Felice, he had come hurrying to Eleuthera, bearing in hand a splendid silver bowl engraved with Megan's name, from Da Cunha's collection.

"I can't tell you how much I regret not having been home when this tragedy—when all this mess—occurred." His mobile face bore a solemn dignity. "Perhaps I shouldn't say it, but, well, I almost believe it wouldn't have happened if I'd been here."

"Then you agree with me? You're putting the blame where I put it?"

Mebane said delicately, "It's difficult. . . . I find myself between a rock and a hard place, as my father liked to say. Maybe I would have been able to get your crop out without upsetting any applecarts, or rather, banana carts." He smiled. "Then again, maybe I wouldn't. It all comes down to knowing how to handle people, doesn't it? That's the true art of politics, knowing when to give in and when to demand. It's never, never easy."

The true art of politics was also double-talk and evasion. Francis felt a slight impatience.

"I know that," he said.

"Personally, I don't think I would have permitted that speech so close to your gates. Still, having the utmost sympathy with your position—if I were in your place I would certainly feel the same— you'll understand, I hope, that I must make other considerations, too. Patrick and I are closely involved. I have spoken to him, I shall speak to him—"

"Not necessary," Francis interrupted. "What's done is done. So you needn't upset your own applecart on my account."

"The art of politics," Mebane repeated, "is the art of compromise. And judgment, always judgment! I'm afraid my friend Patrick still needs to learn that." He sighed. "I sometimes feel I'm walking a tightrope, Francis. I have the organization, building and building with a great public good in mind. So I must keep the balance there. Yet the last thing I want is to lose your friendship over this."

"It's all right," Francis said. "My opinion of Mr. Courzon and your opinion of him need not influence our opinion of each other. It's all right."

"I'm wonderfully relieved to hear that." Mebane rose. "I can't tell you how much. Perhaps some day all this will straighten out. Who knows?" He added quickly, "But the important thing is that you and

I are in a sense allied. We're both concerned with the future of this island, you as a producer, I, it's to be hoped, in government. And I think we understand each other."

Francis bowed his head in acknowledgment. "You will have my support when the time comes."

He meant it. Regardless of the double-talk—he was, after all, a politician!—Mebane was reasonable and decent, a practical man. One could talk to him. One had to respect him.

"If there is ever anything you need and I can do," Mebane said quietly, "you know where I am." His brown hand shook Francis' hand, his heavy gold ring bruising Francis' knuckles. "Your mother is coming along nicely, I'm glad to hear."

"Thank God, yes. I'm putting her on the plane to go home tomorrow."

"A stalwart lady. Give her my best, won't you? And the same to your wife. And the new young lady, by all means," he added in parting.

"That was Nicholas Mebane. See what he brought for Megan." Francis placed the bowl on the bed, where Marjorie sat propped against white lace pillows.

"Oh, gorgeous! Handmade Danish silver, Francis!" Marjorie's fingers slid around the bowl, moving carefully with the grain. She turned it upside down. "Yes, of course, look at the stamp. Danish."

"Very generous. Overly generous." Expensive presents made him uncomfortable. A holdover, probably, from his father's careless taste for luxury.

"Why not? He's terribly rich, everyone says. Anyway, I really do like Nicholas. I always have. And that Doris of his. One feels sorry for a girl as clever and good-looking as she is, having that handicap. Being black, I mean. So you see, I'm not the disgusting bigot you always thought I was, Francis. I just never liked Patrick, that's all. I saw him as a fuzzy-minded troublemaker from the start, you know I did. And I was right, wasn't I?" she finished triumphantly.

He didn't answer. God knew he couldn't feel her sense of satisfaction! Disillusioned both in a friend and a lover, he could hardly find cause for rejoicing. He was a man who had misread directions and strayed into a wilderness. He had been wrong; he had been wronged. It had all moved so fast! Bewildered, he tried to reconstruct events, but the pattern of events was overlaid by the red blur of anger: Kate's, Patrick's, and his own.

A terrible sense of loss overwhelmed him suddenly, so that his eyes stung with burgeoning tears, and to hide his grief, he bent to pat and rearrange Marjorie's fluffy pillows.

"You look absolutely done in. It's been so awful for you," Marjorie said softly. "There's only one thing that could be worse: to lose one's child."

He was grateful to her, grateful at this moment for any human touch, any gentle word. Yes, in a pinch, in this pinch, he had to admit, she had been there when he needed her. Dependable and sensible, she had measured up, even calming her own first hysterical demands to leave the island, even accepting at last his reassurances, his determination not to be driven away. Call it a sense of duty or propriety, call it a rigid code of outmoded behavior, call it what you would, he was grateful for it.

Now he must measure up, too, must pull himself together.

"Yes," he said, thinking aloud, "yes, you remember what my father said? 'Look out for number one. That's the first commandment,' he said. Number one being, in our case, three-in-one."

"Elementary, I should think."

"Not what they teach in Sunday school, though. Well, I'll start in on that Monday, my dear. I've a lot to make up for on account of that crop we lost. Miss Megan needs new shoes."

Marjorie laughed. "Isn't she the cutest thing, Francis?"

"I think she has the Francis nose."

"Nothing wrong with that." Marjorie yawned and stretched.

He could not remember when he had seen her so happy, so expansive, so *soft*. Maybe things would be different now. Maybe, through some miracle, newness and youth would come surging back. That other business, that other woman, had probably been just an aberration, common enough, Lord knew. The man who didn't have such aberrations was the oddball, really.

"Oh, I'm sleepy," Marjorie said luxuriously.

"Take a nap. Want a cold drink or anything?"

"Later, thanks. Some lemonade in an hour or so. You are good to me, Francis."

"A woman who can produce a baby like ours deserves the best," he answered lightly.

Contentment felt warm in him as he went out and softly closed the door. It was only when he was halfway down the stairs that he remembered, queerly enough, that they hadn't kissed each other once since he had brought Marjorie home.

The baby was in a cradle on the veranda. Francis was watching her while the nurse went indoors, when a car came to a halt on the gravel drive and Patrick Courzon came up the walk.

"I've come as soon as I could," he began. "Kate's told me things. I had to talk to you."

Francis did not invite him to sit down. Instead he himself got up and stood leaning against a pillar. "There's nothing to talk about," he said.

"Francis, I was sick when I heard what happened here."

Sick, was he, standing there with his bland condolences?

"Were you?" he said dryly.

"Kate says you're blaming me. And blaming her because of me. She says—"

"I don't want to hear what she says."

"It isn't fair not to give me a chance to talk."

"You're scarcely one to talk about fairness."

A flush, red bronze, mounted in the troubled pale brown cheeks. One could almost feel sorry for the poor bastard! But no, no! And Francis glanced at his baby, who had made a small sound in its cradle. If she had come a week sooner into the world, she too would have perished in choking smoke. And he felt again that awful outrage, that first sickness at the pit of his stomach.

"One doesn't just throw away relationships—" Courzon began.

"Don't tell me what 'one' does or doesn't do!"

"I'm only asking for a chance to straighten out the confusion in your mind."

The arrogance of the man! Having identified himself—and Kate, too, yes, she too—with the scum who had literally brought his house down about his head, to dare to speak of "confusion" in *his* mind! To dare!

"I've told you I have nothing to say to you. You're lucky I'm managing to keep my temper at all. I advise you to leave me alone."

"I'm sorry to hear that, Francis."

"Yes. Well. You had better go. You're not welcome here."

For long minutes he sat watching the dust that had spurted as Patrick gunned his car. He sat there until the dust had settled. His eyes moved across the drive to the fields where his sleek white Brahmans had gone into their afternoon rest. Far down on the left there gleamed a sliver of beach and an angle of glitter where the sun struck the sea. Behind the house the hill rose in tiers, green on green, bananas and palms and varied groves, on upward to the Morne's peak wrapped now in cotton cloud. His kingdom, his benevolent small kingdom! Let storms roar outside, let the social rats race and the politicians moil; here, in this kingdom, peace and a reasonable plenty would continue, if he had anything to do with it.

And unconsciously he stretched out his right arm, flexing the muscles. He looked down again at the sleeping baby. No one, no one, by God, should disturb her peace!

"Scum! Wretched scum!" he cried, so loud that the baby's eyelids trembled.

And contritely, tenderly, he bent to adjust by a hairbreadth the soft, white coverlet.

Seventeen

WITHIN three or four months Megan turned into a pretty child with remarkably fine dark blue eyes. They were both, Francis and Marjorie, a little bit crazy about her. But then, as everyone kindly remarked, it was only natural: they had waited so long and known so much disappointment before she finally came.

Francis kept saying that she had the family nose. He took a certain pleasure in that. Apparently it was a dominant characteristic; you couldn't breed it out. However, it was an attractive feature, giving a kind of pride to an adult face.

Marjorie ordered Megan's dresses from France, via Da Cunha's. From an expensive store in New York, via its catalog, came a marvelous pinto rocking horse the size of a small pony, a swing apparatus for the lawn, a dollhouse, and enough books to occupy the child to the age of ten. Yes, they were a little bit crazy and they knew it and they delighted in it.

She was almost two years old before they knew quite positively, or were forced to accept as a fact, that Megan was retarded.

Of course they resisted the knowledge as long as they could. An undesirable visitor knocks at the door and you do not open it; but when the knocking persists and the undesirable *will not* go away, the moment arrives when at last you open the door. So it happened to Marjorie and Francis.

At six months the baby didn't roll over. At nine months she didn't sit up or attempt to crawl, or say "mama" or laugh aloud. At one year she didn't even try to stand.

A woman at the club, one day when all the babies were playing in the wading pool, remarked quite seriously in Marjorie's hearing, "I can't imagine why they don't do something about that child. Look at her! She's just lying there like a vegetable!"

Megan was reclining in her stroller, content to do nothing. Her fair hair curled in the afternoon heat, which had flushed her face quite charmingly pink.

Alarmed and angry Marjorie reported to Francis what she had overheard.

"Some children are slower than others," he said. "It doesn't mean a thing. Haven't you read that Einstein didn't talk till he was three?" But with the thought of his sister Margaret, a terrible fear slid like cold slime down his back. And at the same time he knew that the fear had come quivering more than once during the last few months, had quivered and been put away.

"Maggie's had seven children and she'd certainly have noticed if there were anything wrong, wouldn't she?" Maggie was an upstairs maid who sometimes took care of Megan.

"I should think so. And certainly the doctor would have said something." He tried to reassure himself.

But certainly the doctor had said nothing, at least until they questioned him.

"I have had my thoughts about the baby," he admitted. "I've had them for quite a while."

Furiously, Francis attacked. "What do you mean? What thoughts? And why the secrecy?"

"To begin with, one wants to be sure. Children don't all mature according to textbook schedules. I didn't want to alarm you until it was necessary." An old man, and tired, he leaned back abruptly so that his chair squeaked into the waiting silence. "As a matter of fact, I don't want to *alarm* you at all, but I did intend to mention it at the next visit."

"It? It?" demanded Francis.

"A degree of retardation. What degree, I don't know."

Marjorie made a sound between a gasp and a cry. And Francis, flung back to the memory of Margaret, could not look at his wife.

"There's nothing actually to be done, anyway," the doctor said kindly, "except to watch developments. And to be patient and loving, which I know you are."

They knew then, that evil day, they knew. Yet they struggled to reject the knowledge. By the time they reached the gates of home they had made a hopeful decision.

"He's too old," Marjorie said, having wiped her first tears away. "He probably hasn't learned a new fact since he left medical school. We'll have to take Megan to someone at home."

"Home" was Boston and Baltimore and Philadelphia and New York. With each repetition of the story they lost a year of their youth.

"Don't tell them about your sister," Marjorie said. "It might prejudice their thinking. Let them evaluate Megan without prior judgments."

It was the first time she had spoken of his sister. That would be according to her code of good sportsmanship and courage: having married him with her eyes open, it would fit her ill to accuse him now. He looked at her with a certain awe. Sportsmanship! This was, after all, no tennis match! And he thought his guilt must be visible to the world, an affliction spread like leprous sores from head to foot.

"The IQ, as we all know," the experts told them, "is certainly not the perfect measurement. Yet some measuring stick is needed. So we say that roughly between fifty and seventy-five gives us mild retardation. Such people we call educable. They can learn to do simple, repetitive tasks and support themselves. Between thirty-five and fifty we call trainable, that is, they can care for themselves physically and—"

Marjorie interrupted once. "I've always read that most of the retarded come from homes where they're unwanted in the first place.
Nobody reads to them or talks to them, there's no stimulation." She
finished bitterly, "You couldn't possibly apply that to us."

"All true. However, there are many other genetically determined
factors. Disorders of protein metabolism, chromosomal abnormali-
ties—Not simple."

"So what do we do now, Doctor?"

"Take her home. Be gentle and encouraging. You'll need to spend
time, teaching as much as she can accept. Later you'll see how far she
can progress in school or whether she can go to a conventional school
at all. It's too early to tell."

In the end, then, they learned no more from the authorities than
the old man had told them in Covetown.

Before going back they paid a last visit to Francis' mother, who
lived alone now with Margaret. His sister Louise was there with her
two toddlers, both of whom, Francis noted, were active and well.

"I'm glad you came," Margaret said, with her gentle, foolish smile.
She had grown strong and fat. Her stockings sagged and her nose was
running. Francis wiped it.

Teresa was ashamed. "It's hard to watch every little thing," she
murmured, almost defensively.

"Of course it is."

When Teresa had left the room for a moment, Louise said, "Margaret takes up her whole day. It's almost more than she can handle."
Margaret had gone into the kitchen. "At the cake box again! The
doctor says she shouldn't eat so much, or she'll be monstrous in a few
years. But if you don't let her, she cries and screams worse than my
babies do. The older she gets, the worse her temper gets. I don't know
how Mother stands it."

Marjorie was staring somberly at the wall and Francis had no
answer.

"Of course, a home is really the solution, but Mother won't hear
a word of it. Mothers don't give up their children, she says. She has
such a *conscience* about it! You know how she is."

"Yes," Francis said, "I know how she is."

They left Teresa's house with their future clear in their understanding at last. All the way back to St. Felice, a menace rode with them through the summer sky, muting their voices and breaking their hearts, while it darkened the sunny head of the child on their laps.

One must never subordinate one's life to another's. That had been given on good authority and they both knew it. Nevertheless, they did it, for theory is one thing and practice is another. Emotion, of course, is still another.

It was a saving grace that they should both be of one mind. They had no need, even, to put their determination into words.

"How is she?" he would ask on coming into the house.

Or else he would have no need to ask, for Marjorie would be waiting in the hall.

"She picked up her cup by herself today."

And he would hasten to watch Megan repeat the achievement.

They did not bicker nearly as much as they had before. It was as if they had no more energy for it, or rather as if these things which had irritated them once were without importance now.

He was so bitterly sorry for Marjorie! It was his fault. Because of Margaret he ought to have taken thought; if she had married someone else, she would not have known this grief! And he felt more stricken because she did not blame him.

But sometimes he felt a curious *flatness,* as if there were nothing left to feel. It was as if he were a plow beast, stubbornly, with patient acceptance, pulling a load. Megan was the load. The sustenance he must provide for her was the load. The load was just something waiting when he rose in the morning to be put aside again when, tiredly, he went to bed.

The plow beast wore blinders. The events of the world beyond his toil were of no interest to him. When he read the papers with their news of endless conflict, both on the little island and the world abroad, he was not touched. He had had enough of all that, enough and too much. It was a relief not to care, not to feel passionate anger about anything or with anyone.

A relief not to feel passionate love, either, with all its honeyed anguish and suspense! You could, after all, live very well without it. You could simply take sex whenever you were hungry for it, just as you simply ate your meals without ado; one didn't need ravenous anticipation to take one's nourishment at table. So it was in bed. The child woke often in the night, crying for attention, and Marjorie had moved into the room down the hall to be closer to her. But he could go to Marjorie whenever he needed to, which was less often than he would have thought possible.

For some reason, then, he remembered the Indian summers he had known in the north; there'd been such fragrance in the air, such tranquil skies and shimmering trees. But it had been a time of withering, for all that.

It had not yet occurred to him that he was too young for Indian summer.

Book Four

ENEMIES AND
FRIENDS

Eighteen

"**W**E'VE asked for full and final independence now," said Nicholas Mebane, coming to the end of his remarks, "and when I return from the constitutional conference in London I shall have it in my hand. Or rather," he smiled, correcting himself, "we shall have it in our hands."

There was a burst of clapping, followed by a buzz of many conversations. Patrick looked around the office, which was now much expanded. The banner still hung on the wall of Nicholas's handsome room, but now across the hall lay a row of smaller rooms from which the rapid clack of typewriters was heard. Everything bore the mark and promise of prosperity. Union leaders, old and young, were all here this morning except for Clarence, who had not roused himself from peaceful retirement to come along. There were three white businessmen, as well as the leaders of the black community, doctors, lawyers, and civil servants, representing the wealth and education of the race.

There sat young Franklin Parrish, just returned from London with a Gray's Inn law degree; his black, vivid face, on which was drawn, Patrick thought, a slight, possible trace of the Indian, was both keen and open. Surely a young man one would choose for one's daughter!

"The structure is ready for transfer," Nicholas was saying. "We

— 293 —

have to admit we've learned a good deal from the British. The art of government is no small art."

Kate Tarbox stood and spoke earnestly. "I should like to say something. We are very small and I hope independence won't cause an inward turning. We need to look out on the world. We have all these links now, air service and radio. The Caribbean has been having its own small renaissance in music and writing and art. We've had exchange students and joint research in tropical agriculture. None of these things must be allowed to die when we become independent." With slight self-consciousness and a pretty flush, she sat down.

Nicholas applauded the little speech. "There speaks the power of the press! The *Trumpet* can do most to keep things alive, Kate, as you have done, and are doing so splendidly. The power of the press!" he repeated, "and of women!" And smiling, he nodded easily toward the next raised hand.

"You'll get nowhere with anything if you don't tackle unemployment." This came from a union man. "Since the mechanical loader was introduced in 1961 we've lost four hundred jobs in the cane fields alone."

Nicholas assented. "I'm familiar with that, although not as familiar as I should be and intend to become. My thought has always been that we ought to lessen our dependence on export crops and raise our standards of scientific agriculture. Our educators ought to get a handle on that." He turned to Patrick. "When I'm elected, and I will be elected, I intend to make you my minister of education. There will have to be a strong tie-in between education and labor problems. It will have to be worked out most carefully, and obviously I'm not prepared to do that this morning, or even tomorrow morning."

A white man, Elliot Bates, the banker, spoke. "One sees here the interdependence of all elements. To modernize agriculture you will need investment capital. I'd advise you to do nothing to discourage it. Just a reminder," he finished pleasantly.

Nicholas's reply was smooth. "We will surely not discourage anyone who can help us build the good life, Mr. Bates. Rest assured."

He stood up. "Now I think we've had enough for one morning. Thank you all for coming."

Patrick and Nicholas went downstairs together.

"That was masterful," Patrick said with admiration. "You had all those different elements working as one. I could almost feel the gathering momentum."

"I love the challenge," Nicholas said frankly. "But let me tell you, the going won't stay this smooth unless we get some money. Plenty of money. Not just for the campaign, I mean, but support for the kind of projects everybody wants. As Elliot Bates said, we need investment capital. You need capital to build a damned chicken coop, for God's sake." They walked on down Wharf Street. "You may not want to hear this, but I was at Eleuthera over the weekend, talking to Francis."

"He let you in?"

Nicholas laughed. "I won't scold you for the sarcasm. Yes, he always lets me in; you know that. We have a very cordial relationship."

Patrick did not comment.

"I really need him on our side," Nicholas said.

"The planters all wear blinders." He could hear the bitterness in his voice and, disliking himself for it, tried to elevate his tone to one more matter-of-fact. "They prefer to believe independence isn't coming. Ignore it and it will go away."

"No, they know better. Anyway, Francis is different. There's a chink in his armor, a softness inside. And he's a tie with his class, don't forget. They're going to vote and I want him to help persuade them to vote for our side."

What I am feeling, Patrick thought, is jealousy, pure and simple. They never knew each other before I brought them together.

He said, "They'll vote for us. The other side's splintered, ineffectual, and they know it."

"I agree. Still, one should take nothing for granted. . . . He said he doesn't want to be involved in politics, although he did give me a nice donation. Maybe it was to get rid of me." Nicholas laughed again, with the confidence of a man who knows things are going his way. "Seriously, Patrick, it's a shame about you and him. A failure of communication, all the way round. I've told him so, too. I manage to mention it every now and then."

"Yes?"

"No soap! He thinks you're a rabble-rouser. He thinks Kate is, too."

He wanted Nicholas to drop the subject at the same time that he wanted to hear more. It crossed his mind that this was like wincing at an accident while being drawn to look.

"Pity about him and her, too. Oh, don't tell me you didn't know!" Patrick's lips closed.

"Loyal in spite of betrayal?" Nicholas touched Patrick's arm. "Sorry, I wasn't mocking. Don't be hurt. You know I respect your standards. I respected them when we were twelve. But the fact is, news gets around this town and an awful lot of people besides you know about Kate and Francis. Or knew. Marjorie Luther seems to be one who didn't, though."

"Well, that's a mercy," Patrick said dryly.

"It really is. I don't like the woman much; Snow Maiden types aren't to my taste, although I must say she's perfectly friendly to me. And one does have to have a heart, after all. It's pathetic, the two of them are so wrapped up in the child. Must be hellish to bring something like that into the world and know you'll have to live with it the rest of your life. Ah, there's my wife now."

Waiting at the curb, behind the wheel of a European sports car, sat Doris Mebane. A row of bracelets slid down her arm as she raised it to wave.

"Patrick! Changed your mind, I hope?"

For a moment, after the last few minutes of agitating reminders, he could not bring his thoughts into focus. Then he understood.

"About Europe, you mean?"

"She would love it, Patrick! Oh, she's dying to go!"

"You would be doing me a great favor," Nicholas said. "I'll be busy with the conference in London, as you know, and I promised Doris two weeks in France while I'm working. I hate to have her go alone.

Désirée would be company for her. And it wouldn't cost you a thing," he added gently.

"I know, and I appreciate the offer, believe me I do. A man doesn't have many friends like you two in a lifetime. Oh, it's hard to explain," he struggled, not wanting to seem ungrateful. "But every family's different, and I just don't see it working out for us right now. Some other time, maybe. And I'd appreciate it if you wouldn't talk about it to Désirée anymore."

"Well, it's up to you, of course," Doris said coolly. Patrick saw that she was aggrieved. "As you said, some other time. Want a lift anywhere?"

"Thanks, no, I'll walk. Need the exercise."

Selfish of him, he thought, going on toward home. But some instinct, and rightly or wrongly he trusted instinct, told him it would be a mistake for his wife to go. She was already drugged on beauty. The beauty of the natural world attracted her, but the charm of expensive objects enchanted her. And Doris would be buying her way through France. It wouldn't be fair or wise to tempt Désirée with things she couldn't own and never would own. This was his one reservation about the friendship between the two wives, a friendship for which, otherwise, he would have been totally thankful.

He passed Da Cunha's, where in the window there stood, as it had for several weeks past, a handsome five-branched silver candelabrum. Several times Désirée had casually pointed it out. He wished he could give it to her. Probably she couldn't help desiring such things any more than he could help wanting books, or someone else wanting music or women or drink.

Lovely Désirée! Again he marveled, again he wondered, at the peculiar chemistry which draws us one to another. Her blackness? As expiation for a subconscious pull toward whiteness? Ah, you analyze yourself too much, Patrick! He knew he did; he had been told he did. By whom? By Francis? Or had it been Kate? Funny how sometimes he confused the two of them in his mind and memory, even though the one had been removed from his life.

He went by the library and the courthouse. Just beyond lay Boys'

Secondary. He stopped to catch his breath after the climb uphill. A mango dropped at his feet, just missing him with its thick splash of yellow juice, and his mind went back to the mangoes in the yard of the little house at Sweet Apple. Then he thought of Agnes. He had been in Martinique a few months ago; it would soon be time to go again, at least before Christmas. She had failed noticeably. He wondered whether it was simply old age or whether some sickness might be at work within her. Yet her spirits were high, her glance as shrewd and her tongue as sharp as ever.

"You're looking thoughtful," Kate said now, coming up behind him.

"I was thinking that we're finally on the way," he fibbed. They passed Government House. "He's a magnificent speaker, our honorable member from St. Margaret's parish. I listened to him last week in the Legislative Council. Very impressive, the whole business, from the silver mace and the bobbies' silver buttons right up to the queen's portrait, though that'll be coming down soon."

"Oh, Nicholas knows how, no doubt of that! He's a vote getter, if ever there was one. The voters will love it that he dresses like a white man, a rich one, and talks like one, too. He's all the things they never will be and wish they could be."

Patrick looked down at the vivid little woman striding beside him.

"That sounds mighty cynical. I don't know whether you intended it that way."

"I'm not cynical. At least, I don't want to be. I think I'm a realist, that's all."

"You don't believe in our party?"

"Of course I do. The others are a lot of self-seeking country bumpkins who wouldn't know how to run a government, and luckily, the people have enough horse sense to see it. As for Nicholas, he's shrewd as they come, but very, very talented. I wouldn't be working for him if I didn't think he was."

"I'm glad. I would hate to think you didn't believe in him completely."

"Completely? Who said anything about that? I believe in what I see from one day to the next. I can't look too far ahead. I've been disillusioned too often."

Francis, Patrick thought, feeling her bitterness as if it were his own. Well, in a different way, it was his own.

After a moment Kate resumed, "I only wish I could be sure he had your heart."

"Who, Nicholas?"

"Yes. His mind's brilliant. It's the heart that worries me."

"Oh, Kate, you're wrong! He's sterling. I'd stake my life on Nicholas Mebane. The man is sterling."

Kate looked up at him. "You're sterling yourself, Patrick Courzon." Then, abruptly, "Tell me, how's Will these days?"

"The same," he said soberly.

Against his will, he was perceiving things he didn't like in the boy who was now so near to manhood. Something ugly lurked there. Will had a quick brain and extraordinary memory. He could trip Patrick up over a fact or a date, even over something that Patrick himself had once said and then forgotten he had said. "I hate to admit I forgot," Patrick would tell him, laughing at himself as mature people should be able to do; yet the truth was that he always felt like squirming under the boy's bold stare.

Kate spoke gently. "I think of him as an empty vessel. He was dry so long, starved and dry, until you came to fill him."

"I try, anyway."

"That's all any of us can do. Try. Well, I'll leave you. I turn off here."

For a minute or two Patrick watched as she went up the lane toward her house. He knew her routine pretty well. First she would let the dogs out for a run, then replenish the bird feeders. She'd go inside and make her supper, which she sometimes ate at the table in the yard, with a book propped in front of the plate. In the evenings she'd write for the *Trumpet* or work on party accounts or make calls. Now and then, he knew, she'd go out dining and dancing with men who came over from Barbados or someplace, men she'd known through family, probably, or during her married years. What she did with them when they brought her home he didn't know; it was none of his business. Whether any of them wanted to marry her or whether she would accept if one should, he didn't know either; he hoped, at least, she had mostly got over Francis. She never said. But she was being wasted, that was one thing he did know. She was being awfully wasted. This was no life for a woman like her.

Thinking of women, he thought as always of Désirée. Thank God, *her* life was not being wasted! She held him with a thousand strands of habit and affection and sex still marvelously fresh; he chafed sometimes, complaining silently about one thing or another, yet knew how tightly he was held.

He smiled a little at himself and his memories. He remembered how he used to tease her over her devotion to the house. The truth was, he had grown most happily accustomed to the orderly comforts that she provided, the cleanliness of the linens and the pretty, appetizing supper table. More than that, much more than that, he had, quite simply, grown accustomed to her spirit, so that without her listening ear, her trust, her little touch of worldliness, her pleasure in every day, without all these and the balm of her understanding, he would have been parched grass, a withering tree. Yes.

And he went on now past the central square where Nelson stood with pigeons soiling his shoulders, past the careenage and out toward the savanna, where half a dozen glossy horses were being exercised by their grooms. On the veranda at Cade's Hotel a pair of pink-cheeked old Englishmen in white suits were enjoying their whiskey and soda. One recognized them as retired civil servants, taking a respite from the English winter. He reflected that someone who hadn't seen Covetown for fifty years or more would probably find very little changed: the boats, the horses, and the winter visitors would all be familiar.

Yet change was here, not only the proud promise of meetings like this morning's, but another kind, tangible and visible, a creeping tide.

From where he stood the roof of the Lunabelle Hotel rose squarely over distant trees. A long concrete rectangle, a slab with hard edges, it was a machine-age intrusion upon the natural world of curves, in which hills arched against the sky and coves were scallops in the cliffs.

He stayed there, looking at the tasteless thing which, not yet one year old, had already surrounded itself with its own small slum. A prediction of what might come unless it were controlled somehow; he must talk seriously to Nicholas.

In back of the Lunabelle a shantytown had sprung up. Here lived the little army that serviced the hotel, people who had come in from the villages looking for something better than what they'd had, but were now worse off. Here were no garden patches and no shade. In the glaring heat their shacks stood naked among pools of stagnant water, foul and glistening like sores on the skin. The place had acquired an unofficial name: the Trenches. In Jamaica, in Kingston, he had seen such a place, worse only because it was larger and, being older, had had more time in which decay could spread and young men, idle and angry, could collect, followed inevitably by all the vices.

Will had friends in the Trenches. The boy was so secretive! You couldn't ever get at him. Remote, and perceptive enough to understand that with his secrecy he was inflicting hurt, he didn't care whether he hurt or not! Patrick had so wanted to love him, did love him, and was not loved in return. He wasn't hated either, simply disregarded, mostly in that cool way just short of disrespect, as Will stood off, thinking his own amused and scornful thoughts.

In the yard, Laurine and Maisie were sitting among their friends talking about whatever it was that girls talked about, clothes probably. . . . They gave him joy, his girls. They were fond of him, which was, when you came down to it, most of the reward that parents wanted: that their children should be fond of them.

He kissed them. "Where's Will?" he asked.

"Back in the shed."

He needn't have asked. Will and his steel band had struck up again behind the garage. They had constructed their instruments out of spare parts, mostly rusty. Will played the tock-tock, the most important of the instruments. He had made it himself out of the bottom half of a kerosene tin. One of the boys had made a tom-tom out of goatskins and a rum barrel. Another had made his own shack-shack out of a bamboo cylinder filled with pebbles.

Patrick sat down on an upended barrel and watched. The watching was as much a part of the entertainment as the listening; the concentrated vigor of the players, their rhythm and sway were a dance in themselves. Sometimes on Saturday nights he'd pass the dance hall near the wharf where the young hung out and he'd wonder whether the girls in their earrings and bright skirts knew that they were basically dancing the calinda, brought out of Africa. Perhaps they did know. The racket now in the shed assaulted his eardrums, but his feet were swinging in time, nevertheless.

"That's great!" he cried when the music stopped and the boys began to leave. "You practically set fire to that thing, Will! Almost burned me to a crisp just watching you!"

Tom Folsom poked Will. "Oh, when it's setting fires, Will sure knows how! Always did. Biggest and best fires of all time." He bent over, laughing.

Will's fist struck Tom a fearful blow between the shoulders. "Damn fool! Damn loudmouth son of a bitch of an ass!"

Tom straightened and sobered, his eyes aghast. And while Patrick stood astonished, the two boys stood staring at each other until, flinching under Will's fury, Tom picked up his books and sidled out.

"What the devil was that about?" Patrick asked.

"Nothing important."

"You were pretty mad about something unimportant."

Not answering, Will busied himself with a pile of music sheets. Patrick frowned, trying mentally to reconstruct the swift byplay.

"Fire. He said something about you setting fires."

"He doesn't know what he's talking about. He's an idiot."

"One of your best friends, isn't he?"

"So?"

There was a silence. Something lurked in the air. Something serious was being hidden. The least suspicious of men, nevertheless Patrick made a connection.

"You ever set a fire anywhere? Tell me, Will."

"Sure. Kids make bonfires all the time, don't they?"

"That's not what I meant." Oh, it was preposterous, what he had meant, too hideous to consider, and yet he was considering it!

"Then what did you mean?" Will looked up boldly.

" 'Biggest fire of all time.' Isn't that what he said? Like the one— at Eleuthera, maybe?"

"Bullshit!"

"I'm asking you, Will: did you have anything to do with that?"

"I did not!"

"Is that the truth, Will?" Patrick's palms were sweating. "Because if you had anything to do with that, I'd not only have to give you up to the law, I'd have to give up *on* you. And that'd break my heart."

"I said no, didn't I? What more do you want?"

I want to believe you, Patrick thought. Please God that you're telling the truth. Those hard, bright eyes of yours—I never really meet them, never get behind them. How can I know who you are?

And taking out a handkerchief, he wiped his hands, swallowed a painful lump in his throat, made an inner resolution to go forward hopefully, and changed the subject.

"We had a fruitful meeting this morning. Thought maybe you'd like to hear about it." Make contact with the boy, share your interests with cheer. Bury those ugly fears. "Nicholas will be leaving soon for the constitutional conference in London. When he comes back he'll have it all signed, sealed, and delivered. Independence." The word fitted the mouth, a crisp, snappy, prideful word. He smiled, wanting to coax a smile from Will, but none came.

Will asked only, "And then?"

"Well, elections, of course. The New Day will surely get in, unless there's some unexpected coalition of all the splinter parties. No, we'll surely get in," he repeated, adding brightly, "And then our work begins."

"What part will you play?" Will inquired.

"Nicholas said this morning he'd want me to be minister for education, which would suit me fine. It's not all that political, or shouldn't be! I won't have a lot of speeches to make, thank goodness. Although I suppose I'll be asked to do a couple here and there during the elections. . . . Well, I'll manage that if I must." Feeling enthusiasm, he sounded cheerful to his own ears.

Will didn't answer. It could be like pulling teeth to get him to talk, but Patrick, accustomed to this reluctance, was usually patient. When a minute or two had passed in silence, however, he became exasperated.

"Well, haven't you anything to say?" he demanded

"Yes. I spit on your elections."

Patrick was astonished. "Spit on them?"

"They have no meaning, your silly elections. They're just the old colonial farce with different actors. We'll still have the bosses. The white man will still have the money and people like you will front for him. Read Fanon. Learn all about it."

"I've read Fanon. There are truths in him and untruths. He's too angry, too violent for me." Patrick paused. "Frankly, I think you're rather young and inexperienced to have a valid opinion about Fanon."

Will looked at him. Often his eyes would slide away in avoidance, but at other times he would switch his head about like a whip so that the eyes came straight at you, narrowed and intent, with a cat's cold, powerful stare. You'd grow uncomfortable and look away, then be ashamed for allowing yourself to be intimidated by a boy less than half your age.

"I only meant," Patrick said delicately now, "you haven't had enough time to learn and judge, to evaluate and weigh. These men with the fiery messages—they're fanatics, Will. They can—and have —lured whole nations to their downfall."

"Downfall? How much farther down can we go?"

"A hell of a lot farther. We can go down into tyranny and bloodshed, a slavery worse than you can imagine. Yes, there's a lot wrong now, but nothing that can't decently be fixed. Think about it, Will. Look at your own situation, a nice home, an education—"

Will interrupted. He had risen and stood tensely, clenching and unclenching his fists.

"How many of my kind don't have a 'nice home'? You think I

should be happy because I live here, but I'll tell you I'm not, I'm ashamed that I do!"

Patrick felt a rise of pity. Thin and tall now, the passionate youth took on again, for an instant, the guise of the terrified and beaten child, tied to a tree. He spoke quietly.

"Must you think so hard about these things, Will? You've so many years ahead to watch the world getting better, to help it if you will. Right now's the time to enjoy yourself, to—"

"It's all right for you to talk. Oh, yes! Pass-for-white! A couple of shades lighter and you'd have it made! What chance is there for anybody like me under this system? Enjoy myself!"

"That's foolish talk, exaggerated—"

"That's why you used to hang around Francis Luther, until he got rid of you the minute you wouldn't do what he wanted."

"That's unjust, Will. How can you know what's inside my head? Or anybody's? I don't judge people by their color, I'll tell you that, though. This morning I was with Kate Tarbox—"

"A fool of a woman! Can't have children of her own—"

"That's a cruel thing to say."

"—and doesn't want anyone else to have them. 'Overpopulation,' she says. Yes, of course, overpopulation of *our* kind! Genocide and nothing but!"

Patrick was suddenly exhausted. Rational argument had always been stimulating for him, a pleasurable challenge, but this blind 'thinking with the blood' had no direction and no end. It was a tiring, infuriating muddle. He got up.

"I've had enough for now, Will. I'm going inside."

He went down the hall. Will's bedroom door was open, revealing not only the usual jumble of sneakers, books and sundries, but also a large blowup of Che Guevara over the bed. Something new.

He went to his own room. Désirée was posing in front of the mirror. Her lemon-colored dress smoothed her body like a stocking or a glove. She knew how to move as models do, lithely and lightly.

"Pretty, Patrick?"

"Pretty," he said, for once not caring very much.

"Doris gave it to me. It's brand new but it didn't fit her. You have to go to New York to get clothes like this. If," she said wistfully, "you can afford them."

"Lovely," he assured her. He had no patience.

Clarence was reading the paper in the front room. He put it down when Patrick came in.

"Were you having an argument with Will? I was passing the shed and couldn't help hearing."

"He's steamed up over revolution and class warfare. It worries the hell out of me. Where will it lead?"

"I'm an old man and you're a young one, Patrick, but he's only a boy and his language isn't yours or mine. It's language, that's all it is."

"I hope you're right."

"Did I hear him say something about Francis Luther?"

"You did."

Clarence was silent for a moment, then said quietly, "I know how wounded you feel. Life hasn't toughened you up and maybe it never will. Remember, I told you long ago not to put too much trust in Luther, didn't I? Later, I got to know him a bit and changed my mind, but still later I found out I'd been right the first time. It's in the blood. The call of the blood—and the money—it's all the same. In a crisis, at a crossroads, a man goes with his interests and his own. As far as that's concerned, at least, Will may be right."

Désirée, still wearing the yellow dress, had come into the room. "You talking about Will? Is he giving you trouble again?"

Patrick didn't want to involve her in the discussion. She was always too ready to turn against Will.

"Nothing much," he said. "Just a mood."

He didn't fool her. "I could take a strap to that boy! Poor Patrick, you wanted a son. Two healthy girls weren't enough, were they?"

Clarence intervened. "No I-told-you-so's, Désirée."

"I don't mean it that way, Pop. Patrick knows I don't. But it's been such a hard job with Will from the very beginning."

"He has his placid moments," Patrick argued.

"Yes. Like a hornet resting between flights."

"He'd had such hardship. I thought just loving him would rebuild him."

"Well, maybe it will," Clarence said cheerfully. "It's the idealism of youth, carried too far, maybe, but still, you have to remember the world would never advance without it. When the rough edges are sandpapered, what's left will be a building block, something solid in the structure we call civilization." He moved his old hands as he spoke, as if piling stones, setting them precisely, and pleased with his own metaphor.

But Désirée was disturbed by Patrick's mood. "Go on out in the hammock and read till I fix you some lunch. You never have any time to do nothing in," she complained kindly.

"I think I'll do that."

In the string hammock, under mottled, moving shade, he lay back with his book unopened. "Building the blocks of civilization," the old man had said. Well, perhaps. Or tearing them down? Destruction wearing the guise of justice? There was an awful lot of that in the world these days. And he lay there, frowning and troubled, wishing he could sleep.

On the front lawn the girls were still holding animated conversation. "He can't even dance!" he heard one say, and smiled to himself. Little women! He was reminded suddenly of Francis, whom he had glimpsed a week or two ago in town with his own little daughter, a soft little thing in a fancy pink dress. Francis, like himself, had so wanted a son, a friend of his blood, a healthy son. Instead, he'd got a sick daughter. The injustices of life, the cool indifference, the "luck of the draw"!

Then he was angry at himself for still thinking about Francis. It shouldn't matter to him! "A man goes with his interests and his own," the old man had said a few moments ago. Was that just nature, then, just bloody tooth-and-claw, when you came down to it?

A young man with his leg shot away in a festering jungle, a baby animal, still half alive, skinned to make a coat for a fine lady, a mother raped by special interrogators in a great stone city: just nature, bloody tooth-and-claw? Every man for himself and the devil with the rest? His head ached.

He woke with a smooth hand on his forehead.

"You needed that sleep," Désirée said. "Come inside, I've made cold cucumber soup."

She had changed from Doris's dress into a blouse and skirt. Her long hair was pinned up in hot-weather style and she smelled of flowers. He felt a swelling of desire, now in the middle of the afternoon! Oh, if he had any sense he'd take his own advice, that which he had given to Will, to enjoy his youth, or what was left of it, and let the world, including Francis Luther, take its time getting better. And swinging himself out of the hammock, he followed Désirée into the house.

Nineteen

F ROM the high walls of Government House the portraits still looked down. Princes, queens, generals, and judges in the velvets and ermines of authority regarded the push and jostle of the crowd as serenely as though the world had not been turned inside out. Music buzzed and voices shrilled in Francis' ears. All day he had been pounded by the enthusiastic noises of oration, churchbells, and gun salutes from the warships in the harbor. The frenzy was still echoing in his head.

Today a nation had been born, an independent nation having its own flag, orange and green with a cluster of stars that rippled up the pole after the union jack came down. A duke had spoken, along with a dozen native dignitaries. Nicholas Mebane's clear voice had carried immense authority, so that it was quite certain, after elections were held three months hence, who the new prime minister would be.

Francis had not paid much attention to the verbiage, since on such occasions nothing new was ever said. Only noble and triumphant platitudes were called for. Problems would come later, in due time. Besides, everyone knew what they were: malnutrition, unemployment, electrification, imports, exports—one had heard them and read of them all before and would do so a hundred times again. The sun had blazed and he had wondered why he'd come, knowing, of course, that "everyone" had come and it would have been very queer not to have done so. His eyes had wandered, as had his thoughts—this old place had seen so many flags!—had wandered across the square to the careenage and the rotting capstan where great sailing vessels had been hauled up to have the barnacles scraped off, to the Nelson statue and then, at the far end, to Cade's Hotel, where he'd wished he could be having a cold drink in the shady garden.

He'd thought of Kate.

In that drowsy, dreaming garden it had begun, although he had not realized it then and probably she had not, either. The recollection had been extraordinarily vivid, even to the emerald ring, later to be discarded, even to her words. Something about "long tides bringing you back." It vexed him now that the memory should be so sharp. There were, after all, so many encounters, affairs, or whatever one wanted to call them, in any healthy young man's years: restaurant lunches in hidden little Italian places, drinks in neighborhood bars or extravagant hotels, "love" in cars and on ships, in bedrooms and on beaches; did one remember them all? Hardly! Why, then, should these particular reminders slide back to bother him, when his mind was so filled with other things, when they only made him angry, when he didn't *want* them?

He never saw her, which was all to the good. He never saw Patrick either, for that matter. He saw very few people, anyway. He hardly ever went to town these days, except for an occasional call at the bank, when he would park his car at the back of the building, transact his business, and be gone within minutes, or from time to time an evening function at the club, to which he went partly to please Marjorie and partly because it was unhealthy to be a total recluse. And there was small likelihood of meeting either Kate or Patrick at the club!

In the four years since everything had happened, the fire and the birth of Megan, he had drawn in, retreated behind an invisible wall of his own construction. He had learned to run the estate, as Lionel said with candid praise, "like a charm." His cattle had won prize after prize at the shows and were now being exported to Florida for breeding stock. In another few years his mortgage would be paid off. After that he'd be able to salt away every available extra cent for Megan, who would long outlive him and would need whatever he could give her. His mind whirled, thinking of these things, over and over.

His mind was in a constant whirl over Megan. Sometimes he would even drop what he was doing, and almost frantic with intent, run to fetch the child and patiently, urgently, repeat some simple number game, some little puzzle ("suitable for ages four through seven," it said on the box) as if through main strength and the power of his love he could *will* her into normality—knowing all the time that it was useless and absurd, knowing, too, that he would keep striving, as his mother still strove for Margaret.

Such were his days. The evenings were quiet enough. It was known that the Luthers were usually at home, so people dropped in from neighboring estates to sit on the veranda and watch the afterglow spread its rosy fire over the sea.

Often Marjorie entertained at dinner. She was pleased to display the house, to set a splendid table with heavy silver and thin French crystal. Surely one couldn't begrudge her this diversion.

As for himself, he liked it best when the Whittakers were invited, solely because they brought along a nephew who came from Chicago for long visits; the young man would play the piano all night if you encouraged him. Sometimes when the others went across the hall for bridge he would play for Francis alone, a Mozart divertimento, a Haydn capriccio or fantasia, music whose pure refinement, lacking all turbulence and bombast, could clear at least for a little while the turbulence in a man's heart and head. No one on this island could play like that—except Kate. Kate again!

"An exquisite piano," the young man said, stroking the keys.

"Yes. A Pleyel. My father bought it years ago in Paris."

"You know, of course, what he is?" Marjorie asked one night after the Whittakers had gone home.

"What he is? A music teacher, isn't he?"

"No, no. There's something wrong with him, I mean. He's a homosexual. Couldn't you tell?"

"I didn't really think about it."

"Honestly, Francis! You never notice anything! The way he uses his hands! And he's at least thirty-five and not married. Disgusting, isn't it?"

"No," Francis said.

Marjorie stared. "Sometimes I can't make you out at all. It's as if you actually try to take the opposite, whatever I say." And she had sighed, and he had gone to his desk in the library to work on his history of St. Felice.

He had surprised himself, these past few years, with his own diligence. Having put out his feelers in New York among rare-book collectors and dealers in out-of-print books, he had surrounded himself with piles of source material and was progressing well, stimulated by this rich hoard to explore and delve. Creeping back into minds and seeing through eyes long dead, he came to know the warriors and the traders, the architects and poets, the anthropologists, the governors and slaves, the flora and the fauna, all the myriad life of this small spot into which and out of which had radiated the energies of five centuries. It seemed sometimes as though he would never reach the end, and indeed he knew that inwardly he hoped he never would. For the work was a refuge and companion; only when he was immersed in it could he know such rare contentment.

Occasionally he thought of a time when it must finally be complete; he toyed then with the idea of embarking on another project, something he might call *Man at Work in His Environment.* Perhaps by then there would be time to travel and take pictures all over the world for such a book. And he bought from Da Cunha's a fine camera against such a day, only half believing that the day might ever come. But it was nice to have the camera waiting on the shelf all the same.

"Quite a change from the first time we were here," Marjorie remarked now, returning him to the present hour and place.

Yes, quite. To begin with, there were ten times as many people as there had been at Julia Tarbox's wedding to the Honorable Derek Frame. But it was the atmosphere that was most strikingly different, the air of jubilance today, written on the face of the black peasant in from the country in his Sunday suit, with his dignity and his hands held awkwardly, as if he didn't know what to do with them, while he stared about at the grandeur. And the brown middle class, here in its finery, was jubilant indeed. The women wore leaf-green and peach and crocus-yellow; their shoes and their hats matched their dresses; they chatted and drank champagne, they greeted and laughed. A spectacle for a Balzac, Francis thought.

"Have you noticed the necklace on Nicholas's wife?" Marjorie whispered. "Someone said Da Cunha had it brought from France."

Diamonds, turquoise, and gold flashed on Doris's coffee-colored neck. She was a handsome woman. The climate agreed with these women and they bloomed; white skin shriveled to leather in this sun.

Marjorie led him to the terrace. "Come, they've saved us a table."

"Who has?"

"Lionel and the Whittakers. I don't know who else. Oh, yes, they've stuck Father Baker there, too. We always seem to get stuck with him, don't we?" She grimaced. "He irritates me, he's so benevolent."

"Perhaps we irritate him." Francis felt contradictory; he didn't know why, but then he felt that way with Marjorie too often. It wasn't decent of him. He must try to watch it.

Lionel looked up with a grin. "Great fun, eh? At least they haven't burned the prison so far."

Marjorie asked what he meant.

"Oh, you know, it seems to be the thing to do. All over the islands on Independence Day they burn the prisons and set the murderers free."

Marjorie shuddered. "Burning again! I suppose I'll always feel I'm living on borrowed time here. Now more than ever."

"Things aren't that bad," Francis assured her.

"I'm not that optimistic." Lionel shook his head gloomily. "I'm finally getting out, you know. I really am. The sooner the better."

"Getting out!" Marjorie cried.

"Yes, I made up my mind this morning, when I saw that flag go up. The trouble is, a lot of others feel that way, too, so who'll buy what

I want to sell? Unless you will, Francis, since you want to stay. I'd make it easy, take back a big purchase money mortgage and let you have the whole lot for a price that might surprise you."

"No," Francis said, decisively. "I've no wish for large enterprises. What I've got is all I want."

Marjorie was eager. "Where will you go, Lionel? You always said you'd never leave!"

"I know, but things change. I'm tired of the uncertainty. So I'm thinking of a nice place in Surrey near my sister." He plunked his fist into his palm. "Damn it, though! I've got to sell fast before these people expropriate!"

Father Baker remonstrated. "Come now! Expropriate! Who, Mebane? He represents the rising middle class and no one else. They don't expropriate. You know that as well as I do."

Mrs. Whittaker's cheeks were habitually sucked in, with an expression of disapproval. "Rising, Father?" she objected, unpursing her lips. "Risen, I would say. Look at them, with their jewelry and cars! That whole section where Mebane's father lived has tripled in size. Have you seen some of the houses they're putting up?"

"You bet I have," Lionel said, "but middle class or not, you're going to see a huge increase in taxes. They've made promises to labor that have to be kept even if it hurts themselves. Expensive promises."

"I'm not too alarmed," Francis said. "Peace and order, that's all I ask for. As long as we have those, a few more taxes won't devastate us. Land taxes have tripled anyway since I came here, and that's been under British rule."

"Exactly," Father Baker said. "Even that government recognized necessity. The world is smaller now. Everybody knows what everybody else has got, and the ones who haven't got anything expect something, for which you can hardly blame them. And that's the crux of the matter."

"But where's the money to come from?" Mrs. Whittaker demanded. "With all respect to you, Father, if you were to strip us at this table and everyone like us besides of every cent we own, that wouldn't mean more than a few cents in the pockets of the poor."

"The answer, of course, is to produce more. Mechanize," Francis said promptly. "It takes us twenty man-days to produce a ton of sugar here. In Hawaii it takes about two and a half days. There's your answer."

"But the unions keep fighting these new machines," Lionel objected.

"True, and that's where education comes in," Father Baker began, but was interrupted.

"This is too gay a party for such serious talk!" Nicholas Mebane, accompanied by an ancient white man in an equally ancient suit, drew up two chairs. "Time enough to face all that business on Monday morning! I'd like to introduce Mr. Anatole Da Cunha. Someone happened to mention your name, Francis, and he wanted to meet you. He knew your parents."

Da Cunha took Francis' hand. "You resemble your mother. I remember her very well. I knew her in Paris. She was a shy young girl, very lovely."

"My father always talked about you. You introduced him to my mother," Francis responded.

Nicholas said proudly, "Mr. Da Cunha made this trip especially to be here on Independence Day. It's a great tribute, a great honor for us."

"I'm almost eighty," Da Cunha said, "and not very well. I wanted to see home one more time, and what better excuse than a day like this one?"

"Mr. Da Cunha is planning a gift for the new nation, a group of paintings that he will send if we will promise to start a small museum here."

"And to encourage the arts," Da Cunha added. "There's too much talent going to waste everywhere for lack of encouragement."

"I'll leave that to my wife. It'll be in good hands," Nicholas said. "That is, if I'm elected."

Laughter, flattering and polite, rippled around the table. Nicholas continued, "Naturally, she loves your island paintings the best. She tells me you always have at least one cabbage palm with its crown of thorns in every one. Is that correct?"

"Yes, that's my signature."

"How fascinating!" Marjorie cried. "We have a few of your works at home that Francis' father gave us. I must look carefully for the cabbage palms tonight." Her eyes widened with a new idea. "Would you like to spend a few days with us and see what we have of yours? We'd love it if you would!"

"Thank you, but I'm a guest of the Mebanes and I leave the day after tomorrow." He turned to Francis somewhat abruptly. "I hear you're a writer."

"An exaggeration. I've been working on a history of the island, of the whole West Indies actually, from Spanish galleons to Arawaks, parrots—and cabbage palms, too. But I don't call myself a writer."

"I didn't know you were living here. I lost contact with your parents years ago."

"Yes, I've become a native."

The old man smiled courteously. It struck Francis acutely that there was more than ordinary interest in the smiling courtesy. But why should there be?

"You're here alone? You're with your wife, of course; I meant, your brothers and sisters?"

"I have no brothers, and my sisters live in New York."

"Ah," Da Cunha said.

Yes, definitely he was curious. Well, he was old and probably eccentric to begin with.

Nicholas obviously wanted to draw him on now to another table, but Da Cunha prolonged the conversation.

"I bought a newspaper in New York. They're saying fine things about your new leaders. It's all very interesting to me. Franklin Parrish, they mention, and another one, Patrick Courzon. But you know them all, I suppose."

"Patrick Courzon is the intellectual," Father Baker said, tactfully enough, since Nicholas's attention had been diverted by a pair of enthusiastic pink-and-blue matrons.

"You know them? You know Courzon?" Anatole asked Francis. "I know them both."

"Unfortunately," Father Baker said, "they've had some differences, Francis and Patrick. I must say I've felt very sorry about it, too, since this island needs all its best minds working together." And he looked reproach at Francis, who colored with anger. Father could be an interfering old fool.

Nicholas, released by the ladies, drew Da Cunha away. Immediately then, everyone began to talk about Nicholas.

"He really is rather likable, isn't he?" Mrs. Whittaker remarked. "One gets to thinking when one's with him that things may not turn out so badly after all."

"I don't know about that," Father Baker said, rather wanly.

"What, Father?" Lionel cried. "You should be jubilant today! This is what you wanted, isn't it?"

"I would be happier if Patrick were going to be running things instead."

"Nonsense! What experience has he ever had? Good Lord, Mebane is a barrister, he's worked on the Constitution, been on the Legislative Council, worked in the Development Bank during federation—you name it! He's a practical man! Mind you, I still want to get the hell away from here, but at least with Mebane one would stand a fighting chance of survival. He's got his feet on the ground and knows how to compromise. Courzon's nothing but a dreamer."

Lionel was right, of course. Oh, Patrick would have his place, Nicholas would see to that, for they had been like brothers since childhood. That was understandable. One had to admire loyalty of that sort. But Nicholas knew what he was about, and he'd picked the right slot for a man as imprudent as Courzon. Only last week he'd told Francis—obviously, he had high respect and regard for Francis to give him as many confidences as he did—that Courzon was to be minister for education. Well, he couldn't do any harm there and, to be honest about it, might even do some good. It was his sort of job.

"Why, even in the Guardian Club," Lionel continued now, "even among his own kind, the colored politicians, so they tell me, Courzon is called a dreamer. They don't think much of him, even there."

"And all the time the world is starved for dreamers," Father Baker said.

Francis turned away. Too much talk tonight, and the wrong talk, too! He was at his poorest in crowds and he wished they could leave now, but Marjorie would be among the last to depart.

She was laughing. Her laughter had always been infrequent; it was more so, naturally, during these last few years. Sometimes her laughter was genuine, especially her loving gaiety with Megan, but her "social" laugh was a high, affected chortle, straining the cheek muscles. It made his own cheeks ache to watch her. He could never see why it was necessary to make such an effort at seeming amused or to be amusing for the good opinion of people one didn't especially care about. Yet most people did it, so probably it was he who was the odd one.

Then he had a new and sudden insight: quite unlike himself, Marjorie *needed* the crowd and the approval in order to survive! When they were alone at home the silence often lay like a heavy cloth, shrouding the two of them and shrouding as well the room in which they sat. Her thoughts must be so heavy, then!

His own could run like quicksilver in his head. The other night he had been reading about Crete and the rosette motif on the murals at the palace in Knossos. For some reason he had needed to talk about it, to share his curiosity with someone.

"It must have meant something, don't you think? Or perhaps only a decoration?"

"I shan't lose any sleep for wondering about it, I assure you," she had answered, not unkindly, but with irony and boredom.

She had yawned and he had felt a profound and lonely sadness.

He drank his coffee, pushing the dessert aside. Tomorrow would be Sunday and a whole free morning with Megan while Marjorie slept late. Maybe they'd sail over to Spark Island. They could take Osborne's four-year-old grandson along—he'd be company for Megan. Or was that only a delusion? Roy was so far ahead of Megan. He tossed in the water like a dolphin; he saw everything and had his chatty opinions about everything; he could relate a photograph of a thousand-pound turtle to the newly hatched young crawling out of the sand holes on the beach where the eggs had been laid. He was a companion, that little boy, following his grandfather so closely that he was known on the estate as Mr. Osborne's shadow.

It was so hard not to be bitter, not to envy Osborne this wealth of his!

Yet just to look at Megan, not hearing the repetitious baby syllables, not knowing with what difficulty she was being trained out of diapers—just to look at her, you would never know she wasn't "normal." She with the soft blond down on the back of her warm, sun-browned neck, she with the double row of tiny, perfect teeth, the cobalt eyes, the— And behind his own eyes Francis felt the painful prickle of unseen, stifled tears.

How he was tied to that poor scrap of a life! And both of them tied to the scrap, the piece of earth on which they lived! Without making himself appear absurdly bathetic, he was never able to explain exactly how he felt about this tie, this solemn linkage both to his child and to the first of his blood who had built upon that land, or how he felt about the land: half guardian and ultimate shelter for that vulnerable child.

"You're in a fog," Marjorie said now, with slight impatience. "Where are you anyway, Francis?"

"In the middle of tomorrow morning," he answered, and she gave him her I-don't-understand-you look.

Something else troubled him. Could he possibly be "using" the child because there was no other deep affection in his life? No one else he would die for? For Megan he would die a hundred times over. Yet so would Marjorie. Often he watched them together, the mother and the little girl crossing the lawn at dusk, with their pale dresses like flowers or moths. In a way of which Megan could fortunately have no idea, it was she who held them all together. She, and Marjorie's compassion, too, for he could not have borne to lose Megan and Marjorie knew it well. Her standards might be rigid and unyielding, but she did live up to them herself; one had to grant that. In this respect, at least, he had certainly not misjudged when, on that first night so long ago, he had recognized the quality and honor that were Marjorie.

She prodded his ribs. "Oh, look! Look over there!"

"Over where?"

He knew instantly what she meant. Moving among the tables toward a large, reserved one at the center of the terrace were Patrick with his wife, a group of young white men and women who were friends and relatives of Kate's, two or three black politicians—and Kate.

"Clever of her to wear pink with that hair," Marjorie said. "Funny, she never did care much about clothes."

Lionel studied Kate frankly, as if it didn't matter whether she saw him doing so or not. "She never needed to care very much. Anything she puts on becomes graceful." The observation was surprisingly delicate to come from Lionel's lips.

"You never mention her," Marjorie said.

"Why should I? We're divorced. Besides, it would hardly be tactful in your house, would it?"

"What do you mean? Because she once had a crush on Francis?" Marjorie laughed.

Francis felt the blood rushing to his neck. "Don't be ridiculous, Marjorie!" His eyes met those of Lionel, who looked amused.

"You know she did!" Marjorie insisted. "I don't say it lasted very long, but—"

Lionel interrupted. "I never mention her in your house, Marjorie, because of the tragedy that happened to us all. You know quite well that's the reason. And also because she's involved with Courzon."

"Involved? I wouldn't be astonished at all," Marjorie said, "if someone were to tell me she's having an affair with him."

The blood was beating hard now in Francis' neck. But he spoke calmly and curiously. "You hate her, don't you, Marjorie? Why?"

Amusement still played on Lionel's face as he watched the little play.

"Don't be silly, Francis! Why should I hate her? Just a little gossip

EDEN BURNING

within the family, no harm in it," she said lightly, as if she had suddenly become aware she was going too far. "I'm quite open-minded, quite unjealous; you know perfectly well I always am. If I weren't, would I draw your attention to how attractive she is? Those earrings are stunning, by the way."

All one could see of Kate were her bared back, the reddish foam of curly hair and the glitter of swinging eardrops.

"They were her grandmother's. I found them in a safe deposit box awhile back. She'd forgotten about them evidently, so I sent them to her. They're not worth much. Pretty, but the stones are very flawed." Lionel lit a cigarette and leaned into his subject, as if he were quite at ease with it, enjoying it. "Kate never cared about jewelry except for funny old antique pieces. I remember the day she gave back the emerald ring. I really wanted her to keep it, you know. I came upon her in the bedroom, packing to leave me. She was sitting naked on the bed. It was quite a picture, stark naked except for the emerald. She threw it across the room at me. Yes, quite a picture. That fellow Da Cunha could probably paint it, make a big splash with it. He could call it *Naked Woman with Red Hair and Emerald,* or something like that."

The muscles in Francis' belly tightened with the old familiar shock and he felt again that outrage—although it was none of his business anymore—at the memory of Lionel and Kate, the memory with which, he knew, he was now deliberately being taunted. Lionel had rare nasty moods like this.

Lionel had "known" her. He had "had" her. But not as I once had her and as I knew her. Creamy and slippery under the shower. The mole on her left breast. That little gap between her two front teeth. Crying over an abused cat. Laughing in bed, that wonderful bed. The quilt has a different kind of bird embroidered in each square. . . .

Not that it made any difference to him! The past was past. She had written him off. She had failed him and he had written her off. His life was very different now. His head and his heart were filled in many different ways.

Lionel and Marjorie got up to dance. For a moment he watched as Marjorie's face appeared above Lionel's shoulder, a face still pure and smooth in spite of sorrow. He followed them until they were concealed in the crowd of dancers. Then his gaze fell on Kate's back; she was talking, her hands flying up in the animated gesture that he had forgotten until now.

A stubborn, fanatical, opinionated, bad-tempered woman, no matter what else! And so to hell with her.

But don't let anything happen to her. Keep her safe in the little house, with the doors locked and the storm outside. She's so small! She likes to think she's bold, but she's only a weak little thing and quite alone. Take care of her.

Something happened, Kate, between you and me. It can't be undone, can it? Something happened.

His hands were cold and he called for a second cup of coffee, really to warm his hands around the cup rather than to drink. His head throbbed so that the music's beat was painful, each crescendo crashing through his skull.

"Something happened," he said aloud.

Returning, Marjorie announced that it was time to go.

"I can see you're having a miserable time." It was a reproach in the guise of generous consideration. But he let it pass.

A wind had risen and Lionel, who had Marjorie's shawl in his hand, helped her on with it.

"Frankly," Francis heard her say very low, "I'm glad Francis refused to buy your property. Please don't offer it to him again, will you? I'm still waiting for him to get tired of all this and go home."

"Don't hold your breath while you wait," Lionel told her. "It's my guess he never will."

"Never's a long time," she replied.

But Lionel was right. He was not going to be driven out by politics or economics, by anything or anyone! He had lost enough for one lifetime: a kindly father dead and a dearly beloved mother left alone; then Kate, a woman out of a dream—until the dream broke; then

Patrick, a Jonathan to his David, or so he had hoped; finally, finally an unhealthy child. Loss enough, yes, for one lifetime.

The land was all he had left. He had fallen in love with the land and it was like loving another life, so profound was the attachment. To abandon it would be to long and ache for it until the day he died.

No. Eleuthera was his and he was hers. There was nothing more to be said.

Twenty

WHEN at last you reach the place at which, reluctantly, you must accept some enormous, shocking change —as when the endearing child becomes the hostile adult or the enchanting lover turns dull and mean or the trusted friend embezzles and cheats you—then, looking backward, it suddenly becomes quite clear. Yes, yes, of course, that was the day, when he said this or she did that, of course, that was the first sign, the start, which you failed to recognize! Or did not want to recognize?

Nicholas Mebane entered office amidst a universal, roseate euphoria. Enthusiastic comparisons were made with Roosevelt's historic first hundred days. "We will not promise miracles," he said frankly, "but there will be immediate and swift beginnings. They will be visible and felt, I promise you that."

And Patrick's heart swelled.

Within two months of the accession ground was broken for a splendid recreation center, with soccer fields, a swimming pool, and basketball courts, a whole range of sports. With the turning of the first shovelful of earth, there was a collective jubilation among the people. At last they were getting something, something they could see and touch!

Next came the establishment of the St. Felice Museum in a great, stone eighteenth-century warehouse behind Wharf Street. Doris Mebane, whose project it was, had overseen the renovation. With taste as refined and graceful as her husband's, she had caused a dry moat along the building's sides to be filled with greenery, while in the lofty, quiet space behind classic arches Anatole Da Cunha's gifts to the nation were displayed. There were some dozen oils and two pieces of marble sculpture. Above the front portal Nicholas had ordered a grand inscription to be carved into the stone: *Pro bono publico.* In the official brochure it was explained that this meant: For the benefit of the people. The building was dedicated with the accompaniment of a string quartet and unlimited champagne in paper cups, the entire middle class of Covetown attending and admiring. A fine beginning, indeed.

Patrick had ideas of his own to offer. At the close of the ceremonies he drew Nicholas aside.

"Something occurred to me last night. It's a school children's project. I was thinking of giving out seedlings, young fruit trees or vegetables or both. We'd have instruction, and prizes, naturally, for the best results. It would serve a joint purpose, a fine activity for the children, and at the same time it'd point up our need to be self-sufficient in food. What do you think?"

"Excellent! Go to it! Draw up a rough plan and present it at the next executive meeting." Nicholas clapped Patrick's shoulder. "Did you ever think, or dare to dream, we'd come so far? Lord, I remember doing Latin verbs together! Not that they ever did us much good. Or maybe they did!" His laugh came from his lips and shone in his eyes, an upwelling of pure pleasure.

"Can we get to work on this, then?"

"Don't see why not. One good thing about it, it won't cost much. We're frightfully low on money. Frightfully." And having been hailed from across the room Nicholas began to move away.

"Give me a minute," Patrick said hurriedly. "I know how swamped you are, but I haven't had a chance for a minute with you in days. I wanted to add, what about giving tree seedlings to the farmers while we're at it? Some blue mahoe or Honduras mahogany? That last hurricane wrecked at least two thousand acres of government-owned forest and there's been no replanting at all. It occurred to me we could combine the projects. It shouldn't cost much."

"You're minister for education, remember? That would come under the heading of forestry."

"I know, but things do tie into one another, they overflow from one department to another."

"I've got to run now. Really. We'll talk about it some other time." Nicholas gave him another shoulder pat. "Just remember, Rome wasn't built in a day. Although I do love your enthusiasm!" he called back.

Patrick drank enthusiasm as if it were rich wine. So much needed to be done! He was too well aware how poorly qualified so many of the system's teachers were; better salaries and improved conditions were, naturally, the solution to that. Driving out past Gully one day he noticed that the roof, which had leaked so badly when he taught there that they'd had to keep a row of buckets on the ready, was still the same old roof, unrepaired. Textbooks, visual aids, the drop-out problem—so his mind ran.

At executive meetings he ran through his list.

"Whoa, not so fast!" Nicholas rebuked one day. "We'll get there eventually, you know."

"Yes, but when?" Patrick felt himself pressing.

"The money," Nicholas said, with emphasis. "Money. We haven't got it."

"But there's the World Bank loan. And you've just raised taxes. I'm not sure I understand why things are all that tight."

Nicholas winked around the room. The committee was a tight group, personally close; it was permitted to make teasing comments about each other.

"Money management, as I understand you, is not one of your talents, Patrick."

There were smiles and chuckles, so that Patrick, too, had to smile. Everybody knew that Désirée handled the money in his house, ostensibly because he was too careless to pay bills on time; he sometimes thought, though, that it was really because she spent everything as fast as it came in and had to rob Peter to pay Paul.

"No, you're no financier," Nicholas repeated, moving on to the next topic, a discussion of ways and means to "beef up" the police force on the streets of Covetown.

For a moment Patrick hesitated. Still unused to his role, it was an effort to speak up. But he did.

"The town's already full of police, it seems to me."

"We need them, don't we? We've too many pickpockets. They'll frighten tourists away if we get a reputation for being unsafe."

"The kids have nothing to do. You remember, we spoke about playgrounds—"

"Well, we've been giving them some, haven't we?"

"Only three in the lower parishes and the last one's still waiting for equipment." He went on thoughtfully, "Anyway, playgrounds aren't the real answer, are they? It all goes back to the economy. Everything does. And these aren't the nineteen sixties anymore."

"Exactly. That's why we need to encourage tourism and immigration. To do that, we've got to have law and order."

"Tourism and immigration aren't the whole answer, since you mention it. I've been wanting to talk about it, as a matter of fact. These people come flocking in for cheap land; they speculate and drive the prices up." Having once begun, his thoughts and his words flowed easily. "We shouldn't sell to speculators anyway, only to people who plan to stay and contribute to the country."

He thought he saw glances and lowered eyes. A sudden sensitivity to the change in atmosphere caused his skin to prickle.

"Hotel construction creates employment," Nicholas suggested mildly.

"Only temporarily. And for monsters like the Lunabelle and those others? No way! That's the kind of investment we don't need. They're wrecking the bay with all that dredging, destroying the natural marshland to make fancy beaches. Destroying the reefs, which kept the beaches from eroding in the first place. But they don't care. It's today's quick buck they're after and to hell with the next generation! Dumping raw sewage into the bay! When the wind's right you can smell the stink a mile away." And he looked around for some nod, some sign of agreement, but there was none; seven or eight faces circled the room, staring ahead without expression. "Look," he pleaded. "You all remember when the bay was full of lobsters and groupers. Now you have to go miles offshore for large fish. Pollution and spear fishing have done that. They're wrecking the seas. I've seen what's happened elsewhere and I've read Cousteau." About to finish, he thought of something else. "Go to the window and tell me we aren't on the way to ruining one of the most exquisite seascapes one might hope to see anywhere in the world! Remember what they did to Diamond Head in Honolulu? You've seen pictures—"

"You're jumping from fish to reefs to hotels," Nicholas interrupted. "We can't keep up with you."

"I'm not jumping. They're all part of the same picture."

There was a silence. Then Nicholas spoke, "Will anyone move that we take the previous remarks under serious consideration?" The motion having been made and passed, he added, "I shall appoint a committee to study land use with a view to preserving the character and ecology of St. Felice."

Three months later the sale of property for another bayside hotel was made public. Patrick went at once to Nicholas.

"I don't understand. I thought there was to be no more construction around the bay, at least not without discussion."

"We had discussion, a couple of hours' worth, at the last meeting, the one you missed."

"I missed?"

"Yes, I called an emergency executive committee meeting while you were visiting your mother in Martinique. I ordered the minutes to be sent to you."

"They were never sent, and to my shame I haven't been in Martinique in months."

"Queer! Well, someone was certainly misinformed. I'm sorry, I'm really sorry. And I do understand how you feel about aesthetics. It's just that we're badly in need of capital right now. I think I can promise that this sort of thing won't happen again, though."

Humiliated and indignant, Patrick nevertheless reined himself in. No sense jumping to conclusions! Nicholas wouldn't trick him! It was almost paranoid to suspect that he would.

Yet he left with the odd feeling that he had been placated, as one diverts a demanding child.

Désirée was stirring something at the stove. He could tell by her back and her stiffened shoulders that she was disturbed.

"I was at Doris's this afternoon. Nicholas must have had some sort of business going on at his house. The men were leaving just as we drove up."

He was startled. "Meeting? The executive committee, you mean?"

"No, of course not, although I did see Rodney Spurr and Harrison Ames. I didn't know the others. There were even some white men. One of them was that very heavy, short man who built the house on the cliff, the one with all the glass, you know."

"Jurgen. He's making a lot of investments here, they say."

Désirée turned around. "Doris made me promise not to tell you, but Nicholas has been saying you don't cooperate."

Patrick was aghast. "Don't cooperate! What the devil does he mean by that?"

"That you—heckle."

"Heckle!"

"I do hope you're not making any trouble, Patrick. You've been friends all your lives."

"And what sort of trouble would I be likely to make? Or do I ever make?"

"I don't know. Sometimes you do climb on your soapbox, though. You can be very stubborn when you've an idea in your head. You never give in."

"You mean I stand by my convictions? May I drop dead if I ever stop!"

"Don't get so excited! But you are stubborn, you know." Désirée's red mouth pouted. "For instance, why wouldn't you let me go to Europe with Doris that time? Quite frankly, she thought it selfish of you and so do I. I've never been anywhere and—"

"I couldn't afford the trip, that's why!"

"I thought surely with you being in government we'd have things easier. But it's really no different from when you were teaching or working on the *Trumpet.*"

"I didn't join the government to get rich."

"Well, you could at least have let me go once with Doris!"

"I'll be damned if I'll let you take charity!"

"Charity! Your best friend! It would have been doing Doris a favor. She wanted me to go. And they've loads of money, anyway. It wouldn't have meant a thing to them!"

"Loads of money," Patrick repeated, thoughtfully. "I don't know. Dr. Mebane wasn't all that rich and he had four children to divide among. I don't know."

"Nicholas is making money on his own! He's investing in hotels and beach front property all over the island. That new nightclub that opened off Wharf Street, the Circe—he owns half of that. Didn't you know? That new hotel they just announced—that's his!"

Patrick sat down. He was quite still.

Désirée continued in the high, petulant voice of Doris Mebane. "Why can't we get some pleasure out of life? Stuck in the same rut, when you could be getting ahead, like Nicholas?"

He answered coldly, angrily. "When do you plan to grow up? Or do you, ever?"

Her eyes filled and he was instantly sorry. She hadn't deserved his temper. This, today, was her first complaint. Although she had never had much of anything compared with many of her friends, she had, he was well aware, stifled her wants and been cheerful with the little he had been able to give her. Now, in their new situation, she must be feeling a certain bafflement. Doris's husband could provide things, while her own husband couldn't and didn't seem to mind that he couldn't. He wished he could explain it to her, but his own confusion dizzied him and he was silent.

With a full heart he went to bed, to lie long awake. So that was what Nicholas was doing! It was, very likely, what they were all doing and why they were silent whenever he spoke. They knew he wasn't with them. So he stood alone! To whom could he talk about it, where turn? He felt a bewildered sense of betrayal. It would have been comforting to confide in his wife, but he did not dare. Her tongue was too loose, too innocent. The only human being he could talk to, when you came down to it, was Kate Tarbox.

On his walks home from the center of town he had to pass the office of the *Trumpet*, where from time to time he stopped off. He missed the place. It was so alive, with the news of the world flashing in, the typewriters clacking and the telephones ringing. And there was always Kate at the editor's desk. He'd used to catch himself, when he worked there, staring at her from across the room. She had the kind of face that is known as mobile, meaning, he supposed, that you could so easily read its moods as the light of humor moved across it, or as stern disapproval closed the lips, or as some lovely contemplation opened the eyes into a wide, soft gaze.

Sometimes, now, he would accompany her on the homeward walk to the corner of her street.

"You look glum," she remarked, as they climbed the hill, the day after the talk with Désirée.

He told her, half reluctant to reveal himself and half relieved to express what he had been stifling.

"I'm troubled," he concluded. "I feel as if I'm standing alone in the center of a circle, with everything vaguely falling away, and I can't reach Nicholas, I don't know why."

"Why don't you tell him what you know?"

"I can't. I promised Désirée. I don't suppose it would make any difference, anyway. It's not my business, is it, how a man invests his money?"

"This is your business. This is different and you know it. It smells bad to me." They stopped and Kate ticked off a list on her fingers. "Look. We were going to electrify the villages and put in a sewer system. On the north side they still dump night soil in the ocean every morning. Nobody talks about it, but we all know they do. We still collect water in cisterns and on rooftops. Nicholas spoke again and again of desalinization plants and hydroponic gardening and canneries. Oh, it was all so *energetic*! Our roads are terrible. We have more cars and more accidents. I know everything can't be done at once, but I'd just like to see some slight movement toward a beginning."

"I don't understand Nicholas," he repeated. His voice was hollow and sad in his own ears.

For a moment Kate seemed to be making up her mind. Then she said, "I want to show you something. Have you got an hour to spare, right now?"

"I'll spare it."

"You'll have to get your car. Have you ever been at the Lunabelle Annex?"

"Over the causeway, you mean? No."

"Over that little bridge you have to walk across, where the new cottages are."

At the remote end of the Lunabelle's beach, out of sight around the point and half a mile from the main building, they stopped the car. Tall grasses grew between the ruts of a secluded, sandy lane.

"Not used very much," Patrick observed.

The footbridge spanned a narrow channel. A circle of quaint, peak-roofed cottages bordered the white beach along the little island's rim. The backs of the cottages looked upon an oversized blue pool, amoeba-shaped. Parasols and expensive chairs stood on the silky lawn between the flower beds. It was very quiet. Only one couple, lying in the sun, looked up briefly as Kate and Patrick appeared and then went back to concentrating on the sky.

"Out of season," Patrick said.

"It's never crowded. This isn't for the public, you know."

"Isolated. One couldn't guess it was here."

"Exactly. Come, maybe there's an open door. Or we can peek in."

All the sliding glass doors were locked. But one could clearly see inside to rooms in which white velvet rugs lay on pink terrazzo floors and wide beds bore gilded carving; in one a lace robe had been left lying on a chair. A nineteenth-century, or possibly a twentieth-century, bordello must have looked or maybe still looked like this, Patrick thought, but did not say it.

"Bizarre, isn't it?" Kate asked, as they walked back between oleander hedges to the car.

"Yes. Who are these people?"

"You can't guess?"

He had some uncertain thoughts, but waited.

"The mob."

He stared.

"I can't prove it, although I suspect it strongly. More than suspect it. These men come down here from the States, bring their girls, do their business, and make their payoffs here in private where the government protects them."

"Payoffs for what?"

"Dope, I think," she said seriously, and as he still stared at her, she went on, "Why should you be surprised? Central America is ridden with it."

He couldn't answer that.

"You're crushed because it's Nicholas." She touched his hand. "Of course, I could be wrong."

"You've got to be wrong," he said. "You've got to be."

On the broad side lawn of Government House they passed a unit of police deploying, smart in their new gray uniforms with scarlet caps and scarlet trouser stripes.

"Stop a minute," Kate commanded. "What do you see?"

When he did not understand immediately, she asked, "You mean to tell me you haven't noticed them these last few weeks?"

"The style, you mean? Nicholas likes a certain amount of ritual and display," Patrick offered, almost sheepishly.

"That's not what I meant. Look again! When did we ever have so many police? Every one of them over six feet tall! They're tough, and they're all new men. There's not one old familiar face, the faces we all knew. I wouldn't be surprised—" she said and broke off.

"Surprised at what?"

"Oh, nothing."

"Women are so damned exasperating! Will you please finish what you started?"

"Frankly, I'm not sure I should have trusted you today."

"Well, thank you! Thank you very much! If that's the way you feel, don't bother to talk to me at all. Please don't."

"Don't be huffy. I didn't mean it the way it sounded. I meant that you're a very loyal person, and very close to Nicholas in spite of the things you've been seeing. How can I know what your conscience, nagging at you in the middle of the night, will tell you to do?"

He softened. "Kate, anything you've ever said to me has gone no farther. You ought to know that." It was the first time in a long while that he had made mention, however oblique, of Francis Luther.

She flushed. "All right, then." She looked around and lowered her voice, although the car was moving. "There are rumors that a national police force is being gathered. They've even got a name: the Red Men."

"Well, wouldn't that be more efficient?"

"Don't be dense, I'm speaking of a paramilitary force. Arrests in the night, mysterious disappearances, bodies dumped along the roads. Know what I'm talking about? You ought to know. It's the history of the twentieth century, isn't it?"

Shock went through him, down to his knees. "You can't be serious! Who told—" He broke off. "Excuse me. Of course you can't reveal it."

"Of course I can't. Let's just say I have—sources."

For a minute or two neither of them spoke. The car had stopped at Kate's house, but she made no move to get out.

"Patrick. I'm terribly afraid."

"It may not be what you think," he suggested softly.

"If I had any guts I'd put it all in the *Trumpet.* But I have none, that's the trouble."

"Kate! Are you out of your mind? Don't you dare!"

"You see, you do believe what you've been seeing, or you wouldn't say that. In a free country, the press has nothing to fear, has it?"

He didn't answer. Here were the old streets, the listless leaves, gray with dust, the muffling, sleepy summer heat, so long familiar, now as threatening as some queer, twisted alley in a foreign place where nobody speaks one's language.

Then he brought himself up short. This was jumping too hastily to conclusions! For all her intelligence, Kate was still a woman; women exaggerated; they were always drawn to the dramatic and the thrilling. He was about to say so when Kate spoke again.

"About Will—keep an eye on him. Tell him not to get mixed up in politics right now."

"Why, what's he doing?"

"It doesn't matter. I can't say any more. Just tell him to be careful." And leaving Patrick with that enigma, she got out of the car.

Feeling faintly irritated by all the mystery, as well as with himself for his own fears, he drove away. It was market day downtown. Schooners from out islands were unloading woven baskets filled with iridescent pink and silver fish, as they had been doing for centuries past. But on the other side of the square a dozen or more young men and women waited in front of the airline office ready to depart for England or America, where they would drive the busses and collect the garbage: a better life, apparently, than they had waiting for them at home. He sighed and came back to his own affairs.

"Keep an eye on Will," Kate had warned. Oh, by all means! And just how was he to do that? Will was a man now, or more a man than almost any other boy his age. You couldn't pin him down!

"Where were you?" one would ask.

"Out with friends," he would answer.

"Yes, but where?"

"Just walking around, down on the beach."

You never could get more out of him than that. And what if you did pin him down, saying, "We know you spend time at the Trenches and we don't want you to go there anymore." What good would that do?

He wondered what Will and his friends really did talk about, what interested them besides Che Guevara and Mao. No, not Mao anymore; he'd gone out of favor, like so many left-wing heroes. At Will's age, Patrick thought, what I cared about were girls and books and wanting to know some more of the world. I wasn't angry like him, I know that much. And I remember I could laugh a lot. Will never does, at least not when he's home with us. No, you couldn't pin him down.

Nevertheless, he asked point-blank that night, "Will, I want to know, are you mixed up in anything political?"

Will gave him a long look. "Why do you ask?"

"Because I'm worried. I don't challenge your right to believe in what you believe, and by this time obviously I know what you believe. But I don't think it's safe for you to be too outspoken right now."

"Right now? I thought this was supposed to be a democratic government. Free speech, freedom of thought and all that." There was a taunt in the way Will said it.

Patrick found himself struggling, put once again on the defensive. "It is a democratic society! But it takes time to develop orderly democratic societies in which people think for themselves." He mouthed and floundered, repeating, "It takes a long time, and in the meanwhile, during a period of stress—"

"Each of us has only one lifetime," Will said. "How long are we supposed to wait? In the meanwhile," he went on before Patrick could reply, "there's been no change. Take the Francis family, the Tarbox family. The worker tends the bananas, and the profits go to a fancy house in England, or maybe the Riviera, or wherever else those people travel to make themselves comfortable."

Back to the Francis family again. Always the Francis family. Strike, and strike the sore spot. Will knew how to do that!

"Tell me, are you so satisfied with what you've had since Mebane got in?" the boy demanded now.

"Not entirely, no, I'm not. But never forget, we've a way to change things when we're not satisfied. The ballot is our defense, a most precious defense. When you think how few peoples in the world have the right to vote, you'll treasure what we've got."

"Vote for this one, vote for that one—it makes no difference. I'll take the Cuban way and you can keep your ballot."

"Oh, it's tempting, isn't it? No vote, just one man, quick and efficient, who gets things done without a lot of committees and talk! Justice and equality at the stroke of the great man's pen! Only it isn't equality. Listen"—and earnestly now, trying to convince, to force the boy to understand it as he understood it, Patrick thumped his fist into his palm—"listen to me! Do you really think people are equal under those systems? Why, the leaders in Russia have every privilege and luxury that kings ever had, things the masses never even see. And what's more, they have the power of life and death over those masses. Equality!"

"Life and death," Will said. He spoke calmly. He looked off, looked at the wall behind and above Patrick's head, as though he were considering whether to say something else or not. Then he stood, leaning with one elbow on the mantel, a habit which made Patrick nervous. Will made such abrupt movements, so rough and sweeping, and Désirée's Royal Copenhagen figurines, those fragile blue-and-white milkmaids and goosegirls, patiently collected at Da Cunha's, were so treasured. But he had never broken one yet.

"You know, of course, what's happening with the Red Men," he said at last.

"Happening?" Patrick repeated.

"Yes." Will was patient, intense and old.

He's never been young, Patrick thought, as eye contact was made between them. And he evaded. "Well, there are too many of them—"

Will interrupted. "It's not what you see, it's what you don't see. It's what they do when they take off the uniform, it's the ones who never wear the fancy uniform at all. And there are hundreds of them, that even you don't know about. Talk of the power of life and death—" He broke off. "But you won't want to hear because Nicholas is your friend."

"He was a brother to me," Patrick said slowly, as if murmuring to himself.

"Well. Brothers do strange things, too."

To know so much, to be so cynical, at seventeen!

"You're in the government, but you haven't the faintest idea what the government is. Don't you realize at all what's going on behind your back? The Daniel sisters' car crash last month—take that, for instance. You thought it was an accident?"

"Everyone thought so."

"Not everyone," Will corrected. "That car didn't skid off the road. The sisters were shot by Red Men and then the car was shoved over the cliff. That's what really happened."

"But why?"

"They ran a whorehouse, a fancy place for tourists on the West-brook Road. They were murdered because they got too sure of themselves and stopped paying off to Alfred Claire. That's Mebane's cousin—of course you know that. Don't you see the whole family's on the take, milking the country?"

"But where do you hear these things, Will? How can you say these things?"

"I say them because they're true." Will smiled. He had a one-sided, reluctant smile, almost wistful. "My friends and I—we have ways of knowing."

Kate and her sources, Patrick thought. He was dazed. From the nature of democracy to Cuba and communism and now to whore-houses and murder, all in less than half an hour! How could he know who was telling the truth?

"I don't know whether to believe all this," he said.

And again Will smiled, that strange, touching smile.

"Believe it," he said.

"The Mebanes are having a housewarming," Désirée announced.

Nicholas's house had been completed in the new community on the cliff at Cap Molyneux. Through Désirée, Patrick had been informed almost daily of its progress, its Italian tile, the pool, and the great curved room. "Like the prow of a ship," she reported.

"I don't want to go," he told her.

"What! What can you be thinking of? Never mind my feelings and Doris's if we don't go, but how will it look? The only member of the government to stay away? And you on the executive committee?"

"The executive committee hasn't met in months and it's only a rubber stamp anyway, as far as I'm concerned. I'm a minority of one." He could hear his own bitterness.

"Well, maybe that's your fault! Anyway, what has it got to do with the party?"

She was right, of course. It would be very strange indeed to stay away, conspicuous and strange. So, still as troubled as he had been during these last weeks, Patrick got himself dressed up and went.

It was an eagle's aerie. On a plateau at the top of the mountain stood a small cluster of new houses. Men retired from industry in North America and Germany and Sweden had built them with a view of endless ocean and more than a thousand feet of jungle below. The Mebanes' house adjoined the Jurgens', where through a gap in the shrubbery the Jurgens' peacocks could be seen, flaunting their fantails as they passed the hidden floodlights.

Patrick walked out to the far end of the terrace and sat down on the parapet. Indoors the buffet table bore flowers, food, and quantities of silver. Here on the terrace people were dancing to the music of the stereo. And he turned his head away, to stare downward at the quiet, black sea. Certainly it was not that he ever disapproved of music, wine, and dance! Rather it was that, in some subtle way, this place and the people here tonight had removed themselves, so it seemed to him, from the struggling, throbbing life beneath them, where even now a weak light streaming from some night fisherman's little skiff brightened the dark water with a moving stain of indigo.

It was cool at this height, almost cold. The cold cleared his head.

Did none of these people see or care what was happening to the country? Surely others of them beside himself must see, although none spoke! Only from below there in the villages came the sounds of discontent and restless hope.

Since Independence Day there had been a surging of the mass, people streaming out of the countryside, seeking mecca in the town. That sour, tragic area known as the Trenches was flowing over. Packs of defiant, idle boys had begun to rove through the streets, mugging and stealing. Did no one see the writing on the wall? His hands clenched in his pockets, so that the nails dug into the palms.

At what point, when and how, had Nicholas Mebane, with his quick, discerning mind, so keen and clear, at what point had he been corrupted and beguiled? Now, below the surface of that mind, lay revelations at which Patrick could never have guessed. It was like peeling off layers of clothing and finding some secret deformity of the flesh, or like finding a stranger wearing the familiar features of another. Was it power alone that had brought this change? Or could it have been there all the time, awaiting its hour all these years, unrecognized by one who loved him?

Oh, people changed, everything changed! That was the one thing you could be sure of. Francis Luther. Better not to think of him. Think of himself. Think of Désirée and his love for her, which, no longer the dazzle of first youth, but deeper now, more clear and tender, could comprehend and smile at her mood when, raising his eyes from the sea, he saw her pass; her laugh was happy as she flashed in her new dress, bought after such decisions made and unmade, as though her fate depended on it. Lovely, kind, and foolish Désirée in the fluttering dress, poor woman-child, to be so enthralled by all this —this tinsel!

Yes, people changed. But not as Nicholas had done.

How many years since those first days at school? "Come on home for lunch," he said, and I went and thought his father's middle-class, clean house on Library Hill was a palace.

Next door the peacocks blared their harsh cry. And Patrick stood up, turning away again from the chatter and glitter to look back over the dark sea. He brushed his hand across his eyes. He could have wept.

The man inside this house was dangerous.

What to do, but admit to yourself that you're afraid? He was helpless. Three or four times he tried to talk to other members of the government, but always, even from his most careful, tentative approach, they drew away, either in alarm and fear or because of their own complicity. There was no way to tell.

And suddenly the storm was upon them all. Suddenly the newspapers of the world made the name of St. Felice familiar to millions who had either never heard it before or had forgotten it if they had.

A prominent feature writer for a popular journal came to the island and sent home an article about the growth of dictatorship on St. Felice. Two days later he was shot to death in the garden of Cade's Hotel, his body, with a bullet hole in the temple, having been discovered there by a waiter.

Passing the scene on Wharf Street, Patrick felt compelled to go in, which was odd, since he was ordinarily one of those who shun the scene of an accident because they can feel the intensity of pain in their own flesh, as if they were themselves the victims. Yet he went in.

Cade's had gone to seed. The twentieth century had at last arrived on St. Felice. The Lunabelle and its kind, with their glass and steel and chrome, their neon and plastic, were proof enough of that. Cade's had remained in the nineteenth century. The sugar bowls still stood in saucers filled with water to keep the ants out. A shabby old Englishman, who either couldn't afford the Lunabelle or would not go there, was having his morning tea on the veranda as Patrick, having seen the spot in the garden where a large red-brown stain was all that remained of a decent, talented young man, went down the steps and out into the morning. For an instant he looked back at the old building where he had brought Désirée for their first gala dinner together, and where they had spent their wedding night. He was deeply moved. Everything was bound together, his life with Désirée, the murdered stranger, the old Englishman, everything. All of us, all in the flow of time. What to do?

He got into his car, having no idea where he was going or why. He knew only that he had to move. He could not have said whether it was despair or fear, in its nakedness and shame, that moved him. As he sped along the road, his vision grew sharp; it was as though he had been given a glass that magnified the world. He saw a dead dog on the road and hoped it had died quickly, without pain; too often one saw agonized animals in the ditches, dying in the broiling sun. On either side of the car the cane grew tall. It was like running a jungle path; a bird's eye would see it as a canyon between green cliffs. He could see the workers moving steadily, cutting in pairs. Once, catching a bar of song in the wind as he went by, he recognized it as a chant to ease the labor. These were the men with whom he had once, in the village, been a boy. And again he felt a rare, exalted kinship with all people, all living things.

At a village rum shop, one of those places where men came to drink and play dominoes, he stopped the car. A jukebox blasted out a raucous tune and voices had to rise above the noise, but no one turned it off. Noise probably gave life to the midafternoon, for the men at these tables were not working; this was slack time, and they were talking about credit—how they would get it and whether it would be enough to carry them through until they could go back to work. Patrick knew they had been talking about it. When he took a seat and asked for his drink they lowered their voices or stopped speaking. He saw that they did not recognize him. He was not prominent enough in the government for his face to have become familiar. It was his clothing and his light skin that told them what class he came from. It was these that had silenced them. They didn't trust him. They were afraid of him. Yet he was of them and he understood them, although, if he were to tell them so, they would surely not believe him. True, he had left them behind; true, as a child in a village like this one, he had already been different from them in many ways. And yet he was of them because he understood them. He had never felt that as clearly as he did now.

He finished his drink quickly and got back into the car. Quite suddenly, he knew what he must do. And he drove rapidly back to Covetown, parked the car at Government House, and went up the steps two at a time. He remembered that, one day as they passed this tall, white portico, Will had remarked that the more things change the more they remain the same, meaning that the color of the men who occupied this mansion had made no difference after all.

He was admitted to the beautiful square room where Nicholas sat.

"Nicholas, what's happened to you? I demand to know."

"Sit down," Nicholas said agreeably. "I'm not sure I know what you mean."

Patrick drew his chair to a place where he would not be staring into the light. Strong men liked to discomfit their visitors by putting them in the face of the light, he remembered.

"What's happened to this government? Suddenly—or not so suddenly—everything's caved in."

"Caved in?" Nicholas's eyebrows made two inverted v's of surprise. "Aren't you being somewhat dramatic?"

"Don't turn me off, Nicholas. You made promises to me, to us all. And you haven't kept them."

"What do you want me to do? Rub Aladdin's lamp and make your wishes come true overnight? Well, I can't do it!"

"I said, don't turn me off, Nicholas. There's a stench in this land. A stench the world calls fascism."

Nicholas looked across the desk at Patrick. His glance traveled to the open-necked shirt, of which, Patrick knew, he disapproved; then it traveled around the room, fastening first on a crystal paperweight, then on the bunch of keys he had taken out of his pocket, and finally on his own finger, where shone a diamond on a narrow gold band. Then he spoke.

"The world, meaning a handful of reporters, doesn't know what it's talking about. If there's any stench, as you put it, it's wafting from the other direction. Good God, you know what's going on? You know Moscow, through Cuba, is exporting terrorism all through this region. Listen to me, my friend. We face serious trouble. Maybe you don't realize how serious. You know what's being smuggled into this country? Arms, Patrick, rifles and hand grenades, landing on our beaches night after night. I haven't wanted to make it public knowledge because the people who are doing this will take advantage of the slightest unrest, of a thing like a teachers' strike, for example, anything, to further their cause. And we can't afford to let them do it unless we want to give in and give up right now. We have to fight strength with strength. Only a strong government—"

Once Nicholas had had the power to mesmerize him, but no longer.

"This is no 'strong government.' This is a rotting government."

"I don't like the sound of that, Patrick."

"Do you think I like it, either? Oh, Nicholas, what's happened between you and me? From the very beginning, after all our hopes, you shut me out, me and every idea I had. You gave me a sinecure and got rid of me. Why?"

"Because I found out early on, during those first few weeks, that you had no grasp of affairs. You live a boy's life in a man's world. It's one of your most appealing and most exasperating qualities. You want utopia right now. But there is no Santa Claus, Patrick."

Through the window on the side of the room Patrick could see the bay and the cupping hills, with the pale-green water lying at the bottom of the cup. The Lunabelle and the steel-framed cubical skeleton of new construction severed the sky. He pointed and heard himself speaking.

"I understand you're a part owner of all that."

Nicholas started. "I? Who told you that?"

"Doris told Désirée originally. But it's common enough knowledge by now, I suspect."

Nicholas leaned across the desk. "Women's talk! Damn women!"

Eyes like lumps of coal, Patrick thought; hard and dull, with sudden glisten when a streak of sunlight strikes the turning head. I've made him furious.

"Yes. I've put a few dollars in here and there. Is it any business of yours how I invest my money?"

"Yes. There's conflict of interest." Patrick's voice rose, sounding high as a boy's, so that he had to clear his throat.

"You're a nitpicker. I'm running a government, planning a stable future for thousands of people, and you're upset because I've earned something for myself."

"You're not planning a future for anyone except yourself. You only want money and the power to keep making it. Don't you have enough now?" The high voice again, sounding like pleading.

"Grow up, Patrick." Nicholas's anger had receded. "And get out of politics. You don't understand it. You never will. You'd be better off back in the classroom before it's too late."

"It's too late already."

"Quit, Patrick. Don't make me throw you out."

"I won't quit. And I won't let you throw me out."

"Let me give you some advice. What you really should do, what any sensible man in your shoes would do, is to go off to the States. We may be in for some hard times here. You could go off to the States and pass. Actually, you could have done that long ago when we were in England."

"I couldn't have and can't, and if I could, I wouldn't't."

"Of course, with Désirée it might be somewhat difficult." Nicholas smiled. "But you could get rid of her if you wanted to. Maybe Kate Tarbox would go with you instead."

"You bastard! If there's anyone who'll leave here, it'll be you. Yes, when you've ruined the place with prostitution, gambling, and dope so it isn't fit to live in, you'll leave and meet up with your money in Switzerland."

I've struck home. He will vault over the desk and come at me.

But anger had made Nicholas go rigid. "If my wife weren't a friend of your wife's, if I didn't have some memory of our being boys together, I'd make you pay for what you're saying."

"Yes, you could have me shot like that poor fellow at Cade's Hotel."

"What do you think a communist government would have done to him? And, while we're talking, what do you think it would do to a woman like Kate Tarbox? You think I don't *know* what she's saying? Luckily for her, she's been smart enough to keep her fuzzy ideas out of that newspaper of hers. Besides, she has friends among the planters and some of them are my friends. So no matter what I think of her lies—"

"She doesn't lie, Nicholas."

The men stood up and faced each other.

"I want to tell you something else, Patrick. There's no reason why

I should, but out of the friendship you've just tossed away, I will tell you. We know about your son Will. We know about his meetings and his plans. They're a slippery lot, his people, but even a slippery fish ends up in the net. Tell him to remember that."

"I can't do anything about Will." Patrick's heartbeat changed to a reckless pounding. "He's a harmless boy—"

Nicholas mocked him with a look.

"Nicholas, I'm going to run for office. You've got an election coming and you'll have to go through the motions or there'll be real turmoil here, turmoil that even your Red Men won't be able to contain. And I'm going to oppose you in that election."

The black eyes still mocked.

"I had loyalty to you," Patrick said quietly, "but it's been strained beyond bounds or bearing. So now I'm going to fight you."

Nicholas smiled. "You do that. You won't get very far."

Twenty-one

FRANCIS and Nicholas stood in Eleuthera's hall, talking confidentially.

"I quite realize that he's not your type, Francis. Somewhat vulgar, shall we say? But you ought to listen to him, just once. They've come down from the States with money unlimited. Your Uncle Lionel's probably going to make a deal with them, you know."

"Yes, he told me."

Lionel had been exuberant these past weeks. "First offer I've got and it happens to be dazzling," he'd said.

Well, you could hardly blame him for being dazzled. He could go to England and live for the rest of his life on the invested income from the sale of his lands. Fleetingly, irrelevantly at this particular moment, Francis wondered about the woman whom Lionel had cherished all these years. Most certainly he would not be taking her to England! Francis had only seen her once, when he'd been arriving at the airport in Barbados and Lionel had been leaving. They had pretended not to see each other. She'd been a stunning woman, reminding him of— yes, of Patrick's wife, except that Désirée was jet and Lionel's woman was milky tea.

Nicholas brought him back now to the subject. "Did you know that the High Winds people are interested, too? The old man's over seventy and his sons don't want to run the estate."

"They haven't told me."

"Well, people don't talk about these things until they're signed and delivered. It's always a good policy to keep one's business close to one's vest. At least I've always found it so. Listen, Francis, you've got more beach than High Winds has, by far. And beach is what they need for a hotel project as big as this. You're in a position to ask almost any price you want for the place."

"I don't want to sell Eleuthera, Nicholas."

"But one has the impression," Nicholas said politely, "that your wife does. Isn't it true that she wants to go back to New York?"

So, one "had the impression"! Of course, everybody knew everything in this little place. And Nicholas, especially, had means of finding out whatever he wanted to find out.

"I have good reason to believe," Nicholas continued, "that you could get a couple of million."

Francis looked out to the lawn where Marjorie, already dressed for dinner, was sitting with two men. In their city woolens, the men obtruded on the pastel glimmer, the gauzy trees, the perfection of the waning afternoon. He wondered what conversation she could possibly be having with that pair. Frank Aleppo's wraparound glasses swathed his upper face. Francis hated it when people hid behind dark glasses; they reminded him of the black youths from the Trenches who went swaggering around town these days, except that these two men were white, so white that their skin in this warm light had the greenish cast of a reptile's underside. Aleppo's suit was hand-tailored. To be sure, Francis was accustomed to men who wore expensive clothing, but this man, these two, didn't wear it—they flaunted it.

"I don't like them," he said abruptly, aware that he sounded petulant as an adolescent.

Nicholas laughed. "With all respect to you, Francis, that's really not the issue, is it? Business is business. In justice to yourself and your family, you should at least give it some thought."

Why was Nicholas so anxious? Because of course he'd have a piece of the investment. It amused Francis to think that Nicholas assumed he wouldn't figure that out. There was, after all, no sin in putting your money where you chose. As Nicholas had just said, business is business! A clever man, Nicholas Mebane, so clever that he didn't realize other people could have quick wits, too. But he was charming, all the same—an eminently civilized man.

Francis frowned. One had heard some troubling things of late, things about torture and secret police and drugs and God knew what else. That was the news of the world, wasn't it, from Argentina to the Soviets? But way out here at Eleuthera he'd seen nothing unusual going on. Maybe the one thing he had noticed, the prevalence of the Red Men in town and on the roads, was all to the good. There'd been a lot of petty and not-so-petty crime last year, but ever since this force had been established it had diminished considerably. Or so one heard. Personally, he'd had no experience of it, nor had anyone he knew.

As for the other business, there was possibly a kernel of truth, a bit of "roughing up" going on. But most of it was exaggerated rumor. All that stuff about a ravine where they threw your remains if you spoke out against the government! How could he relate to such atrocities a man like the gentleman standing with him now? Anyway, no matter what government was in power, one was better off keeping within the law, earning one's honest living, and staying away from the disputes. He himself was no man for the political fray. He'd heard somewhere that Patrick Courzon was to run against Nicholas in the next election. The more fool he, Francis was reflecting, when Nicholas spoke again.

"I've reserved a table for dinner at the Lunabelle. I've also invited some other people who've been doing business with Mr. Aleppo. I hope you don't mind."

"No, certainly not." He never enjoyed himself at places like the Lunabelle, but that was not something one would tell the prime minister.

"Senator Madison Hughes will be there, just flew down from Washington yesterday. Also my neighbors, the Jurgens. I don't believe you've met them, a very wealthy Swedish couple? American citizens, though."

Their citizenship was of no interest to Francis, but it was Nicholas's habit to furnish details, especially when he thought they might be impressive. The truth was that planters had no liking for the members of the foreign retirement community; their interests were often at odds. The winter people cared nothing about the welfare of the island except as it concerned themselves; they lived on the island without being of it. But that was something else he didn't care to discuss with the prime minister.

Marjorie came to the door. "We're ready if you are," she said pleasantly. She would despise Aleppo and his young friend, Mr. Damian, but they would never guess it.

"It's too bad your wife can't be with us," she said to Nicholas as they drove off.

"I'm sure she'd rather be where she is." He laughed. "Every year I let her take a few weeks off to go to Paris. She adores it. But then, why not?"

The car had descended the hill and was passing the beach when Aleppo said, "Wow, what a spread! Could we stop a minute and take another look?"

The four men got out, while Marjorie, whose shoes were silk and perishable, waited in the car. Nicholas and Aleppo walked ahead up the strand, both their pace and their flung gestures revealing animation. Damian was less enthusiastic. He sat down on a rock while Francis stood and waited.

"You own this river?" he asked languidly.

"Nobody owns it. It just happens to run through this land." Something about the other man's languor made Francis disagreeable.

"What's it called?"

"Spratt River. They seine sprat at the mouth, near the cove."

"What do you call this place? This beach?"

"The whole cove is called Anse Carrée. You can see it's almost square, and that's what the name means." Saying so, Francis looked up to where the two sharp sides of the cliff turned at right angles into a sheer drop and then down to the third side, a mild slope onto the broad clear beach.

Damian followed his gaze. "Fantastic!" he said with growing interest. "You made a smart buy all right! How long you own this place?"

"My family has owned it for three hundred years."

There was a silence. Damian's somber eyes squinted into the sun and back at Francis.

He doesn't believe me, Francis thought, and there being no more to be said, he walked a few steps to the water's edge and stood there looking straight out through the dazzle to where, if you were to keep on going, you would bump into Spanish Sahara.

Drifting at his feet in shallow water a sea anemone waved its delicate feelers. He picked up a stick of driftwood and gently touched the creature, who, withdrawing from the touch, rolled itself into a knobby ball.

"What's that?" Damian had come up behind him.

"A sea anemone."

"What do you know! Crazy-looking thing!"

Suddenly Francis felt sorry for the man. He didn't know why. Perhaps it was because he was so out of place.

"The sea is filled with strange things, plants that look like animals and animals that look like plants. Coral is an animal, you know. But some of it looks like trees. You can see whole gardens growing underwater." He didn't know why he was telling all this, either, except that it had something to do with that feeling of being sorry for this little man with the bored, superior air.

Nicholas and Aleppo came back, still talking vigorously.

"This is solid rock here," Aleppo was saying. "You could build eight, maybe ten stories, five hundred rooms eventually, adding wings, with the casino on top. There'd be a fantastic view. Nothing like it anywhere."

"Something like the Lunabelle?" Francis asked dryly.

"The Lunabelle, let me tell you, is a dump next to what we'd put here."

"And the house? What would you do with the house?" He felt himself tensed, as with the imminent expectation of pain.

"Tear it down, probably. Unless maybe it could be kept for a clubhouse. We'd have to go into all that. And you know what? I'd have elevators going up the side of the cliff from the beach. You ever seen that? People would get a kick out of it. Look up there, will you! What a location!"

Francis followed the man's pointing arm. At the top of the limestone bluff a pair of sooty terns rose and dove toward a clump of gilded elkhorn coral, having spotted some prey moving there as the tide went out.

"Water gets choppy at high tide, I imagine," Aleppo said. "But we could always dredge."

"Those are coral reefs out there."

"So?"

"So—if you dredge you'll ruin them. It took thousands of years to create those reefs."

"Mr. Luther is a naturalist," Nicholas explained to the uncomprehending Aleppo.

"Very amateur," Francis said.

"All the same." Nicholas was embarrassed. He was apologizing— but to which one of them?

Some prickling anger drove Francis on. "Flamingos used to breed here years ago in the flats between the river and the ocean."

"You don't say," Aleppo murmured.

Patrick Courzon had told him that the day they'd met. He had forgotten that until just now. And he went on, although he knew they were not interested, "I've been trying to bring them back. I bought two pairs a while ago and now they've got young."

"We could name the place Flamingo Hill. No, Flamingo Beach," Aleppo said. "How about that? Can you put them in cages? Some big fancy cages on the lawn?"

"You cannot put them in cages," Francis said. Why had he permitted Nicholas to bring these men?

Nicholas intervened with ease. "We'd better start. The reservations—"

They got back into the car.

Skirting the old stone houses of Covetown's center, with their flowering back-gardens and Georgian facades, they passed along mean roads where the town met the countryside; mangy dogs, scrabbling chickens, and rusty, derelict cars, along with more children than one remembered noticing only a month before, crowded the front yards.

Of a sudden they came upon the Lunabelle's angular bulk and those of its latest neighbors encrusting the hills around the bay. Flags snapped in the wind at the end of the long drive between royal palms. At the portico a black man smiled and sent for another black man to take the car away. And Francis experienced a flash of déjà vu: from a portico like this you followed the luggage to the room, and they brought a rum punch to welcome you, and the soporific wind blew through the jalousies and you heard the steady, repetitious crash of the Atlantic coming up against the breakwater and you went outside and Kate wore a yellow bathing suit and her hair hung like a mermaid's, and then you came back in and she took the suit off and—

"You come here often?" Aleppo inquired, making conversation.

"No. My wife does. She spends more time in town than I do." He was aware that for some reason he had purposely drawn a distinction between himself and his wife.

The enormous, airy lobby displayed at its center a fountain with a naked nymph. Around its sides a row of little shops displayed their French perfumes, their Danish silver, English china, and Italian silks.

"Oh," Marjorie cried. "Da Cunha's branch is open!"

"Francis," said Nicholas, "you'd better come look. Your wife sees something she likes."

Francis peered over Marjorie's shoulder at a pale blue pendant hung on a twisted chain of coral, blue, and gold.

"That," Marjorie said, drawing in her breath, "is absolutely the most beautiful piece of jewelry I have seen in my entire life. Absolutely. The beads are sapphires, Francis."

"Very pretty. But I can't afford it."

Nicholas laughed. "You could very soon though, if you chose to."

A young woman came from behind the counter. "Can I help you with anything?"

She was very dark; her eyes were delicately tilted and her long, heavy hair was Oriental. The men, struck by her presence, took a moment to answer.

"Some other time, thank you." Nicholas and Francis spoke together.

"Half black, half Chinese," Nicholas explained as they walked toward the dining room. "Her father had a grocery store. Ah Sing, the name is—or was; he must be ancient by now or dead. And his daughter is rising in the world. You see how it is, we provide employment with these places, we create opportunity."

"Much envy, too," Francis answered.

"Ah, Francis, you're so gloomy sometimes!" Marjorie complained.

Heads were raised as the prime minister walked into the dining room with his party of whites. Except for the waiters, he was the only black in the room. But he appeared to be unconscious of it, aware and pleased that his status was acknowledged.

The senator and the Jurgens were already at the table. The senator was handsome, a man who would age or had already aged well, with that air of powerful health which stems from a youth spent out of doors in almost any location west of the Mississippi. The Jurgens were thickset. They had the odor of money. Francis could smell it, not ordinary prosperity, but enormous amounts of it, obscene amounts of it. He was a stout, graying blond; she was pink, with loose pink skin and a loose pink garment which, so Marjorie had taught him, was called a caftan. She wore many diamonds. Fat cats, Francis thought, caught in the strange mood that so often beset him when he was forced to a gathering he didn't want to attend. It did this to him, bringing out a sharp, a nasty, critical awareness. He didn't like himself for it, but there it was.

Introductions were made and Nicholas said, "The Jurgens have the most marvelous house. With your taste," addressing Marjorie, "you would find it enchanting."

"It's the house next door to yours, isn't it?" Marjorie responded.

"Yes, but there's no comparison." Nicholas spoke modestly. "As Europeans, they have a special feel for gardens. Their lawns, and the pavilion at the far end, so Italian—"

"In spite of our being Swedish. You really must come to see us sometime, Mrs. Luther. Harold's retired, you know, so we're only here for three months. Then we go to Europe, and we have some family in the States, too. We do love it here the best though. I have two maids," she confided, "and one of them cooks better than the chefs at this hotel! For only twenty dollars a week each."

Francis glanced at Nicholas. Embarrassment shot through him so that he could feel its heat. But Nicholas gave no sign.

"People really don't need much cash here, do they?" Mrs. Jurgen's rhetorical question was gay. "No heating bills, no overcoats, no boots. And the villages are so quaint, all those picturesque little houses— really delightful."

"Delightful," Francis said. "With the toilet in the back yard."

He received from Marjorie a sharp kick on the ankle.

Mrs. Jurgen, thinking apparently that he had meant to be humorous, laughed. But Aleppo had understood.

"We could change all that. We could put this place on the map, I tell you. Remember how Havana used to be? This could put it to shame. We could make this another Riviera, build marinas, build a jetport, have excursion trips direct from Europe for deep-sea fishing, tarpon, whatnot. Believe me, there'd be a bathroom in every house on the island then, and a whole lot more!"

"Especially," Mr. Jurgen, who had not spoken before, put in, "especially with a common-sense man like this one at the helm of government." His plump cheeks, drawn into a smile, narrowed his small, pale eyes. "Frankly, he's the only reason I'm willing to invest. I feel secure."

"I shall have to merit confidence like that," Nicholas joked, "by making sure I get reelected."

Jurgen waved his cigar. "No problem! Those others—that fellow Courzon and the rest—mosquitoes buzzing. Nothing more. I'm not worried, I assure you."

The dinner arrived. Only a French or a Swiss chef could have created such marvelous soufflés and sauces, or such variety of flambéed desserts, borne proudly high as the waiters moved between the tables.

A trio of young men came to sing before a microphone. They were dressed as if they had just been brought there from the cane fields. Perhaps they actually had been. Their voices were warm, resonant, untrained.

> *Oh, island in the sun, willed to me by my father's hand,*
> *All my days I will sing in praise . . .*

And Francis put himself in their places at the front of the crowded room. What were they seeing? White faces burned pain-red, white breasts straining out of silk, mountains of food, the flicker of jewels. He wondered what they could be thinking about what they saw.

To these others here, surrounding him, it was all quite natural, quite unremarkable. Eating slowly, almost disregarding the talk at his own table, Francis observed the scene and listened to snatches of conversation.

"Darling!" people said, throwing their arms about each other. Then came the cheek-peck, the cheek-graze. "How are you! You look simply fantastic! I haven't seen you since dinner at the George V!" Or the Dorchester, or better still, some place less frequented, like Porto Cervo in Sardinia, or even some really far off "little" spot where "tourists don't go": *We were the only Americans in the whole place.*

Then, as always, he was brought back to the present. "You're a thousand miles away," Marjorie scolded in a whisper.

"Three or four thousand, actually. Sorry."

"Please, Francis."

Her eyes pleaded. "Do be sociable, do give forth a little, can't you?"

She wouldn't want to offend the prime minister. She didn't mind his being black, because he was the prime minister. She was having a good time. She loved wearing her beautiful dress, loved being here. Her eyes were brilliant and very large. She was thinking of two million dollars.

When dinner was over they walked outdoors, where terraces descended in tiers to the beach. The tide had gone out, exposing at the end of the beach the roots of beach grape and mangrove, along with a fringe of debris: clotted petroleum tar, bottles and cans. Floodlights plucked all these out of the darkness.

"Poor maintenance," Nicholas remarked. "I'm surprised."

"More than that," Francis said. "Look at the silt in the water. It's from dredging. That silt cuts down the light; the algae are smothered and the coral dies. They've destroyed the protecting reefs to get construction sand, that's what's happened here. Yes," he said, "dredge the seas, bulldoze the hills, and what next? It's a rape, that's all it is."

"Oh," Nicholas said lightly, "you sound like—" and stopped.

Like Patrick Courzon, Francis thought. That's what he had been about to say. And it was true—Patrick had always talked like that.

"You can't stop the twentieth century," Mr. Jurgen remarked, somewhat exasperated.

"You can plan your development instead of raping. Raping," Francis repeated. It was a reckless, angry word, and it suited him just then.

He was conscious, as they turned back to the cars, of Marjorie's furious glance.

Nicholas rode with the Luthers, who were to take him to his home. When they were almost there he reminded Francis, "I hope you don't mean you won't give consideration to the Aleppo offer, Francis. In spite of what you've been saying, it would be not only a great thing for you but a bonanza for the country. Take my word for it, please do."

"Oh," Marjorie said angrily, "naturally we all know the planters don't want development because they'll lose field labor. We all know that."

"That's not my reason," Francis said with some heat.

Nicholas made no comment. When they reached his house, he gave Francis his hand. "Well, it's all been quite bewildering and sudden, of course. But you will think it over?"

"I'll do that," Francis said out of courtesy.

"Thank you for a marvelous time," Marjorie called. "The dinner was perfect." When they had driven away she turned upon Francis. "You were absolutely ridiculous—I must say it. All that talk about algae and dredging! They thought you were eccentric and boring. I don't know what you hoped to gain with that kind of talk."

"I didn't hope to gain anything. It was just a mood. I wanted to get things off my chest. Am I not entitled to a mood like anyone else?"

"You sounded like some sort of hippy ecologist. . . . Like that younger Da Cunha brother who's always writing articles."

"That young Da Cunha cares. It's the older generation that doesn't give a damn about anything but money."

"It seems to me you like money well enough!"

"Yes, I like it. But I work for mine fairly—"

"Work! Yes, nobody could deny you do that! Worrying about banana rot and labor and too much rain or not enough rain—and for what?" She spoke rapidly. "Listen to me, Francis. Megan has to get away from this place. She has special needs. When she gets a little older she'll need schooling she can't get here. And this is our chance to provide all that, plus having a decent life of our own with no more worries. I swear I'll never forgive you if you don't take it, Francis. Never."

He was silent and she repeated, "Never. This time I mean it."

He was thinking that once her voice had had a ring as sweet as chimes. The sweetness had rung through to his very bones. He tried to remember when it was that it had stopped doing so, and could not. Driving now along the narrow mountain road in the darkness, he felt a penetrating sadness; it was like knowing there had once been a song you loved, and now you had forgotten it, forgotten even its name.

He said quietly, "I don't want to talk any more tonight, please. It's been a long day and for some reason I feel especially tired."

"Damn it, Francis! I hate it when you shut me off. You think you can just turn me off and on like a faucet whenever you feel like it."

It was an effort to answer, to open his mouth. "I told you, another time. I don't want to shut you off. All I want is to get home and sleep."

"Damn it, then. Get home and go to sleep!"

The car door slammed. The bedroom door slammed. She still slept across the hall. He wondered whether the sound had awakened the child. It was his last thought before he fell asleep.

But he slept badly, waking in the middle of the night, unable to fall back. Soon after dawn he got up and went out to walk.

Where the foothills of the Morne sloped steeply upward behind the house the path was scarcely used. Wet ferns showered his legs as he passed. The silent droppings of the pines were slippery underfoot. Now the woods were waking, loud with bird song and a thousand small rustlings of unseen life. Once, glancing up, he thought he saw a parrot, an instant's astonishing flash of emerald and orange in the sheltering gloom. If it was a parrot it had probably been *Amazona arausiaca,* a variety now hunted almost to extinction because a single specimen could bring five thousand dollars.

"It's disgusting," Kate had cried passionately. "They smuggle them out in tire tubes and suitcases. Naturally, most of them die on the way. I can't bear to think of it." She had reminded him of his mother's fierce pity for the weak.

He came back down the steep path. He had no wish to get to the day's work; he would have liked rather to lie down in the ferns and perhaps go to sleep at last, but the notion was eccentric, for if anyone were to come upon him lying there like that they would think he'd lost his mind. And he thrust his way on through a jumble of bananas, palm, and cane gone wild, emerging at the bottom of the path into a vision of splashing light, of clouds fleeing westward over the clearing where the great house lay among flamboyant trees. He stopped to look at it, his great house, and saw Marjorie coming toward him over the grass.

"I saw you on the hill. I wanted to say I'm sorry if I was nasty last night, Francis."

"That's all right. I wasn't in such a great mood myself."

She laid a hand on his arm and mechanically he put his over it. How he had loved her once!

And they stood a moment looking at the morning light, stood together, each wanting so much to understand and to be understood.

To ease the stress he made a neutral remark. "The river looks like silver from here."

"Oh, rivers! One makes such a fuss about rivers! The blue Danube is a muddy brown brook, that's all it is. But you've never seen it, have you? You've really never gone anywhere."

"I haven't had the time."

"Of course you have. You just came here and never left it. Never wanted to. If you left here you could travel. You've still got that camera on the shelf for your next book. What was it to be? *Man at Work in His Environment*, wasn't that it?"

"I guess so," he said dully.

"I nag you awfully about leaving, don't I?"

"I wouldn't say 'nag.' You just talk about it."

"Oh, you always cover everything with euphemisms. Don't you know you do? I nag."

It was true, he thought, surprised. Even in my private thoughts, I cover up. Like my mother, I'm too private. And I don't face the truth, it's true.

"I don't believe in covering up, Francis. Not anymore. So I'll tell you flat out: I *hate* it here! I always have. There was just no easy way to leave before this. But now there is."

"Have you thought of Megan?" he asked.

Her eyes widened. "I don't understand you! What a question!"

"It was stupid of me. I phrased it badly. I meant—this place is shelter for her, given what she is."

"But she can't hide here, Francis! She needs special education to bring out the little she's got, so she won't be just a—a vegetable! There's nothing here for her, you know there isn't! And you can't tell what's going to happen here anyway, with the political situation what it is!" She began to weep. "Oh, if we had a normal child!"

"Don't," he said. It tore him to see her weep over Megan. Because of him, his blood, his sister, his genes. His fault.

"And with all that money she would have security for the rest of her life! If you love her so, how can you be so selfish?"

He said thickly, "I love her."

"I'll tell you something, Francis. I'm not excited now. I'm thinking clearly and I'm quite, quite calm, not angry at all. But if you don't take this offer, I'm leaving. I'm taking Megan, and somebody in my family will shelter us until I can find a place for us."

"Is that the way it is?"

"That's the way it is."

Her eyes met his. Hers were austere and steady in their gaze. And he knew that she meant what she said.

"Let me think," he said. "Oh, let me think."

Her face closed. "All right. Just don't think too long."

She went back inside, and he walked down the hill toward that silver river to sit on a rock with his chin in his hands. On a bush close by a yellowbird was gathering twigs for a nest. So still he sat that the bird was unconcerned with his presence. Just so had he sat one day not long ago with Megan, showing her how a bird goes about the making of a nest. It had even picked up a piece of cotton torn from somebody's shirt. He had showed her that. And he had thought: Just something, some little thing missing in the making of her, some juice in the brain, some electrical connection, what? And she would have been whole and who knew how intelligent, how creative. Oh, God, he begged now, speaking aloud, and the yellowbird fled.

The air was filled with the fragrance of wild ginger, and he knew the white flower could not be too far away. One of his colts went galloping through pangola grass behind the rail fence that he had himself helped hew and set in place. Well, if he were to leave, he'd be leaving things in very different shape from what he had found when he came. The drenching sweetness of the ginger swept over him. Oh, my God, the place bewitched you! And he thought of his mother: could she, too, have felt this wrench when she left? Was that why she had never wanted to come back, and not, as some people thought, that she had hated it? Human behavior! How can you hope to understand it, when you can't even understand yourself?

And he sat there for a long time until he heard Megan's voice from somewhere above. No doubt she would be looking for him, his shadow, his Megan, his poor simple girl.

Slowly, stiffly, he rose and went up the hill. In the shelter of the old library he picked up the telephone.

"Mr. Aleppo," he said. The word stuck in his throat. "Mr. Aleppo. I've considered the offer and I've decided to accept. You can draw up the papers for me to show my lawyer."

Aleppo said something about having to go back to the States, something about time, a few weeks or a month or so.

"Take your time. Whenever you're ready."

"You're doing the right thing, Mr. Luther. Come back in a couple of years and you won't recognize your place."

"I'm sure I won't."

"You're a gentleman, Mr. Luther. I've met all kinds and I know a gentleman when I see one."

When he had hung up the receiver he went outside and walked around the house, with no purpose except the walk itself, the need to move. A voice sang from the cook's radio in the kitchen wing.

> *Oh, island in the sun, willed to me by my father's hand,*
> *All my days I will sing in praise . . .*

He went around to the front of the house. Somewhere inside Marjorie was waiting, determined and frightened, too, he knew. Well, he would just go in and make his peace. A man had to be strong enough to lose gracefully. He'd made a start here and he could make another.

Not far from the front door grew a great acoma, very old. His mother had said, "My grandfather used to touch a tree as though it spoke to him." This same tree, it might have been, as he came in at this same door. And before he went up the steps into the house Francis reached over to lay his hand on the ancient bark, and spoke to it softly, without words.

Twenty-two

IN a shady grove near a beach another crowd had gathered, the second one in a day that was to provide three of the same in various parts of the island. Blue paper streamers, emblazoned in gold with the words *Vote for Courzon,* dangled from the trees and festooned the skirts of the long sawbuck tables on which the food was laid out. Patrick, standing in line for calalu stew and soursop custard, reflected that he hadn't had such food since Agnes had cooked it, for Désirée had no taste for what she called peasant food. Then he wondered what Agnes would say if she could see this day. Next he thought about the connection between those kids dancing over there to a frantic rhythm band and the issues which were tearing their country apart, issues about which, according to theory, they were expected to think carefully before casting their votes. Well, it was a gradual thing, the evolution of a democratic government! It had taken, after all, quite a few centuries in England between Magna Charta and one man, one vote.

As for himself, after the first nervous, hesitant week or two, things had begun to pick up, "things" being his own sense of confidence. He was even becoming inured to the long days, the late nights, the voice gone hoarse, the food to be stuffed down his throat, and the hands

— 363 —

to be shaken. All in all, he was doing better with this campaign than he would have expected a normally reserved, almost a reclusive, man to do.

Men were rushing about now, trying to quiet the crowd. Someone bellowed, pleaded, and commanded over the microphone. It was clouding up and they'd want to get the speech finished before the rain came. Patrick glanced over the assemblage. There was the usual cluster of journalists, some, now that this part of the world had drawn the rest of the world's attention to itself, having come even from European countries. More white faces fringed the crowd: a few curious tourists, the planter Fawcett and the Whittaker nephew who was known to be "liberal," the youngest Da Cunha son with friends, and of course, Kate and her staff, who followed all the campaign speeches, Nicholas's as well as Patrick's. All of these stood forth from the dark-faced mass.

When the noise ceased the hush was absolute. They were waiting for what Patrick had to say. And as always, he gave himself a mental reminder to speak in strong, clear language. He might not be able to bewitch them with passionate oratory nor impress them with his manner and dress, but he could surely speak to them in language they would understand about things they would understand. He reminded himself also: never underestimate the intelligence of the "common" man.

His points were simple and consistent. He had said before, and would say again, that they were a farming people, that they would remain a farming people, and that such industries as they must establish would stem from agriculture.

"We are told about world markets and such things as balance of payments, all fancy expressions to describe and explain why we are poor, why some of us go to the cold north to pick apples in another country, why shoes cost so much, as do soap and even sugar, which although we raise it here ourselves, so many of us can't afford to buy.

"Yes, you've heard all this. Our present leaders asked for your vote because they promised to do something about these things. Now, we all know they can't be changed overnight; the structure of years can't be overhauled in hours. But you do have to make a beginning! Here we are, approaching the third year of this administration, and I see not one small sign, none at all, that anybody cares to alleviate any of our pains. Have you?"

A roar went up: "No! No!"

"What I do see is a display of fantastic luxury in high places. I see men in red uniforms—expensive ones, by the way, as are their fancy barracks and their new cars. Yes, men in uniform with large fists in white gloves and"—he paused—"men without uniform, who stalk and spy among you, extorting taxes, often known as contributions. Contributions, mind you, while they rob and beat, terrifying you in your homes at night, silencing your tongues."

And while he spoke, other recollections, sharp as hooks, attacked him: the farmer who, having written an open letter protesting taxes, was found dead in his field when he failed to come in for lunch; the son of one of Clarence's old union friends who'd come home, after three days' detention on some vague charge, with an empty socket instead of an eye; his own Will, who'd returned one night with torn clothing and a knife slash. "A fight over a girl," he'd said only, but he hadn't left the house for a week.

"Even under colonial rule we never knew terror like this. People never disappeared. People weren't afraid to talk out loud in public places."

The silence was so deep that he thought he could hear them all breathing, or hear a long collective shiver and sigh. Behind him on the platform he did hear his bodyguards shifting in their seats. They were wary and nervous.

"You lay it on pretty thick, Boss," one had told him only yesterday. "You're not afraid?"

"The foreign correspondents are my safeguard. If anything should happen to me," he'd answered, "wouldn't it prove that everything I've been saying is correct?" He almost believed that himself.

Plowing back into the substance of the speech, making promises, but not too many, promising only to give his honest effort and, above all, to remove the terror, he rose at last into a peroration and stood to acknowledge the applause.

The dark peasants gathered their children and departed. I must have had great-grandparents who looked like them, he thought, or maybe great-greats. Who knew? For a moment, half unconsciously, he stretched out his hand to look at it, then remembering where he was, put it quickly into his pocket. . . . Two young blond photographers from some news service were taking pictures of Patrick and the crowd, while he, looking back at them, felt again, as so often, that old confusion—*I am of them, too*—a confusion that would never leave him, he knew well.

When, after the last applause, he turned to step down from the platform, the rain came. The sky opened. The soaking rain pounded a furious drumbeat on the earth, so that the foreign newsmen, astonished at its vehemence, went scuttling to their cars.

Patrick's car was a station wagon seating nine, among them Kate and her two young cousins who worked on the *Trumpet.* Franklin Parrish sat in the rear with Patrick, who could sometimes stretch out a little there to rest.

"The rain will be over by the time we get to the next place," Franklin said. "This was a very responsive crowd, I thought. Not one heckler in the lot. You know, Boss"—although Patrick disliked the appellation *Boss* and had told Franklin so more than once, it still slipped out occasionally in pure affection—"you know, Boss, I'm beginning to think we might make it after all."

"We'll see," was all Patrick said.

The other side had the money and the power. Best not to think farther ahead than each day's uphill climb. Still, he was grateful for Franklin's confidence. The young man's intelligence and enthusiasm nourished and sustained him. If he won, he was resolved to put Franklin into a position of importance and trust. Not that the young man needed Patrick's sponsorship, for he was obviously destined to rise in the party ranks through his own abilities, his firmness, his tact, and his welcome smile. He was a fine speaker with a natural talent, unlike Patrick, who had taught himself through his persevering observation of Nicholas Mebane. Franklin was clever enough, too, to utilize a few politician's tricks.

"Look at me," he'd say. "I am one of you." Referring, of course, to his color, which was as dark as any worker's.

Patrick smiled inwardly. It was pretty clear that Parrish was having serious thoughts about Laurine and that she, now almost twenty years old, was having thoughts of her own. Patrick and Désirée had even talked about it. Désirée had raised objections: "He's too black," she'd said. And Patrick had put her arm next to his own, making an elaborate play of doing so. "Too dark," he'd said, in such a mock-tragic tone that she had begun to laugh at herself. "Thank goodness for your sense of humor," he'd told her.

The car, last in a short procession, turned inland and uphill. Alongside the road Patrick observed a farmer, helped by his neighbors, building a house. They were wattling and thatching. There would be food and drink for them all when the job was done, he knew. And he laid his head back on the seat, closing his eyes, thinking of the kindly comfort there was in such a continuation of old ways during this time of speeding change.

He'd seen more of country life during these weeks of his campaign than he'd seen in a long while, ever since he'd begun to live in the town. He'd gone looking for votes in the sugar factories, where, although the windmills were gone, the workers still skimmed the boiling foam and tested the liquid thread between the forefinger and thumb to judge when to strike. He'd eaten chicken and yams and drunk mint tea with prosperous farmers in their comfortable homes. Oh, yes, there were many such farms on which the descendants of slaves worked their own fields, played with their children, and married off their daughters to the sound of music! He'd talked to teachers while children played cricket on the village green, exactly as he had once done. He'd talked to planters at the Agricultural Show; most of them, he knew, would be on the other side, with Nicholas, for "law and order"; nevertheless he'd tried to show them he was for better law and order. . . . Certainly it never hurt to try. And he remembered now, apropos of nothing, that he'd seen Osborne there, standing before a pen, guarding a handsome cream-colored bull. There to collect the prize for Francis, probably! A queer pain shot through him, making a shudder and a chill.

He opened his eyes.

"You dozed some?" Franklin asked. "You needed it. Did I tell you that young Da Cunha sent us a check?"

"The older brother's for Mebane, I take it? Like the father?"

"The father, yes, of course. The brother, though, doesn't care one way or the other. Whatever's better for business is what he'll be for."

The road was dry and dusty, for on this side of the Morne it had not rained. They drove through a string of villages, where, the caravan having been expected, people had come out to stare, more often now to wave and cheer. It occurred to Patrick suddenly that he might really, after all, win! The prospect thrilled him and scared him, too: what had he let himself in for? He pushed the thought away.

"You've made an impact," Franklin said positively. "More than we've realized, I think."

"We've still a long way to go."

"True. But if we lose, we'll try again. We'll have to, that's all."

Franklin was actually enjoying himself, which was surprising. One wouldn't expect a bookish fellow like him to like this business. The strategy of government was one thing, but the hullabaloo of an election was quite another.

"If we lose," Patrick said, "you'll carry on. You and your generation."

Franklin was astonished. "Why, you're a young man! What are you talking about?"

Kate, sitting in front, had overheard. "You're only forty-one, Patrick! How can you talk like that?"

They were right, of course. Still it was good to see many young people ready to go forward, a man like Franklin's cousin, for example, that thin fellow with the odd green eyes, home on vacation from the University of the West Indies, so reasonable, intelligent, liberal, never fanatical. And he thought of Will, then blocked out the thought.

"I wish," Kate said, "I had the courage to come out flatfooted for you. This business of presenting both sides equally as 'news' just sickens me."

"You're doing a good job this way," Franklin told her. "At least, you're printing Patrick's message so people can judge for themselves. The other way, if you took sides, they'd just close up your paper. You know that."

"You're a great help, all of you," Patrick said softly.

The road mounted through cane fields toward more hills; ahead, you could see the dance and dazzle of the heat; on the platform the sun would burn; he would be glad to get this over with for today.

"Good God," Franklin cried, as they approached the meeting place, "there must be two thousand here! It's the largest yet!"

From miles about they must have collected, to stand now sweating and fanning themselves with their straw hats, drinking beer and nursing their babies, while they waited for the afternoon's event.

Patrick got out of the car and mounted the platform. He saw, with his new "political" eye, that there were many young in the audience, so he began by addressing them.

"The world is harder for the young today. There are more of you, and you have higher aspirations, which you should have. I think I understand the young because I'm a teacher. So you'll forgive me if I'm long-winded, like a teacher." He paused for the laughter, aware that it was a good thing to begin a speech with a little joke, preferably at one's own expense.

"A great responsibility rests upon the educational establishment . . . not to raise everyone to the top of the heap, which is a quite obvious impossibility, in spite of the worldwide propaganda to the contrary, because men are not equal in their capabilities . . . nor to lower everyone to the same bottom . . . to want that is only futile envy and revenge . . . no, to give every person the chance to climb up if it should be in him to do so. . . . That and that alone is the voice of fairness, decency and common sense. . . . I ask you to listen. . . . I favor a mixed economy, government to do those things that governments do best and free enterprise to do the rest."

Patrick's eyes moved over the crowd, which was listening, with interest. At the far edge of the field, where trucks and Hondas were parked, he thought he saw a flurry of arriving cars, latecomers. The heat was dizzying and he hastened on toward a close.

"I made a little joke before about talking too much. I've really tried not to. I hope you'll go home and give thought to what I've said, then come out and vote against this regime which will, if allowed to continue, drive you first to despair, and in the end, I'm afraid, to communism."

"Dirty communist yourself!" a man cried. Cries came from all over the field. "Smash the son of a bitch! Yeah, dirty communist himself!"

Cries came as a line of men shoved forward from the rear of the field.

"Shut up! Shame! Throw them out!"

Somebody hurled the first stone. A woman screamed as a man fell with the blow. Then, with the suddenness of an earthquake or explosion or any cataclysm that gives no warning, the field erupted into chaos.

From all sides and as if from the sky itself came a bombardment of stones. Chairs and tables went hurtling. From somewhere came the stench of rotten eggs: precious eggs! Men wrestled, women wailed in turn and fell on one another, trying to flee. In the confusion, it was impossible to tell who was assaulting whom. Some seemed to be joining up with the invading ruffians. A hail of paper bags descended on the crowd to burst and spatter their incredible contents of excrement and garbage. Police, appearing out of nowhere, melted into the crowd, some attempting to attack, some trying to restore order, and some observing, doing nothing.

"Stop it! Stop it!" Patrick heard his own frenzied, futile screaming. His throat strained with his screams, even after he had been struck with some foul liquid that soaked his shirt and knocked him, for a moment, to the ground. It was unbelievable, first this attentive meeting and an instant later this vicious brawl!

Somebody helped him up. Out of the savage mob men mustered in a ring, three deep, around him. The outer ring, as they pushed him through the uproar toward his car, sustained a bloody battering. Men armed with clubs and nail-studded boards went flailing. Patrick saw

Franklin dodge a blow. Stumbling and shoving, they edged toward the car.

We won't make it, Patrick thought. Strange way to meet your end, in an open field on a blazing summer day, at the hands of Mebane's thugs.

And suddenly the crowd fell back. A dozen or so young men, coming from behind the row of cars which Patrick and his men were trying to reach, stepped forward and threw.

"Tear gas!" Franklin cried. "Run, run!"

Over their heads and behind them the acrid cloud sprayed. The engine was already racing in Patrick's car; it was in motion before the doors had even been closed, and they were out of the field, onto the road, with tires skidding in a foam of dust when a last stone smashed through the windshield.

"The tear gas?" Patrick gasped. His eyes stung. "Whose?"

"Our own people. We were prepared for something like this. We knew it was bound to come eventually," Franklin said.

"My God, I hope there weren't too many hurt!"

"Bastards! Are you all right, Patrick?"

"Yes. A stone got me in the shoulder. And I stink. Other than that, I'm all right."

Désirée was furious, scolding and weeping as she brought clean clothes for Patrick. "You idiot, you could have been killed!"

They were on Clarence's porch. Crippled with arthritis, he had taken to the old custom of sleeping out of doors in a hammock.

"I hear it's a triumph wherever you go," he said now. "Franklin and his boys tell me. Next time I'm coming along for the thrill, if I have to get someone to carry me."

"Triumph!" cried Désirée. "Thrill! Is that what you call this?"

Clarence ignored his daughter. "I've news for you. This afternoon, while you were out there, the trade union congress voted unanimously to support you."

"Well, I shouldn't think they'd want Mebane," Patrick said, pleased.

"No, but you might think they'd want the left wing, mightn't you?

And they don't. They don't want the radicals. They want you."

"Everybody wants you. They'll destroy you with their wanting," Désirée mourned. Then anger seized her again. "You're nothing but big, overgrown boys, the two of you, sitting here boasting over this —this horror! You're naïve, that's what you are, naïve."

The adjective amused Patrick, since it was one he had always privately applied to her.

"I wish you could see yourselves," she went on. "Neither one of you has faced the truth of what life is!"

"Well, well," Clarence said. "Suppose you tell us, then."

"I'll tell you what it isn't! It's not knocking your brains out, eating your heart out, sacrificing your health and safety for other people, when they don't give the least damn about you! Do you actually think all these people here in this dinky place really care who's elected?"

"Yes, I do think so," Patrick said.

"Well, you don't know what you're talking about! All they want is food to feed their faces with and enough rum, and bed on Saturday night—"

Patrick smiled at her modest words.

"—and you think they'll ever thank you for giving them the means to get what they want?"

"I'm not looking for thanks," Patrick said.

"The more fool you, then! Go! Go! Get yourself killed!"

He sighed. "I don't suppose I'll ever make you see, Désirée. And don't be melodramatic. I'm not going to get myself killed."

"Oh, if I'd married a preacher I would not have had to put up with this holiness! You're so damned holy, Patrick!" She amended the judgment. "I don't mean you're a hypocrite. No, you really mean it all; you care. But I'm not like you. I want things first for ourselves—"

"I've tried to give them to you, I've done the best I could," he said stiffly now, aware at the same time that his words were perhaps self-pitying and sulky.

"Oh, I know. But I don't want only *things*, Patrick. Not so much anymore. It's peace I'm talking about now. I just want peace."

"I'm trying to give you that, too. Don't you understand how I'm trying to give it to us all?"

She sighed. "You've had no supper. Shall I fix a tray here on the porch? I've fresh broiled yellowtail with lime juice."

He was too utterly done in to be hungry. Nevertheless, he stood up. Food had always been her remedy, her way of expressing her concern and giving love.

"I'm ready. We'll go inside," he said, putting a hand on her shoulder.

She caught his hand, kissing the palm, then turning it over and kissing the back. She cradled his head, comforting and protesting.

"Oh, dear God, what have they done to you! The animals! What have they done! But animals don't do things like that! Still, I'm so proud of you, Patrick, no matter what I said. I'm angry at you and proud of you and I'm so afraid. Oh, my dear, my dearest, I'm so afraid!"

Twenty-three

"**D**ID you know Rob Fawcett's supporting your good old friend Patrick for election?" Marjorie asked as they arrived at the Fawcetts' anniversary party.

"No, I didn't, and I wish you wouldn't be sarcastic," Francis said.

"Erstwhile friend, then. Sorry."

Not wanting to talk about Patrick, he was, at the same time, curious. "Fawcett never mentioned it to me."

"He wouldn't. He's a gentleman. He knows how we feel."

Francis liked the Fawcetts. They had a depth often lacking in this ingrown, tight community where relationships could yet be so superficial; their house held music and vitality and good talk. Tonight Whim Longhouse, illuminated like an ocean liner, floated in the darkness; out of its windows streamed a glitter of celebratory light.

Francis followed his wife as, in crisp lime-green taffeta, she rustled up the steps. Her spirits were high, higher than they had been since the day of Megan's birth and this, of course, was because they were at last "going home." Her increasing animation silenced him, although he knew he had made the right, the inevitable decision. He simply didn't want to talk about it.

Everyone was already outside on the rear lawns. The Luthers were

late; they usually were, because Francis would never leave home until
Megan was asleep.

"You go on out. I'll phone home first," he said.

"But we've just left home!"

"Forty minutes ago. I want to make sure of things. It's the first time
we've left her with this new maid."

The rule was that whenever the parents were away, a maid must
sit in the room next to Megan's until they returned. The idea was
Francis'. He supposed it was neurotic to be so apprehensive, but that
fire was always with him; he never came up the driveway at Eleuthera
without seeing the ruin all over again and feeling terror in the pit of
his stomach.

When he had made the call he walked past the dining room, where
the dinner would be served later in the evening, and through the great
drawing room. Here was a comfortable clutter of overstuffed Belter
furniture, all curved and curlicued. "So tacky!" Marjorie always said.
The walls were hung with ancestors in broad, heavy frames. He
wondered whether they were fake or real and decided, knowing the
Fawcetts' candor, that they were very probably real. So even these
nice people had a need to worship their ancestors! Well, it was all
right as long as you didn't get to thinking you were better than people
without ancestors—as if we didn't all have them, even though they
hadn't left their portraits behind!

He was oversensitive to everything tonight, he knew, without knowing why. It was just one of those times when, because of glands or
hormones or something or other, his worries tormented him. He felt
as if he were in limbo, still here on St. Felice, but not really here
anymore, because his mind had already lurched on ahead to the new
place, to the new start. It was almost like assuming another identity.

Yet at the heart of it all was Megan. Going on six, past kindergarten
age, with each passing month she made plain the difference between
what she was and what she ought normally to be. Her future was
becoming more cruelly certain. And silently Francis groaned, while
he went outdoors toward the clatter of music and voices.

Little round tables for hors d'oeuvres had been set up at the edge of the terrace, under a triple row of maria trees so tailored that their intertwining branches formed a flat and solid roof of leafage. Candle flames wavered in hurricane lamps, each set in a ring of red hibiscus blossoms. The bar stood under a flaring tulip tree, against a background of marble-striped croton leaves. For a moment Francis stood looking over a scene now grown familiar, the pastel luster of the well-dressed crowd, the black waiters, soft-footed and white-gloved, and the wealth of flowers. Already, he saw, the men and women had separated. He wondered what the women could find to talk about, since they saw so much of each other at the club most days. The men, who did not see each other that often, had politics to talk about, of course. Now, spotting his host, he went down the steps.

"Congratulations on twenty good years," Francis said, shaking hands. "I'd like to be around to celebrate your fiftieth."

"If we make it, God willing," Fawcett replied. "It's a pity you won't be with us here if we do. You'll be missed," he added.

He meant it, Francis saw, murmuring his thanks.

"Yes, losing a man like you is a great loss for this place."

"I haven't done anything," Francis replied, feeling embarrassment.

"Not lately," Fawcett said steadily. "But you could again."

Old Whittaker interjected, "Listen to me, Luther, and don't pay attention to what anybody tells you. You're doing the smart thing. Half of these people—I don't mean you, Fawcett, you've got your own way of looking at things—but half of these people would quit tomorrow if they could find a buyer. They'd sell out like that!" He snapped his fingers. "They just haven't been as lucky as you, that's all."

These remarks were unusually lengthy for Whittaker, whose small pink mouth was usually pursed, as if to open it were an effort not worth attempting. His wife makes up for his silence, Francis thought with some distaste, not welcoming his unexpected ally.

"My wife tells me," Whittaker continued, "you're planning a New York apartment and a country place on Long Island."

"I couldn't stand being cooped up in the city all year."

Now his depression settled as if someone had placed a shawl on his shoulders. Limbo, yes, that's where he was. At home there were cartons and boxes in the hallways. Marjorie had already begun to drag things out of attics and closets, to sort and give away. He supposed, or rather knew, it was foolish to impart life to inanimate objects, yet it hurt him to discard his schoolbooks—which no one would ever use —or Megan's crib, which they would never use again, either, or so many dear old possessions.

"We simply can't drag all this stuff back with us," Marjorie declared. "It would cost a fortune, and where would we put it?"

He was too sentimental, by far.

And accepting from a silver tray a drink and canapés, he sat down among the men, to let their conversation wash over and past while he only half heard. The talk was the same talk that had been circling through the clubs and the great houses for months past.

"The burglaries in Covetown are not to be believed, especially in the hotels. They don't put them all in the papers, you know."

"The tourists bring it on themselves, flaunting their money and their jewelry. What do you expect?"

True, Francis thought, but not all that simple, either.

A large, bald man on the other side of the table—Barnstable, his name was, from the south end of the island—was telling a story amid much laughter.

"So when my cook's father died I went to pay a condolence call. Way the hell and gone out in the country it was. But good Lord, Sally's been with us eighteen years! They sit up all night at the wake, of course, but what I didn't know was, they tell jokes and drink and dance, a regular party! They even poured rum down the dead man's throat. He was sitting up in a chair—"

"Who was?"

"The corpse!"

"I don't believe it!"

"True, though, I swear it. What do you expect of these people, anyway?"

The waiter was passing a mushroom quiche. Francis, wincing

acutely, glanced up at the man's face, but the face was bland. I
wonder what they tell about us? he thought.

And he looked back at the large, bald man, who was still laughing,
pleased with his contribution to the entertainment; then he watched
as a covey of butterflies, attracted by the lights, went fluttering into
the bougainvillaea and clung there, like black velvet bows pinned to
a veil.

"So you were at one of Courzon's rallies," someone remarked to
Rob Fawcett.

"Yes, I wanted to hear him for myself. The newspapers don't dare
print it all."

"You were impressed, your wife says."

"Yes, I was. I'm not going again, though. I'm too tall a target for
a bottle or a brick."

"They've gone utterly mad. A kid was stabbed not two blocks off
Wharf Street a couple of days ago in some political brawl."

"I didn't see that anywhere."

"I told you, they don't dare put half of it in the papers."

"I give us ten more years on this island at the outside."

"Too generous, by far. I'd say four or five, more likely."

"No, no, not with Mebane running things. I'm not that pessimis-
tic."

"Ultimately some crazy will throw him out and take everything
over. It'll be like Cuba, mark my words."

"The next three days will tell the story. If Mebane wins the election
we'll be all right. He'll quiet things down."

"I doubt it. The pot's boiling too fast."

"Give the man a chance! How much time has he had?"

"Enough to fill the jails with his fancied enemies."

This, outside of the host's, was the first dissident voice of the
evening. Issuing as it did from a newcomer to the island, it produced,
in domino effect, a series of surprised and disapproving frowns.

"Aren't you exaggerating, Mr. Trumbull?"

"On the contrary, I've not said a fraction of what could be said."

Mr. Trumbull, being of that breed of lawyers known as liberal, wore an emotional expression. He was very young and had, for some reason probably connected with his liberal sympathies, recently opened a practice in Covetown. His somewhat babyish blue eyes looked startled, as though he had suddenly realized he stood almost alone.

A second later, though, he had an ally.

"Mebane's a brute, a canny, cultured brute."

This voice came from Whittaker's nephew, the musician. More disapproving faces were turned toward him, but there was no immediate protest, for the Whittakers were one of the wealthiest families on the island and they were pleased to humor their "odd" nephew. And, Francis recalled, there was oil money on the young man's mother's side.

Their host spoke quietly. "I couldn't agree more. What the rest of you call straightening out, what you call law and order, are only euphemisms for a police state."

Whittaker opened his little pink mouth. "You're entitled to your opinion, Rob, and so is my nephew, but I would advise you both to be careful of what you say. This is no time for loose talk."

"Mr. Whittaker is right." Francis spoke up clearly. He hadn't intended to speak at all, had deliberately closed his mind to all affairs except his own. Now he surprised himself with his own positive reaction. "Even you who favor this government are admitting, aren't you, that you don't feel safe?"

"Do we understand then," someone asked, "that you're voting for Courzon?" There was malice in the question, for Francis' feelings toward Courzon, as well as the reason for them, were well known.

"I don't intend to vote at all," he answered curtly. "What I'm thinking is, A plague on both your houses."

"Well, of course, you're leaving. But for those of us who want to stay, who have to stay, it's no pretty prospect. Personally, I believe Courzon would pauperize us all. He may mean well and sound good, but in the end we'd have nothing."

"What have you got now?" asked Whittaker's nephew.

The senior Da Cunha, sumptuously suited as befitted a merchant of his class, came over now and took a vacant chair. He was obviously excited.

"I've just come from town. Here, look at this." He held up a newspaper. "A special edition of the *Trumpet* just out this afternoon. I'll read it to you. Listen, it's an editorial by Kate Tarbox.

" 'For many months now and through various means we have been gathering information about the men who run what they are pleased to call our government. Now, on the eve of a decisive election, the time has come to reveal who and what this government really is.

" 'To begin with, it is not a government at all. It is a private enterprise of gentleman-criminals, defended by a secret police, a band of swaggering thugs, well paid out of your taxes, earned by your labor. Our country has become a safe harbor for shady enterprises, where narcotics and weapons are traded and dirty money laundered. Public monies have been directed to the pockets of the prime minister and his friends; safely hidden as they now are in as many as nineteen different banks as far afield as Switzerland, it would take a legion of lawyers and untold years to recover them for the people to whom they belong.' "

"Good God!" said Whittaker.

Da Cunha resumed. " 'These men make themselves heard almost daily on the subject of communist subversion, Cuban style. The truth is never mentioned: that communism was able to take over in Cuba because the mobsters had first laid the country in ruins.' There's more," Da Cunha said. "Here, I'll pass it around."

"She didn't sign her name to that?"

"She certainly did! Here, look, in big, black letters. Here's the windup. 'If you care about your country, if you care about yourselves, you will go to the polls on Thursday and vote them out. You will vote for Patrick Courzon.' "

"Fool of a woman!"

"Why? That's what I call guts!"

"Sure, if you call it guts to commit suicide."

Grudgingly, "Well, she does stand up for what she thinks. You have to hand her that."

"She won't be standing up long at all, I'm afraid. Not after this."

"Too bad Lionel's gone to England. Divorced or not, he'd have stopped her. He was always fond of her, even after the divorce."

"He wouldn't have been able to stop her. You don't know Kate Tarbox. She does what she wants to do."

"I wonder whether somebody should ride into town and—" Rob Fawcett began, when his wife came running up.

"Rob! Rob! I've just heard, Emmy had the radio on, and she just heard they've called off the election!"

"They've *what?*"

"Called off the election! No election on Thursday! For reasons of national security, it said."

The Whittaker nephew smote the table. "Of course! Because Courzon is winning, don't you see?"

"But they say, they say, one of the waiters just came late and he's terrified, he says things are frightful in Covetown! They've got police everywhere, arresting people. They've confiscated every piece of the *Trumpet* they can lay their hands on. And he saw"—Mrs. Fawcett trembled—"a man beaten up. They smashed his head in, right near the telephone building, it was—"

All of a sudden the party was over. The candles, no longer festive, glimmered wanly in the looming darkness. Everything is in the eyes of the beholder, Francis thought queerly. All, all had become in these few moments vulnerable, the house with its music, its crystal and silk, its orderly men and women gathered, all breakable, destructible and powerless.

Rob Fawcett made a vigorous effort, saying cheerfully, "There's nothing any of us can do tonight. We might as well have our dinner. My wife tells me it's going to be a good one, too."

Something seized Francis. *They've confiscated every issue of the Trumpet . . . smashed his head in . . .* And I shall sit at table holding a lobster fork and a wine glass, while she— Blood rushed to his head, not thought, just blood and strength, so potent, so compelling that his legs moved and his mouth spoke before he had commanded any of them.

He caught Marjorie's arm. "Make any excuses. The Whittakers will drop you home on their way. I've got to go to town."

"What are you thinking of? Covetown, now?"

"I have to. Please. I'm in a hurry."

"Francis! Francis! Have you gone out of your mind?" Marjorie's voice was a long, scared wail. "Francis, come back here!"

But he had already leaped into the car and gone down the driveway, out of hearing, out of sight.

Lights were on in the villages. Knots of people stood before the general stores and the rum shops as if they were waiting to be told what to do. Fear lurked among the trees beyond the headlights of the car. Doom rode the night air. He pressed the accelerator to the floor. There was one thought in his head, one purpose, and nothing could have stopped him. He knew, he knew. It was a good thing that neither police nor militia stood in his path, for he would have driven straight through them. He sped. If he could have flown, he would have.

Down the hill toward the town he came careening, and in the outskirts wheeled with screeching brakes around the corner of the street which he had not entered in so long. He jerked the car to a jolting stop before her house and jumped out.

The house was dark, but the front door was open. He rushed in, switched on the light and raced through the rooms. Kate's dogs were lying on the kitchen floor. The poodle was dead and the yellow mongrel had been piteously, brutally wounded. Lying in its blood, it opened its eyes toward Francis, as if to plead, then turned them toward his bowl and his ball, his dear familiar things, as if to question, and sank back and closed his eyes.

Now Francis was sure of what he would find. In a frenzy he called her name—"Kate! Kate!"—and bounded up the stairs. In anguish he slammed doors wide. The rooms were empty. Then something made him open a closet in the hall—and there he found her.

Face down in a pile of shoes and tumbled clothing, she lay naked, tied and gagged. Crying, sick with horror, he picked her up.

"Oh, my God!" he heard himself say over and over.

Without moving, she lay on her bed. He looked at her in despair. He was outraged, he was helpless, he didn't know what to do. At least she was alive. . . . But no doctor would come out tonight. Could she be dying? Then he bestirred himself. He went downstairs and found brandy. Which would be better, brandy or water? In the bathroom he got water and a wet cloth with which to bathe her forehead. And sitting on the edge of the bed, he covered her lightly, decently, with a sheet, then soothed and soothed with the cloth, thinking, Kate, oh my Kate, what have they done to you?

She opened her eyes. For a long minute she looked at him. "I knew you would come," she whispered.

"How could you know?"

"I had a premonition that this would be our day. I even called you this evening before everything happened, but they said you weren't home. They said you had gone to a party."

Things joyous and painful moved at the same time in his chest. "You called me?"

"Yes, I was so terribly afraid! I thought I might be needing you . . . so to hell with all my pride."

"Ah, God," Francis said.

She whispered. "My back hurts awfully."

When, carefully, he turned her over, he saw why. Three raw stripes lay across her back. The flesh had been savagely slit open by a whip. Droplets of dried black blood clung to the edges of the torn flesh.

He was sick at the sight. "Kate, did they—do anything else to you?"

"Only what you see."

In the bathroom he found a jar of unguent, gone liquid from the heat. Gently, he poured it over the wounds. "I don't know whether this is the right thing, but it can't hurt until we can get a doctor."

"Take my necklace off, please. It hurts."

Still warm from her body's warmth, the beads slipped through his fingers. They were blue beads, cheap and pretty; in some odd way they made him remember the marvelous emerald she had worn when he first knew her. And everything that had happened since those first days slid away as if it had all been written on flimsy paper, meant to be discarded. What remained was a story inscribed in a permanent volume, beautifully illustrated: Kate on the breezy hill at Eleuthera and in the hotel garden and in this house. The time between then and now had simply vanished tonight. All the sullen, stupid anger, the proud resentments—all, all were gone.

He took her hand. "Tell me what happened," he said.

"Well, Franklin Parrish had just left. You know Franklin? He'd just brought me a copy of a speech for the *Trumpet*. And then, only a few minutes later, they came. There were three of them. I'd had the doors locked—I always do, anyway—but they broke a kitchen window and got in. The dogs—" Kate started. "The dogs. Where are they?"

He didn't know how to tell her, but in his momentary silence she heard the answer. He had to hold her back.

"No, don't go downstairs. Please. Kate, they're dead."

She began to cry. "You're sure they are? Not just hurt?"

He remembered the mongrel, then, the one she called Beans. "I'll take care of everything. I don't want you to see. Kate, my darling, you're lucky to be alive yourself."

"Killed them? And what for? It took months for me to get that poor thing to trust people after I found him, he'd been beaten so—"

"I know. People beat children, too." He covered her lightly. "Now lie there. Promise me you won't move. I'm going downstairs. I won't be too long."

In the kitchen the dog Beans had died, too. Poor animals! Poor Kate, whose tears were cried for them rather than for herself!

In the pantry he found a flashlight and, fearful of turning on a brighter light, fearful of attracting attention, went out to the yard. God knew what other terrors were still roaming tonight.

It had been raining for a week up until the day before, and the loam was soft. It took no more than ten minutes to dig a proper grave. Then, bitterly angry, he picked up the two small bodies, still faintly warm, still limp, and laid them gently in the grave. He passed his hand over the soft wool before he took up the shovel again.

And standing there, while burying two dogs, he felt a wave of fierce emotion, such as one could not sustain too often if one were to keep one's balance. All he had ever felt for life and living things, brother-hood, kindness, pity, was overwhelmed now with regret and shame for having shut himself away so long from what was truest in himself.

When he had finished he put the shovel down and stood looking up into the sky. It was utterly black. On the main road at the end of the street an ambulance wailed. A moment later motors roared and tires squealed around the curve. Police cars, he thought. Then silence fell again, a profound silence, as if the night itself were cowering in fear. Afraid of the morning, he thought, and so am I.

He wished he had a gun. The best weapon he could find in the kitchen was a carving knife. From the refrigerator he took a pitcher of cold tea, which he brought up to Kate, while he laid the knife on the floor where she would not see it.

Weakly, she braced herself against him while she drank the tea. In the faint night-light from the hall he could discern white garments hanging in the closet; he remembered the fragrance of vetiver.

"That was quite an article you wrote. You should never have done it, Kate. It was a crazy thing to do."

"I just got so mad, so fed up."

Then he heard himself ask, "Did—did Patrick know about it?"

"No, he wouldn't have let me. Nobody knew except me. . . . I wish you were friends again, Francis."

He didn't answer that, but laid her back on the pillow when she had finished the tea.

"I wanted so many times to call you," she whispered. "I used to look in the telephone book just to see your name in print. Weren't we fools, Francis? A pair of stubborn, arrogant fools, the both of us."

"Yes, yes, we were. I more than you."

Now she saw the knife on the floor. "Do you think they're coming back?"

"I don't think so. They did what they were sent to do." And answering her unspoken question, he added, "But I'm not going to leave you."

It was still so ominously quiet outside. Fearfully he thought of Marjorie and the child. At least they were not alone. Osborne was there, as well as loyal people in the house. He picked up the telephone.

Had she got back all right from the Fawcetts' house? Was everything all right at home? Yes? Good! No, no reason to worry, he was going to stay in town at a hotel and he'd be back in the morning, or as soon as the roads were safe. No, he couldn't explain now. He'd only wanted to make sure things were quiet at home.

Turning the covers back he lay down beside Kate, being careful not to touch her tortured back. She fell asleep, but he could not. A catherine wheel whirled in his head, the wheel on which the saint had been broken, and he knew he was too exhausted to sleep. Once Kate woke and called his name.

"I'm here," he said at once. "Don't be afraid. I'm here." She slept again.

In the middle of the night he became aware of the ticking clock which, in his agitation, he had not noticed before. It seemed to him that, as the night waned, the clock raced faster, increasing its frantic, nervous pace: tick-tick-tick-tick. And he wished the night would linger, for who knew what sights the morning would bring?

But gray light came on schedule, sweeping the ceiling. Birds, unaware of any difference in this day, began their bright calls. Kate stirred.

"Darling, I'm here," he said again.

And turning her to him, still careful not to touch her back with even the feather-touch of a finger, he placed her head against his shoulder. For a long time he lay with his cheek against her hair and felt the beating of her heart.

A rattle of gunfire startled them wide awake.

"What was that?" Kate cried.

"Nothing, nothing," he soothed. "Lie back and sleep."

But she sat up, alert. "Guns. It was guns, wasn't it?"

"Yes." He went to the window. There was nothing to see. He turned on the clock radio. No voices came from it.

"They've closed the station," he said grimly. "I wonder whether the telephone's out, too."

When he lifted the receiver there was a buzz. Suddenly he decided something.

"Who're you calling?" Kate whispered.

"Nicholas," he replied, still grimly.

"Don't!" she cried.

But Nicholas was already on the line.

"This is Francis Luther." His anger was at the place where coldness burns. "I'm here with Kate Tarbox in her house."

"Ah, yes, of course."

"Is that all you have to say?"

"No, I can say she's a very stupid woman and she's lucky those people didn't kill her."

"They almost did. How long do you think a human being can survive in a closet?"

"Unfortunate. I'm really sorry. I was shocked."

"You're not talking to a child, Nicholas. 'You were shocked'! It came as a complete surprise to you!"

"As a matter of fact, it did. Politics is a strange business, as I've always said. One gets involved with some rough types. What happened was, some of these fellows got angry at the lady's lies about me and decided to do something. That's the long and the short of the whole business."

"Nicholas, I repeat, you're not talking to a child!"

"You really think I was responsible? No, I still have loyalty to my friends—it's one of my weaknesses—even though they don't always reciprocate. Kate Tarbox is, besides being foolish, Lionel Tarbox's ex-wife; she's a friend of my friend Patrick, who has gone somewhat soft in the head, unfortunately. And I see that you—shall we simply say that, in spite of the past, you would care rather much if anything happened to her?" The bland, persistent voice permitted no interruption. "A pity, all these messy affairs! We could all get along so nicely here, live so well in this nice place, if only these mosquitoes like Tarbox would stop buzzing in our ears, undermining confidence—"

Francis got a few words in. "Confidence in your police and—"

"The police wouldn't be necessary if the citizens behaved themselves. And now, if you'll excuse me, Francis, there's a busy day coming up." The telephone clicked.

Francis hung up and stared at Kate, his look conveying total hopelessness.

"You remember, I never believed in him?" she asked softly. "There was just something, a feeling I had from the beginning. I never knew where he stood. Oh, I'd rather have someone like Lionel to deal with, any day! There could be no doubt where *he* stood! Listen, have you never thought why Nicholas was so conveniently away when we had the strike five years ago? He didn't want to have to declare himself, that's why, and run the risk of making enemies on either side. He played it both ways and left it to Patrick to take the blame," she finished, with her old indignation flaring.

When she turned he saw that the ugly welts on her back had swollen.

"We'll have to get a doctor today," Francis said immediately and was wondering whether to hazard the streets or who might answer his call, when a persistent knocking was heard at the door below. He picked up the knife, feeling at the same time both foolish and wary. With the knife in visible position, he opened the door a crack.

"Is it you, Francis?" said Patrick Courzon. Rumpled and weary as he was, it was plain that he had been up all night. "I just heard. Is she all right?"

"Come in. Yes, all right except for her back, where they—whipped her."

Patrick was grim. "Things are bad. There's a fight on now for the radio station and the airfield. But a lot of people have come out of the woodwork to our side. Almost half the men in the police barracks came over to us about four o'clock this morning. We've got about fifteen dead so far." He was breathless. "It's chaos out there, bloody chaos."

For a moment Francis felt choked, unable to express his regrets or his embarrassment.

"I've been here all night," he said irrelevantly.

"You'd better get back to Eleuthera while you can. Things are quiet in that section so far. I'll have men here to watch this house." Patrick turned to leave.

Francis put out his hand. "Now's not the time, I know. I just want to say I've had what you might call a kind of revelation since last night." And, speaking these few words, he felt an inner easing of the spirit, an ebbing of embarrassment and regrets.

Patrick pressed his hand. "Wish us luck then," he said, smiled briefly, and was gone.

It was after noon before Francis arrived at home. Avoiding police stations and villages where confrontations might be occurring, he had taken a long, twisted route over dirt roads, some little more than mountain trails. The car's radio had kept him informed of events: the station had been retaken. Small battles seemed to be exploding all over the island; barracks were seized; arrests were made; the airfield was sealed off (so I can't send Marjorie and Megan home, he thought, with sickening fear); a cache of weapons was found in a cottage enclave belonging to the Lunabelle Hotel. At one point Patrick's voice came over the air, advising tourists to stay in their hotels and assuring them they need have no fear. Well, Francis thought, it must mean something that Patrick has the radio station, mustn't it?

Yesterday at this time he would have been on the other side or, rather, on no side at all. And he wondered what it was, what slumbering conscience or stifled yearning, had brought him to Kate last night and turned him back in time to what he had been five years before.

Marjorie too was listening to the radio when he came in. "I was furious with you," she said. "Then I decided it was a waste of my energy. You're impossibly eccentric and I should be used to that by now. But do you mind telling me where you went?"

"I saw Patrick," he told her, not untruthfully.

"Patrick! What on earth for?"

"I've been wrong about him. Terribly wrong, and I admit I have."

"I can't believe it! This attachment again! I thought we were rid of him. What is this fascination he has for you?"

"That's absurd, Marjorie. It's a question of principle, not fascination."

"So now you're on his side!"

"Yes, after the things I've seen. I've had a late awakening, that's all."

Marjorie sighed. "Well, I don't suppose it matters, since we won't be here, anyway. I only wish we were moved and rid of the whole business. Frankly, I'm scared to death. I suppose you aren't, though."

"I am very scared, I assure you."

If Nicholas's people firmed their hold— He shuddered to think of Kate and Patrick and so many more, whose names were unknown to him, who would suffer. God only knew what they would suffer.

The radio crackled all afternoon. There was an audible commotion in the street outside the station, until an obviously terrified announcer declared that the attackers had been repelled. Well into the evening the bulletins continued, but no decisive move in the turmoil was disclosed. And the troubled land waited.

After a while Marjorie went up to bed. Francis went into his library, the one room in the house that was distinctly his own. There was nothing he wanted to do there; simply, there was comfort in the room, in the familiar Chinese ivories on the shelves, his books and that very fine Da Cunha, *Cane Cutters,* which his father had given him. Going to the window, he pulled back the curtains. Someone, Osborne probably, had seen to it that the floodlights were on, a safety measure for this night of unknown dangers. The lights, concealed low in the shrubbery, made paths of silver in the darkness. It was perfectly still and so beautiful a night that in a sudden gesture of impulsive gratitude he stretched out his arms to it.

He feared for so many in this hour. There had been no relief of his own burdens: his child still lay helpless in her bed upstairs, a child who, for all that she was his "shadow," would never be able to share thought with him; his wife lay upstairs, too, bound to him through their child, but never able to share love with him. And yet he felt such vast and awesome gratitude.

*　　*　　*

The rapid events of the next three days were reported throughout the world.

"In an astonishing display of loyalty and power, the party led by Patrick Courzon has restored order to St. Felice. More than three hundred soldiers and police, aided by hundreds of citizens, including many teenagers from various clandestine left-wing groups, combined to oust the government forces. White flags of surrender fly over government strongholds, while the green-and-white Courzon emblem is everywhere displayed. A curfew has been declared. . . . The dead and wounded number so far about seventy to eighty. The election will be held as scheduled. . . .

"The whereabouts of the prime minister are unknown. It is rumored that he has taken refuge somewhere in the country until after the election. The minister of justice was arrested, and it is rumored that he is being held in secret custody to protect him from the wrath of the public. . . .

"The Courzon party has won a decisive victory. It has now been established that, shortly after the results were made known last night, Nicholas Mebane and a large party left on a yacht which had been waiting offshore. It is thought that after a short stay in New York many of the members of his former government will depart for Europe, where they maintain residences. . . .

"The new prime minister, taking office, promised a cheering crowd that he will restore and maintain decent, democratic government with full guarantees of the rights of the individual."

Kate cleared the supper dishes away. For about a month now, ever since Marjorie had gone to New York with Megan to visit her family and look for an apartment, this evening routine had been evolving, so that by now, after his day of customary work at Eleuthera, Francis felt that he was coming home to this kitchen. Here tonight the lowering sun touched alike with a tawny antique light the hanging philodendron, the simple dishes with their brown scalloped edges, and Kate's white dress.

"We can have our coffee outside," she said. "It's got much cooler."

In the yard, shade filtered through the leaves, laying a dusky bloom upon the coffee tray. This evening, gravity lay also upon Francis. Two more days and Marjorie would be back. They would be that much closer to departure time. Everything was speeding; things hovered and impended; there could be no swerving away, no turning back.

Kate was feeding pieces of cookie to the two curly black puppies whom she had acquired from the pound after the death of the other two.

"Not good for them to have sweets," she said, as if Francis had objected, "but now and then I like to give them something . . ." Her voice trailed off. "John Lamson wants to marry me," she said.

For a moment he was not only shocked but confused by the unfamiliar name. Then he remembered. Yes, somebody's brother-in-law had a cousin who practiced law in Curaçao, someone who flew over on occasion for the big parties. . . .

"You know," she said, as if she were asking him to recall some trivia. "With Republic and Southern Oil?"

A picture developed itself. Yes, shoulders and height and a hearty, positive manner.

Jealousy almost took Francis' breath away. It was a physical thing, a blow between the ribs. For a moment he could say nothing. Then he saw that she was waiting, plucking, probably without knowing she was doing so, at the fabric of her skirt. So, let her! he thought angrily. Let her go! And then I won't have to fall asleep knowing she's less than an hour's distance from me, nor pass this street whenever I go to town, nor walk into a crowded room both hoping and not hoping to look across the faces and see her face. Then he remembered that he himself was going away.

He murmured, "And will you? Will you marry him?"

"No. I compromised the first time. No."

Bravely, he made himself say, "Perhaps you ought. It would be a good thing for you, better than being alone."

"No, I said."

He set his cup down so hard that the spoon jumped on the saucer. "Oh, I wish, I wish—" he began.

She stretched out her arm to touch his lips. "Don't. I know what you wish."

So they sat silently. The sky darkened until there was only a pale, milk-blue streak left far down at the edge where the earth dipped away from the sun. A late bird, half asleep, gave one startled chirp; a dog, scratching, thumped his hind leg on the flagstones. And again Francis felt that sense of racing time, of vast opening distances and endless loss.

He looked over at her. She was sitting with her head bent, staring, so it seemed, at nothing. It was so uncharacteristic of her, to seem that small and frail. He had to do something, anything to make her move, to speak, to be his Kate.

"Would you like a late swim? We could have an hour before I go back," he offered, feeling as though he were offering a present to a child who has been hurt.

"We can't. I forgot that Patrick and Désirée are coming over with a present for me. Something Désirée bought in France."

"Poor Désirée! I'm glad she finally got to go."

She brightened. "Yes, it was his birthday present to her. He couldn't really afford it, what with two weddings coming up, but he wanted to."

"Laurine's done well. Franklin Parrish is a catch. A good man and a man with a future."

"I like him better than the one Maisie's got, although her mother's ecstatic over the engagement."

"Do I know who he is?"

"The Hammond family. Estate Ginevra."

Francis whistled. "Knowing Désirée, I should imagine she would be ecstatic. That's a rather nice little place. I've never been there, though; only passed it."

"Well, different circles," Kate said somewhat wryly. "The father's only about an eighth black, I should think. The Hammonds were in the colonial service for at least two generations, maybe more. He has a *manner*. Patrician, I guess you'd say."

"You were there?"

"I was invited to lunch with Désirée and the bride. The host was telling us that his great-great-grandmother was the mistress of Lord Whitby. Funny thing, I was thinking while I was there, one of my great-greats, I'm not sure who, was a Whitby. So maybe he and I have some ancestors in common."

"Did you mention it?" Francis asked. For some reason, he was curious.

"No. I don't know why, but for all my lack of prejudice I felt uncomfortable," she said honestly. "So I didn't."

"It's still in us then, no matter what we say?"

"To some extent, yes. We're not angels—yet." She smiled. "Ah, here they are."

A car had stopped, and a moment later Patrick came around the corner of the house with Désirée.

"Prime minister," Francis said, rolling the words on his tongue. The title had dignity, and was only Patrick's due.

Patrick carried a flat package in brown paper. "Can we take this inside to the light?"

The election and the longed-for trip had given Désirée new animation. Now, wearing a dress which, Francis guessed, she must have bought in Paris—for what woman could visit Paris without bringing back one dress!—she was excited with the ceremony of making a gift.

Patrick, releasing the string, opened to view a painting simply framed with a narrow band of gilded wood.

"It's Anatole Da Cunha's," Désirée cried. "I bought two for you to choose from, but this isn't the one I like. The other's fishing boats, really lovely, only Patrick insists this is the better one and you should have it."

Under an arbor, beneath grapes hung like stalactites, sat a young pregnant woman, wearing a brown dress. Her thin white hands were folded on the great, swelling curve of her body.

"But it's such a *plain* picture! And who wants a pregnant woman?" Désirée complained. "Of course, it is a Da Cunha—"

"Take my word for it," Patrick said, "there is no comparison between the two. This is the one Kate must have."

"It's beautiful," Kate said, very moved. "Beautiful. So patient, waiting there for the child, not knowing who he'll be! But that's an experience you've had, Désirée, so you must know. It's beautiful," she said again, softly.

"Well, I'm glad, then. You know how it all came about? There was an item in the paper about Anatole Da Cunha's death. He never married, you know, just lived with the same woman for years. And she needed money—strange how often these people who're good enough to become so famous don't leave any money. Well, there were eleven pictures she had to sell, so I ran over to look at them. I even cabled Patrick for public funds to buy the lot for the museum but he said no, there are things the country needs more right now. So I just bought these two myself. Anyway, by the time I got back they were the only ones left."

"I shall hang it over the piano," Kate said. "It's the most wonderful present I've ever had, I want you to know. Now stay a while and we'll have a drink to celebrate my present."

"You're sure we're not intruding?"

"Sit down," Francis said.

The lamplight fell across the picture, which Kate had propped against the piano, casting a spot of brilliance on the face. The artist had painted a three-quarter view; a rich fall of hair encircled round-lidded eyes and a strong nose. There was, Francis thought, with growing wonder, an incredible resemblance to his mother. This is how she must have looked in her youth, he thought, pensive, tender, and always with something reserved, held back within herself.

His eyes kept returning to the portrait. And shifting into a direct line of vision, he scarcely heard the conversation. It was almost as if, by fixing his will upon the picture, he could force an answering gaze from those living eyes. Absurd! But he did not move, just sat there allowing himself to be entranced. The young woman with her fine, resting hands and bowed head, had brought a kind of peace into the room.

"You look tired, Patrick," Kate observed.

"I am," he admitted. "I just got back from seeing my mother in

Martinique. She's dreadfully sick and that's a worry, of course. But I suppose the real thing is an inner tiredness. The truth is," he said, thrusting his face up abruptly, so that one saw new lines beneath his eyes, "the truth is, I suppose, that I'll never get over the pain of Nicholas. That struck deep, deeper than I realize, maybe." No one contradicted him, and he went on, "You know, I'm relieved that he and the rest escaped the country. We'd never recover what they took, trials would cost a fortune, and there'd only be more anger and more damage. As it is, we can look forward to a long, long struggle. There are an awful lot of people on this island who want to get revenge for what Nicholas's people did."

Kate brought in a tray of drinks and Francis served them. He raised his glass.

"Good health to us all!"

"And especially to you, Patrick," Kate added, "since you're the one with the load on your shoulders."

"Yes, it's a load. But we're off to a good start, all the same. One good thing I did, I made Franklin my minister for finance before the wedding. Otherwise," Patrick laughed, "I'd be accused of nepotism. Maybe I will be anyway, but I don't care. There isn't a better man anywhere for the job." He spoke eagerly, seeming suddenly to need to talk. "We're working on slum clearance. I want to get rid of the Trenches before they fester and spread any farther. I've got some private investors, a Canadian firm, and the government will guarantee the loan. Another company got in touch with me this week about a food processing plant for tomato paste. Well, we can surely provide enough tomatoes in this climate! Then I'm negotiating with the International Monetary Fund, and oh yes, what else is on the fire this week? A bill to require plantation owners to sell to any tenant who wants to buy his house and plot of land. That's long overdue."

Francis said quickly, "I've already done that, did you know? My sugar lands across the road aren't part of the Eleuthera deal. I've sold to every tenant who wants to buy. And I've given some as a gift to a few of the very eldest," he added, not concealing his satisfaction in having been first to do voluntarily what the law was about to force others to do. And then, suddenly aware that he might have seemed proud, he added again, "It's not that I want to boast about it. I only wanted you to know."

"It is much appreciated," Patrick said, somewhat formally, so that Francis knew he was touched and too shy to reveal how much.

"Well, I always did what I could. I wanted to. And there were others like me."

"Not very many," Patrick said. He sighed. "The problem is, everything's too slow. That's what's bothering me. We haven't much time to put things in order."

"Aren't you perhaps too apprehensive? Are things that bad? No one's starving here, after all. There's new hope since the election—"

"These are very dangerous times. Nicholas was correct in much of what he said, except that he tried to fight one evil with another."

"And line his pockets," Kate said indignantly.

Patrick went on as if he were tabulating quantities, almost summing up for himself.

"It's true, I had help from the left. I don't delude myself. Those young men who fought the secret police, who recaptured the radio station, so many of them came from the ranks of those with whom, it hurts me so to say, my Will is involved—though he denies it. Yes, it's true they helped." Patrick stopped, and the room was absolutely still, with the others leaning intently toward the pool of light in which he sat.

"When you're desperate you take help from anybody at the moment. But now—now I don't need to be reminded that the Soviets are in Cuba and Cuba is here, so to speak. Here or next door, which is almost the same thing. Yes, they're all here, the training camps for terrorists, the Soviet AK-47 rifles, squadrons of aircraft, forty-knot patrol boats, maritime facilities for submarines, jeeps and trucks, all next door. As soon as they think they can knock me and my kind out of here they'll be in St. Felice, too."

The words hung heavily in the air. So, then, it would be the same as having Nicholas back, or worse, Francis thought. Is there no end to it? And he answered himself, No, none, without eternal vigilance.

Then, as if he had had an afterthought so deeply painful that he had tried to suppress it, Patrick said, "They are already subverting our young."

"Oh, Will," Désirée protested. "Will! How he makes you suffer! I wish—"

"We all know what you wish," Patrick told her. "That we had never taken him in."

"Well," she responded, quietly enough, "don't you wish it, too? Tell the truth!"

"I couldn't have done otherwise. If I were to see him again as he was that day I would have to do it all over again." He looked away for a moment, then back at the picture. "But let's talk of happier things. . . . That is a wonderful work of art. I don't think Da Cunha could ever have done anything better." He turned to Francis. "So you are really leaving?"

"Yes."

"When?"

"Next month. They've got the papers ready to sign next week, so we can leave in June." Francis caught Patrick's eyes and held them with his own. "I'm terribly ashamed. I haven't said it before, but it's something you must surely have been thinking. The way in which I'm leaving, I mean. These people, this casino and all it entails—I hate it all. I hate what it does to the country and I'll tell you one thing: I'm glad that under your aegis there will be no more of it." Francis threw his hands out as if he were pleading to be understood. "But given the situation, with no other buyer in sight— And I have to leave. I have to."

"I know," Patrick said. He paused. "Excuse me. Do I—do we— know you well enough to ask, What about Kate?"

He felt a stinging behind his eyes, a warning of tears, and was painfully embarrassed.

"She understands," was all he could say.

It had grown quite dark. The night life in the scrap of jungle which remained in back of the street rose loud and shrill, a whirring and peeping, a rhythmical buzz and chirp. Désirée, with a gentle tact for which Francis was grateful, moved to the subject of her daughters' weddings: quite possibly it would be a double wedding, because although Maisie was only seventeen and young to be married, he was such a marvelous boy. . . . So she prattled until, in a little while, she and Patrick left.

When they had gone, he sat on with Kate. She had taken out her embroidery and now, with a frown on her forehead, sat working at it, not speaking. Francis said suddenly, "You know if it weren't for Megan—you do know that, don't you?"

"Darling Francis, I do."

"I'm so guilty. I brought her into the world, when I should have known better. I gave Marjorie that burden. Gave Megan that burden, too." His voice trembled.

"But I've told you again and again," Kate said patiently, "you mustn't think like that. It won't help anyone for you to walk around with all that guilt."

"I can't leave Megan," he said for the thousandth time and, as he had also done before, went on. "Ah, what a pity! You're the one who should have children, Kate."

"If I had, I would probably never have left Lionel. Poor old Lionel! I don't know why I always say 'old,' because he isn't."

"He was old when he was born, I expect. Like me," Francis said glumly.

Kate put down the embroidery. "Like you! I've never heard anything sillier!" She reflected. "You know, I sometimes think Lionel's never really felt anything much in his whole life. But maybe people like him are better off. When I left him, it was only the humiliation that upset him, no pain, while I—" She did not finish.

And Francis, watching her with her head bent again over the needle and the fine white cloth, thought of how she would be when she grew old, thought of it for no reason that he could have explained except for a cruel awareness that he would not know her when she was old.

Suddenly he asked, "What will you do now with your life?"

"Oh, go on living here and working on the paper. This time around I'll expose the leftists—"

He interrupted. "For God's sake, don't do anything crazy again! Take care of yourself. I couldn't bear it if—"

He got up and sat on the floor beside her chair with his head against her knees. She stroked his hair. From her body, as she leaned to him, came an aura of warmth and the sweetness of vetiver, that fragrance of grass and morning that seemed always to go with her.

"I've been thinking—it's better, after all, that you're leaving. I couldn't just live here like this, sharing you with Marjorie and your child. It's done, it's always been done as long as men and women have lived on earth, but it's not for me. And yet if you were here, I'd want to do it. So I'd be cutting myself in two, you see."

He kissed her fingers and her wrists where the blue veins crossed, then her arms and her neck.

"Come upstairs," she said.

This was their time of day. Always a stripe of light lay over the place where, naked, she came toward the bed: a light from the hall, or sometimes from the window when the moon was right. A creamy ghost, she materialized out of the darkness, then unghostlike, firm and desiring, lay down beside him. . . .

The old clock on the landing banged ten metallic strokes. He sat up and switched the lamp on.

"I'd better start."

Kate rose and took a robe from the closet. In flowered cotton and with bare feet she followed him downstairs. When, at the front door, he bent to kiss her, she put her arms around his neck.

"No, wait! Francis, wait. I have to tell you—I didn't want to tell you before."

Something in her face alarmed him. "What is it?"

"This was our last time. That's what I want to say."

"What do you mean?" he cried.

"Our last time to be together." Her eyes were wet and brilliant.

"Oh, no!"

"It has to be. Francis, listen, it has to be. Marjorie will be back the day after tomorrow. In another month you'll be gone. What's the use of prolonging things? Another month together won't matter. It'll only be that much harder for us both."

"It couldn't be any harder for us than it is right now."

"It could. Oh, my dear, make it now! How many times can people be expected to go through this—" She did not finish.

He held her close. "Brave Kate. So brave."

"I don't know whether I am. You like to think you'd be stalwart and have dignity and all the rest of that stuff if you were told you were dying of cancer. I hope I could be if I had to—"

"God forbid!"

"Maybe that would be easier than this."

"I'll come back," he said desperately. "I'll come back every year for a while—"

"No. It wouldn't be any good that way. It has to be finished, like an amputation, and then one has to teach oneself to live with it."

He could only hold her more closely.

"Oh, it's worse now, isn't it? Far worse than when we fought and were so angry at each other. Besides, I'm five years older now. Five years have made changes. In you, too."

"I love you, oh I love you, Kate," he said. Scraps of thought passed through his head, scraps of bright paper torn in a breeze: I love the quilt with the birds and the dishes with the scalloped border, even your two sleeping puppies and the creaking gate; I love your pink slippers under the bed and your tortoise-shell brush on the dresser, the way you sing in the kitchen and your temper and your two separated teeth; I love you playing Brahms, you dancing, your hair blowing in the wind, you, you— He was crying.

She pulled away and wiped his eyes with her sleeve. She opened the door. Before them the night sky hung white over the black, serrated outline of the trees.

"Listen, I told you once about the Inca priests and how they used to kiss the rising sun. Remember to kiss it in the morning, Francis. And wherever you go, wherever you are, I'll know you're alive and in the morning when I see the sun I'll think of you."

He never knew afterwards how he got to the car or how he drove home and reached his room where, still in his suit and shoes, he threw himself on the bed and lay there, face down, until day.

Twenty-four

Through the day's last light Will
made his way downhill toward the Trenches. Below him, the glint of
tin rooftops and jumbled derelict cars dazzled the eyes; the silvery
shimmer would have been beautiful if one had not known what
caused it. Above and to the left across the bay, the settlement at Cap
Molyneux, in its wreath of dark and luscious leafage, crowned the
mountain. To give Patrick credit, Will mused, he had not succumbed
to any such lures. Even if he could have afforded them, he wouldn't
have, of that one was certain. When his term was over, Patrick would
simply go back to the old house, now rented out for the duration, on
Library Hill.

Will had refused to move into Government House, refusing also
Clarence's invitation to come stay with him. He just "lived around,"
with friends, whenever he could. Anyway, he was often out of the
country these days.

Tonight he was on his way to an important meeting. Walking
lightly in sneakers, he had a wonderful sensation of flowing, flowing
with time in a purposeful direction. So absorbed was he with this
pleasant sensation that he almost failed to notice the man who hailed
him now from the cross street. Then he recognized the dark shiny suit
and reversed collar of the old priest, Father Baker.

"Walking my way, Will?"

"I turn off at the Bay Road." He was not in a mood to talk, or to listen, either, to any pious liberal mouthings.

"I've just been visiting my old cook on Merrick Road. She's been ill."

Will glanced at him sidewise. "Not afraid to walk alone down there?"

"No. Should I be?"

"I wouldn't think it the safest place in the world for you."

"One can't walk in fear all one's days. And faith is my substitute for fear."

"Faith in God?"

"Of course," Father Baker said simply.

The exchange began now to interest Will. It was like a game.

"You think God hears your prayers and answers your needs?"

"He hears, but He does not always heed, for reasons of His own."

"Tell me then, why should He have bothered to create us if He was going to be indifferent to us?"

"I didn't say He was indifferent. If He were indifferent, He wouldn't have created the earth at all, or us to live on it."

"But I reach a different conclusion. I say no God worthy of the name could have created this mess we're in. That's why I'm sure He didn't create it, that He doesn't even exist."

The old man was silent for a minute. It was probably cruel to bait him this way. And Will was opening his mouth to say something softer, to blunt his jab, when Father Baker spoke.

"Very well, let me ask, Do you believe in man?"

"Certainly I believe in man. I see him. He exists."

"In the power of man, then, to reason and struggle and achieve?"

"Sometimes, yes. Very often, yes."

"That means you believe in yourself, in your own will to do good. So in the end you will come to faith. For good is God, and God is good."

Not choosing to argue further, Will shrugged. The gesture, he knew, conveyed irony and dismissal.

They walked on. The old man's tired, panting breath was audible above the sounds of their steps.

"How is your father, Will? I don't see much of him these busy days."

"All right, I guess. I don't see much of him, either."

"Salt of the earth," Father Baker said. "We're lucky to have him. Well, I leave you here. Take care, Will."

Recrossing the road, Will took one look back at the old man, who was walking on with his face turned toward the sky, as if he were following a flight of birds or simply inhaling the soft air. Easy meaningless words, he thought, with a certain contempt and yet not without understanding. The priest meant well, but he was totally without knowledge of the world. Spouting his kindly generalizations—Will had heard them often enough—about brotherhood and God and loving! While all the time he'd been sheltered away behind the protective walls of the school and the church, respected and unchallenged because of the cloth he wore. A man of words, a theorizer, an onlooker, not, Will reflected, really very different, except in degree, from Patrick. Well, no, that wasn't exactly true, for surely Patrick had gone down into the fight, that you couldn't deny; but even so, there was something too innocent about Patrick, too innocent and therefore, in the last analysis, stupid. Stupid.

Now in the falling day the last busses from Covetown were passing out to the country, rattling by with people hanging out of the windows and bundles tied to the roofs. In bold orange and pink and blue they announced their names: Pleasant Dreams, Grateful Shores, Golden Joy. Now, what in heaven's name did their occupants have to be grateful or joyous about?

Halfway down a short lane Will stopped to pick up his friend Clifford, calling in at the door, "Clifford home?"

"No, he say he be back in a minute. Come in and wait."

Will climbed into a house built on stilts and made of corrugated iron. From the front room, furnished with a table, chairs, and a small oil stove, one could see into the only other room, which had a large bed and blankets on the floor where the children slept. The walls were decorated with magazine photographs of movie stars, both black and white, along with Christmas cards of jolly horse-drawn sleighs and snow-covered pines, these last the greetings from various children and grandchildren who had gone north.

"Sit down," the grandmother said. "He be back in a minute. He went to get some canned milk for the kids."

There were, Will knew, some six or seven "kids" in the house, nieces, nephews, brothers and sisters of Clifford. The grandmother, whose hair was just beginning to go gray, was still vigorous enough to do cleaning at the Lunabelle.

"You going to a meeting?" and without waiting for Will's answer, "I go to prayer meeting every week. And Credit Union meeting twice a month. You going to a prayer meeting? Clifford never tells me anything."

"Well, sort of, you might call it that."

The woman looked at him closely. "I hope you don't get in no trouble. Don't pull Clifford into none. We never had no trouble in our family. A good name, Drummond. Came from Drummond Hall, way back."

He was about to reassure her when Clifford came in. His appearance was always a kind of astonishment: he was the palest tan, with kinky hair of the same shade as his skin—a bleached African.

He put the milk down on the table.

"Ready?"

Will got up and they went down a few alleys to the meeting place. Some fifty or sixty youths had already collected in a courtyard, where chairs and a small podium had been set up behind a dance pavilion, open to the sky. The whole affair was open, there being now no need to hide. You had to give Patrick credit, he had kept his word about free speech.

Candles, flickering in bottles, illuminated the faces of the expectant audience: black faces, working-class faces, except for the presence of several young white women, pallid and earnest. Holdouts from the sixties, Will thought, glancing at their stringy hair; trying to prove something, trying to feel as if they belonged here. His glance swept away. Well, let them. Let them have their great adventure.

The speaker came to the podium to be introduced. Will had heard him before, in other countries, and knew what he was going to say, yet was impressed again by his easy dignity and the music of his Oxford speech.

"Who are you?" He began speaking so softly that a forward movement of the shoulders rippled through the audience. "From where do you come? Why are you here? I'm told that most of you don't know your own history, though it's not your fault that you don't. Listen to me, I have traveled. I've been in Africa and seen the forts along the coasts where our great-grandfathers were collected, torn from their forests and their tribes and brought in chains. There's where they started the long voyage to places like this one where we are tonight.

"In the course of three centuries some fifteen million men and women made that voyage. This you must have heard, how for eight weeks or more they lay manacled in their own filth and vomit, fed barely enough to keep alive; how, maddened and desperate, manacled as they were, so many jumped overboard, dragging each other to death. Surely you have heard that!"

Indeed, they had heard it many times, but they were fascinated nevertheless. Without stirring, with open mouths, they waited for more. The speaker took from the podium a sheet of paper, which he waved in the air.

"Listen! I have here some quotations from a historical document which I found in the Covetown library. I took it from the last will and testament of a planter who lived here when the island belonged to the French. It lists the value of his possessions, among them his slaves. Listen! Pierre, twenty-eight years old, worth four thousand livres. A strong young man, you see. Next, Georgette, seventeen years old, also four thousand livres. A strong young girl, you see. Next, Marnie, aged sixty-eight, an old woman; she was only worth two hundred livres, because she wasn't fit for much, there weren't many years' work left in her. Naturally, you don't know what that money was worth in that time. Well, I'll tell you. You couldn't get a silver dish in Da Cunha's today for the price of that old woman, and you couldn't have done so at that time, either." He held his hands out, as if weighing things on a scale. "A woman. A silver dish."

Steaming them up, Will knew. All these facts were true, but so far removed in time that they had become irrelevant. The only value in them was shock value, to make these people angry—which had its purpose, to be sure. The real tasks of the movement were done quietly behind the scenes, not by orators like this one, shrewd and eloquent as he was, but by anonymous, cool men doing their assignments in small, tight groups, working in and out of Cuba and throughout the region. And Will had a feeling of proud exhilaration to be trusted, at his age, by men like Cortada, overseer of guerrilla affairs for the Communist party in Latin America and the Caribbean. To be trusted with great things!

No one moved, not a chair squeaked, as the speaker's voice rose. "But how much better off are you today? Are you not still strangers in this land? Look up onto the hills where the glass-walled houses stand so proudly and the hotels tower, or look at the estates where for centuries the owners have sat in luxury among the cane fields. . . .

"Ah, but now you have your own government, they tell you! Yes, a lot of mealymouthed incompetents who, aping the European, have merely substituted themselves for your former masters. Nothing at all has changed except the color of the skin, nothing at all."

At the back of the assemblage two men, who had been standing there, met Will's eyes and nodded. He looked at his watch. It was time to leave; walking along the beach, he would be taking a different route from theirs and ought to start. Unobtrusively, followed by Clifford, he stepped outside.

"Great man! Great speech!" Clifford whispered.

"Yes," Will said. Clifford was clinging; it would be hard to shake him. And this night's business was no business for Clifford.

"Where're you going now, Will?"

"To my grandfather's. I promised the old man."

"You have to? Sure you don't want to get a girl?"

They were passing the barroom where the girls sat around waiting. The jukebox blared past the swinging doors.

"I can't, I told you." He wouldn't have, anyway. He wasn't interested in girls right now. There was simply no time. No time.

"Well, guess I'll go home, then."

They walked back toward Clifford's house. The sky held only a curve of moon, narrow as a machete, and clouds were hurrying to cover even that. It was a good night, well chosen.

Clifford mused, "I was just thinking how you told me once you set fire to that place, Eleuthera. You know, I didn't believe you then, I thought you were boasting. But I believe you now." There was awe in his voice. "Don't worry. You know you can trust me."

It had been a mistake to tell Clifford, even though he really was trustworthy and a friend. It was a mistake to talk at all. You could never regret anything you had kept to yourself.

"A dumb thing to do. Childish. But I was only a kid. What did it accomplish, after all? I've learned better now." He said no more.

When he had left Clifford at his house, Will went as far as the corner; then, out of sight, he doubled back toward the shore. From a board shack came the sound of hymns. Prayer meeting, he thought scornfully. Waiting for heaven. He passed another bar and a smoky yard where crouching men watched a cockfight. Rotten amusement! Rotten life, he thought, as he came out onto the beach.

He had three miles to go, around the farthest visible curve of shore to the lonely cove where tall cane marched almost to the edge of the sand. There they would meet the boat and unload the rifles and grenades. The beach was deserted now, because the seas between Christmas and March were too rough for all but harbor fishing. This was the resting season for the fishing trade, another point in favor of the night's work.

The sand reflected the dun sky. Across the inlet he could barely see the strip of beach on which hotel guests baked themselves while beggars hawked straw hats, baskets, and worthless shell trinkets. He almost tripped over a pile of cane trash. Clarence had shown him how this trash, floating, attracts garfish in schools, and for a moment, recollecting this, he had a feeling of nostalgia for the lore and homely wisdom of old Clarence.

A lone man was mending a boat on the sand as Will rounded another curve. The whole side of the boat had been staved in.

Will stopped. "What happened to it?"

The man looked up. "Oh, just grudging."

"Grudging?" He wasn't quite sure what that meant.

"You know, like when somebody's jealous you got a better boat, or some good luck or something, they cuts your nets, you know?"

"Oh," Will said. "Sorry."

And he walked on. So the poor destroyed each other. This was what poverty did to people.

The rising tide lapped at his sneakers. He took them off and trudged on. Clams clicked on the flats, making a syncopated rhythm. Not far out a small yacht floated by, returning to the yacht club after a cruise, no doubt. It was so close that he could see a table set on the deck and people eating; he could hear their voices drifting inshore. Having wine with their lobster, I suppose, Will thought. Ought to be blown up!

Go on, haggle over elections, unions, legislation, and arbitration! Instead of getting out there and grabbing like men. People like Patrick, with their talk, talk, endless talk!

People like Patrick. And he had a flash of memory, with the very taste in his mouth of chocolate and bananas. The kind hands. *No, I don't beat my children.* The earnest face, bent over a book or explaining and teaching and admonishing. Sad, in a way, to have lost him! For they'd lost whatever there had been between them, as far back as—yes, the day Patrick had asked him about the fire at Eleuthera, and he'd denied having anything to do with it, and known all the time that Patrick never wholly believed him. Sad.

Still, the man was a fool and always had been! A well-meaning fool was what he was. Will kicked the sand. You can't afford to be sentimental when you're making a revolution. Not the way things are.

Now, rounding the last turn into the cove he could pick out the shapes of cars and a small truck with headlights off, parked in the shelter of tall beach grape. The boat was already hovering offshore, with only the dimmest lights, just lanterns, probably. Low voices hailed him and he walked toward them.

No, you can't afford to be sentimental about anything or anybody when you're making a revolution.

Not the way things are.

Book Five

PARTINGS AND MEETINGS

Twenty-five

HER thin hands plucked and clawed at the blanket. When the pain flowed away Agnes lay back, moving her head so that her gold hoops brushed the pillow.

"Maybe I'll sleep a little now," she said.

Patrick got up and went outside to the yard. If he could vomit he might rid himself of the foulness. He wasn't quite sure she was sane or whether he could possibly accept what she had been telling him in there, in the small dim room where she lay.

The woman whom he paid to care for her sat on a bench, shelling peas into a bowl. As he approached, she stood up. She was in awe of his title, but more in awe of the fine black chauffeured car, although it had only been hired to bring him from the Martinique airport.

"Sit down," he said.

Trembling, he walked to the end of the yard. A double line of bamboo gave shade to a neat patch of vegetables. A row of yams followed along a strong new fence. He looked back at the house which he had bought for his mother when she refused his request that she return to St. Felice ("It's fitting to die on the earth where you were born," she'd told him). It was a good house with a tin roof and running water. In a little while he collected himself and went to sit on the bench with the woman.

"How is she?" he asked.

"She's dying. It's the cancer that's killing her." The tone reproached him for not seeing what was obvious.

"I don't mean that. I mean her mind. Does she talk sense? Can you believe what she tells you?"

"Why, of course you can! There's nothing wrong with her head. Try giving her short change, and you'll find out."

"She doesn't ever rave? Imagine things?"

"Who, she?" The woman was indignant. "Sharp as a tack, I tell you!"

He went back inside and sat down by the bed. "Did I wake you, Maman?"

"No, I was awake. You know, there's some pleasure in lying here with nothing to do but remember. Everything is so clear, I can even see the colors. Did I ever tell you about the Maurier house? Oh, I must have! They had three thousand acres and such gardens, you can't imagine. They used to say the gardens were like the ones in France and it was true, when I went to France I saw it was true." The voice ran on, murmurous and so soft that Patrick had to strain to hear it. "They used to go to Paris every year, with servants, too. I never went along, I was too young. I think they went to visit their money in the bank, people said they had ten million dollars; maybe they did, I know the Francis family had nothing alongside of them."

"I want to talk about what you told me before," he insisted. His voice sounded almost harsh in his ears.

"Yes. Well, she said she would come back to St. Felice to die. And she almost did, didn't she? I heard about the fire, you know. Why didn't you ever tell me yourself?"

"Why should I have? I don't like to talk about horrors, especially to you. And I didn't know it—had anything to do with me, or you."

The sour smell of sickness made him gag. The gloomy green flicker of sunlight through slatted blinds made him dizzy. And he passed his hand over his sweating forehead.

"Yes, yes, she told me. I remember it well," Agnes repeated.

"Told you about a fire?"

"No, no"—with exasperation—"no, about not coming back, I meant. But she did come anyway. I wonder why? Oh yes, yes, a son ... I forget so many things these days, Patrick—it's the pain medicine —but not the old things. I remember them all."

"And you're sure you can't be wrong? Wrong about this, for instance?"

Now came a flare of her quick familiar anger. "What am I, a fool? You think I'm making up a fairy story to amuse a child?"

It was his turn to ask her, "Why didn't you ever say something before?"

"I never wanted to hurt her, what do you think? I shouldn't have said anything, even now. Tomorrow I'll be sorry I did. I'm sorry already."

Loyalty! Loyalty to an old family, an old code, to the end!

"Patrick! You're not going to speak of this to anyone?"

"You don't want me to, Maman."

"All my life I kept it in here"—she touched the sunken flesh above her heart—"in here. Not because I wanted to keep *her* secret, not just that, anyway. It was because I wanted you all for myself. . . . Ah, you're a big important man now! They say you'll be traveling all over the world."

"They exaggerate. Only a few trips here and there to raise money for the things we need."

"You still don't believe what I've told you about yourself, do you?"

"I—"

"Give me your hands. I'm dying, Patrick."

"I know, Maman."

"You won't see me again."

"I know that, too, Maman."

"Then would I lie to you? I swear that everything I've said is true. I swear it."

He held her hands—old, dry hands that had hemmed workmen's tough cloth, cooked for a child, rocked a child, and polished a rich woman's silver. She, she had been his mother, not that other pale woman in the pale north, chilly as snow! And kneeling there, he held those two good hands until, in a little while, she fell back into sleep.

Sadly, he got up and went outside into a surge of yellow heat. The air was the color of ochre. Now he grew cold; a chill ran up his arms and down his back. He picked up a flat stone and hurled it to the ditch across the road, where it fell into rainwater, making a small, dirty splash. And he picked up another, one after the other, hurling with all his strength, while his driver waited, curiously watching.

They started back to the airport. The driver, who had been chatty on the trip out, was silent. Now and again Patrick met his eyes in the rearview mirror. I must look ghastly, he thought. Outraged. Destroyed.

His heart raced. His mind raced. That woman—that girl—had brought him forth and thrown him away. But then—a young girl, younger than his own Laurine and Maisie! And he thought of the double disgrace that had attended his beginning, shame of the girl, given her time and class, and death of the boy. Would it have meant death for him if he had been white of skin? Yes, yes, probably it would. Or possibly. The economic, the social, status would have been a factor, surely, in assaying the crime, if crime it had been. One had seen too much and felt too much in one's own weak flesh to decide precisely, justly, where blame lay.

Pity, pity for the terrified girl who bore me!

But then, consider a young boy "of color," confronted with some tremulous, forbidden loveliness, fragile in white, perhaps, with pearls like those Kate Tarbox had, careless pearls worn like common rope.
. . . Kate's flowered skirts graze her seductive legs and in my mind I have removed the skirt, touched taut, rosy flesh, even though I know quite surely I am nothing to her but a friendly brain in a body which could, for all she cares, belong to a woman of seventy or a boy of ten.

Imagination flashed its pictures, that imagination which both blessed and bedeviled him with the ability to see at once all sides of any question. That boy, intelligent and yearning as he himself had been ("You're always reading, you always want to know too much!" Agnes complained), was he not familiar? How many such had he not seen on the schoolroom benches, dreamers of eager dreams, scattered among the apathetic and the louts!

What a crazy business, life! And his mind raced on again: Teresa Francis at Eleuthera. Virgil, righteous, tough old man of legend. Drummond Hall. The fine, proud places. Francis. Francis and I.

He leaned forward and tapped the driver on the shoulder.

"I need a drink."

"Yes, Boss. There's a bar right down the road."

"I meant water. You can stop there and bring me water."

He got his drink and they drove toward the city, past blue and yellow rotting houses trellised and gabled like the fairy houses in tales he had used to read aloud to his little girls, then through the city to the airport from which the plane would bring him home in an hour. And he remembered the interisland schooner on which, among crated coconuts and clucking chickens, he had slept all night with Maman in a time of innocence.

When he came into the house Désirée was waiting.

"How is your mother? Did she eat the cookies? Did she like the sweater?"

"She thanks you for them all." He turned away, wanting to hide. Then because Désirée was waiting for more, he said, "She's dying. It won't be long."

"Oh, Patrick, I am sorry!" She had never truly forgiven Agnes, but she was soft, and she meant her words.

They had dinner. He was still not used to the cool, high dining room with its whirring fan and its servants; this night, especially, he would have liked to be eating a supper cooked by his wife in their own old house. When they were finished, he went upstairs and sat down with a book which he wasn't able to read.

Instead, the day's incredible disclosure stood before his eyes, written in glaring letters. It seemed to him that, if he did not tell someone, they would burst in a spangled eruption, would explode and spill over and flow, even as Mount Pelée had done so many years before. It was all as large, as powerful, as that. And he heard himself saying the words, *"Do you know who I am?"*

"Patrick," said Désirée, coming in. "Are you all right?"

"I've a headache," he said, "one of my sun headaches. It's nothing that won't pass."

She put light fingers on his forehead. "I don't believe you. It's something sad, something else, not just Maman. What is it?"

He shook his head. "No, nothing."

She moved back in distress, her bracelets jangling.

"Do you still love me, Patrick?"

He smiled. "I've been a fool over you since I first saw you."

"That isn't the same thing. I'm not only talking about bed, you know."

"Neither am I, my dear."

"I think—do you want to know what I think? If things had been different in your life, you'd have married a more educated woman."

He looked up, wondering and touched to the heart. That she should harbor even the smallest doubt about herself! None of us knows another.

"But things aren't different, and it's you I have and you I want and always you."

Sweet Désirée, firm center of a world spun wild this unbelievable day. And he drew her hand down, holding the fragrant palm against his cheek, needing her familiar comfort.

"I worry so about you," she said.

"You needn't. I'm all right."

"They pressure you too much."

For a little while she stood beside him. When he released her hand she left the room and he sat for a long time watching, as the clement evening gradually covered the bay. When night fell like a violet curtain shaking in the wind, he was still sitting there.

He thought of many, many things; of how a stone strikes and the pond stirs, of how words fall and the walls tremble. He thought of his dark daughters, with their Carib strain and that of the Arawak women whom the Caribs took. Now to all that was added the blood of Eleuthera's masters! And from deep inside him came a sound like a groan, as of something twisting and wrenching his chest, while before the eye of his mind there passed the stereotypical images of great-house ladies, an impossible mélange of haughty shoulders and soft faces, of whiteness and blondness, of silk and pearls. Who, who of them was she? And as so often in times of his most profound distress, he held up his hand, examining the whorls of the fingertips and the lines of the palm as if they could tell him something. Strange, all of it so strange and sad! That it should matter so much!

Then suddenly a faint and wry amusement twisted his lips. What would Marjorie, cool Marjorie, have to say if she knew? He suspected she'd make it rather hard on Francis. And with a premonition of loss and loneliness, he thought of Francis' departure: Perhaps that was a reason to speak?

Pressure, Désirée had said, not even understanding how much or of what kind, or how painful!

Oh, sometime, surely, he would have to tell what he had learned this day! He wasn't going down to his death, nor would he let Francis go, with such a truth unspoken. No matter whom it might hurt, it would have to be said.

Yet he came to know, as the hours went by, that the time was not now. There was enough of turmoil and tension at this moment in the life of each of them without creating more. Why burn Eleuthera again?

No, let them rest awhile, the living and the dead. Let them all rest.

Twenty-six

PATRICK moved the desk chair closer and shoved the telephone to one side. He still thought it was somehow comical to have three telephones. Perhaps they had been a necessary adjunct to Nicholas's position, affording him a sense of power and giving the impression that this desk was the place where things were made to happen. But Patrick had no need for them.

He picked up his pen again, returning to what he thought of as his "speech from the throne," or "state of the state" message, his first since he took office, a first accounting.

". . . negotiations for cooperative factories," he wrote. "Two Canadians and an American, having confidence in the economic climate on our island, want to produce a light cotton cloth in distinctive designs, using our local talents. A furniture manufacturer . . ."

He got up and walked to the tall windows from which, beyond descending treetops on the slope, one could see the harbor and the ancient structures along Wharf Street. There lies the power, he thought, there in the row of banks with the brass plates and the great names of London, of Canada and New York. If they will give us loans, we can— And he stood there while numbers went running through his head.

At the same time he was observing the life that pulsed in the town. There the banana boat was being loaded. A long line of women joined with a line of trucks as it wound toward the dock. There, as if a gift were being offered, each woman received a stem of bananas to balance on her head, and in a dancer's posture, to carry to the hold of the ship. Nothing of this had changed.

His eye traveled down Wharf Street to the low brick building where Kate would probably be working late on the *Trumpet,* bearing what she had to bear with dignity and grace. It was this very dignity that saddened him so. Tears would have been less painful. Yet he understood that Francis also must do what he had to do. Few things were ever simple. How could you weigh the relative values of a child and a woman? Especially if the woman was Kate?

Now a water taxi bounced across the harbor, lightly as a skimming gull. It stopped at the dock across the street from Da Cunha's door. Wharf Street had a row of new boutiques—little boxes—arrived in the wake of the hotels, but Da Cunha's was still king of the shops. How Désirée loved their dresses and their scarves and all the pretty trifles! And suddenly he remembered her—oh, it must have been before the girls were born—whirling in a white dress that she had bought there. He could see it quite clearly, billowing and short, printed with scarlet poppies. Fearfully expensive, he had thought, for those few yards of cloth! She had laughed and told him he didn't know anything about it, which was true. But she had looked so beautiful, and still did. Da Cunha had offered her a discount now because he'd been elected, but he hadn't, against her protests, allowed her to accept it. A matter of principle, it was, to owe no one for favors.

He felt he was making a good start. Even after this short time he could sense that the planters who had, to say the least, been lukewarm toward him, were beginning to support him with some conviction. They saw that he was trying to hew to a decent middle way. Last Saturday he'd called upon every citizen to give a day's work to the country, planting trees, repairing schools, or cleaning up the hospital grounds. The response had been—well, beautiful! The comments everywhere had been enthusiastic. He'd got out and put his own hands to work, too, which had done wonders for morale. Yes, a good spirit was rising.

Of course there were angry holdouts from Mebane's time; that was only to be expected. Those who had been making fortunes out of the drug traffic, for example, were not likely to be pleased with the new regime. Between them and the left wing, which was ever present, ever burrowing and undermining, there was plenty to worry about.

The Russians were entrenched in Cuba, and through the entire area the Cubans were spreading not only their advisers and technicians but their shotgun shells. It was very, very hard. You couldn't patrol every distant cove, especially on the ocean side, all night and each night.

He knew, he was almost sure, that Will was deep in these affairs. He couldn't prove it, any more than he could prove that the boy Will had set fire to Eleuthera, although he had never ceased to be plagued by the horror of the thought. One had one's gut reactions, that was all, and too often one's gut reactions were correct. They hardly ever saw Will these days, though, having come at last to a parting of the ways, an unsaid agreement to disagree. And he remembered the last time they had really talked together. It had been on the final night in their house and they'd been standing in the kitchen. Patrick had been saying something about the Cubans having thirty thousand troops in Africa and when Will had defended them Patrick had argued.

"You're going far beyond social justice, Will. You're making it all so simple, aren't you? Ask the thousands who are fleeing Cuba; ask why they've had to build a mine field at the Berlin Wall to keep workers from quitting the workers' paradise. Yes, too simple, Will! And what's more, you're entering an area of confrontation with a country which, for all that some like to say about it, has been the greatest force for human rights and freedom that the world has ever known. Ever. Yes, I'm talking about the United States," he'd said and thumped the table. But his words had petered out to empty air.

So we move again toward violence, he thought as he looked down upon the drowsy little town. It hasn't erupted yet, not fully; contained, it merely smolders. But if the high winds come, then—

He went back to the desk. Yes, tell about that, too. No sense writing a cheery message full of halftruths and clichés. Tell it all. And end with a good, strong peroration about having faith in ourselves, in our courage and abilities, something like that. An upbeat ending is what's needed.

Maybe he ought to take the rough draft to Francis for an opinion. This was an important speech, after all. But the real reason was his compelling wish to see Francis. Now. Tonight. Several times since his return from the visit to Agnes, he had got into the car and started toward Eleuthera, then as abruptly turned around and come back. It was as if he were afraid to face Francis, afraid that his excitement, and yes, his love, would show. But tonight, now, he would go. The speech was a good excuse.

The yellow two-seater sports car, an expensive toy, was the one that had belonged to Doris Mebane. Hasty flight had caused it to be left behind. It had, then, become public property and the council had offered it for sale. When no one bought it, they had sold it to Désirée for a nominal sum.

"Far too conspicuous," Patrick argued, but Désirée had some savings of her own and she was in love with it. Patrick had never ridden in it.

What foolish impulse made me want to try this thing out? he wondered, as he rolled along the coast road. A flash of lost youth, maybe? He'd never desired flashy things and still didn't, yet this was fun. The motor made a rich sound, the husky throat sound of a passionate woman.

At the Point he stopped the car. This was a sight not to be missed. The sun rested now on the rim of the sea, streaming a mauve and turquoise radiance across the lower sky. Oh, how we buzz and buzz our lives away! First school, then business, politics and money and God only knows what else. But all the time there is this, too.

Along the beach at the water's edge two small boys came trotting on spidery legs. All of a sudden they stopped and threw themselves at the face of an incoming wave. When it swallowed them, shattering itself into spume and foam, it released and threw them back onto the sand. Again and again they went, waiting for the rise of the wave, the glossy dark green curve, slick as glass; over and over they hurled themselves and were hurled back. Their shrieking laughter carried down the beach.

Life in essence! The elementals: the salt water out of which we all came, and the sun in which we lie, drinking the heat of it. Take away everything that man has made and done and this is what's left. How good, how joyous, to see those two thoughtless kids coming out of the sea! Life from the sea! A mystery. All, all a mystery. . . .

And love for the world overwhelmed him. Here we are, and at the moment of our deepest love and understanding, we depart. All this delight! Stretch out your hand to reach the sun ray or moonbeam. Touch it! It's gone! You can only hold it for a moment.

Releasing the brake, he turned the little car back toward the hills.

Eleuthera came into sight above the trees like a classic columned temple. It would be good to see Greece one day, he reflected, to travel with Désirée at last when his work was finished here. How she would love it!

Francis and Marjorie were reading on the veranda. He stood.

"Prime minister," he said, smiling.

"I've brought my speech," Patrick said, feeling suddenly awkward. "I thought you might be good enough to look it over."

"Thank you, I'm honored."

Marjorie gave greeting and got up. "I'm going to bed early, I'll leave you to your talk."

Her heel tap sounded briskly in the hall and clicked up the stairs.

"She has a cold coming on," Francis explained, after a moment's silence.

"Please, am I intruding?"

"You are not," Francis said with firmness.

Again silence fell. The night was so still that the neighing of a horse three fields away caused them to start.

Francis spoke softly. "Nine years! That's how long it's been since the day I met you in the schoolhouse. What a storm that was!"

"I don't know where the time's gone, as the old folks always say. Mostly I feel very young; I guess you'd say I still am, but sometimes I'm brought up short, to count the years that are left."

"Yes. Everything becomes sharper when you think about time. You walk out in the morning and suddenly you've never seen a fresher green. You've never smelled such fragrant coffee. Yes."

So they sat for a while, talking of the speech, talking of this and that, until abruptly, darkness fell. In northern places it approached slowly, Patrick remembered now, but not here.

A calf lowed in the barn nearby. "I don't remember your barns being so close to the house," he remarked.

"They weren't always. I guess this is the only place around that has the barns this near. But I've always liked the sound of animals. I had them build a cowshed at the same time they rebuilt the wing, after the fire."

He can speak of it now, Patrick thought. It's not between us anymore. And he said, "I used to like hearing the hens settle down at night when I was a kid. I kind of miss those last contented clucks."

"Has it ever occurred to you that our tastes are very much alike, yours and mine?"

"Alike?"

"Oh, I think so. Kate always says—said so."

For an instant it seemed as though Francis were going to say more; there was a pause while his fingers drummed on the chair arm, but apparently he changed his mind, for the silence lengthened.

It became necessary to fill the silence. "At least," Patrick said lightly, "you're not a politician!"

"You want to know something? I don't think you really are either. I don't mean you're not doing a good job, I mean that I don't think it's your first choice. I think you'd rather be standing up before a class, teaching."

"Yes, but there still are moments when I like what I'm doing, I have to admit. The cheers, you know, and the praise. Well, we're all human, and there've been great days, like the day our flag went up and we became a nation."

"Ah, yes. For a place you can drive across in an hour's time, this nation has some pretty large problems."

When Patrick didn't answer, Francis apologized. "Sorry. I didn't mean that the way it might have sounded."

"I understand, and you're right. We're on the brink of worldwide decisions here, in a strategic place. You have only to read the newspapers and look at a few maps." A figure came suddenly to mind. "Russia gives Cuba a million dollars a day in aid. The whole world's being terrorized."

"Yes. Undermined. The object is to make chaos. Undo whatever we do as fast as we do it."

There's Kate talking, Patrick thought, and answered, "You ought to get together with my new son-in-law, my soon-to-be. You know, he's one of the best things that's happened in my life. Not just that he's marrying Laurine, but knowing he could take over for me if need be."

"I've heard you say that before, and I don't know why you talk that way."

"Don't worry, I plan to be around a long time! But it's a good feeling all the same. My other son-in-law, Maisie's young man—well, he's a disappointment. He's leaving the country, going to Canada. Taking Maisie, naturally." And as Francis made no comment, Patrick went on fretfully, "Some of our best people are leaving. Dr. Sparrow has already gone and Dr. Maynard's going. Talk about a brain drain! When what we need is more people like them coming in, not going out."

"Well, they feel there's better opportunity elsewhere. You can't blame them, I suppose."

"You can blame them! Don't they know or care that it takes time to build a country? And how are we going to do it with them deserting us and the enemy almost within the gates? Oh, I lie awake thinking and thinking. I get so mad sometimes I can't think clearly anymore."

"But you've made a very fine beginning, Patrick, in your short time."

"I've done what I could. One thing is that nobody here need be afraid of the government. We have no political prisoners. You can think and say what you want as long as you keep the peace. Nobody's beaten up in our jails. That stuff's over and done with."

Francis hesitated a moment. Then, not looking at Patrick, he spoke. "I haven't ever told you. . . . I'm ashamed of myself. When Nicholas was here and there were rumors of those things going on, even a rumor about a ravine where the bodies were thrown, I didn't believe them even when Osborne told me where the place was."

"You could have gone to see for yourself."

"I didn't take it seriously."

"I understand."

"I suppose I felt that if I found it was true, I'd have to involve myself—"

"Are you still up, Francis?" Marjorie spoke from the doorway, then, seeing Patrick, clutched the frill of her dressing gown about her throat. "Oh, excuse me, I didn't know you were still here."

Patrick stood. "My fault. I've kept him talking too late."

"Oh, talk as long as you like," she replied.

The two men went down the steps to the car.

"I'm sorry you're going to leave us, Francis," Patrick said.

Francis nodded. The light from the veranda revealed the face of an aristocrat. Not in any narrow sense, Patrick thought, but as the inheritor of an excellent body, of intelligence, and basic honor, this was an aristocrat.

"I hope things won't be too hard," he said next, "not for you nor for anyone."

Francis took his meaning. "You'll look out for her, will you? Don't let her do anything foolish."

"I won't." He didn't know when he had been so moved. And he put his hand to his mouth as though to stop the words that were in his head: Trust me, Francis, because you and I are—

Francis put out his hand in dismissal. It was the gentle dismissal of a man who is asking for privacy and a relief from tension.

"We pin our hopes on you, Prime Minister. And on men like you all over the world," he said rather formally.

"Thank you, Francis. I sometimes think—there's something I'd like to say—" He stopped. Not now! The words had come out without his willing them to.

"Say what?"

"Nothing. Nothing important. It's too late tonight. What do you think of this car? Isn't it outrageous?"

"Not at all. It's a gem. Come back again, will you, before we leave?"

"I will."

When he reached the end of the driveway he looked back through the rearview mirror. Francis was still standing with his arm upraised in a wave. An impulse grasped Patrick, so that for an instant he made to swerve and go back. But in the second instant it released him and he was able to steady himself and head the car toward home.

Francis watched the taillights, two red fox eyes, vanish at the turn. He stood until, in a little while, headlights flashed a white path through a gap in the trees far down the hill road.

How much had moved and changed since he had first come to know this good and decent man on that stormy afternoon nine years before! God go with him. He was fighting the good fight, as the saying went. God go with us all. Shelter helpless Megan, please. Let Kate laugh again, let her be warm and loved. He felt a choking in his throat.

A small wind was blowing off Morne Bleue, agitating the wind bells into a clatter of chimes. And he waited on the steps, unwilling to go inside, almost mesmerized by the sound, by his own emotions and by the flawless night.

Oh, this must be one of the most beautiful places on earth! Human pain was so piercingly incongruous here; to suffer in bleak deserts and on raw northern tundras was comprehensible, but not here in this soft air, under this white moon, with the grass so sweet.

At last he went in to take a handful of cookies and a glass of warm milk, for he hadn't been sleeping well. In Megan's room he adjusted the coverlet and moved the teddy bear from where it had fallen on her. He listened to her tiny breath and tiny stirrings. What dreams would flit through that poor brain? And again there was that choking sensation in his throat.

In his own room a new magazine lay on the bedside table; the combination of milk and reading might quiet his racing heart, he hoped, and send him the peace of sleep.

It was eleven on the dashboard clock when Patrick's little car slid between fragrant hedges down the last moonlit mile and turned in at the great gates.

The shot crashed through the windshield and struck him in the forehead. The car plunged, screeching, into a granite pillar, then burst into flames and, in a few searing moments, was consumed on the lawn in front of Government House.

Twenty-seven

Now once again the island shuddered and thrashed like some great wounded creature of the sea. For three days it struggled and bled.

The international news services made these reports in succession:

As leftist groups and rightist adherents, left over from the Mebane regime, lay blame upon each other for the assassination of Prime Minister Patrick Courzon, St. Felice bows beneath another wave of violence. An attempt to seize the radio station was repelled yesterday by forces loyal to the government, but in other areas key installations have changed hands three or four times during the last forty-eight hours. Two army barracks have already gone up in flames. Government forces have uncovered quantities of arms belonging to dissident elements of several persuasions. Among the caches were Molotov cocktails, gelignite, and several types of small arms.

Looting and vandalism in Covetown are gradually being brought under control. Banks and shops are still boarded with plywood and a six-to-six curfew has been set by Mr. Franklin Parrish, the acting head of government.

On the third night after the assassination calm has been restored to St. Felice. The dead number fifteen to twenty, with as many wounded. Over one hundred arrests have been made, ring leaders rounded up and the curfew lifted. Correspondents report remarkable cooperation on the part of the citizenry, which is weary of conflict and shaken by the tragedy.

On the fourth morning Patrick Courzon was buried. The cathedral in Covetown was filled; crowds teetered on the steps and filled the street outside.

"He was a man of the middle, without hatreds," Father Baker began, in the dry voice of an old man, straining. "His political ambitions were small. There were others far more ambitious and far more skilled in the art of politics. But what he possessed was infinitely precious and rare, an innate goodness and the will to persevere on a rational course." For an instant the old voice broke, then resumed: "Who did this to him? That is the question which absorbs us, and will continue to absorb us."

In essence, Francis thought, the ones who did it were the ones he loved most: Nicholas and Will. And he looked down at the front pew where Will, who had just flown in a few hours before from wherever he had been when Patrick died, was sitting with Désirée and the daughters, all in deep black, and with Clarence, who was weeping.

"Both sides had their reasons for eliminating a man who stood so firmly, so honorably, in the way of their desires, a man who believed so passionately in the worth of the individual and in peaceful solutions."

"Thank God we're leaving this crazy place," Marjorie murmured in Francis' ear.

He did not answer. Suddenly he was washed by a wave of sickness. His own emotion, combined with the heat of bodies closely jammed, overwhelmed him. Seated in the path of the sun as it streamed through pastel stained glass, he was dizzied by spots of lavender moving on his knees.

And it seemed to him that heat was rising everywhere; he imagined he felt the presence of fire, just as, waking in the night, one can imagine the acrid fumes of smoke—so it must have been on that other night. Now, though, it was not only a house that was on fire, it was the planet; the skies of every continent were ominous; the very air, the very flowers, burned.

He must have made a sound, for Marjorie turned to him with an expression of curiosity and alarm.

"Don't you feel well?"

"So hot in here."

"It's almost over, thank heaven. Look, look who's over there, will you?"

And he saw that Kate was sitting a few rows down across the aisle. She was wearing a little round straw hat. Her funeral hat, she called it, because it went with anything and was suitably decorous. She kept it in a clear plastic box on the top shelf of the closet with her tennis racket and a red-striped sweater. Yes.

He hadn't seen her in two weeks and he would never see her again. He would never have time to know her entirely. It was strange to think that actually he knew Marjorie so much better! Marjorie existed in familiar territory; he was not at home in her territory, but at least he could find his way around in it. Marjorie was always predictable; you could never predict what Kate would do. One thing, though, you could say and never be wrong. A tag of Latin from years ago repeated itself in his head: *Nihil humanum mihi alienum.* Nothing human is alien to me. Or nothing animal, either. And he had to smile, watching the little straw hat, remembering her dogs and her birds, her stray cats and her indignations.

They were standing now, and the nausea receded. While the organ recessional poured overhead, the coffin was borne out. The crowd on the street had been forced back to let it pass. From the high steps Francis looked down upon what is always described as a sea of faces, an apt enough description, to be modified here, he thought, to a sea of young faces. How many of them there were! The island, the whole earth, was bursting with impatient, restless young.

Someone touched his arm. This time he looked down into an old face, into a quilting of wrinkles on Chinese cheeks.

"Did you happen to know him?"

"Yes, very well. Did you?"

The old man wanted to talk. "Just when he was a boy. But I remember him clearly. In Sweet Apple, it was, where I had a store. Ah Sing's store." And he folded his hands into his sleeves, a gesture he had brought from his homeland more than half a century before. "He's not a person you would forget."

Francis nodded. "No, you wouldn't."

And he looked back at the sorrowful, respectful crowd. Calm now, all of them calm. Next time we might not be this lucky.

"I'm not going to the graveyard," Marjorie said. "I suppose you are?"

"Yes, and afterwards to the house. The family is going back to Clarence's. Désirée wanted to."

"Well, you go then. I never knew them all that well, anyway. I'll get a lift."

Neighbor women had taken over the house and sent Désirée upstairs to rest, leaving the front room to the men. Clarence, Franklin, and Will were by themselves when Francis went in.

"It could as easily have been one of Mebane's men," Will was arguing. "Far more easily. You always blame the left!"

"I didn't say it couldn't have been one of Mebane's," Clarence retorted. In his grief he had aged; his dark face was powdered with gray. "But also, it might not have been. You aren't going to tell me your heroes don't kill? Russians and Cubans and the rest who are going to deliver this world from all evil—they don't kill?"

"You don't understand," Will said. "You never did. You never will."

"I understand that you don't care, that this death is nothing to you." In anger, Clarence half rose from his chair.

"I don't think he meant—" began Franklin, his tone admonishing *Don't be too hard on him,* when Will made his own defense.

"You think I'm indifferent because I take a larger view! I'm sorry, of course I'm sorry! But how much can you grieve for one man in a world where millions suffer?"

Clarence was contemptuous. "It's the same with all of you. Oh, the wringing of the hands on behalf of the masses! But where is the human feeling for the family or the friend? Pity in the abstract for the masses, yes, but for the individual, none. Torture even, and the gulag for him."

"I have pity." Will stood his ground. "But Patrick was misguided. He was ineffectual. All his nice words, his laws and rules—crumbs! They'll come to nothing."

"Yes," Clarence said bitterly, "that's very true, if you and your kind have anything to say about it. You'll make sure that they come to nothing."

Will stood up. He has the eyes of a fanatic, Francis thought. I should hate to be at his mercy. And yet—so young, so bright, so— wasted!

"Where are you going?" Clarence asked.

"The Trenches. I have friends there."

"Friends! You're still welcome to stay here."

"No. Thanks anyway."

"Where will you be going after that?"

"Grenada in a couple of weeks, I think."

"And where then?"

"It depends."

"Cuba?" Clarence persisted.

"I don't know. Maybe. Yes, maybe. I'll see you again before I go."

When the screen door had slammed behind Will, Francis spoke. "Caught in a vise." It was the first thing that had come to his mind.

"Yes, very sad." Franklin spoke quietly. "And there are many, many like him. You can see we have our work cut out for us."

"Strange. Patrick always said you would take over for him, and now you are."

Franklin nodded gravely. "I know. I'm going to try to do what he was trying to do. That is, if I'm elected after I fill his unexpired term."

"You will be," Francis said.

Franklin made a pyramid of his hands, regarding it thoughtfully. "There's just so much! Deal with terrorism. Stop the brain-drain. I'm hoping the United States will stand by with economic help—"

Clarence interrupted. "Good thing Will didn't hear you say that about the United States." He was still fuming.

Franklin smiled. "Well, Marxism dupes the young. It sounds so hopeful, doesn't it? Funny they don't ask themselves why there've been more than six million refugees from communist governments. It's a case of *wanting* to believe. Phony miracle cures like any phony miracle cure!" He returned to the subject. "Yes, I'm looking to the United States as the—what's the phrase? The last best hope on earth? It's strong, it has always been generous and above all, it's free."

The voice was confident, but not brashly so. And Francis thought, Patrick judged well. He suspected that Franklin might prove to be even stronger than Patrick. For one thing, he was younger, but might it not also be that he had no internal conflicts about his own identity and his place in the world?

"I had such a crazy feeling," Francis said, "during the service this morning. It was a terrible illusion that the whole world was on fire. For a minute or two I was sick with it. I feel a lot better now, though, after hearing you."

"Fires can be put out," Franklin replied quietly, as Désirée came down the stairs.

She was a tall black stem; her head was a dark flower. There were two blacks, the matte cotton of her dress, and the gloss of her long hair. A beautiful woman, even on this day.

Hearing her descent, the women came in from the kitchen. "What are you going to do?" someone asked, while another remonstrated gently, "You don't have to decide a thing now, honey. It's much too soon. Take your time," this being the usual advice that is given to widows all over the world.

"I don't know," Désirée murmured. "I don't know."

"You can go with us, Mama," Maisie said. "You can be with us in Chicago. You always wanted to leave here, anyway."

"Yes, I always wanted to leave, but your father never did."

"If you stay, Mama," Franklin said, "you can help us make what Patrick wanted us to make of this country. Of course, one can't promise anything, one can only try."

Désirée's large, grieving eyes moved around the room, out to the hall, out to the porch, and back in to the kitchen, covering the familiar spaces of the home in which she had grown up. For a few minutes no one said anything, nor did she. Then she spoke.

"I'll stay. Yes," she said simply, "I'll stay. I'll live as we—as he planned. As I would have lived if he—" she did not finish.

Now the family would want to be alone, Francis saw. He stood up and said his good-byes. Franklin Parrish saw him out to the porch.

"I believe," he said, as Francis looked back up the walk at him, "I still believe we can make it so decent, so beautiful here—" and he threw out his hands in a gesture as moving, as graceful as a blessing.

When he got home Francis put his car in the garage and walked away from the house. Down the hill he went, crossed the little river at the footbridge and found his familiar flat rock on the beach, where he disturbed a tribe of squawking black birds who had been flurrying in the beach grape behind the rock. For long minutes he sat very still. Then he picked up a flat green disk of grape leaf, traced its rosy veins with his fingertip, threw it away, and was so still again that the birds dared to return, bold on their stalky legs, and so close that he could see into their shallow, cold, yellow eyes. And still he did not move.

When at last the birds flapped away he was still sitting there. Silence enveloped the little crescent of beach; the wind, which had been so faint, now died; even the mild waves made no sound as they approached and receded. There was only the thin, high buzz of silence. Like a ceaseless insect hum in grass it was, or like the streaming of blood in the arteries of the ear. The sound of silence.

Not long ago, and yet it began to seem very long ago, he had sat in this same place, had walked up and down here, up and down, then gone back to the house and announced his capitulation.

He got up now and began to walk, up and down, to the far edge of the beach and return, back and return.

"You can't live isolated," something said inside his head. "Can't live without—can't live—"

And an idea which had been unacceptable, alien to everything he

had believed and the way he had looked at life, suddenly and sound-
lessly, unfolded and revealed itself as do those tightly furled paper
flowers that when placed in water ripple open and gently spread their
brilliant petals.

He could not live without her! And desire for her overpowered him,
a cruel hunger, as if he had been starved. He was filled with a con-
sciousness of her presence. He looked up to the hill where she had
stood on that first day, here on this dear ground, and it seemed to him
that she was standing there now, that her arms were out to him,
begging him to stay. Kate! And he was filled with a rush of love, for
her, for this land, a love for everything alive. That caterpillar crawling
near his foot, a curious creature, black-and-yellow–striped with a red
head; it too wanted its life, its own short, free time in the sun. And
he stepped aside to spare it. How much time did it have, and how
much had any of us, when all was said and done? So little! Kate!

And now he rushed, he ran, he leaped the little river, he raced back
up to the house.

Marjorie was sitting on the terrace before a silver tea tray. She had
changed into country clothes, meaning pastel; it would have been
incorrect to wear light colors to a funeral in town. At sight of him she
set the cup down.

"Well! I must say you look like death warmed over."

"It's not been the happiest day of my life."

"Hmph! We're lucky they didn't follow him and decide to kill him
here. We might all have been shot on account of your precious
friend."

Francis sat down. He wet his lips. He had a flash of memory, of
himself as a child being angry at adults for being so stupid as to marry
each other, when even a child could see they didn't belong together
and never could.

"I want you to go," he said. "Take Megan. Leave here. Without
me."

"You what?" She gave a high laugh. "*You* want *me* to go?"

"Yes. Let's make a final end to the waste."

"Waste? What are you talking about?"

"I'm talking about our time. There isn't all that much of it in anybody's life. What are we proving by staying together? There's nothing left and you know it. You want to leave here and I don't. It comes down to that."

She rose from her chair, clattering the tea things. "You want to marry Kate Tarbox, you mean!"

"Yes," he said simply.

"I knew you went to her that night the elections were called off, when you rushed away from the party! I knew it! But I didn't want to look like an idiot by accusing you if by some chance I was mistaken. Oh, the bitch! The whore!"

"I don't want to hear that, Marjorie."

"That first time here at Eleuthera, I knew it, too! I saw it!"

"You knew more than I did, then."

"I ought to mutilate her face so you wouldn't look at it anymore. Throw lye on it, the way the natives do here."

He was astonished. "Why? You don't care about me, about us. You haven't in a long, long time."

She didn't answer. Furious tears were falling and she groped for a handkerchief, not finding one. He gave her his.

"You don't care," he repeated. "We hardly ever sleep together anymore."

"Really," she mocked, "for such an ardent lover as you are—"

He interrupted. "I know I haven't been for a long, long time. Doesn't that tell you anything? I'm young, I'm healthy." His voice rose passionately. "This is no life, two solitary beds—"

"Oh, for God's sake! Moderate your voice, you fool! Do you want the servants to hear such talk?"

"The servants! The servants! They're human beings like you and me. Don't you think they have eyes in their heads? I don't have your sense of propriety—"

"Keep your voice down, I said! Megan is napping! Do you want to frighten her awake?"

At once he whispered, "If we hadn't had Megan we'd have ended this long ago, Marjorie. We've been using her, both of us have. And

I should never have brought you here. It was wrong of me. It wasn't fair to you."

"You know damn well I've tried to make a go of it. I've run your house and entertained your guests and been a credit to you."

"Yes. Yes, you have." But the chasm between us is wider than St. Felice, he thought, and would have opened if we had never heard of the place.

"I do my best to take care of the defective child you gave me, too."

This cruelty silenced him and he bowed his head while she continued.

"My child wouldn't have been like this if it hadn't been for your family."

"You don't have to remind me," he said dully.

"Apparently, I do, since you seem quite willing to dump us. Trading us off for a tract of land and a new woman."

He raised his head. She wanted to cheapen his feelings, he understood that. He wasn't going to let her.

"I'm not 'dumping' you," he said angrily. "I intend to take perfect care of you and Megan. Always, even if you should—establish yourself. No matter."

"Establish myself! In what, please tell me? What chance have I had to learn anything? I've thrown my life away for you!"

He wondered scornfully what things she would have learned and done if she hadn't "thrown her life away" for him. But no, that wasn't fair; she was an intelligent woman and this was nineteen-eighty; in other circumstances she would have done other things.

"Or maybe you meant establish myself with another husband? A rich one?"

"Whether you do or not is immaterial. Megan is my responsibility. But I hope you do find another husband, someone more suited to you than I've ever been," he added bitterly.

"And what about Megan? All of a sudden, you're so willing to part with her! A new development, to say the least."

"We'd have to anyway. She'll have to go to a special school, eventually. You know that." His heart ached. "Oh, don't you see how sorry it all is? For you, for me, for Megan? But from the day she was born we've lived as if we'd abandoned all hope for ourselves, and that's not right! No human being should be required to do that. We'll do the best we can for her, all our lives, but—"

"You bastard."

"Why? Because now I'm the one who wants to end this charade? It was all right last month when you threatened to walk off with the child if I didn't do what you wanted me to do. That was all right! It's your damned pride that's injured now, that's all. 'What will people say?' Well, you needn't worry. I'll be chivalrous. I won't talk."

"You bastard."

"If it makes you happier to say that, keep on saying it."

"Oh, go to hell!" she cried, with her fist against her mouth.

He knew she was ashamed of weeping before him and he looked away.

"Oh, go to hell," he heard again. The door slammed and her high heels clattered on the stairs.

A few days later he rose early and looked in the mirror at a face gone haggard, spent with turmoil and lack of sleep. As if he were counseling it, he spoke aloud to his face.

"Yes, it's better to be honest, even to go through this pain. Divorce is terrible. It's a rending, a breaking. Destruction. When you marry you're sure it will last. But what did I know? Nothing. Nor did she. Glands, that's all it was. That and illusions. Strange to think it's all turned to hatred. No, not hatred. Anger. She's more angry than I am, though. A woman's pride. There must be someone who's right for her. A Wall Street type. Someone less—less what?—than I. . . . Less intense, maybe. She's better off, in a way, than people like Kate and me. We look into each other's souls, we want everything from each other. Well, you can't help what you are."

At the edge of the terrace he had built a large feeder, filled with sugar, for the yellowbirds. It had been intended to amuse Megan. But her attention span was too short, not more than half a minute. They were standing there now, when he came downstairs, Marjorie pointing out the birds while Megan, not interested, looked in the other direction. It struck him that Marjorie already looked like a visitor, a stranger.

Hearing him, she turned around. Her eyes were darkly circled and he felt a sudden painful pity.

"Well?" she said. The syllable was clear and cold as a chip of ice.

Once again he made an effort at conciliation. "Well, I hope you're feeling better, that's all."

"As if you give a damn how I feel!"

"Believe it or not, I do."

"If there's anything that disgusts me, it's a hypocrite!"

"Whatever other faults you've found in me, I can't think hypocrisy is one of them."

She bit her lip. Her lower lip was raw.

"As long as we're going to do this, wouldn't it be better to do it decently and quietly, Marjorie?"

"Decently and quietly! The next adjective will be 'civilized,' I suppose. 'A civilized divorce.' "

"Why not? You want to go. Why not go in peace?"

"In peace! With another woman waiting to move in while my bed's still warm."

Megan was staring. He wondered whether any of this could be making an impression on the mind behind those apathetic blue eyes. And he spoke very gently.

"In case you are having any—thoughts about yourself, I want to tell you something. You're a very desirable woman, Marjorie. This isn't a case of someone else being more attractive. You're a lovely woman. People turn to look at you—"

"A hell of a lot of good that does!"

She put her face in her hands. She walked to the end of the terrace and sat down with her back to him. In her proud reserve she was struggling silently with herself; he knew, having seen her do it often enough. Sad, he turned away to the morning's moist glitter.

After a while, hearing the chair scrape, he looked up.

"All right, Francis. Call it quits." She spoke rapidly. "I'll go to

Mexico or wherever the lawyers say it's quick and easy. I don't want any complications." And with some bitterness, she added, "I'm sure you'll be overjoyed to hear that."

"I'm not everjoyed about this at all, Marjorie."

"You'll have to keep Megan with you until it's over."

He nodded, the lump in his throat being too thick just then for him to speak. Instead he picked Megan up, rubbing his cheek against her hair.

"Daddy," she said, then struggled to get away. He put her down.

"I'm sorry I said some things I didn't mean, Francis. About throwing lye. And about your giving me Megan."

"Of course I knew you didn't mean all that. People say things when they're angry. I do, too."

"No, you never do. I don't think you ever said anything really nasty to me." For the first time since this crisis had begun, she looked straight at him.

He was touched. "I'm glad you'll remember me that way."

Horses, being let out to pasture, whinnied beyond the fence. A child, one of Osborne's boys probably, called out, making cheerful morning noise.

"You know, Francis, I must say, in all fairness, it hasn't been entirely bad here."

That was one thing about Marjorie: regardless of her angry pride, she was usually able to be honest and, upon reflection, to soften both the anger and the pride. He had always thought of this trait as her morning-after quirk. Also, because she was a realist, she knew when it was time to advance and when to retreat.

He said now, "I want you to be happy, Marjorie. I really do."

She clenched her fists. "How I hate to fail! I ask myself how it could have been different. You can't know how I hate to fail! Hate it!"

Her vehemence did not surprise him. "I know you do. You can't bear not having things perfect. It would be better for you," he said gently, "easier, if you could. I only hope you'll find—"

"You hope I'll find someone else to love me? I'll tell you something. I don't think all women really need to be loved, not the way you're talking about, anyhow. I'm never unhappy being alone. Oh, you're thinking of my going to parties and all that, but that's not what I mean. I'm talking about the inner self. Maybe I don't really want anybody, after all. That's why I couldn't give you what you wanted."

Perhaps it was true and perhaps this was only bitterness. If it was bitterness, and he hoped that was all it was, it would pass.

He put his hand on her shoulder. "I told you, though, I'll always take care of you. You needn't worry."

"I never doubted that, Francis. But I've been thinking—I did a lot of thinking last night—maybe I'll start a business in antiques or get a job in the field. I'd be doing what I want to do, in a place where I want to be."

"You'd be good at it."

"Yes, far from the madding crowd. Surrounded by beautiful things right up to the deluge. I'm certainly not one for politics or civic betterment, as you well know." She gave a short laugh, almost as if she were laughing at her own expense.

The child was trying to eat grass.

"No, no!" Marjorie cried, taking it from her. The child screamed and the mother picked her up, comforting, straining under her weight.

And Francis, watching, knew that he was tied to the mother through the child and always would be, tied with a strong cord, not to be sundered.

"It's not the way we wanted it to turn out, is it? But it's no one's fault. Remember that, Marjorie."

She nodded. "I'll take Megan down to the beach."

"I'll be in the office if you want me."

And they walked away, in opposite directions.

Twenty-eight

F RANCIS and Kate were to be married in the ancient Church of the Heavenly Rest, that rugged pile on top of the cliff with the sea at its feet and the forest at its back. Early that afternoon Francis and Tee drove cross-island together.

They had been talking since her arrival two days before, talking of Kate and Margaret, of Marjorie and Megan, of politics and farming, talking as they had not done since he had been a boy coming home from school to the little yellow upstairs sitting room where she would be waiting to hear about his day.

Now suddenly a silence fell upon them. Too many emotions had come too close to the surface. Even the marvelous fulfillment of this his wedding day came close to pain; always, joy quivers in the lee of sadness.

Yesterday he had put Megan on a plane to join Marjorie in New York. Thank God, the parting had held no pain for the child at all, otherwise he could not have borne it. She had simply walked away, sucking a lollipop, not looking back. Oh, he would see her again, of course he would, but it would not be the same. It had ended, tied neatly in a package, addressed and sent away. End of a phase.

His mother touched his arm.

"You're thinking of Megan."

"Yes."

"She will be better off with Marjorie. A good school, a residence for her special needs—"

"But you! You say this to me while you yourself will never—" He stopped. This was the one question it was fruitless to ask her. But, to his surprise, this time she answered.

"There are no rules always right for everyone. Every one of us is the result of what came before."

Curious, he glanced at her, but her face was averted and his glance fell across her dark head to the silver-green of cane along the road.

"I may know what I ought to do and be unable to do it." Her voice was a murmur, so that he strained to hear. "But you mustn't think of me as some sort of sickly martyr; I'm really living very well—"

He interrupted. "Of course I know that! I know how you live. And yet—I must tell you—as close as you've been to me, to all of us, I've always felt, I feel as if some part of you is hidden. It's like a locked door, a curtain. . . . I think my father felt it, too."

She didn't answer, but turning, gave him an unfathomable look and dropped her eyes.

"Well, I knew—we all knew—yours was a strange match. No two people could have been more different from each other."

Still she made no answer.

"In your time, though, I realize divorce wasn't all that simple. Also, you had four children."

And again she looked away, her eyes wandering over the wind-bowed cane, her voice murmuring something he barely caught: "I would never have broken his home." He thought he heard her say, "I owed him everything," but wasn't sure and couldn't ask, because abruptly she raised her head and with a little toss admonished him. "Enough of me! I've come for a wedding and I want to hear about it."

"Well, you know it's to be the ceremony, that's all, especially since you have to go home right afterwards."

"I'll come again in the winter, I promise."

"I'm glad. You'll love Kate when you know her better. She'll love you," he said gratefully. "A couple of cousins are all she has. They're coming today. And our new P.M. will be there. Also his mother-in-law, the widow of the last P.M. You remember, I've told you about Patrick."

"I remember."

"I miss him." He had a flashing recall, a glimpse of night, of headlights streaking the lawn and Patrick saying something, hesitating, wanting to tell him and not telling him—what? He blinked, returning to the present. "His mind—oh, perhaps it sounds pompous or foolish, I don't know—but his mind just seemed to reflect my own so much of the time. It was almost a mirror-image. Made him very easy to talk to."

"I should imagine. Did he have a good life, would you say?"

An odd question, Francis thought. What's a good life?

"I'm not sure what you mean."

"Oh, was it all a dreadful struggle, did he fit in here after his English education, did he have enough money—"

"He never wanted very much. Yes, I'd say he got along all right. And he loved this place, he really did. I think he'd had a very healthy childhood here, in simple circumstances, and he was awfully fond of his mother. Some of these native women are so warm, the most extraordinary mothers, you know. And he had a good marriage. Désirée's charming, you'll see."

It had showered on the other side of the island. A shine was on the leaves and the old stones when they drove into the churchyard. Kate, in pink, with a pink cap on her bright hair, was already there. She kissed Tee.

"I'm so glad you're here. I know it can't have been easy for you to see St. Felice again."

"I wanted to come." Tee laughed. "Besides, I'm afraid I shall never learn to say no to Francis."

"Nor shall I."

The two women stood a moment regarding each other and then

each, as if content that her earlier estimation of the other had been correct, turned toward the door.

Désirée, with her daughters and their fiancés, followed by Kate's cousins, went in with them. Désirée had brought a pink bouquet to place on the altar; except for it, the church was bare.

"We're early," Kate said. "Father Baker's not here yet. I feel like Juliet eloping with Romeo to the friar's cell."

"Patrick and I were married here on a windy day just like this one," Désirée remarked.

Kate was horrified. "I would never have done this to you if I'd known! I took for granted you were married in town."

"It doesn't matter. Look how beautiful it is!"

Through the open doors one could see a stretch of ocean and lines of speeding whitecaps.

"Isn't this fascinating?" cried Laurine. " 'Here lie the remains of Pierre and Eleuthère François, infant sons of Eleuthère and Angélique François, died and entered into paradise . . . year of our Lord, seventeen hundred and two. Our tears shall water their grave.' Fascinating!"

Father Baker had come in on rubber-soled feet. "If you look back far enough you'll find that practically everybody on this island has the blood of a Da Cunha or a François or both in his veins."

"I'd like to place a stone here in memory of Patrick," Désirée said. "I don't know whose blood he had, but anyway—" Her voice trailed off.

Tee put her hand on Désirée's shoulder.

"It would be very fitting for him to be remembered here," she said gently. "Will you see Father Baker about it and let me make the contribution?"

Désirée began, "I don't understand—"

"He was—they tell me he was—an unusual man. So I should like to do it in his memory. Please?"

"I thank you, then," Désirée said simply. Her mouth smiled, but her eyes held bright tears and, to Francis' astonishment, his mother's eyes held them, too.

"Here's Francis' plaque." Father Baker drew the group toward the new, white stone on the west wall, then read the sharp-cut lettering aloud.

"In loving memory of my father, Richard Luther—" The other half was blank.

"For me, when my time comes," Tee said.

"Really?" Kate asked curiously.

"Why? I can't live here. Still, I should like to lie here at the end, among my people."

Francis glanced at his mother, his sensitive ear catching every nuance. *Can't* live here? Not, I don't *want* to or I wouldn't *like* to, but *can't*. And for the thousandth time, he wondered why, in spite of knowing her so well, there was still so much he did not know, and never would.

Laurine broke into the silence. She had a pretty voice, gay and a little husky.

"Enough of memorial stones! We're here for a wedding."

"You're right," Father Baker said. "Come." And he opened his worn black book to begin.

"Dearly beloved, we are gathered here—"

The old words made music in Francis' ears, but his mind was too full to grasp their meaning. His mind was searching *himself*. He had never thought of himself as a religious man, and yet here in this moment it came to him that you had to have something strong to hold to if you were to survive. You had to believe that you were doing the best you could, whether it was ending a marriage that ought never to have taken place or beginning one that should have taken place long ago; whether it was caring for a needy child (and are not all children needy in one way or another?) or combatting evil men. If you were doing right, you would prevail. He had to believe that. Perhaps he was religious, after all.

And then it was over, and he kissed his wife, and they all went outside to stand looking at the ocean, as though they were reluctant to break the spell of the hour by parting.

"How happy Patrick would have been for you both today!" cried Désirée. "He loved you so much."

"We loved him," Kate replied. "Everyone did who knew him. I wish you could have known him," she told Tee.

"I wish so, too," Tee said.

The little party hesitated on the verge of separating. And Kate cried out, "Look, look! Up there!"

All followed her pointing hand. Through a palm grove in the rising jungle behind the church a gaudy stream of birds in raucous flight appeared and, as quickly, vanished.

"Parrots," said Father Baker. "It's deserted enough here for them to feel safe."

"Lovely, lovely!" Désirée was entranced. "Do you know, I was born on this island and lived here all my life, but I've never seen parrots wild. Have you?" she asked Tee.

"Yes, once. A long time ago."

Tee walked to the edge of the cliff. Now, as if by accord, all eyes followed her. Graceful, still young, she stood looking out to sea, shading her eyes from the light. Standing so, in her blown skirt, with her head high, standing strong and supple against the wind, she might have been carved on the prow of some old, proud ship.

"This must be the most beautiful place on earth," she said at last. "Isn't that what you always tell me, Francis?"

"But you're leaving it," Kate protested.

Again Tee smiled her slow, grave smile. "Yes, yes, I must." She looked at her watch. "In an hour, as a matter of fact."

Laurine and Franklin had arranged to take her to the airport so that Kate and Francis could go directly home.

"Be happy," Tee said now, kissing Francis good-bye. "This time you will be. I knew that the first time I looked at her."

He wanted to say so much, to say, I wish you could have had the same; to say, Maybe, do you think maybe, it's not too late for you and you will find someone, too?

But he said only, "Bless you and thank you for coming, and safe journey home."

Then she raised her hand in farewell and was gone.

When he took the wheel of their car, Kate covered his hand with hers.

"A very special woman, your mother."

He nodded, too full for a moment to speak. "And you," he said then. "A very special woman, too."

It was Saturday market day in Covetown as they drove through. Heaps of silvery fish, alewives, sprat, and mullet lay in their baskets along the curb. A troop of Girl Guides, wearing the brown uniform of their English heritage, were lining up to see Da Cunha's pictures.

"It hasn't changed all that much," Francis observed.

"Hasn't it?"

"Oh, you know what I meant." He leaned over to kiss her. "Yes, of course, everything changed just half an hour ago."

They turned up the driveway to Eleuthera. "Home," he said.

Osborne was waiting to welcome them. "I can't tell you how glad I am, how glad we all are, that you're staying!" he exclaimed, pressing Francis' hand. It was only the second time in their years together that he had revealed so much of himself.

Francis and Kate crossed the drive to the veranda, crunching on loose gravel.

"These heels!" she said.

He glanced down. "You have beautiful feet, my dear."

"Beautiful feet? Is that all of me that you've got to admire on our wedding day—my feet?"

"The rest I'll save till later," he told her.

"Oh, look, that plane has just taken off! Do you suppose it's Tee's?"

The plane was still low enough for its windows to be seen from the ground. He wondered whether Tee might be looking down and if she would be seeing Père on the veranda and her old white horse in the paddock.

"Do you remember the day you brought me here?" he asked abruptly.

"I remember everything. The lizards and the goats and the silence and your face."

"You still talk poetry."

And they looked at one another. It was a long look, a trembling look, until she turned away and said something ordinary to stop the trembling.

"I'll just go in a minute and see to the dogs."

He had to laugh.

"Don't laugh! It will be quite an adjustment for them in a new place, they'll be worried."

"All right," he said. "I'll be there in a few minutes."

And he watched her go through the door, into his house.

But he himself was too stirred to be shut inside just yet. He was a newborn man. He was Eleuthère François, standing on this spot for the first time. He was a man of tomorrow.

My God, it was a day to throw your head back and shout into the wind! There, down there, shout where the waves break on the rocks in smashing, jubilant spray; shout where the Morne, rising tier upon tier and dark as dreams, spreads its multitudes of green; cry out where the clouds drift over the living land and on every side, far and away and as far as you can see, the moving water glimmers.